SAVAGE KIN(
BOOK THRE

FILTHY
SAVAGE

LILIAN
HARRIS

Editing/Interior Formatting: CPR Publishing Services

Proofreader: Judy's Proofreading

Cover Design: Wildheart Graphics

TO MY DAD. LOSING YOU WHILE WRITING THE LAST PART OF THIS BOOK WAS ONE OF THE HARDEST THINGS.

MISS YOU.

TRANSLATIONS & PRONOUNCIATIONS

- Fionn – "Fee-yun"
- Eriu – "Air-ooh"
- Iseult – "Ee-salt"
- Tynan – "Tie-nan"
- Cillian – "KILL-ee-in"
- Bratva – Russian organized crime or Russian Mafia
- Pakhan – Head of Russian Mob
- Mo ban dia – My goddess
- Tha seo cearr – This is wrong
- Bidh tu am bàs dhomh – You'll be the death of me
- Chan eil mi làidir gu leòr – I'm not strong enough
- Daragaya – Dear
- Maya milaya – My darling

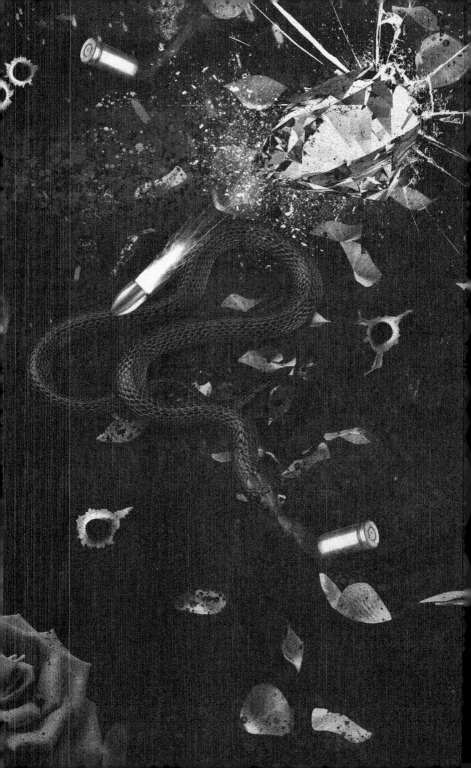

ONE

AMARA

"Stop making a scene." Xander's lip curls, anger radiating through his irises.

"How…" I swallow down the ache in my throat, the gentle wind swaying through my hair. "How can you do this to me? I saw you kissing her."

There's no way he can deny it. I've seen him with my own eyes.

The betrayal…it shattered me.

He shakes his head, blowing a harsh breath, and once he looks at me, his gaze intensifies. His stare fills with disgust, roving up and down my body.

"Because you bore me."

Those words bulldoze through the center of my chest, and I fight the tears that come. His cruel laughter only whispers more pain through my already broken heart.

Not sure why I've bothered for this long. I knew our relationship was at the end of its rope, but I guess I wanted to hold on. I thought coming to Necker Island for his best friend's engagement party would be good for us. But I was wrong.

"Did you sleep with her?"

Why does it even matter? He kissed her. That should be enough. But I want to know the truth.

My throat burns as I push down the tears, refusing to cry. Yet they slip down my cheeks anyway, betraying me and the strength I hoped to have through this.

He pinches the bridge of his nose. "I don't know why the hell I'm still with you. You're so whiny."

Your father never loved you. He saw you as a burden. It's why he left. It's all your fault.

Those words echo, causing me more agony.

No. Can't think about that. Not now.

"Pity, probably," he goes on. "Because no one else would want you. You know that, right? No one would put up with a boring-ass bitch like you."

People pass by through the outdoor patio of the hotel we're staying in, glancing at me while I fight not to fall apart. Fight with everything I have not to be weak.

But his words…they've dug so deep, every inch of me wishes to die. He knows my every insecurity, and he uses them against me on purpose.

I swipe my fingertips under my lashes. "How can you be so cruel?"

"It's the truth, Amara. Sometimes it's good to hear it." He grabs my hip and pulls me in.

I just want him to finally admit that he's cheated. Maybe then I'll finally grow a backbone and walk away.

When I caught him with some blonde an hour ago, his tongue in her mouth, I confronted him after she disappeared. But he denied it. Said the photo I snapped of them was nothing. He forced me to go to this engagement dinner, even though it was the last place I wanted to be.

After I saw the same blonde woman moments ago sitting at another table beside ours, I was sick to my stomach and stepped out here for some air.

Of course, he followed me.

I'd had a feeling he was already sleeping around before we took this trip, but I had no proof, except how secretive he became when I wanted to look at his phone and staying at work later than he normally would. My gut just kept screaming that he was cheating, but I didn't want to believe it. We were still having sex regularly, and I convinced myself I was just being insecure. I wanted to make the relationship work.

It's obvious I was the only one who cared. At least he wore a condom every time we slept together. Still going to have to get tested, though.

His mouth falls to my ear. "If you really wanna know, yes, I fucked her. Twice, actually. And I enjoyed every damn minute of it. Happy now?"

I suck in a breath. Backing away, I almost trip in my flat sandals.

"I hate you," I cry with a whisper, my bare shoulders shaking. "I hate you so damn much."

He laughs, smiling as a couple passes us, the woman's brow creasing.

"Stop embarrassing yourself and grow up," he whisper-shouts. "I'm a man. I have needs. And you've never been one to excite me. Gotta think about other women when I'm fucking you."

I sniffle. "How can you say that?"

He chuckles under his breath, shattering the rest of my soul. "At least that chick can fuck. And she sure as hell knows how to suck dick."

Fat tears stream down my face. I wish I could leave this island and run far away from him. From my life. From everything that hurts.

"Give me my plane ticket." I swipe my fingertips under my eyes. "I'm going back home."

His snicker radiates down my body, digging into my skin. "You're not getting shit. We're leaving tomorrow, and not a moment earlier. I don't want my friend to think we're having problems."

I'm the one laughing now. "Why would you wanna be with someone you don't even like? You're a joke, Xander. I'm done with you."

My eyes pop.

I can't believe I just said that.

Don't know where that bout of courage came from or if it's here to stay, but I meant every word.

The tip of my nose burns as I look into the eyes of the man who once swore he loved me.

Now? There's nothing there. Except lies.

I should've ended things months ago. It's hard to explain why I clung to something that wasn't there. Will never be there. He'll never be who I want him to be.

He chuckles dryly, grabbing my arm until I wince. "We're over when *I* decide we are. Now shut your fucking mouth and let's go back inside before people wonder what's taking so long."

"Let go of me!" I attempt to fight him off, but he only squeezes his fingers tighter.

"Suddenly got a big mouth on you, huh?" His eyes scan my body, covered in a pale blue sundress that hits my knees. "Maybe I should take you back to our room and show you what happens when you talk back to me." He grabs a single strap and starts lowering it.

I gasp, fear taking hold as I yank it back up. He's never taken me against my will, but right now, there's something dark in his eyes. Something sinister.

"Don't touch me." Terror crawls up my spine, my pulse quickening. "I'm leaving now."

"No, you're not." His fingers cinch until my skin throbs. "You'll never leave me. You're like a leech."

"I—"

"Get your fucking hands off of her." The sudden deep, growly voice of a stranger behind him causes me to jerk, my eyes expanding.

When I glance past Xander's shoulder, I find a tall, intense man. His eyes are so green, I can practically see the ocean if I stare just hard enough.

My stomach flips. Maybe from fear. Maybe from something more I don't yet understand.

He catches my gaze for a moment, eyes falling to my trembling mouth before he zeroes his irate attention on my boyfriend.

Xander drops his hold on me, looking the stranger up and down. I don't know why he isn't afraid. This man is huge, a good seven or eight inches bigger than him. His tuxedo swells with the ripples of his bulging biceps, his chest wide and powerful.

A sudden feeling of protection wafts over me, like a safety net of some kind, though that makes no sense. This man is no hero in my story. No one ever is.

The stranger's eyes go to mine once again, his thick chestnut brows tight, and for a moment, it feels as though there's concern there.

My heart lurches.

But before I can wonder if he was worried for me, his expression hardens again.

Maybe it was pity.

"Mind your business, man." Xander turns back around, grabbing my arm again.

When I wince, the guy grabs him by the back of his neck and yanks him around violently, clutching his shirt in a tight fist.

A muscle in the stranger's jaw pops as he bores a glare at my boyfriend. "Maybe I wasn't clear enough. If you touch her like that again, I'll kill you."

My stomach clenches, and it's definitely not from fear.

This man just stood up for me.

No one ever has.

"Who the *fuck* do you think you are?" Xander attempts to get free, but it's to no avail.

He's used to having control over everyone. His family comes from money, and when you have money, you think you own the world.

The veins on top of the man's hand jerk like they're attempting to break free and wrap around Xander's throat.

From my periphery, I find more men in tuxedos walking over, two of them with the same green eyes as the stranger, and another with blue eyes and longer dark hair. Are those two related to him? They must be.

Xander notices them too, and for a moment, his eyes flash with fear. My mouth lifts into a quick grin as I enjoy the look of horror on his face.

He's afraid. I don't think he's ever been afraid.

"I don't know what the hell you think you saw," Xander explains. "But that's my girl, and how I handle her is not your fucking business."

The man brings his face nearer, glaring down at Xander with an intense, virile stare. "I've made it my business. What are you gonna do about it?"

Xander doesn't relent, his upper lip twitching.

This guy only clutches his shirt tighter. "You're gonna leave. Now. You're gonna get your shit and get the fuck away from her before I permanently remove you."

The warning isn't idle. He means it.

"Is that a threat?"

"It is. Do you want a demonstration?"

Xander's eyes fill with passing terror before they grow with disdain. "Whatever. You want the whore, you can have her. She's boring in bed, anyway. Half the time, I can't even get it up looking at her."

My face flushes, completely humiliated, and I can't help the small sniffle falling from my nose.

This man's eyes are instantly on mine, and I'm even more ashamed.

Inhaling a deep breath, I hike up my chin. I won't let this asshole bring me down anymore.

"Maybe it's your dick." The guy clenches his jaw. "Because from looking at her, she's definitely not the problem."

My vision grows.

Did he just…

Did he mean…

No, of course not. A man who looks like *that* would never find someone like me attractive. It's almost laughable to even imagine him liking me. It's sweet that he's defending me, but I don't need someone to say things they don't mean.

He drops his fist off Xander, but from the looks of him and the way his hands ball at his sides, it won't last long. "You have five minutes to get out of this fucking hotel. I don't care where you go, but you're not staying here."

Xander coughs up a laugh. "Yeah, okay."

"I guess you're hard of hearing." He draws nearer, until his face almost touches Xander's. "We own the place. So unless you want to see what happens to people who don't do what we say, I suggest you get lost before I lose more of my patience."

He owns the hotel? Holy shit.

Xander glares at me, muttering something inaudible before stalking off.

When he's finally gone and the stranger's eyes lock with mine, something passes through me.

Something that makes my gut flip. Something that feels almost like yearning. Or maybe a deep desire to have a man care for me for once.

Stupid Amara. Conjuring up fairy tales in your head. Don't you know by now? Fairy tales don't exist for girls like you.

His eyes scan my body, but not in a gross way. Like he's assessing me for injuries. When his attention lands on my arm, his nostrils flare. My eyes round when I remember the fading black and blue from another time Xander grabbed me.

"He did that to you?" A flash of rage passes through his features.

I shrug. "It's okay. It happened a while ago."

My gaze darts to the ground, unable to look at this man anymore. Too embarrassed from it all.

He approaches, hand lowering to my chin, and I break out with goose bumps when he lifts my gaze up to meet his. The raw intensity there, the way he looks at me—not at my body or my mouth, but at *me*—causes more tears to come.

When has anyone ever looked at me with such care?

I know it's pathetic to think I matter to him. We just met.

Xander was nice at first too. But they change, don't they?

"It's not okay." His smooth, raspy baritone causes me to choke up on my emotions even more. "No one has a right to put their hands on you." He glances at my trembling lips. "How about I get you some food?"

"Uh, no… You don't have to do that."

Wiping at my lower lashes, I think of ways to get away. It's not good for me to be around him. To be so inexplicably drawn to this man.

The last thing I need is another man to complicate my life.

I don't want to leave, though. I want to stay right here. With him.

Because for the first time, I feel safe. *He* makes me feel safe, as stupid as that may sound.

It makes no logical sense. No way to explain why I feel this way, but I do, and I want more of it.

"I know I don't have to." A gorgeous smirk tugs on his cheeks. "I want to."

Warmth cruises down my limbs, like a blanket I want wrapped around me on a blistering cold night.

"Okay." The word slips out before I can stop it.

But it's too late to take it back, and I'm glad.

It's like my mind is warring with itself. On one hand, I want to get to know him better. On the other, I don't want to grow attached.

Even if Xander and I are done, it's too soon for someone else. And more so, this guy is way out of my league.

"Do you have the keycard to the room you two were sharing?"

Oh, no.

My pulse jumps. I completely forgot that Xander has our room key. What the hell am I going to do? I don't have a penny to my name. Every dime I make at the coffee shop goes to household expenses and rent.

Shaking my head, I say, "He kept everything."

His chiseled jaw tightens, that emerald glimmer turning darker. "Alright, don't worry. What's your room number?"

"6693."

"Okay, I'll get you a suite and move all your things to it."

I hit him with a wide-eyed stare.

A suite? I'm sure he misspoke.

"I don't have money."

"You don't need money."

I almost cry, and I swear, my heart skips a beat. A half-smile curves one side of his face, and it becomes harder to breathe.

I shouldn't be feeling anything for him. Nothing at all. Not this attraction, nor this need to spend more time with him.

He could be dangerous, for all I know. But he doesn't seem dangerous. Not to me, anyway.

"Why are you being so nice to me?" My voice drops.

"Because someone has to be."

Emotions hit the back of my throat. Why does his voice calm me so much? And why does it feel like I've known him all my life? It's weird, really. To meet someone and feel like you've always known them.

When his full mouth twitches, I wonder how it'd feel to kiss him. To run my hands through his hair.

My God, this needs to stop.

He's gotta be thirty. Doubt he'd be interested in a nineteen-year-old anyway. He probably dates older, more sophisticated model types. I definitely don't fit that mold. Though I try to look away, I can't seem to untether my gaze from his.

Someone clears their throat from my left, and I suck in a breath, finally remembering we aren't alone. The other men he's with are still right here, not saying a word.

I give them a quick glance, and a chill runs down my arms. Their expressions are tight, their stances exuding power and superiority.

Who are these people?

"Come on, let's get you settled into a new room." He breaks through my thoughts, waiting for me to follow him.

I glance at the men again—who are now falling further behind us as we walk away—and keep pace beside the man whose name I don't yet know. Only a hand's length remains between us; I'm nervous to get nearer.

Even this is too close. Though I want more.

My heart grows frantic.

But when he cuts the distance between us until his arm almost touches mine, the warmth of his proximity makes all the nerves sizzle beneath my skin.

"Do you like weddings?" he asks out of nowhere, staring at me with that awfully sexy smirk. "Because one of my brothers back there is getting married in about three hours, and I could use a date."

My eyes flicker to his. I hadn't expected that.

I shouldn't go. It'd be stupid to risk growing more attracted to him when I'm already feeling all these things. But I could use a little bit of fun. Something to help me forget all my problems before I have to return to the hell that awaits me back home.

"I think I'd like that."

His grin spreads.

What's the worst that could happen?

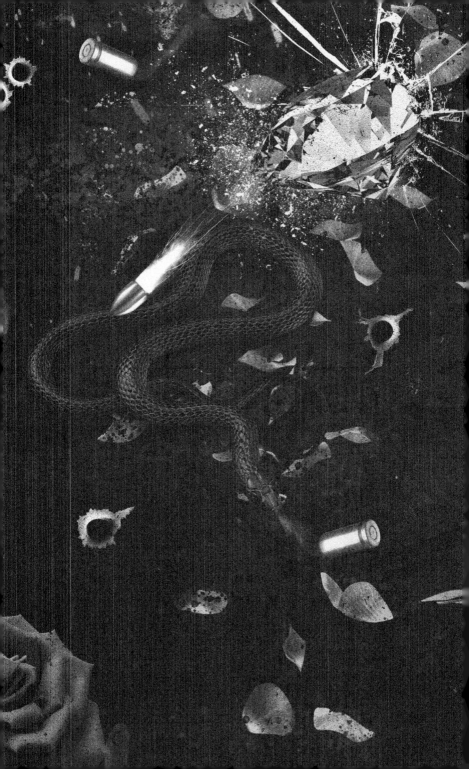

TWO

FIONN

Damn, she's pretty.

Can't help staring at her as we make it inside the hotel.

Gorgeous, thick raven hair, eyes filled with warm honey twined with specs of gold.

I noticed her earlier while I was out on the patio having a drink with my brother-in-law Devlin and my two brothers, Tynan and Cillian.

But she was with that asshole. He's lucky all I did was kick him out of our hotel. Really wanted to do far worse. Maybe carve him up and throw him in the ocean.

That does sound tempting…

But it's Tynan's wedding day, and getting all bloody hours before would definitely piss off his fiancée, Elara.

Next time, he won't be so lucky.

As soon as I saw him grabbing her, something in me snapped. The girl looked like she was crying from where I sat, and that only enraged me further.

When I got close, when I saw how fucking sad she looked, how beautiful she was, I wanted to kill him.

Gazing over at her, those hips swaying beside me, I attempt to control the damn need to throw her up against the nearest wall, cup her face, and kiss her.

The more I try not to think about it, the more I start to wonder what she looks like without that dress on. What she tastes like. What she feels like when she comes.

Shit. I've gotta stop. She's clearly too young. Small little thing that I'd enjoy tossing around in my bed. On the floor. In the shower…

Tie her up, dangling from the ceiling.

Groaning, I dig two fingers into the bridge of my nose.

Her attention flashes up to me and concern fills her features. "You okay?"

"Yeah. Headache," I mutter.

"I'm sorry." Her voice grows with worry. "Do you have meds?"

You're the only medicine I need right now, baby girl.

"Just gotta eat a little something." I force a tight grin, and those pink lips of hers wind into a shy smile, making my dick swell.

Great. Can't even control myself when she does something as simple as smile at me. I'm in fucking trouble.

She's maybe five feet, curvy frame, a small kissable nose, and hair that's begging me to fist it. But it's her eyes I've most enjoyed looking at. That beautiful hazel hue seemed dull when she was with him. It made me want to tear the bastard's heart out and feed it to him for hurting her.

She gives me a nervous glance, and my jaw twitches as I try my damndest not to act on what I'm feeling.

Slide my fingers into her hair. Tease her mouth with mine while my fingers climb up beneath her dress…

Fuck.

I can't.

Even if her age wasn't a factor, this is not the time or the place. I'd only be taking advantage of her.

We trek toward check-in and I secure her a room, ordering the staff to move her things from the one she shared with that prick.

Once that's done, I lead her toward the elevator and we ride up in thick silence, heading to her new room. When I scan the card and let her walk in first, her mouth pops open.

"Oh my God… It's so huge."

It is. And it wants inside you.

Turning away, I grunt internally, rearranging my slacks and trying to tame my raging erection, while she struts further into the two-bedroom suite with her back to me.

"I would've been fine in a regular room." Her voice drifts as she stares in awe at the large living space with two cream leather sofas and a shaggy gray rug between.

This unexplainable desire to do more for her, to give her everything, overtakes me. My palms land on her shoulders, and she jolts, though remains rooted, like she enjoys my touch as much as I enjoy touching her.

I let my hands ride up and down her velvety skin, my mouth sinking across her ear. "I wanted you to have one of the best rooms in the resort. You deserve it."

"Thank you," she whispers, goose bumps prickling where I touch her.

That has a smirk tipping up my face. She either likes me just as much or is terrified. I prefer to think it's the former.

A knock on the door startles her, and I reluctantly go to open it, finding a bellhop with her luggage.

"Here you are, sir."

He rolls it inside, and I hand him a one-hundred-dollar bill.

His attention snaps between me and the money. "Thank you, sir."

I nod and shut the door behind him.

"You're generous." She kneels, unzipping her luggage to remove a few shirts and pants, plus a white one-piece swimsuit.

"Try to be. They work hard."

That has her smiling as she places all the items in the dresser, though my mind is on her in that hot little swimsuit. My cock pulses as I lean against the wall beside her, picturing her wearing it for me. Straddling me while my hands sink into that round ass.

I should convince her to take a swim with me tomorrow.

"What's your name?" I ask, needing to know the name of the woman who's currently occupying every dirty thought in my head.

"Um…" Her eyes dart between me and the luggage, like she has to think about whether she wants to trust me with it.

"I'm Fionn. It's nice to meet you."

"I'm…I'm Emily." A grin gradually flashes over her soft mouth.

"That's a pretty name."

"Thank you. Yours too." Her cheeks turn slightly pink as she shyly looks up at me. "Never heard that one before."

"Yeah, it's Irish. My parents liked the rare ones."

"That's nice." I catch it as her face falls for a moment, but she erases it in an instant. "Are you close to them?"

I gnash my teeth. "My mother passed away a long time ago, but yeah, I'm close to my father and the rest of my family."

Her brows furrow. "Oh, I'm sorry. About your mom, I mean."

"Thanks."

I don't like thinking about my mother. The shit she went through. How she was burned alive by Sergey, Pakhan of the Bratva at the time and Konstantin Marinov's father.

I fight the thoughts and concentrate on the beautiful woman before me, my gaze leisurely sliding down her body, not doing a damn thing to hide my desire. Her arms come around her, like she's trying to hide from me.

Too bad she can't.

"I've gotta know, why the hell were you with an asshole like that?" The thought of him has my blood boiling. "I hope you're not thinking about going back to him."

No fucking way will I let that happen.

Just say the word, and he's already dead.

"No, I think this is it."

"Better be."

Her lips thin with a sad smile while my features grow tenser at the thought of how he must've treated her all this time.

"I don't know why I was still with him." She settles on the edge of the bed, while my pulse beats louder in my temples, wanting to kiss that emptiness out of her eyes.

Wanting to do far worse than that.

These damn thoughts are going to ruin us both.

She's too young. Too innocent. Too utterly tempting.

And I know right now this woman will be my downfall.

"Shit," I mutter, running a frustrated hand down my face.

"What?" Her brows furrow.

She's going to start thinking I'm talking to myself, which I guess isn't that far off.

"You're too good for him."

Her body sags. "You sound like my friend."

"Maybe you should listen to her."

She releases a heavy sigh, staring up at me. "I know I do. Deserve better. But I'd spent so much time watching everyone else date that I started to feel…I don't know, like no one would ever want me, you know? Then he came along." She shrugs, her face growing crimson like she's embarrassed. "I probably sound pathetic. Because of course you wouldn't know what it's like to feel lonely. I'm sure you have a hoard of women chasing after you."

I almost chuckle. This woman thinks she has me all figured out.

But she has no fucking clue who I am. What I want. She knows absolutely nothing, and that's probably for the best.

A girl like this doesn't belong in my world. Yet I find myself moving toward her, somehow needing to be in her aura.

Her breath hitches when I stalk another step forward, a smirk tilting my mouth.

"Well, babe, it looks like right now you're the only woman who has my attention."

Her cheeks turn pink.

Is she that unused to a man flirting with her?

"You're beautiful. You know that, right?"

She lets out a dismissive laugh, fingers fumbling to push a long strand of hair behind her ear. Something I very much want to do myself.

"You're sweet, but I know you're just trying to be nice, which I appreciate. You don't have to say anything. I know a man like you would never even consider a girl who looks like me."

"A girl like you?" My tone turns rough. "What the *hell* does that mean?"

"You know…" She stares at me like I'm supposed to understand. "I'm not razor-thin. My stomach rolls when I sit." She gives her midsection a glance. "And my thighs touch when I walk, so I definitely don't look like a fashion model, which—let's not kid ourselves—is probably the kind of women you date. Which is fine." She raises both hands in the air, unable to stop rambling in the most adorable way. "I'm not judging. Those types of women are beautiful. Me? Well…I'm just me. And a man like you wouldn't be caught dead with someone who looks like this." She gestures at herself with a sway of her hand.

I chuckle dryly. "Wow. You have me figured out, huh, baby girl?"

How wrong you are, little rabbit. One night with me, and I'd show you just how gorgeous I think you are.

"Deny it, then." The words fall out of her lips in a hurry, and her eyes widen for a moment like she's surprised she even said it.

When I let out a small chuckle, her brow arches and she curls her arms over her chest, causing my attention to fall to her tits, just the right size at more than a handful.

Wanna do more than that. Wanna bend you over and fuck away all your bullshit insecurities.

The shock on her features expands the closer I get.

If she wants me to deny it, I'll do just that.

The space between us evaporates when I force her legs apart, fingers tracing up her knee until her skin prickles and her breathing comes in gasps.

"Is that what you think?" I draw her dress higher until the thick strip of her white panties peeks through. "That I care what size you wear? Or what kind of clothes you own?" A slow, dark chuckle emanates from my throat. "I'd tear your goddamn panties with my teeth right now if I thought it was the right thing to do."

"Oh God," she whispers, squeezing her knees around my legs.

My fingertips slowly slink up her arm, thumb brushing over her pretty lips, ones I want wrapped around my cock desperately. "The things I could do to this mouth."

She shivers, inhaling deeply, gaping with equal part shock and lust.

"I'm not what you want," she murmurs, and I hiss when I feel her tongue slipping between her lips, accidentally swiping across the pad of my finger. "Stop toying with me, Fionn."

A growl rumbles in my chest. "Who are you trying to convince, little rabbit? Hmm?"

She bites her bottom lip, and I'm ready to just say fuck it all and take what I want.

When the hell have I ever denied myself a goddamn thing?

"If you knew how attracted I am to you, how badly I wanna fuck you, you'd run."

Her eyes round, body shifting, like she's trying to satiate the arousal building between those thick thighs.

Would be easy to slip her panties to the side and feel just how wet I've made her. I squeeze my other hand at my side, trying like hell to behave. But it's never been in my nature.

She was right about one thing: I don't know how it feels not to constantly have the attention of women.

But that doesn't mean I haven't felt loneliness before.

Being an enforcer for the Mob means women are always throwing themselves at me or running the other way. But what I truly want is someone to come home to.

Sex is sometimes the loneliest thing when there's nothing tangible to hold on to after it's over.

Fuck, if I admitted that to my brothers, I think they'd have me examined. But being thirty-one now, I've realized I'm sick of the games and the clubs. I crave stability.

I want what Tynan and Elara have. What my sisters, Eriu and Iseult, have too.

And this little rabbit may be just what I need.

She'd probably bolt if she knew what I do. Enforcer for the Mob may sound a bit better than killer, but it's what I've always done. It's what I'm good at. And I'll never stop for anyone, not that I could. Once you're in, you're never getting out.

Unless you're dead.

I stare down at the stunning woman before me. Her doe-eyed expression has me clamping my teeth, desperately needing to prove to her how wrong she truly is about what I want in a woman.

"The only thing stopping me from ripping off this flimsy dress and filling your pussy with my cock is…" I hook a finger under the strap of her dress. "…knowing that it's the last thing you need right now." I drag the strap lower, barely clinging to my sanity.

Her inhales are harsh as she lets out a sinful moan.

Fuck me. She sounds even better when she moans.

"Tha seo ceàrr," I groan, reluctantly letting her go before I do something she may regret tomorrow.

Her face grows flushed and her expression is so damn innocent, I'd corrupt her and enjoy every damn minute of it.

Moving back, I grip the back of my neck, attempting to control my untamable desire. "We should probably get the hell out of here before I do something I can't take back."

She nods feverishly, tongue slipping out to run over her bottom lip.

Fuck me. This is getting harder by the second. And I don't just mean my dick.

"How about we go get some food?" I suggest. "My brother's reception doesn't start for four hours, and I can't wait that long."

She clears her throat, fingertips feathering over her lips—exactly where I touched her, like she's committing it to memory.

"Okay, uh, yeah…" As she tries to rise, her stomach growls. "Guess my body agrees with you." She giggles, and that shit is infectious as hell.

"When did you last eat?"

I give her my hand and help her up. She tries to slip it from my grasp, but I hold on to it tighter. Really like the way her tiny hand fits in my large one. I rub circles on her skin as she gazes up at me.

"Um, breakfast?"

"Shit, babe, it's three. Why the hell haven't you eaten yet?"

She shrugs, her cheeks growing crimson.

Damn. When she said she didn't have money, she meant it, didn't she? I swear I'm gonna find that fucking asshole and cut off his balls for not taking care of her the way he should've.

The thought is really enticing. No one has to know…

Before I can stop myself, I'm tilting her chin with the back of my free hand. "Hey, it's okay. You don't have to be embarrassed with me. I'm not like him. I'll take care of you."

The suddenness of her tears filling her eyes guts me. Wonder what her life is like back home.

"Should we go?" She slips her hand out of mine, and this time, I let her.

Don't want to push this skittish little thing any more than I already have.

THREE

AMARA

I lied.

I gave him my best friend's name before I could stop myself. But the idea of him knowing who I am, where I'm from, made me panic. I can't let this man find me. See where I live. *How* I live. It's too humiliating. It's best if he never finds me.

If today is the only day we spend together, then so be it. It could be a day I never forget, and I'd rather hold on to that than have it ruined by the realities of my existence.

He grabs my hand again, and his firm grasp has me fighting a sob.

To have a man like this—a strong, kind man.

It feels nice. Too nice.

It's as though he'd break through every wall to keep me safe. Like he'd never hurt me.

But I don't actually know him, do I? He could be just about anyone.

We settle into a booth at the casual restaurant inside the hotel, and when the waitress with a chest triple the size of mine approaches, he doesn't even look at her.

Xander always looked at other women right in front of me. Like he didn't care. I swear the more I remember everything he's done, the more I wonder what the hell is wrong with me. How could I have allowed it to go on for so long?

Fionn's bright green eyes linger on mine, forcing me to focus on him as he orders our drinks. The way he gazes at me has my heart racing like mad, enjoying the way he takes me in, like he's touching me without ever doing so.

"What do you wanna eat?"

I glance down at the menu, shocked at the prices. Forty dollars for a burger and fries. Thirty for a plain salad. This is crazy.

"Uh, maybe I'll have the mozzarella sticks."

They're a bit cheaper, but not even by that much.

"What?" He chuckles. "You can't just eat that. Do you like steak? The steak is really good."

I've only had it once, and I remember how much I enjoyed it, but there's no way I can justify the cost. One hundred and fifty dollars, to be exact.

"Emily…" He reaches for my hand from across the booth. "If you want it, just tell me. You don't have to worry about how much it costs, babe."

My heart skips a beat. I hate to admit how much I like the way he calls me "babe."

He smirks, and it shoots right to my belly, making me warm and completely aware of how much I'm attracted to him.

My stomach growls again.

Screw it. I should get that steak. I haven't had a nice meal in forever.

There you go, Amara. Finally doing something for yourself for once.

"Steak sounds nice. Thanks, Fionn." Even his name is sexy.

When the waitress returns with our drinks, he orders two steaks and mozzarella sticks, then hands her the menus. I sip on my Diet Coke, biting on the tip of the straw.

All the while, I take my time looking at him. Really looking.

His deep, dark mahogany strands are coiffed back—fuller at the top, tapered on the sides. His face looks as though it was carved by the gods themselves. The snake-and-floral tattoo on his right hand stretches to the tips of his fingers, making him appear dangerous. The veins on his neck throb beneath his skin, making it hard to concentrate on anything else besides how hot he is.

My body grows taut at the sight of him. At the words he said to me earlier, the way he wanted me...

I swear I've never felt anything like this before. I'm aching for his hands, his body, for every inch of him.

Who am I right now? These feelings are a little scary, but exciting too.

The desire to run my fingers across the stubble of his jaw, to touch him everywhere, fills my mind. In my thoughts, I can do whatever I want to him and have him do the same. Though I could never be that brave in reality.

It's no surprise I find him attractive. He's older. Confident. Has protective instincts. He's objectively handsome in a very masculine, dominating kind of way. Any woman with eyes would agree.

I wish I had more experience with men, but Xander is the only man I've slept with, and I definitely don't want him to be my last. I don't have much to compare it to, but he never really cared if I got off. He just expected me to jump on top of him, and once he came, I was forgotten. I never even enjoyed it.

But being around Fionn, I've felt more in every inch of my body than I ever felt with Xander.

I want to know what good sex can actually be like. Emily swears it's way better with a man who puts his woman first. Who enjoys getting her off multiple times before he comes himself. Xander never did that.

I'd like to believe there's someone out there for me. Someone who'll respect me and love me enough to be loyal. Or, you know, get me off? That's not too much to ask.

I let out a sigh.

"What are you thinking about?" His husky tone slices through my thoughts.

Wondering how it'd feel to fuck you.

My face heats up. I never speak that way out loud.

"Nothing," I finally answer, while he orders me a refill.

I hadn't realized I'd sucked the holy hell out of this drink. It didn't stand a chance against my nerves.

"Just thinking about things I have to do when I get back home."

Like deal with *her*…

Makes my chest cinch every time I think about returning. I often picture myself running away and starting over. But I'd miss Emily too much. Wish I could afford my own place, but I can't.

"Where are you from?"

Damn it. I can't tell him that.

But the city is so big, there's no way he'd find me with just a generic first name like Emily. "Boston."

"Wow." His brows hike. "No way." He leans back into the leather. "I'm from Massachusetts too."

Of course he is…

"Really?" I force a smile, hoping we aren't close. "Where?"

"West Sherwood." He grins. "About a hundred miles from you."

I feel a bit relieved. That's nowhere close to Boston.

"What do you do back home?" His discerning eyes take me in, like he's trying to solve a puzzle.

"Uh, I work at a café." I play with my straw. "It's not much, but—"

"Don't do that." His forehead creases as he drops his elbows on the table and leans in, staring at me with disapproval. "Don't diminish what you do. You're still young. Your entire life is ahead of you."

My laugh is small as I fight not to tell him how wrong he is. There's nothing waiting for me in the future.

"Yes, I'm only nineteen, but—"

"Shit, I didn't realize you're that young." He presses two fingers into his temple, face twisting up with obvious tension.

"Sorry?" I grimace.

Knew he wouldn't be interested in girls my age.

He blows a breath. "Don't be."

"How old are you?"

"Thirty-one. Now, what were you saying?"

"Oh, it was nothing."

"Here you are." The waitress returns with our plates, placing them before us.

The steak looks perfect, with a medley of garden vegetables and mashed potatoes with some sort of yellowish sauce. He stares at me as I start to slice off a piece, popping it into my mouth, and as I do...

"Holy shit." I let out a moan.

I don't think I've ever tasted anything this good. It's so tender, practically melting on my tongue if that's possible.

He chuckles. "Good?"

"Amazing!"

That has him smirking, cutting into his own.

He continues to watch me eat, like he enjoys it. His eyes radiate with so much gentleness, I wonder if I'll ever meet a man who treats me this nicely.

Then I think about how Xander was at first, and my happiness deflates.

"So, how about you?" I ask, needing to stop him from staring at me so intently. It's hard to eat when he watches me like this. "Are you in business? Heard you say you own this hotel."

He nods. "Yeah. My family and I run restaurants, hotels, bars, a farm too. A little of everything."

"Ah, so you really do have money…"

Shit, why did I just say that? Need to learn how to keep some thoughts to myself.

A rugged half-smile tilts up his face, and my body coils with need. "A little."

"Lucky you," I whisper, wishing I had just enough to survive on without wondering if we'll eat the next day.

"Hey…" A crease forms between his brows. "Do you need money?" He reaches for me again, clasping my fingers tight from across the table, his thumb drawing circles on my skin. "I can write you a check, no questions asked. Just give me a number."

I jerk back with a small laugh, and my hand slips from his, feeling instantly cold. "No. My God, I'm sorry. I'm so embarrassed. I didn't mean to sound like I was asking you for money."

"You weren't." He reaches for me again, placing his palm over mine. "It was just an offer."

My body warms at his touch.

Slipping out of his grasp, I pick up my drink, sucking in huge gulps. Of course I could use the money, especially because I need to buy a plane ticket back home.

I'll have to call Emily and ask her to lend me some cash. I won't accept this stranger's money.

"You're sweet for offering, but I'm fine. I swear."

"If you change your mind, let me know," he throws in casually, continuing with his meal.

"I won't."

He lowers his fork, locking his gaze with mine. "Look, I know we just met and you have no reason to trust my intentions, but I want nothing in return. I just wanna help you."

My eyes water, and I peer down at the table. "I do appreciate that, but I'll be okay." My lips pinch tight as I return my attention to him. "I'm not looking to be your charity case, Fionn."

A muscle in his jaw pops. "Is that what you think?"

"Why else would you offer me money?" I tilt a brow. "Do you go around asking people if they need money on a regular basis?"

"No." His stare only intensifies. "But I can tell you need some help and I wanted to offer mine. That's all."

Straightening my spine, I pick up a mozzarella stick, dipping it in the marinara sauce. "Well, I appreciate that, but as I said, I'm fine."

His mouth tenses as he stares hard at me, like he wants to argue some more. Instead, he lets out a frustrated exhale as he continues to eat, and I do the same, the tension thick between us.

"So tell me about your family." I clear my throat, trying to change the subject and erase this unease that's caused a wedge between us. "They must all be so happy with the wedding."

He nods stiffly. "Mm-hmm. My brother never wanted to get married."

"Oh?"

Then he's filling me in on everyone in his family, and I'm thankful he's dropped the money conversation. He's apparently one of five siblings, with two sisters and two brothers. Must be nice to come from such a large family. All I ever had was myself. My dad split when I was only two, and my mom never had any more children.

I often wonder about my father. Who he is. If he's still alive. My mother won't tell me his name, and I've not been able to find my birth certificate. She's hidden it somewhere just so I don't find him. Whenever I try to bring him up, she shoots me down, angrily dismissing my questions.

When will you learn he doesn't love you, Amara? He never has.

Those words are like a knife to my heart. Did my father really not love me, or is she just lying?

"You okay?" he asks, bringing me out of these awful reminders.

"Yeah, sorry." I tug a few strands behind my ear. "I'm looking forward to the wedding. I've never been to one."

He grins. "Wait until you see how we party."

My eyes suddenly widen. I just realized I don't have anything formal to wear. There are only two dresses in my small luggage, and he's seeing one.

"Do you think I can wear this?" I glance down at my sundress.

"Of course you can."

But just one look at his tux says otherwise. What choice is there, though? My other dress is way more casual than this.

We finish our food, and then he's paying for the meal and walking me out toward the elevator.

As he stands beside me, his arm brushes mine, sending jolts of electricity shooting through my body. Both of us stare straight ahead at the elevator doors, waiting for them to open.

All the while, I wonder what he truly thinks about me. Does he really find me attractive? Is my age really a big deal? I mean, thirty-one isn't that old. Though the thought of getting naked in front of him makes my stomach turn.

"Thanks for everything," I tell him, meaning every word.

And I don't just mean for the food, but for Xander too.

"Anytime." His husky timbre lands in my gut and grips like thorny vines.

His eyes fix on mine, his jaw visibly flexing. My breathing grows shallower, unable to fight this connection I feel in my core every time he looks at me. His stare drops to my lips, and before I can wonder what he'll do next, he takes a step forward, his body growing nearer second by second until it's almost pressed to mine.

My stomach somersaults as a finger slowly brushes a strand of hair away from my face, his hooded gaze capturing mine where I stand.

As I remain here gazing up into his eyes, I wonder if he'll kiss me, wishing he would.

Seconds tick by, and he doesn't even try.

My heart instantly sinks when he backs away, running a hand down his face just as the elevator arrives.

We ride up together in complete silence—so heavy around us, I can feel it.

When the doors open, he's the first to get out, waiting for me to follow. A few steps to the right, and we're beside my room.

He hands me a keycard. "I'll get you in a couple of hours."

"Okay. Where are you staying?"

My eyes enlarge when he gestures toward the room next door. "Oh."

He chuckles dryly before his face turns intense. "Don't look that excited."

Those eyes hungrily scan my body, and my nipples grow achy and tight.

I clear my throat. "I just didn't realize you're right next to me."

How am I going to sleep knowing this man is next door?

His hand lowers to my chin and he grasps it firmly, causing every inch of me to come alive. His eyes sink into mine—so deep and forceful, all I want is to be kissed by him. To feel something. Anything. It's been so long since I've felt things besides anger and sadness.

I want to get lost in someone and forget my problems for a night.

His thumb brushes over my lips. "I wanted to be close by in case that asshole comes back."

My skin tingles. He cared enough to watch out for me twice now.

"Thank you," I whisper, the air around us thick with something I can't name.

Temptation? Yearning?

His jaw flexes, eyes glassy as he peers at my parted mouth. I grow slick between my thighs, never once having felt this much desire for a man before.

"Go on inside," he rasps, like a warning. Like if I don't, he won't be able to stop himself.

I don't want him to.

When I bite my lip again, he growls.

"Fuck." His croaky, hungered baritone sets my skin ablaze.

My heart races as he drops his mouth lower, and when it strokes mine, I let out a little moan.

But it's not enough. I want a real kiss. An earth-shattering kiss.

"I need you to go inside, little rabbit." His hand sinks into my hair and he tugs my head back, not letting me go.

Little rabbit.

My chest swells at the nickname.

His warm breath cascades down the column of my throat, and my palms grasp his biceps, hard and strong, causing my body to turn molten. I'd let this man do anything to me right now.

Forget my insecurities. Forget everything but the two of us.

My God. Emily was right, and I haven't even slept with him.

"You're killing me." His whispered breath across the shell of my ear has me clenching my knees, aching for him, needing to feel him inside me.

His head moves back an inch, eyes boring deeper before his mouth falls closer.

And closer.

Oh God. He's gonna kiss me. Really kiss me.

Just when I think he's about to, he pulls my forehead to his.

"I need you to go inside before I do something I can't take back."

Before I can argue that I want him to, he pushes off me, taking the keycard I forgot I was holding and opening my door.

"Go on." A hand at the small of my back ushers me into the room, and my face falls.

I stare up at him, my body flushed, need filling my veins while his eyes drink me in, unable to stop himself.

"I'll see you in a bit." His nostrils flare, eyes hooded.

Then he's closing my door, leaving me there wondering how I'm supposed to forget a man like him.

When his door slams shut, I lean against the wall, a mess of emotions, unsure how my life could've changed this much in such a short time.

FOUR

AMARA

A s soon as I'm done with my shower and throwing a robe on, there's a knock on the door. Nervously, I tuck the belt tighter, hoping it isn't Fionn telling me we're leaving for the wedding earlier than anticipated.

The thought of seeing him again fills me with both excitement and nervousness. After what happened earlier, I don't know how to act around him. And knowing I'll be gone tomorrow and will never see him again makes me sad too.

With a sigh, I look through the peephole to find a woman I don't recognize. She's wearing a hotel staff jacket and holding some bags.

She probably got the wrong room. Because I definitely didn't order anything.

"May I help you?" I ask, opening the door to the attractive blonde.

"Are you Miss Emily?"

"Uh…" My face scrunches in confusion. "Yes?"

"I'm Hannah. Fionn sent me."

Still puzzled, I glance at all the stuff she's holding. "For what, exactly?"

"Well, he chose some dresses for you for tonight's wedding and wanted me to bring them over, as well as do your hair and makeup."

He did *what*?

She appears excited, while I'm staring at her all bewildered.

I can't believe he did that. A smile tugs at my lips. The man continues to surprise me.

How has a stranger done more for me than anyone else in my life? The thought causes a pang in my chest, but I brush it off.

"Sorry. Please come in."

She struts inside, placing the stuff on the sofa. "I have two gown options in two sizes for you to try on."

She removes the garment bags and hangs two on each of the doors of the closet.

Once she unzips them, my eyes grow. "They're gorgeous."

My fingers run down the red silk gown with sparkly straps, a V-cut, and a small sweeping train. There's no way I can pull that off, but I still want to try it on. The other is black with a rhinestone belt and a strapless sweetheart neckline. They're both stunning, and when I look at the price tags, I gasp.

Oscar De La Renta.

Each one twenty grand. Two. Zero.

Oh my God... Now I know what Cinderella felt like.

Except I don't have a fairy godmother. He's more of a...rich, sexy godfather.

I want to head into his room and tell him how crazy this is. He shouldn't be spending this kind of money on me. I'm not his girlfriend or his wife.

But maybe to a man like him, this is pocket change. To me, though, twenty grand is life-changing. I could do so much with that money, like pay the overdue bills we have.

"So, which is your favorite?" Hannah calls my attention.

"They're both beautiful."

"Oh, good. I'm so glad you like them. How about you go and try them on? There are shoes in this bag too." She lifts one up.

"Sure." I nod.

She brings all the items to the bedroom, waiting on the other side while I decide what to wear first. Settling on the black one, I slide into a pair of small-heeled silver sandals, which are surprisingly comfortable. It's like he knew I wouldn't be able to walk in super high heels. Then I'm stepping into the gown, pulling up the side zipper.

With butterflies in my stomach, I head for the full-length mirror, and when I see myself, tears fill my eyes.

I look beautiful.

When have I ever thought of myself that way?

Emily would die if she saw me right now. I'm unrecognizable, and Hannah hasn't even done my hair and makeup yet. I barely wear any makeup, and that's because I don't know how to apply it even after watching tutorials, so I can't wait to see what she does.

Heading for the door, I come out to show Hannah.

When she sees me, her brows shoot to her hairline. "Wow! It looks like it was made for you." She seems genuinely excited for me. "He chose some jewelry for you as well. I can help you put it on so you can see how it all looks."

I nod, choking up on my emotions. I'll never forget this day for as long as I live.

She removes a couple of small black boxes, opening the first to reveal large sparkly studs.

"Wow. They're so pretty."

"I know." She starts to put the first one on, then the next. "Best part is you get to keep them." She removes a matching bracelet, thin with diamonds that sparkle like bright stars.

"Really?"

I've never owned anything remotely this expensive. I mean, I don't have to know the cost to know it's highly valuable.

"Really." Hannah puts the boxes back in the bag. "He bought them for you."

Wow. My head spins at the sweet gesture.

But I'll have to hide them from *her* when I get home, or she'll sell them.

"Want to try the red dress on now?"

"Yes."

I don't even want to take this one off, but I want to see what the other one looks like too.

"Wait until he sees you!" She gives me a knowing look.

"Oh…" I wave off her comment. "It's not like that."

Her face upturns in surprise. "Really? When he came into the salon, he made it seem like you two were dating."

"He did?"

"Yeah. I'm sorry if I overstepped."

I swallow the thick knot in my throat. Why would he do that?

"No, we just met today. He's been nice, but that's all this is."

"Hmm. Okay." She shrugs a single shoulder. "It's just that I've known him for a few years and he's never done anything like this for a woman before."

That's probably because the other women could all afford twenty-thousand-dollar dresses.

"Let me go try on the other gown."

The faster this conversation ends, the better.

"Sure, I'll be here. After you choose one, you can put your robe back on so I can start on your makeup."

"Thanks." Returning to the bedroom, I slip into the red one, keeping on the same shoes.

When I return to the mirror, my breath freezes in my lungs. I instantly know this is the one. The dress hugs my waist and thighs, then flares out. I've never worn something so beautiful in my life.

When Hannah sees me this time, her mouth pops open. "Wow… This is the one."

I laugh. "I think so too."

My hands run down the softness, and I love how it makes me feel: classy and sexy.

"May I make one small suggestion, though?" She grimaces.

"Sure." My pulse bangs in my ears, unsure of what she's about to say.

"If it were me, I'd skip the panties on this one."

"Oh…" Glancing down at my hips, I can make out the outline of my underwear. "Is that what women do with dresses like these?"

"Mm-hmm. Some." She smiles, trying not to make me uncomfortable, but fails, because this is embarrassing.

I've never gone anywhere without underwear before. But I don't want to draw more attention to them either.

Ugh. This is so weird.

"Thanks for letting me know. Guess there's a first time for everything." My face heats up, and she lets out a laugh.

"You'll be fine, I promise. I remember the first time I did that and felt just like you. But now it's second nature." She removes a square case and unzips it. "We can start on your makeup now if you're ready."

"Yeah, sure. I'll go change."

Excitement builds. I've never had a makeover before.

When I come back out, I settle on the chair she's grabbed while she spends the next half hour on my face. Then it's time for hair.

When she's done, she examines me carefully. "I think you'll be really pleased."

Picking up a mirror, she tries to show me, but I stop her.

"I want to put the dress on first before I look at myself." My cheeks burn from how wide my grin is.

"Of course."

She starts returning everything into her bags while I head into the bedroom, sliding back into the shoes and dress.

With gradual steps, I head for the mirror, my throat growing tight with anticipation. When I finally see myself, I barely recognize the girl staring back at me.

"Oh my God…" I whisper, getting closer to look at my makeup.

My cheeks are shimmery with a soft pink blush. My eyelids have a deep brown hue to them, and my brows are perfect and filled. I part my pale pink lips, looking at my intricate updo, a few strands surrounding both sides of my face.

It's then I see Fionn in my mind, wondering what he'll think.

When I come out this time, Hannah gushes, "Boyfriend or not, Fionn is gonna lose his mind."

She winks, heading out the door, and as soon as I'm alone, my hands grow clammy.

And I realize there's nothing I want more right now than for Fionn to want me enough to do something about it.

FIVE

FIONN

I can't get her crushed expression out of my head.

Her disappointment burns through me.

She would've let me fuck her. Right there in that hallway. But damn, I knew it was wrong.

There's nothing I want more than to stalk right through the adjoining door and see her. To tell her how badly I want her.

Maybe once she's back home, I can take her out. Get to know her better. Let her get to know me.

Who the hell knows why I'm so damn drawn to her? There's something there, though. Something I want to explore.

"Fuck." I laugh.

She's just a kid. What the hell am I even thinking? But she seems way more grown up than any of the twentysomethings I've fucked.

Jesus. I've gotta get this girl out of my head before I rip off her clothes and bury myself so deep inside her, she'll never be able to get away.

As soon as she asked me about her dress, I knew she was embarrassed because she had nothing to wear. It wasn't hard to get her something she'd hopefully like. Don't know her well enough to know her style, but when the sales associate showed me those two dresses, I knew she'd look incredible in either.

Grabbing my cell, I head out of the room and knock on hers.

She opens immediately. And when I see her…

I didn't know my heart could do that. Beat so fucking loud, I hear it like a drum in my head.

"Holy shit…" My tone drops, and she smiles sweetly, batting those long lashes.

She's all made up, but I don't care much about that. She was beautiful without any makeup on too. But this dress…it leaves nothing to the imagination, yet is also just right for a black-tie event.

As I let my gaze wander down her curves, my hands burn to touch her, to feel every soft inch of her. Soon, I'll be forgetting all the reasons why I shouldn't make her mine.

My cock throbs the more I stare, and I groan low in my chest, barely holding on to my control.

How the hell am I supposed to be with her all night and not kiss her?

Or fuck her.

Or do anything.

"Is it too much?" She appears unsure, and I grab her hand and kiss the top of it.

"It's perfect." *Can't get the thought of you up against the wall with that dress around your hips out of my damn mind.* "You're breathtaking, Emily."

Something passes in her eyes when I say her name, though it disappears quickly.

"You really didn't have to go through all this trouble for me." She glances down at her feet, like she's not worthy of a man doing something nice for her. "But I really appreciate it."

Her attention returns to me, and my need to get her naked and in my bed all night long plays on a loop.

I cup her cheek, my gaze boring deeper. "I enjoy making you smile, and the way you smiled when you opened the door said it all."

Her face practically glows.

Gonna find out if that shithead is the only reason you're so damn sad, and if there's anyone else hurting you, they won't live long enough to do it again.

"Are you ready to go?" I slide my fingers through hers. "My brother needs us at the ceremony in ten. Will you be okay sitting by yourself for a bit?"

"Yeah, of course." She's nervous, I can tell.

"I'll have you sitting next to my father's wife, Fernanda. She's nice. You'll like her."

We start toward the elevator, entering it as it arrives.

"Don't fuss over me. This is your brother's wedding. I'll be fine."

I have no doubt that she will be, but she has no idea that she's about to walk into a room full of some of the most dangerous people in the world.

AMARA

We head down to the lobby and past check-in, looping around toward the back and into the outdoor area where the ceremony and reception will take place.

"There you bloody are."

An older man with a heavy Irish accent approaches as soon as we step in, his thick gray brows tugged in concern. Pale green eyes bounce between us, and I start to wonder if this is Fionn's father.

"And who might you be?" An easy smile forms on his face.

"I'm Emily."

"Hmm." His eyes narrow at Fionn. "Is she your date?"

"Maybe." He glances down at me with a smirk. "Don't pester her, Dad."

Dad. I was right. I can definitely see a resemblance.

"It's a pleasure to meet you, sir."

"Sir," he scoffs. "No need for formalities, darling. Let's get you seated at the front with my wife, Fernanda."

It's like he read his son's mind.

We head to the first row, where an older woman fingers her shoulder-length brown hair before rising to greet us.

"Hey, sweetheart," his father says. "Want to introduce you to Fionn's date, Emily."

"Emily." The woman's face is warm and kind as she looks me up and down. "It's so nice to meet you, and you look exceptional."

Her arms wrap around me and my eyes close, feeling the warmth of the embrace everywhere. I bet she's a good mother.

I brush those thoughts away as Fionn says, "I'll be back soon."

"Don't worry about her." Fernanda grins. "Us girls will be just fine."

He gives me one last glance before he's heading toward the men I saw with him earlier, when he was ready to kill Xander.

"So…" Fernanda settles back down and pats the seat beside her. "How did you two meet?"

I'm not sure how much to tell her, but then again, why not? What difference would it make? I have no plans of seeing her or Fionn ever again after I head back home.

"Well…" I play with my nails, nerves hitting my gut. "We just met a few hours ago."

"Oh! I have to hear this story." She swings toward me, eagerly waiting for me to start.

My body tenses. "I was here with my boyfriend until…well…"

My pulse beats louder in my ears.

Just say it. It's okay.

Her features tighten.

"Until Fionn saw him grabbing me, and he…he intercepted and kicked him out. And here we are." A nervous laugh bubbles out.

Her face grows concerned. "That boy usually hurt you?"

My eyes close for a moment while she drags in a long, shallow breath.

"I know I don't know you and you don't know me, but I understand." She places a comforting hand on my forearm. "Before I married Pat, I was married to a cruel man who hurt me any chance he got."

Tears form as I concentrate on her, mouth pinched, clearly trying to mask her own pain.

"I never wanted to marry him. My mother forced me into it and I had no choice. Divorcing wasn't an option, either. I couldn't get away from him, and every day I prayed I could. The point is, if you have a chance to escape, take it from me, do it before it's too late. Don't go back to him. Ever." She takes my hand and squeezes it. "You're young. Beautiful. You have your whole life to look forward to. Don't let this guy take it all from you, you hear me?"

With the backs of my fingers, I wipe under my eyes, nodding.

I know she's right. Of course she is. But hearing her say it out loud… It really brought out all this festering pain to the surface.

I wish I had a mother like her. Someone I could talk to. Someone who could give me advice or even just listen.

"Let me." She removes a handkerchief from her handbag and gently pats under my eyes. "Wouldn't want you smudging this beautiful makeup. Did you do it yourself?"

"Oh God, no." I grimace. "Fionn arranged it."

"Did he now?" Her brows rise with a smirk.

"Yeah." I let out a nervous giggle. "He was just being nice."

"Right." She nods. "Nice. Except I just never knew him to care this much about a woman before."

As soon as I try to respond, the ceremony begins.

When I look out, Fionn's eyes catch mine, and I start to hope that there's some truth to what Fernanda just said.

SIX

AMARA

As soon as the ceremony is over, Fionn disappears for a few minutes before he makes his way toward me. He slips his hand through mine, holding it tight as we stride into the cocktail hour as though we're together.

There are less than a hundred guests here, yet it's still overwhelming for me to be around so many people I don't know.

"Gonna introduce you to the rest of my family before they start introducing themselves," he jokes just as a tall redhead struts our way.

Her bright crimson gown fits her like a glove, her chin hiked up as she starts closer. She's got this aura of power around her, like with one look, she'd kill anyone standing in her way.

In fact, looking around the tented cocktail reception area, I find most of the people here to be powerful-looking. A chill skitters down my spine, but I ignore it. Must be the money.

"Who's that?" I whisper to him just as the woman and I make eye contact, her mouth curling into a salacious grin.

"My sister Iseult. I'd say she's all bark and no bite, but I'd be lying."

Before I can ask what that even meant, she's right in front of us, holding out a champagne flute for me.

"Thank you." I take it just as her eyes dance to her brother's, giving him an expression I can't decipher.

"Got yourself a secret girlfriend you forgot to tell us about?" Her face twists playfully, and he grows irate…though from the look on her, that was exactly what she wanted.

I stifle a laugh.

"She's not my girlfriend," he mutters, and those words sting even when they shouldn't.

Of course I'm not, nor will I ever be.

"What do you want, Iseult?" he continues, clearly needing her to stop.

"Just came to say hi to my favorite brother and his date. Didn't even know you were bringing one."

"Didn't know I needed your permission." He smirks. "And you don't have a favorite brother."

"That's what *you* think." She winks, focusing on me this time.

I reach out my hand for hers. "I'm Emily. We actually just met."

"Nice to meet you. I'm one of his sisters. There's quite a lot of us in the family, but don't worry, we're all friendly." A slow-growing smile widens on her lips. "Most of the time."

Laughing nervously, I glance at Fionn, tension thick in his features. It's obvious his sister enjoys torturing him. It would've been so much fun growing up with someone like her.

When I get older, I want to have lots of children so they never feel alone.

"Well, I hope we see more of you, Emily." Her eyes play before she's peering over at an irritated Fionn. She laughs as she leans closer toward me, whispering into my ear. "My brother has never introduced us to a woman until now."

Before I can wonder what she was attempting to mean by that, he's pulling me away.

"Let's go get a table. Bye, Iseult."

She chuckles. "Don't you worry. I'll steal her away at some point tonight and fill her in on all your darkest secrets."

He scoffs. "Pretty sure you've got more of those than I do."

"True. But I'm not the one she's sleeping with."

"We're not—ugh," I stammer, but she's already marching out of view.

She's got the wrong idea here. Fionn and I will absolutely never sleep together. It's pretty obvious he has no interest in me, not really.

Scratching the side of my neck, I glance nervously at him.

"Ignore her. She lives to mess with us."

"Yeah, I gathered that." My mouth pinches into a melancholy smile.

I want that so badly. I want a family. A real family.

We make it to the various buffet stations and Fionn grabs us two plates, while I'm still full from the steak. But the food here looks amazing and I kinda want to try everything.

"It must be nice to have siblings," I say, finding him peeking over as he hands me my plate. "I have none, and let me tell you, it sucks. I hated not having anyone to play with as a kid, and as an adult, it's been crappy not to have someone to confide in, you know?"

"I'm sure." He nods. "We were all close growing up, and as much as my sister fucks with me, I'd kill anyone who hurts her. Who hurts any one of them."

"That's what I mean." My mouth forms a thin line. "It's nice to have that."

His eyes go to mine, raw emotions painted within them. His hand reaches for me, knuckles brushing over my jaw, his gaze landing on my lips.

"I'm sorry." His voice whispers across my flesh, like a slow-moving flame licking across my skin.

I see it now, the way he wants me. I can almost feel it.

Yet he does nothing about it. Like he isn't sure if he wants to be attracted to me at all.

He lets out a harsh breath before turning away, and a heavy feeling pummels in my gut. He's never going to kiss me, is he?

"Why do you do that?"

I'm not even sure why I'm asking. But I'll never see him after today. Who cares at this point?

"Do what?" He places more food on our plates.

"Never mind." I head toward the first empty table I find, and he's right behind me, pulling a chair beside mine.

Ignoring him and the thundering way my heart beats as he places a palm on my knee, I stuff a baby tomato into my mouth.

What else is there to say? No matter what he's said, I know I'm not really his type. He's probably embarrassed that he's even remotely into me.

"Emily…" His thumb massages my skin, and I grow weak. Pretending I am Emily. That I'm someone else, someone he truly desires.

I know I shouldn't care. But a part of me wants something to happen. Maybe he can be the guy who actually shows me how good sex can be.

"Don't." I attempt to push his hand away, but he keeps it there, cupping my knee tighter.

He sighs. "Look…you're young. I can't. I'd break you."

Age? Is that what this is about?

"Maybe that's what I want." I hold his stare as he clenches his jaw. "Maybe I need someone who'll break me in half, then put me back together."

Who is this person talking like that? I'm suddenly braver than I've ever been, and I like it.

"Don't fucking say that to me, little rabbit," he grunts, grabbing my chin as he drops his mouth nearer, lips roughly stroking mine.

Shivers spread down my arms.

Oh God, this feels too good.

He groans. "I'm so close to forgetting all the reasons why I shouldn't take you upstairs to my room and taste every gorgeous inch of you."

I swallow thickly, aching for him between my thighs. "But you won't."

My chest rises and falls, pulse pounding in my ears.

He pulls back, a dejected look on his face, giving me the confirmation that I was right. This is a waste of time.

"I should go." I tug on my slit, still feeling his touch on my knee as though it's still there.

Just leave so you're not rejected again.

He drags in a long breath, pinching the bridge of his nose while I fight the tears and start to get to my feet. I'm too emotional to deal with a man who can't decide if he wants me or not. I need to text Emily for money ASAP so I can leave tomorrow.

"Don't." He grabs my wrist, face contorted with tension. "Stay."

"No." I shake my head, peeling his thick fingers off of me as I look down at him. "There's no point. Whatever this is…" I gesture between us. "It's not going anywhere, so it's best if we stay away from one another."

Before he can stop me, I swing around and storm toward the exit, hearing him muttering.

"Emily?" Iseult calls and I turn toward her. "Where are you going?" Her gaze turns to slits while she inspects my face. "Did my brother do something? Do you need me to kill him? You can choose how." The curve of her lips deepens into a smirk.

Sniffling, I let out a short breath of laughter. "Thanks for the offer, but I think it's best if I go. Thank you for having me. Tell your father and Fernanda I said goodbye."

Didn't even have time to meet the rest of the family.

Rushing out, I practically run toward the elevator. Once it arrives, I dash inside, and when I press the button for my floor, a hand stops the doors from closing.

My heart grows heavy when I see him. His strong, powerful form fills the space between us, his green eyes seemingly darker than they were a moment ago.

He stalks closer. And the nearer he gets, the more my heart beats faster.

When his powerful body meets my soft one, he pushes me up against the elevator wall until I can't so much as move.

His nostrils flare as he peers down at me, and my stomach clenches.

If a look could spell danger and primal need, this would be it. Like he wants to devour me right here. Right now. A craving so deep, I feel it rattling my bones.

I swear if he doesn't kiss me—if he doesn't do anything—I may be the one who'll kill him.

His deep-chested growl has me tugging my bottom lip between my teeth.

"Bidh tu am bàs dhomh," he says in Gaelic.

Before I can ask what that means, he wraps his fingers around my throat, his mouth dropping to my ear.

"What made you think you could walk away from me, baby girl?" He tips up my chin with his thumb, his tongue slipping out, taking a swipe across his full mouth.

"Please…" I beg, yet I don't even know what I'm begging for.

He grunts. "What do you want? Hmm?"

His free hand reaches behind us, pressing a button to stop the elevator from going further. A chill prances up my nape. What is he gonna do to me? And when was I ever this excited?

"Why did you come after me?"

I need him to say it. That he wants me.

His eyes turn laden with desire, fingers straining across my neck as he uses his other to slowly drag up my dress.

I've never been a fan of my thighs. They're too big. But right now, I don't care one bit if he sees them. Sees any part of me.

"I came because there was no other choice. No way I can just let you go like that."

"Oh God…" My head falls back as he continues to hike up my dress. "Touch me," I whisper, my lips trembling, my core throbbing for everything I know he can give.

When the pad of a single finger traces my pussy, I buck and cry out shamelessly.

"Jesus. You're not wearing any panties for me, love?"

"Hannah told me women don't wear any with these types of dresses," I utter breathlessly.

He groans, a slow-burning touch feathering my clit. My hands cling to his biceps, nails sinking into the muscle through his shirt.

"Remind me to give her a big fucking raise for that."

"Fionn!" I cry as he firmly strokes me there, making me quiver, my eyes rolling back.

"Look at me, mo ban dia."

And I do, too lost to keep wondering what those pretty words mean.

"Keep those eyes right here while I touch you." He plays me faster, and I let out a series of moans. "Yeah, that's it. Let me hear you beg for it like a needy fucking slut."

My gaze widens at his words, but I don't hate them. In fact, I like them. A lot.

Before I can analyze whether I've lost my mind, he thrusts his fingers inside me all the way.

"Yes!" My nails sink deeper into his flesh while I try to keep quiet so no one hears me.

"Fuck, you're tight," he growls, stretching me, sliding deeper with each stroke, and this intense feeling starts to burn inside me.

His hand around my throat tightens, the rhythm of his movements growing more urgent.

"Is this what you wanted?" His mouth feathers over mine, voice deep and hoarse. "What you needed?"

"Yes," I cry out.

His palm tightens around my throat, igniting every dead inch of me. He rams deeper, and my knees buck from the sensation, inching through my entire body. His large, towering form overpowers me, and I like it. Like being in his control.

I don't feel scared or suffocated. I feel free.

He thrusts faster, his thumb brushing over my clit. "Hear how wet this pussy is for me?"

I nod, toes contorting in pleasure.

Gradually, he pushes his body into me, arching his hips until I can feel his hard and heavy erection against my belly.

"Still doubt how bad I want you?"

"I—I don't know…"

His jaw clenches, and he reaches behind him and allows the elevator to move once again.

Slipping his fingers out of me, he pulls them into his mouth, sucking my taste off of them.

My eyes fill with shock. Can't believe he just did that.

Roughly he grabs my jaw, staring deep into my eyes and running those fingers over my lips. "Taste yourself."

He forces them into my mouth, and my eyes hold his as I suck them.

"Good girl," he hisses, grinding his teeth. "I know I shouldn't…" His forehead meets my own, his ragged breath hitting my lips. "But I'm too far gone to stop now."

"Then don't."

He bows back, eyes holding me hostage, like they don't want to let go. Before I think he'll change his mind and leave me here, he smashes his lips to mine.

He groans like he's lost to this. Our hands are everywhere. His tangled in my hair. Mine trying to untuck his shirt so I can feel his skin.

My God, I finally understand what lust truly means. Because this? This is magical.

I kiss him back, not knowing if I'm even doing it right. Trying not to think about that.

My heart beats heavily in my chest, ready to rip right out. This is too good. The way his tongue forces its way into me, the way he sucks my bottom lip, giving it a little bite. This kiss is like nothing I've ever experienced.

When the elevator dings, he slowly moves back, hands grasping each side of my face, eyes swimming with yearning.

"Let's go." He drags me out.

And with my pulse thundering, I follow him, unable to wait another moment for this to finally happen.

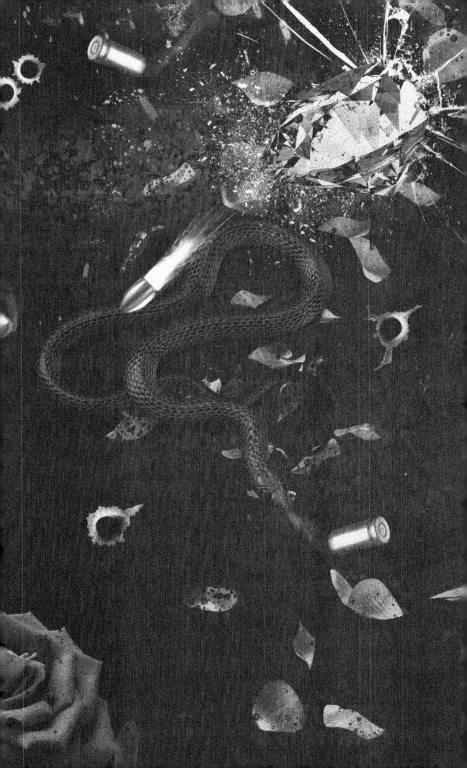

SEVEN

FIONN

Pushing her up against the outside of my hotel door, I clasp the side of her throat and drown in her wild eyes, filled with the same need coursing through me.

That kiss…shit. I don't think there's ever been a woman who made me want to kiss her that badly before.

Now, all I want is to do it again.

And again…

Want her in my bed. In my car. On the motherfucking floor.

But I'd be taking advantage. We both know that.

Would it make me a bigger asshole to fuck her now, or to make her wait for it until I know she's over that prick?

"Emily…" I drop my forehead to hers, exhaling a harsh breath.

She scoffs. "Are you serious right now?" Angrily, she pushes at my chest with both palms, glaring at me with hurt in her gorgeous features. "I can't believe I thought you actually liked me."

"Fuck, babe, I do. But—"

"No." She slides away from me, and I let her go.

Holding out a hand, she stops me from moving forward, tears forming in the corners of her eyes. "Save it. I'm going to my room. I don't want to hear anything else. Goodnight, Fionn."

This right here breaks my heart. But maybe it's for the best.

She doesn't belong in my world anyway. Too sweet and good. All the things that I'm not. It's better to let her go now before things go further.

She starts for her room, giving me one last broken look, and I'm close to stopping her.

But I don't.

Once her door is shut, I mutter a curse and head into my own, my fist flying straight for the wall, but I barely feel the pain. Bet she's over there crying, thinking I didn't find her attractive or some messed-up shit like that.

Gotta get her out of my head, though. She'll be gone soon. Hell, I don't even know her full name, and maybe it's best I don't.

Reaching into my jacket pocket, I remove a pair of her used panties. The ones I stole from her room after the wedding ceremony was over, when I disappeared for a few.

Bringing them to my nose, I inhale her scent. It feeds the fiery obsession simmering in my bloodstream.

I want her. Need her. Want to consume her.

It's not normal. I know that. But when the hell have I ever been normal?

Fuck.

I wanted these panties as soon as I saw them peeking beneath her blue sundress in her room. Now they're mine.

Balling them, I return the simple white cotton back into my pocket.

Didn't expect her to wear anything lacy. But I don't give a shit. With me, she wouldn't be wearing any.

Slipping out of my jacket, I work my tie off next, unbuttoning the shirt, needing to take care of this hard-on in the shower with thoughts filled with that sexy goddess next door.

Just as I'm about to do that, I hear a noise from her room.

Like she's crying.

Motherfucker. I'm a bastard.

Heading toward the adjacent wall, I try to get a better listen. Maybe I should go over there and talk to her.

But the more I hear, the more I wonder if I'm hearing right.

"What the…"

She's moaning. And it's not from tears.

"Shit."

Is she touching herself?

My head falls backward, my fist around the crown of my cock as I stroke it through my trousers.

I shouldn't. Nothing good will come from it. But it's all I want. All she wants. What kind of man would I be to deny her?

Just one night. That's all I need to get her out of my system.

Before I can talk myself out of it, I've got the universal hotel keycard in my hand, opening the door that separates our rooms. Everyone in my family has one. But she doesn't know that.

Not yet, anyway.

The door silently opens, and her moans fill my ears.

Holy shit.

Her bedroom's to the right of the living space. She's so close, I can taste her.

My footsteps fall with a low thud, my blood filling my ears.

When I get nearer, I find her door slightly ajar.

And she's there, fucking naked, the dress hung over a chair, her thighs spread open, fingers working her pussy. Her nipples are large and beaded, just waiting for me to taste and suck each one.

Want to bury my face in her sweet cunt and watch her let go around my tongue.

"Yes, Fionn," she cries, eyes shut, teeth scraping her bottom lip.

I let out a growl when hearing my name.

Fuck.

Her eyes instantly pop open, and at first, she doesn't notice me. Maybe there's a chance I can still save this. Watch her some more.

She gasps when our gazes connect.

Damn it. Too late.

"Oh my God! What are you doing here?" She yanks the blanket up to cover herself.

I snicker, pushing my way in. "Well, I was gonna stand here and watch you make yourself come thinking about me, but instead, I'd rather join you."

Her face turns crimson, teeth nipping her bottom lip.

There's no way I can deny her or myself now. Not when I've seen her like this, touching herself while saying my name like that.

"Chan eil mi làidir gu leòr," I mutter.

My jaw clenches, cock throbbing painfully. All rationality slipping away.

"What was I doing to you, little rabbit?" I advance closer. "How was I fucking that sweet pussy?"

Her chest grows flushed.

So perfect.

"Were you bent over, gripping the sheets while I took you roughly from behind?" I advance another step, and she backs into the headboard, body trembling with each ragged inhale. "Maybe you were riding me, using my body how you like. Is that it?"

She nods.

And my control instantly vanishes.

"Fuck it."

In a flash, I'm on her, grabbing her jaw and kissing her with everything I have. My fingers slide into her hair as I force my tongue into her mouth, sucking hers into mine.

When I back away, she swallows, trying to catch her breath.

"Fionn?" she whispers with a trembled breath. "What's happening?"

My fingers are on my cuffs, undoing them quickly, needing her like oxygen.

She watches me as I start on the buttons, releasing the shirt from my body while she bites that damn lip. My eyes grow heavy-lidded. I want this woman badly enough I'd scorch the earth just to have her.

I fling my shirt over the chaise, stepping out of my shoes before I fall closer to her needy, irresistible body. As I stare down at her, my palm wraps around her throat.

"You're watching me lose control." I tip her chin up with my thumb. "I can't resist you anymore."

EIGHT

FIONN

As soon as I say that, her breath hitches, brows furrowing. With one quick move, I snap the comforter free from her body, exposing every inch of her to my greedy eyes.

I take her in, my gaze sloping down the hills and valleys of her curves, wanting to get lost in them. With my free hand, I stroke a rosy nipple, pinching it between two fingers, causing her to gasp in pleasure.

My hand tightens around her throat. "I heard you through the wall, little rabbit. Heard the sweet sounds you were making. Was it on purpose?" I tug the other nipple, and she shuts her eyes with a cry. "Did you want me to hear you so I couldn't resist?"

"Maybe?" She whimpers, staring up at me hungrily.

"Well, here I am, baby girl." A growl crawls from deep in my chest. "And now there's no going back."

She's nervous. It's not hard to see how much. Yet she also wants

I'm done fighting it.

I tilt her chin up even more, and her eyes latch on to mine, glassy and desperate. Relentless as hell too.

What a beautiful sight.

"Remove my belt. And if you fuck up, I'll punish you."

Her gaze grows, yet she doesn't resist, sitting up on the edge of the bed. When she clutches the buckle with tentative hands, her fingers shake and it slips from her grasp. As it does, I grab her hips and flip her facedown on the bed, slapping her ass hard until she yelps, my fingers sinking inside her wet cunt before I slap her again.

My body falls over hers, hips circling into her ass, lips brushing behind her ear. "I warned you. Now be a good girl and don't mess up this time."

She nods with a whimper as I rise to full height, waiting for her to turn back around. When she does, her breathing's labored, her face flushed, but her fingers are surer this time as she undoes the buckle and yanks the belt free, refusing to look at me.

"Don't stop now. Pants too."

She pants, finally giving me those eyes I crave.

Wonder how many men she's been with and how much experience she has. Doubt it's that much from the way she's trembling.

That's okay. I like that better. Gonna teach her everything.

She unhooks the button of my trousers, the zipper too, before she's looking up at me with unsure eyes.

"Drag them down."

She bites her bottom lip and my fingers sink into her hair, groaning from the feeling of her soft strands.

Her small hands pull my pants lower, taking my boxers with them until I'm stepping out of them.

"Good fucking girl." I roll her long hair around my wrist and snap her head back when she tries to look at my dick. "I like how well you listen. Keep it up and I'll reward you." I tug harder. "You'd like that, wouldn't you?"

"Yes," she gasps.

My growl of approval has her pulling that bottom lip into her mouth.

"You keep biting that lip and I'm gonna pry that mouth apart and see how much of my cock you can fit before you're gagging on it."

"Oh God," she moans, so damn dirty I barely recognize the shy little girl she was earlier.

I release her, and her eyes immediately land on my jutting erection. A slow grin appears on my face as I drag my fist up and down the thick shaft, my thumb rolling over the three king's crown piercings.

She stares at it, her tits jittering from her uneven breaths. "I—I've never seen a pierced one before."

My chuckle has her glancing up. "How many have you seen exactly?"

And why do I wanna wipe the memory of every single one from your head?

"Just one."

"His?" The word comes out with rage hung around each letter.

She nods, and I hate that he got to touch something so beautiful. To hurt her…

Fuck. I need to kill him. I won't be able to go on knowing he's alive.

When her finger grazes the tip of my dick, I forget all about him.

"Keep touching it, baby." A grunt escapes.

Nervously, she reaches for the piercings, tracing each one slowly. "Did these hurt?"

"At the time, yeah. Now, not at all."

"Do they feel good?" Her innocent eyes suck me in.

I cup her jaw. "They will for you."

"Oh…" She swallows.

I laugh to myself. She has no idea how good it can be.

"Stroke me, baby."

"I don't really know how to do it right. He always said—"

Grabbing her throat, I grind my teeth. "Don't fucking finish that sentence. He doesn't exist here."

"I'm sorry."

"Wanna make it up to me?" I hit her with a half-smile.

"Yes."

My pulse beats faster. I'm a lucky bastard to have this sweet little thing staring up at me, all innocent and shy.

"Grab my cock. Right at the base."

Shaky fingers curl around me, peering up expectantly like she wants my instructions, and my dick jerks at the obedience.

"Squeeze it tighter."

"Like this?" Her small hand doesn't reach all the way around.

"Yeah, just like that. Now stroke me and keep your hand real tight."

She fists me up and down, and shit, it feels so damn good.

"Yes, good girl," I grunt. "That's it. Tighter."

She submits to my every demand, and it only makes this a lot more dangerous. Her submission is exactly what I want.

She gyrates her hips as she works me, pressing her ass into the bed while I grind my teeth, wanting her cunt wide open and my tongue inside it.

"Lie down on the bed now." I pull her hand away. "Think it's time I got a better taste of that pretty pink pussy. Finger-fucking you just wasn't enough."

Her lips tremble as she stares up at me with both arousal and shock, covering her tits with her arms.

I let out a small laugh, a single finger rolling down her arm until goose bumps spread. "Come on, baby. Don't be shy now. You wanted this, didn't you?"

Clasping her wrist, I drag her palm down, then the other, until her tits are mine to see. To own. To use.

All of her is mine.

Her face flushes.

"You're beautiful, Emily." My palm runs down her sternum. "Don't hide this perfect body from me, baby."

"It's far from perfect," she whispers, pissing me the hell off.

I have her throat in a tight grasp before she can say another negative thing about herself. "If I said you're perfect, it means you are." My hand cups her jaw, thumb stroking her full mouth. "If you say one more bad thing about yourself, I will punish you. Much harder this time."

Her gasping turns wild, eyes filled with this irresistible innocence.

I let out a deep, dark laugh. "I wanted you from the first moment I saw you. Wanted to fuck you until you lost count of how many times you came. And you wanted it too, didn't you? Wanted me to fill your cunt."

Her breaths grow unsteady.

"Yes," she whispers. "I wanted to know what it felt like."

Confusion settles in my brows, my thumb rolling over that full, fuckable mouth. "What *what* felt like?"

Her face flushes, and she tries to look away.

"Eyes on me, little rabbit."

Her unsure gaze only enhances my need to protect her. She's so damn innocent, it kills me.

"Tell me what you want. Swear I'll give it to you."

She pinches her eyes closed. "He never made me, you know…"

Shit.

"He never made you come?"

She shakes her head, lowering her eyes to her lap.

With every second, the reasons to kill that motherfucker only increase.

I incline her face with the back of my hand. "That's not your fault.

He was fucking selfish. Let me show you how a real man treats a woman."

Pushing her down onto the bed, I slowly force her thighs apart, even as she resists, and settle at her feet.

"Promise, I'm not him. I won't come until you do. On my hand…" I spread her wider, groaning when I take in her pink, glistening pussy.

With a palm, I work her clit, making her back bow, the sounds of pleasure spilling from her lips.

"On my tongue…" My thumb circles her there. "Then on my cock, before you're coming on my mouth again."

Two fingers thrust halfway in. And damn, she looks good. Back arched, tits in the air, eyes slammed shut with her pleasure as she fists the sheets.

"Fionn…" Hearing her moan my name makes it unbearable not to flip her on all fours and claim every perfect inch of her.

Gonna find out where she lives. Maybe move her into my home. It's big enough.

She cries out as I give it to her harder, fingers curling, taking her deeper. My cock is damn near painful.

"He's the only one who's been inside this little pussy?"

"Mmm, yes."

I groan with disapproval. That bastard doesn't deserve her.

Her mouth parts and quivers as I add a third finger while she tries to snap her knees from the pressure.

"Gonna erase every memory you had of that asshole." I force her legs open with one palm.

"Nothing to erase," she rasps. "He's never been any good."

I laugh. "Has he ever eaten you out?"

"What?"

I still my fingers inside her as she looks up.

"Has he used his mouth on you?"

She shakes her head. "He thought it was gross."

"So I'd be the first one?"

Her unending deep breaths, her face turning crimson… Fuck, it just makes me hungrier for this woman.

"Yes."

A smirk tips up one side of my face. "What else have you not done?"

My fingers slide out of her, dragging down to her ass. She gasps when I use her wetness to slip one finger in to my first knuckle.

"He ever take you here?"

She shakes her head. This day is getting better by the minute.

"Have you ever been tied up?"

Her brows shoot up, and she shakes her head.

I chuckle low in my chest. Of course she hasn't. Her apprehension just makes the idea of it even better.

My knuckles roll over the slope of her breast, lower, down her torso. "Would you like to be, little rabbit? Want to be at my mercy?"

"I…uh, I don't know. Maybe?"

"Brave girl." A grin spreads. "How about we start slow and see what you think?"

"Okay." Her breathing grows more labored.

"Trust me?"

"Stupidly, I do." She laughs nervously.

"Nothing stupid about it. I'd never hurt you, mo ban dia."

"I believe you."

Maybe she shouldn't. She knows nothing about me. What I do. Who I am. The things I could do to her.

"What does that mean? Mo ban dia?"

My gaze rakes down her body, drinking her in like bourbon. "My goddess. You're damn perfect, you know that?"

She swallows thickly, lying there like a queen.

My queen.

"If you were my girl, I'd have you walking around naked for me every minute of the day, just so I could bend you over and fuck you whenever I wanted."

Sliding a hand under her, I grab a fistful of her ass, so damn round, I wanna bury my face in it too. Rising to my feet, I grab my shirt, tearing it in half.

"You ready?"

With a shaky breath, she nods.

Taking both of her hands, I sit her up and tie her wrists behind her back. "How does that feel?"

"Okay," she murmurs.

I settle behind her, pulling her back up to my chest, widening her legs while my fingers rake the insides of her thighs.

"If you don't like something," I whisper into her ear, "and want me to stop, you'll use a safe word. What do you want it to be?"

"Uh…cranberry?"

I let out a hoarse chuckle, my cock jerking against her ass. "Okay, cranberry it is."

If she likes this, there's a chance she'll enjoy the rope too.

Probably getting ahead of myself.

My hands fall to her full hips, massaging her flesh as she quivers.

"What's your name? Your full name."

"Why?" she breathes, momentary fear slinking in her tone.

"Because…" My fingers slide between her thighs, feathering over her warm flesh. "Once I fuck you, I'm not gonna wanna stop, so I'd like to know the name of the woman I can't stop thinking about."

I sink a single finger inside her, and she moans, her head falling against my shoulder, breaths rolling out of her in succession as I watch myself touch her.

Two fingers slide in and out slowly. "Think I can tease the information out of you?"

"Oh God! Probably," she cries as I pinch her clit a little. "My—my name is Emily Daniels."

Emily Quinn sounds so much better.

Don't know what the hell I'm thinking, but I can't get this woman out of my damn head.

She circles that ass over my dick, and I fist her hair, grinding my teeth as I pummel deeper, the noise of her soaked pussy twining with her moans.

"Yes, yes, oh God, Fionn!" Her cries morph into gasps, the walls of her tight cunt sucking me in, and I know she's about to come.

I pump into her faster, swirling my finger around her clit until her entire body spasms and she's screaming for me.

"Yes! Fionn!"

My pace increases, wanting every damn drop.

"Such a good girl, coming for me so good." I yank her hair tighter, kissing just under her ear as her release completely takes over, body quivering, eyes pinning shut. "That's it, keep coming for me."

Sliding out, I slap her pussy. She jerks, whimpering when I do it again. I need inside her so fucking bad, I'm unable to wait.

Getting to my feet, I flip her over in a flash, heading for my wallet to get the condom I have.

Our eyes stay glued as I tear the wrapper with my teeth and slide the latex down over my dick. I walk over to where she still sits obediently, legs spread, waiting for her next command.

Grabbing the back of her head, I search her eyes, my heart beating like mad. "You're driving me crazy."

"I am?" she whispers.

She still doubts it?

A slow smirk spreads across my face. "You are."

Then I'm lifting her in my arms as she gasps from the shock of it. Her legs wrap around my hips, her eyes practically begging to own me.

Holding her up with one arm, I feather my knuckles down her cheek. "You don't know how special you are."

"I—"

But I don't give her a chance to tell me I'm wrong, crushing her lips with mine until her feminine sounds vibrate across my mouth. My hands are buried in her hair as my tongue enters, sweeping over hers.

Dragging back, I hold her stare, unable to stop. "Gonna make you come harder this time. Make you squirt on my cock over and over until you're begging me to stop."

"Please," she breathes, hungry for it again.

Poor thing has been deprived. Gonna show her how good it can be.

Throwing her on the bed, ass up, chest down, I spread her knees wider, while she looks at me from over her shoulder. I make myself comfortable behind her, my knuckles running down her spine while I clutch her ass, spreading it open.

"Perfect." When I lower my face, my tongue invades between her cheeks, the tip pressing into her entrance there before I suck her clit into my mouth.

"Oh God!" Her toes curl. "That's different."

"Good?" I chuckle.

"Yes." Her pained, lustful cry says it all.

Rising, I clutch a fistful of her hair, pushing her face onto the mattress, her bound wrists falling against the small of her back.

"There's no chance I'm gonna take it easy on you, little rabbit."

"Don't."

Her jagged breaths, the way her brows bow and her features twist… I know she wants it just as hard. She wants me to push her all the way, and I'll take great pleasure in it.

I press a thumb and a finger into each one of her holes, filling her up from both ends, slowly thrusting. Her pussy clamps around me and her moans grow more urgent and needy.

"Look how good you take it."

"Yes, please…" She can barely get the words out while I increase my rhythm, and just as she's about to come, I stop.

"No, no…please."

Getting on my knees behind her, I stroke my cock and circle the crown against her entrance.

"I'd say I was sorry…" I grab her hair in a tight fist. "But I'm not."

With one jerk of my hips, I'm inside her, and nothing has ever felt this good.

AMARA

He fucks me. There's no other way to describe what he's doing. The bed shakes.

My voice. My cries of need—loud and unabashed—unable to catch my breath. I beg him to take me harder, and I don't even recognize who I am right now.

I like who I am with him. It's as though, in a short time, he's shown me who I can be.

His palm pushes into my cheek, his other hand slapping me hard across my ass. "That's it, baby girl. Take every fucking inch and come on it."

His animalistic grunts, the sweat coating his forehead… It's so raw and masculine.

I've already come four times, him doing exactly as he promised, and I don't know how many more I have in me.

"Yes, please don't stop." I'm so close, I can almost taste it.

It's as though he knows my body better than I do. My hair is in his fist as he pistons inside so deep, it's like I'm floating.

I had no idea what I was truly missing. And now that I know, I don't know how I can give this guy up.

But I'll have to.

He tugs my hair, holding on while he rams inside me, like he's trying to ingrain himself into my body until we're one. The sound of our skin meeting as he pounds into me only intensifies every lustful feeling. The harder he takes me, the more that sensation inside me grows, like I'm going to explode.

"Yes!" I scream, my fingers curling at the small of my back as everything in me shatters, the most intense orgasm taking hold.

"Fuck, you're so damn sexy squirting all over my dick."

I did what?!

But I have no time to think. He increases his speed until he growls, pressing his hips into me as he releases into the condom.

His movements slow, his arm curling around my front as he kisses down my spine. "You're so damn special."

My eyes burn at the words. It's the second time he's said that, and he doesn't even realize how much it actually means to me. I've never heard that before.

"You okay, baby?" He tugs my chin to the side until our eyes meet, his cock still inside me.

"Mm, yeah." A lazy smile fastens on my lips. "That was… everything."

I let out a yawn, and he chuckles, undoing my wrists and massaging my skin there before he's sliding out of me and tossing the condom away.

When he returns, he stands over me like a god out of Greek mythology—strong, powerful, deadly even. He has this look in his eyes, like he knows what he's capable of. But I'm not at all scared of him.

"I want you in my bed." He slips his arms under me, and without a fight, I let him carry me into his bedroom.

Gently, he lowers me on the soft mattress before sliding in beside me. As he tucks my satiated body against his chest, his fingertips stroke up and down my arm.

"Go to sleep. We'll talk over breakfast tomorrow. Then maybe have a swim."

That sounds nice.

He pulls the duvet over us, and I burrow my cheek closer against his beating heart, this sense of comfort and peace overtaking me.

I want more than anything to tell him who I am, but I can't. My mother would ruin everything.

I have to accept this for what it is: a single night of pleasure, one I'll never have again.

"Night." A tight smile forms on my lips because he has no idea that I won't be here when he wakes up.

Leaving him is the best thing I can do for the both of us.

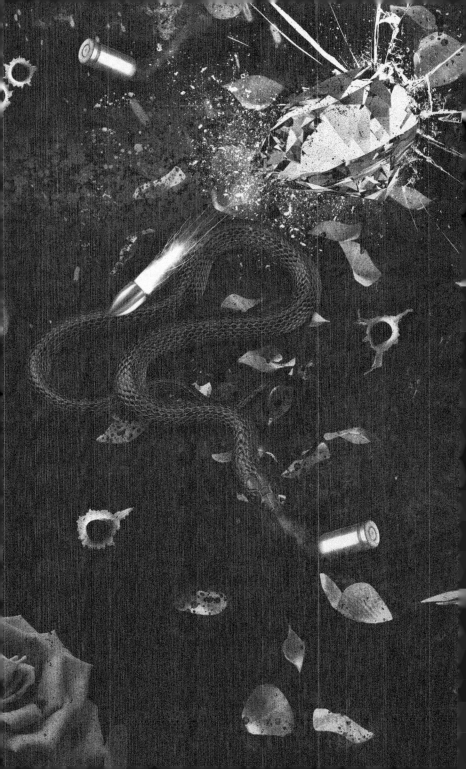

NINE

FIONN

"Good morning, little rabbit." I groan, stretching my limbs, a grin curling over my face at the thought of doing what we did last night all over again.

She doesn't say anything, and when I open my eyes, I realize why. The bed is empty.

My pulse quickens, and I rise to a seated position, staring down at what I was holding. Instead of her, I was hugging a damn pillow.

"Fuck!" Rushing to my feet, I look around my suite, running into the shower, not finding her there.

She probably went back to her own room.

Grabbing a clean pair of boxers, I slip into them and throw on some sweats, running a hand down my face as I head toward the door separating our rooms.

But it's locked. She's definitely there.

"Emily? Wanna get breakfast?"

I knock once. Twice. But no one comes to the door.

"Fucking hell." With the universal keycard in hand, I open the door and walk right in.

As soon as I do, my rage pummels through my blood.

The room is empty. And her luggage? It's gone.

"What the hell?" I open a drawer, the one she put her swimsuit into, and find her clothes gone.

She left. Why the fuck would she do that?

"God damn it." I hurry toward the exit, and as I do, I notice a piece of paper on the nightstand.

It's in my hand in seconds.

When I read her words, there's no doubt that she's gone.

She fucking left me.

I'm sorry, Fionn.

But we knew this was nothing more than a one-night stand.

Thank you for everything. I'll never forget you.

Emily

"Fuuuck!" I crumple up the piece of paper in my palm and stuff it into my pocket, stalking out of the room toward the security office.

When I make it to the lobby, I find my brothers there with Devlin, my baby sister, Eriu's, husband.

Not even saying hello, I march past them.

"What made you angry as shit this morning?" Cillian calls out, trying to get my attention. "And where's your shirt?"

He chuckles while I shut my eyes, curling a fist. I'm *so* not in the fucking mood.

"Where's your girlfriend?" Tynan calls as I turn to face them.

"You sure as hell rushed out of the wedding pretty quickly, and we never saw you again."

"Leave him the bloody hell alone," Devlin says in his heavy Irish drawl. "She still in your bed? Gonna get her some breakfast?" He smirks.

"That's husband material right there." Cillian has another laugh at my expense.

"Speaking of husbands…" Tynan starts to get up. "I gotta get my wife some coffee before she chews my head off for being slow." He grins, like the thought is pleasing.

I don't crack a smile, and they definitely notice from the narrowed expressions on their faces. Usually I'm the one who's cracking jokes, but not this time.

I can't believe she's gone. I thought we had a connection, but she just fucking left like it meant nothing.

I need to find her.

"She's gone." My jaw clenches.

That gets even more of their attention.

Tynan's brows crease. "Where?"

"How the hell do I know? She left while I was sleeping."

I'm so damn pissed at myself for not waking up.

"I'm heading toward security to look at cameras to see what time she sneaked out. Maybe I can still catch her at the airport."

Getting off the island isn't that easy. She'd need to catch a ferry first.

"You did always sleep like a log." Cillian snickers.

Devlin smacks him on the chest. "Read the room, man."

He raises his hands in apology. "Is her phone turned off? Can we track it?"

"Don't have her number."

"Oh, come on," Cillian scoffs. "Why the hell not?"

Definitely feel like an idiot. Don't need him reminding me.

"Things happened fast. Didn't have time."

"Got it." He smirks. "What's her name?"

"Emily Daniels, and she lives in Boston. That's all I know."

"We can work with that." Tynan slaps me on the shoulder. "Let me text Elara that I'll be a bit late."

"No, go. This is your wedding weekend. You don't have to be stuck with my shit."

But he's already got his phone out, typing to his new wife.

He laughs. "Elara said you're an idiot."

Groaning, I run a hand through my hair. "Tell her I already know that."

That's what I get for growing attached to a girl I had no business sleeping with.

Maybe I should forget her. Let this go. She's not right for me.

But the thought of never seeing her again, someone else having what I've deemed as mine... I can't live with that.

My fingers tighten into fists. Her boyfriend stayed here. All I need to do is find him and get her number and address.

"Come on," Tynan says. "Let's see what we can get from the security cams."

We start for the back of the hotel, finding the head IT guy before a set of computers typing some shit.

He glances up, scratching the grays at his sides. "Sirs, what can I do for you?"

"Move," I demand.

His eyes expand as he gets to his feet, letting me have at the computer.

When I find the boyfriend's info, I snap a picture of it before going through the security cams from last night.

Moments later, I find her.

Four a.m. She left at four in the damn morning so I wouldn't see it. Because she knew I'd stop her.

Her eyes scan the hallway as though she's afraid of getting caught. And for a moment, she glances at the security camera, and I freeze it.

"A flight to Boston left here an hour ago at eight a.m." Tynan's voice only infuriates me.

When he clasps my shoulder, I fling it away.

Tracing her face with a finger, I remember how much she trusted me with her body last night. I know it took a lot for her, but she trusted me anyway. That meant something to me.

Switching screens, I type in her boyfriend's name and number, and after a few minutes, I have a face.

"What the hell?" Cillian mutters behind me. "That's not him."

"No. It's not." My chest tightens, heaving with fucking rage like I've never felt before.

He used a different name.

Growling, I slam a fist to the top of the desk. "Gonna need to look up every Emily Daniels in Boston, assuming she didn't lie to me about that too, and run her through facial recognition once we get back home."

One way or another, I'm gonna find you, little rabbit, and I'm gonna punish you for this.

AMARA

Wiping a tear from my eye, I press my face against the window of the plane, finally in the air and able to breathe easier.

I hated just leaving him like that, but I had no choice. I didn't want him to stop me.

There's no way he'll be able to find me. He doesn't know my name. He has nothing, except Xander. But Xander never uses his real name when he books hotels. He's crazy secretive about people knowing his identity, and I'm pretty sure he paid for the room with his father's business card.

When I shut my eyes, Fionn is there, those green eyes searching mine as though reaching into my soul.

It's stupid how much I liked him after knowing him for a few hours. There was something there. Something tangible and real. It held potential. I know it did.

But it's gone now. And my heart is broken.

He'll wake up soon, if he hasn't already, and find my note. I wonder if his heart will break too.

I don't want it to. He's a good man. I'm sure he'll get over it. Any woman would be happy to take his pain away.

Me? Well, I'll be thinking about him long after I get home. Hanging on to every moment we had together because it was something incredible.

Invisible Amara. That's how I've always felt. But with him, I wasn't invisible at all.

He saw me. Really saw.

The back of my throat stings, but I ignore it, taking my soda and drinking a few gulps.

Maybe if I sleep, I'll feel better.

With a sigh, I shut my eyes and fall into darkness, unsure what's waiting for me on the other side.

"Look!"

A little girl with eyes that look like mine grins at a woman. Her face is blurred, but the baby girl this toddler is holding is clear as day.

Her little mouth pinches and she coos, grabbing the toddler's finger.

"Look, she loves me." Her eyes round with excitement and love. So much love, I can feel it.

"Yes, she does, sweetheart."

The woman doesn't say the child's name, but she's me. I know she is. Everything about her feels familiar.

But the newborn? I don't know who she is.

The baby starts to cry, but the little girl shushes her, calmly rocking her as she smiles. "Don't cry."

But as she continues to rock her, the baby flickers, like she's withering away on a television screen.

"Mommy?" Terror fills the child's voice.

My *voice.*

"Mommy! Help!" She rocks her faster. "Don't go! Please! Mommy, help me!"

The girl wails, but the woman is gone now, the baby in her arms slowly disappearing.

Her legs.

Her chest.

Like in slow motion.

Until her face is gone too.

The child screams, her body trembling, tears leaking out of her eyes.

The room is now empty. Black.

And soon enough, the girl...she disappears too.

Gasping, I startle awake.

The woman next to me gives me an annoyed look.

I clutch my chest, my heart beating frantically.

That dream, it's back. It's been weeks since I've had it. Why now?

I hate it. Every time it comes, it scares me, and I don't know why. It started when I was maybe ten. Like out of nowhere. I'd have the same dream a few times a week.

I was happy when it stopped a few months ago, and I thought it was over.

Clearly I was fooling myself.

I still can't make sense of it. I've asked my mother, but she tells me it's just a dream. Means nothing. Yet I have this sense that it somehow does. Like it's telling me something.

But what? What does it mean? That I'm losing myself? That I have no one to care about me?

I already knew all that.

Maybe it's some kind of sign that I should look for my father. That I'm missing some connection to my past or something.

I don't know, but once I get home, I intend to find him. To find what's missing.

Maybe that'll help me stop thinking about the man I left back on that island and all the things we could've had.

TEN

AMARA

A s soon as I land, Emily's there, grinning as she waves from her white sedan.

"Hey! You're all tanned and sexy." She helps me with my luggage before we shuffle into the car and she's taking us on the road.

"Yeah, guess I did get a nice tan." I slide my hair behind my ear, releasing a sigh.

Her dark eyes narrow. "What's the matter? Did the asshole call you?"

"No." I stare out the window, feeling a pang of guilt over not telling her about Fionn.

We tell each other everything, but I'd rather not talk about him. Easier that way.

"Then what's wrong?"

I shrug. "Just hate that I have to go home." Blowing a breath, I give her a small smile. "Sorry, don't mean to be all doom and gloom."

"I don't blame you." She places a hand on my forearm. "You've had it harder than anyone I know."

"It could always be worse." I force a smile. "Thanks again for picking me up and for the money. You're the best, you know that?"

"I know." She cocks her chin.

"I promise I'll pay you back ASAP."

"Oh, shut up. It's a gift."

My mouth widens. "Absolutely not! I *will* pay you back."

"Okay." She shrugs, smirking. "Whatever makes you happy, but I'll just give it back to you."

My eyes water, and I try not to cry.

She's always been the one person I can count on in this world. Don't know what I'd do without her. She even stayed back and didn't go to the college she wanted to attend all because my mother forced me to quit high school.

She said she had cancer. She never actually did.

Knots form in my gut at the memories.

Unfortunately, I didn't know that. Not until it was too late.

AGE 17

I stare at the letter from my dream school, the one Emily was already accepted to last week, unable to open it. Every day, I've checked the mail, hoping I got accepted too.

"I don't think I can look." I clutch it against my chest. "What if they said no?"

She rolls her eyes. "Then they're idiots. You have a better GPA than I do. Of course you got in."

My pulse hammers as I start to open it.

"Plus, I'll go wherever you do anyway." She runs her fingers through her shoulder-length chestnut waves.

"You've always wanted to go to UCLA. Of course you'll go."

She shoves me playfully. "Stop telling me what to do and open it!"

"Okay, okay!" I grimace, my stomach twisted up with nerves.

My fingers start gently tearing open the flap.

"Amara." My mother's voice comes through before she shoves the door open. "Oh, hi, you're here," she mutters at Emily, who has perfected her stink-eye when it comes to my mother.

"What is it, Mom?"

She sighs all dramatically and starts further inside, and I know instantly it's nothing good. I'm sure she's gonna tell me she's quitting that job she got at the supermarket last week, or maybe her latest boyfriend stopped selling her drugs, so she found another. It could be literally anything with her.

"I've got some news, and it ain't good." Her eyes pinch closed, and her chin trembles like she's crying, but I don't see any tears.

"Mom? What is it?" Fear grips me as I steal glances at Emily, who seems more curious than concerned.

"Can you leave so I can talk to my daughter alone?" She scowls at my friend, who folds her arms over her chest.

"Think I'll stay."

"Mom, it's fine. Whatever it is, you can tell us both."

"Okay." She sighs, her body deflating. "Not like she won't find out anyway."

Emily's eyes connect with mine, and fear passes through me. Maybe something is wrong this time. Really wrong.

"I've got cancer," she blurts out like she's telling me what she wants for dinner.

I suck in a gasp. "What? I—I—I don't understand."

"I know," she huffs. "I went for my gyno visit last week and the doc told me the news. Said it's pretty bad. Need to get chemo and radiation and all that starting in a few days."

"Oh my God!" I jump off the bed, throwing my arms around her.

No matter how terrible she's been to me, she's still my mother. "I'm so sorry. You're gonna be okay, right?"

She barely hugs me before pushing me off, and that little part of me that has always wanted her love dies even more.

"I hope so. The doc wants me to quit my job, though. Says I can't be doing manual labor when I'm on chemo."

"Right. Of course. We'll figure it out. You just focus on getting better."

"Well, that's the thing." She clears her throat. "I already figured it all out."

"What do you mean?" Confusion swirls as she pushes her knotty brown hair behind her shoulder.

"Being that I can't work and you're more than capable, I decided it's gonna be you who'll be working because we're gonna have to pay rent or we'll end up on the street."

"Uh, okay. Yeah, of course. I can get some shifts at the movie theater after school. They were looking for people."

She laughs, shaking her head. "That's not gonna cut it. You're gonna have to quit school and work actual jobs instead of going to college. That whole going-away-to-school plan you had going ain't gonna work out for me anymore."

"What?" Emily fires before I can get a word out.

My world spins, tears burning behind my eyes.

"Are you telling me you're gonna force your daughter to quit high school just so she can go work to support you when you have never held a damn job for more than a week?"

My mother moves toward her, nostrils flared. "You have some nerve speaking to me like that, you little rich bitch. What do you know about the real world when Mommy and Daddy hand you everything on a silver platter? You've never had to work for a thing in your life."

Emily's features go visibly tight. "And I know my parents would never tell me to quit school just so I could work. They'd do whatever they could to make sure I graduated and had an education."

She tsks. "Please! An education? The only education a girl needs is to know how to use her body to get what she wants. That's all, honey. Maybe you'll learn one day."

Emily's mouth twitches like she's about to say something else, her expression so rage-filled, I don't think I've ever seen her this way.

"I'm going now. Gotta call your school to tell them you won't be coming back."

"Nonono! Please, Mom!" I rush over and grab her wrist. "I—I swear, I can work two jobs. I can help! But please, I need to finish school. I need to go to college!"

My heart feels as if it's being torn piece by piece, but she merely snickers.

"Sorry, honey. But sometimes we gotta make sacrifices for people we love, and this is yours."

My hands shake as I sob. "Please! I've never asked for anything. But I'm asking, Mom. Please let me do this! I can help us. I can get better jobs with a degree. I've always wanted to go to—"

"Stop making a scene, Amara. You look pathetic."

My heart still stings from her words. Her lies.

She fooled me. Made herself appear sick. Even faked doctor's appointments that her boyfriend was pretending to drive her to. He was just as much of an asshole as she was.

She wanted to ruin my life. That's why she did it. Ruin my chances of getting an education and going away to college somewhere far away.

Now I'm stuck here. With her. Working to pay rent that she won't pay. If I don't, I'll have to move. Everything is so expensive, I can't afford it.

At least I've got Max, my golden retriever. Bet he missed me. I hated leaving him with my mother, but I had no choice. Emily's mom is allergic to dogs, or she would've taken care of him.

"Maybe you can move in with me. My parents said you can take the basement and—"

"No." I run a hand down my face. "I appreciate that, but I'd never inconvenience your family that way, Em. Especially with your mom's allergies."

She sighs. "Well, the offer is always there."

"I know. You're too good to me, and if it wasn't for you, I'd have no one, so thank you for being my friend." I drop my head over her shoulder. "I mean that."

"I love you, stupid. Don't make me all weepy. I hate crying."

Laughing, I squeeze her forearm.

Less than an hour later, we're pulling up to my home—the shutters cracked, the wooden fence with broken pieces across the dead grass. I hate everything about this place.

My chest tightens as I stare at it. "Thanks. I'll talk to you later."

"Okay." Her voice grows sympathetic. "If you need me, just text me."

"I will." Dragging a breath, I start out of the car.

Once the door closes, I head up the stairs while she waits for me to get inside. The neighborhood isn't the best. It's great for Mom, though. She can easily buy crack on the corner.

A pang hits my chest as I enter through the door, waving at Emily before I face her.

Will I always live here? Never having anything better?

Shaking my head, I steel my spine and head past the foyer with its yellow paint peeling. The landlord was supposed to fix it months ago, and he still hasn't come around. Guess I'll have to call him again.

"Max!" I glance around for him.

He usually runs right up to me. Wonder if he's sleeping upstairs.

"Max!"

"Stop yelling."

Mom shuffles in, her white shirt stained with spots of brown, her dark hair a disheveled mess, like she hasn't brushed it for weeks—which she probably hasn't. Her red-streaked eyes are glassy and spaced out as she tries to maintain her attention on me. She scratches the side of her dark hair, and I hate that I look like her.

"Where's Max? Have you fed him while I was away?"

It was only three days, but knowing her, I have to ask.

She snickers. "He ain't here."

All the blood rushes out of my body. "Wh-what? Where is he?"

She shrugs.

"Max!" Moisture forms in my eyes. "What did you do to him? Max!" A sob escapes.

Her laugh only enrages me.

"You think if you yell, he'll magically appear or something?" She rolls her eyes. "He ran out of the gate. You know there's a hole there. It's your problem you never got it fixed."

When she starts to walk away, I grab her arm, my heart shattering into pieces. "You're the parent! I'm the child!" Tears stream down my face and my body trembles. "You were supposed to watch him when he went out! That's what I told you to do."

I never should've gone away, but Xander insisted I go to the engagement party, and now Max is gone!

She flings my hand away. "Don't fucking touch me, you ungrateful little bitch! Next time, get your mutt a sitter. I ain't his keeper."

"When did he run away?" I holler, my blood pumping faster in my ears.

He can't be gone! Not Max!

I let out another sob. Maybe there's a chance he's still close. If he hears me calling for him, he'll come.

"I don't know. Sometime during the first day you left."

"Oh my God," I whisper, my vision blurring, my throat going dry.

He could be anywhere. Someone could've taken him. There are people here who use dogs for dog fighting.

"No!" I break down, while she struts away as though she didn't just send him to a death sentence.

Wish it was her instead.

"Don't cry." Emily grips me tight, though she's crying too. She loved Max. "I can't believe she didn't look for him or anything. My God, what an evil bitch."

Swiping under my eyes, I separate from her. "Let's go put up those flyers in as many places as we can. Maybe someone nice took him."

But I'm just grasping at straws. The chances of that are slim.

"Okay. I also put up notices in different online pet groups in the area. We'll find him."

I'm not so sure.

Hours later, we've put up flyers everywhere and given them to every business we could. If there's a chance he can be found, I'll do anything.

Defeated, we head for Emily's car.

"I should go and unpack to keep my mind occupied, but I don't wanna go home and see her or see Max's bowls in the kitchen." Another sob wracks me as I enter the passenger side.

She grabs my hand while starting the car. "How about I help you? That way it'll go faster. Then maybe you can come by my place for a sleepover. We can order Chinese, watch *Dirty Dancing* for the seventeenth time, and dream of men like Johnny."

She's trying to distract me from the pain; I know that. It's not what I need, though. I want to be sad. I want to scream and cry and smash something.

I pinch the bridge of my nose. "I don't think so."

"Come on. I don't want you to be alone and cry all night. That won't help Max."

It's better not to be alone, but I don't want to eat and watch a movie like nothing's going on. Like Max isn't out there all alone, wondering why I'm not there to bring him home.

The back of my nose stings and tears trample down my cheeks.

"Can we watch *Marley and Me*?" I sniffle, swiping under my eyes.

With a pout, she nods.

That movie will have us both sobbing like always, now worse than ever.

We return to my house, and I don't see my so-called mother anywhere. Maybe her new boyfriend came to pick her up. Hopefully, he keeps her.

Entering my room, I lock the door behind us. It's not much, but I've made it a home. Got a cheap bed set and some decorative pillows that Emily gave me. My luggage is in the corner where I left it before I called Emily, begging her to help me find Max.

"I don't have a lot to put away," I tell her as I lay the luggage flat and unzip it, removing the clothes I need to hang back in the closet while tossing the dirty ones in the hamper.

All the while, I'm thinking of Max and where he could be. He's probably terrified.

"That's okay. I'm here regardless." She starts unzipping the side pockets where I have my toiletries while I head for the closet.

"So, did you like the island?" she asks. "I've never been."

"Yeah, it was pretty. But I didn't get to do much since we only did what Xander wanted."

"Fuck that guy." She snickers.

"Yeah," I laugh through the tears. "Fuck that guy."

"That's the spirit."

We move in silence for a few minutes, almost done with everything.

"Um, Amara?" Her voice grows tense.

I glance at her from over my shoulder. "Yeah?"

"Who's Fionn, and why does he think your name is Emily?"

My eyes swell, a cold rush running down my arms. How the hell does she know all that?

"Um, no one?" I twist around toward her.

"Really?" She settles a hand on her hip, a brow hiked up. "Then what's this?" She holds out an envelope.

My heart beats faster. "I have no idea."

"That's interesting." She looks down at the envelope and reads. "You're no charity case, Emily, but I thought maybe this would help. Fionn."

When she opens the flap, she reveals a wad of cash. More money than I've ever seen.

"Holy shit…"

She arches a sassy brow. "Still wanna pretend you don't know who Fionn is?"

I groan, slapping a hand over my face.

"Spill. Now."

"Fine." I huff out a breath, taking the envelope from her and tracing his name.

I can't believe he did that. When did he even have a chance? He did have the key to my room. It's how he came in when I was doing *that* to thoughts of him. I'm sure he sneaked off at some point.

Staring down at the cash, I can't believe this is all mine. Then again, I can't in good conscience use it.

Can I?

Though he did intend for me to have it, and he *is* rich.

No. No, I can't.

But I don't even know where he lives to return it. I could try looking him up with just the first name.

I stare at the cash again.

My God, how much is in here?

"I'm waiting." Emily plops on the bed, curling her arms over her chest.

"Well, while I was on the island, I met a man."

When I'm finished telling her everything, she can't believe her ears.

"And you didn't get his number? Amara! What the hell? What were you thinking?"

I lower onto the bed, releasing a jagged exhale. "I was thinking that a man like him wouldn't want some poor nobody like me. And he was also very hot and cold, especially at first. My age bothered him most of all, I think." I huff out a tired exhale. "Then I thought, what happens when my mother finds out he comes from money? She'd do something to ruin my relationship. You know how she is. Look what she did with Max."

"Oh, Amara, I'm so sorry." She squeezes my hand. "But you can't live this way. You can't make decisions based on what you think she'll do. You have to escape from under her thumb."

"And how do I do that?"

"I don't know, but we have to figure out a way. Maybe you could get your GED and do online college classes."

"Yeah, maybe."

When I'm rich...

I take the money and split it up into ten piles, hiding each one in a different location in my room where I hope my mother doesn't find it. But if she locates one pile, maybe she won't look for more.

I still can't get over the amount. $9,900. I have never seen this much before.

This money will really help me, and I swear to not waste a dollar unless necessary.

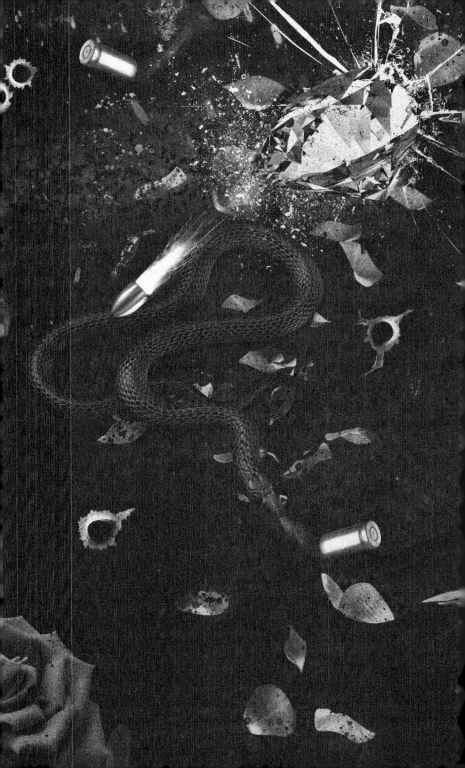

ELEVEN

FIONN

I pour myself a glass of bourbon, leaning into the leather chair in the underground casino we run. When I toss it back, the liquid burns down my throat, not alleviating the rage, which grows with each damn day.

My little rabbit has been gone for three weeks. I swear not being able to find her is going to kill me. And every *fucking* day, I lose even more of my sanity.

But I know I'm gonna find her. No matter how long it takes.

She *will* be mine.

There's a knock on the door, and I know it's one of my men here to bring a gift. A gift I can take all my aggression out on. Who better on than the guy selling crack in my casino?

"Come in."

The door opens, and my two guys are dragging a beaten-up, sorry son of a bitch, blood dripping from his mouth.

"Ah, finally."

LILIAN HARRIS

They drop him on the ground while I start undoing my cuffs.

"So…" I drag my sleeves up, kneeling before the whimpering, pathetic asshole. "You thought you could come to our club and sell here?"

"I—I'm sorry, man. I made a mistake. I—I—I didn't know it was Mob territory."

Cracking my neck, I let out a long sigh, heading toward the closet behind the desk. When I return with a black case and drop it on the floor beside him, he cries.

My body jerks with a dry chuckle. "I'm gonna spend the next hour teaching you not to shit where we eat."

When I remove a hammer, he tries to get to his feet, but my men push him back down.

"Now, are you a righty or a lefty?"

I swing the hammer in my grasp, seeing her face in my head. Those gorgeous eyes I've been dying to get lost in for the past twenty-one *fucking* days.

But she left. She fucking left, and I can't seem to find her.

With a roar, I swing the hammer down, crushing his right hand. His scream only feeds my fury.

"P-p-p-please, no-no more!" he wails.

While he begs, I drop the hammer on the floor and remove a knife from my desk, running a hand through my hair.

My eyes shut, and I see her, the way she lay in my arms that night as I held her.

Reaching into my pocket, I squeeze her panties. I carry them with me at all times like a damn lunatic. I ball my hand, heart hammering.

Fuck, I need to kill something.

"Pry his mouth open."

My men do as they're told while he fights them, both of his eyes so bruised, I'm surprised he can see at all. When the men have him held down, I grip his tongue and slice it off.

104

Blood. So much of it, yet all I want is more.

Need to hurt someone else.

That woman has fucking ruined me!

And until I find her, this is what I've become: a madman riddled with an obsession he can't escape.

AMARA

"You should go home," Kerry, my boss at the café, says as I head out from the restroom.

The nausea hit me out of nowhere today, and I can't seem to stop hurling into the toilet.

But I can't go home. I have to work. We need the money, and I have to pay Emily back for the plane ticket. I refuse to use the money Fionn left me. It's only for real emergencies, and this isn't one.

"No, I'm fine." I clear my throat, but as soon as I do, I rush into the bathroom again.

"You're going home, and that's final," I hear her say. "And take tomorrow off too."

Great. I probably picked up a virus.

Washing my face, I head for my locker to grab my handbag, seeing a missed text from Emily.

EMILY

Hey, are you around later? Wanna grab dinner?

AMARA

I don't think so. Leaving work now because I can't stop throwing up.

EMILY

Oh no! I'm coming to get you. I'm not far.

AMARA

I'm fine with taking the bus.

EMILY

Absolutely not. Stay there. I'll text when I'm outside.

Ten minutes later, and I'm in her car, her eyes assessing me with pity.

"You look like shit, and I mean that in the nicest way possible."

"Thanks so much." I throw my head back. "I don't know what's going on with me."

"Maybe we should go to a clinic to check for the flu or something. It's going around."

"I don't feel like I have the flu."

She accelerates her BMW, a new car her parents got her, turning a corner as she glances at me for a second. "You never know. I'd rather you be careful."

"I think I just need sleep."

She huffs. "You need a doctor. Not gonna have you dying on me."

"You're being dramatic."

"Really? Need I remind you how Sierra died? Hmm?"

"No," I mutter.

But not everyone's flu develops into pneumonia, which then kills them. Her best friend from childhood, whom I never met, is why she has become paranoid when people get sick, so I'm willing to go just to appease her. She's been a great friend. My only friend. I don't have a way to pay her back for all the times she's helped me, but I can do this.

"Fine, I'll go. But only because I love you."

She grins, her brown hair swinging in her short ponytail.

I hope there's no copay for this. But of course there will be. I can use Fionn's money for that, though.

"If you feel better tomorrow, maybe we can do dinner."

I really don't want to. I don't have money to throw away like that, and I don't want her paying for me like she usually does.

"There are a few new people from school I wanted to introduce you to," she continues, ignorant to my inner turmoil.

"Why?"

She's in college, making friends, while I'm here working a shitty job, knowing I'll never get the opportunity to do the same. I realized long ago that no matter what, my mother would find a way to keep me from going to college.

"Why?" She glares at me like I've grown two heads. "What do you mean, why? Because I want us all to be friends."

"I have you. I don't need anyone else."

She rolls her eyes. "Stop your shit. Whenever you feel better, I'll plan something. You'll love Lilith and Patricia. They're cool."

"If you say so."

"I do say so." She smacks my knee playfully, blowing a big breath, her expression crestfallen.

"What is it, Em?" I sit up straighter.

"I just…I just hate this for you, you know? You should've been in college with me." She scoffs. "Your mother ruined it all."

She ruined a lot of things.

Pain hits my chest when I think about Max. He's still nowhere to be found. We've looked at every shelter. Asked every person we can. But there's still no word.

Tears burn my eyes, but I push them away. I'll never stop looking for him, but every day, the hope dwindles away.

She pulls up at a clinic, heading in with me. Someone at the front desk checks us in, and we settle in the waiting area. My foot bounces the entire twenty minutes until they're calling me inside.

"Ms. Edwards," a nurse greets me. "What brought you here today?"

"I'm nauseous and have been throwing up all day."

"When did it start?" She types on her tablet, glancing up at me.

"Today. I'm sure I'm fine. Maybe I ate something bad."

"Can you check her for the flu or strep?" Emily intercepts.

"My throat doesn't even hurt." I stare at her, mouthing *shut up* while she rolls her eyes at me.

The nurse laughs. "I'll let the doctor decide that. She'll be in to see you in just a moment."

Once she leaves, I look over at Em. "Seriously? Strep?"

She shrugs. "Better safe than sorry."

The door opens again, and a woman no older than my mother walks in, the same nurse behind her.

"Hello. I'm Doctor Evans. I've heard we haven't been feeling well." She looks over at the notes on the screen of her own tablet.

"Yes. Maybe some anti-nausea meds will help."

"Well, let's run some tests to get to the root of the problem first."

"Thank you!" Emily scoffs in that *I told you so* way, and I roll my eyes at her.

The doctor checks my ears and throat, then makes sure my breathing is good before she makes more notes. "Let's take a urine sample and do a throat and nose swab to rule out the flu, strep, or COVID."

The nurse proceeds with that and sends me to the restroom with a cup. After I'm done, I place it in the designated slot and return to the office.

"We'll wait for urine and the other test results and be back," the doctor tells us while I grow more irritated.

This is a waste of time. I'm not sick.

"What's the urine for?" I wonder.

"Oh, we just want to make sure you're not pregnant."

A laugh swells. "I'm definitely not pregnant. There was always protection."

"Well, that's not always a guarantee, so we want to make sure." They start to head out. "We'll return in a bit."

Once they're both out, I snap my head to Emily.

"Pregnant?" I whisper. "Are they serious?"

"Well, when is your period due?"

I scan my brain, forgetting when the last one was. I'm not that great at keeping track, and sometimes my cycle is all over the place.

"Crap. I don't know. But I used a condom with Xander."

"And Fionn?" She raises a brow.

"Him too."

She pulls out her phone, typing something before looking up. "According to Doctor Google, condoms are ninety-eight percent effective at preventing pregnancy when used correctly, whatever the fuck that means, but for most people, it says it's eighty-five percent effective."

My shoulders sag. "Fan-fucking-tastic."

If I'm pregnant, there's no way I can keep it. I can barely feed myself, let alone a child. Not like Xander will want anything to do with it.

It could be Fionn's.

Oh my God. It could be Fionn's.

Okay, I'm getting ahead of myself. I'm definitely not pregnant. Just have a stomach bug, that's all.

The doctor returns, and my pulse slams in my ears. Once I notice her serious expression though, nausea hits me again.

Oh, no.

"Well, it looks like you are pregnant."

"What! No. The test has to be wrong. I used a condom. I always use a condom."

"Well, they don't protect from pregnancy one hundred percent."

"Oh God." My face falls into my palms.

"It's gonna be okay." Emily curls her arms around me.

"We'll leave you to it," the doctor says. "Take your time. But I do suggest making an appointment with your gynecologist."

"She will. Thanks, Doc." Emily tightens her arms around me while tears fill my eyes.

I can't have a baby. I'm not cut out to be a mother. I've never had one to show me what to do or how to be one. I took care of myself.

On top of that, if I keep this baby, I'll have to move. How will I afford that?

But there's no other option. I won't raise my baby with my mother. I won't allow her to grow up the way I did. That's nonnegotiable.

She will have more.

AGE 8

"Mommy, I'm hungry."

She laughs with her new boyfriend. He pours white powder on the table and sniffs it.

"Mommy!" I shout, my stomach growling again.

I had a few slices of bread yesterday and some cookies I found where she keeps her snacks.

"What?!" she shouts, grabbing her boyfriend by the back of the neck and kissing him. When she pulls away, she stares at me. "So go eat! What the fuck do you want from me?"

"We don't have anything in the fridge."

"So go make something! My God, do I have to do everything?"

You do nothing.

I don't say that. I just walk back to the kitchen and figure out what to eat. Opening some cupboards, I find a box of ziti.

I've never made pasta before, but how hard can it be? She's done it.

There are pots under the oven, so I grab one and fill it with some water, then pour the pasta into it. Carefully turning on the stove, I wait ten minutes like the box says, watching the water bubble.

If I can cook, maybe they'll let me live by myself. What do I need her for?

When I hear them making noises, those kinds of noises, I rush to my room down the hall and grab my earplugs. At least they work.

When the food is done, I grab a fork and throw some pasta on a paper plate, eating on the floor in silence.

It would be nice to have a table. But Mom sold ours.

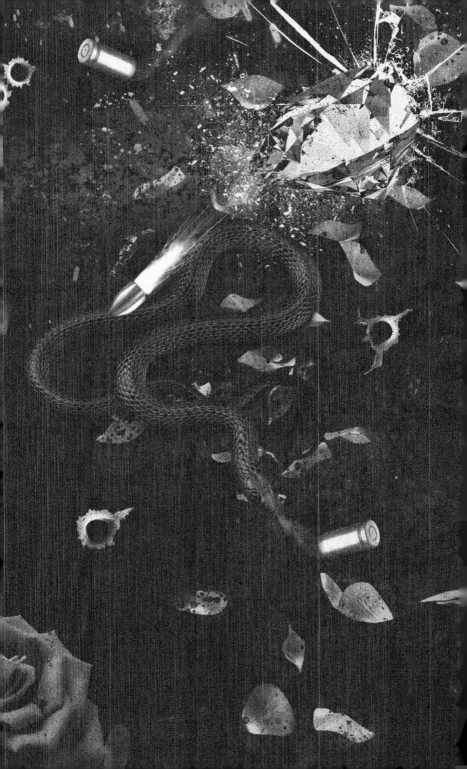

TWELVE

AMARA

"**D**on't be nervous. They'll love you!" Emily grabs my hand as we head up the steps to this new waterfront Italian restaurant that opened up in Boston.

I really didn't want to come, but she insisted I needed something to get my mind off this pregnancy. She arranged a girls' night with her friends Lilith and Patricia, who she was dying for me to meet.

"I don't even know if I can eat anything."

"Then get a drink. A virgin, of course." She's all excited, and I'm ruining it. "Come on, we'll have fun. When was the last time you went out?"

"Um, I have no idea."

"Exactly."

She drags me up the rest of the way, while all I'm thinking about is the baby I'm going to have. It's only been three days since I found out, and the shock hasn't worn off.

As soon as we enter, two girls wave at us.

"Great, they're here!" Emily waves back.

Oh, goody...

Meeting new people is not my favorite. There's usually conversation involved about where I'm going to college, and I either have to lie or tell the truth and slowly die of mortification.

I stuff these thoughts away and promise to make the best of it for Emily's sake. A maître d' leads us to a table, where two girls stare at me with huge grins.

"Ladies, this is Amara, my best friend in the world."

"So good to meet you! I'm Lilith. Emily hasn't stopped talking about you since the moment we met." She glances at Emily, her large brown eyes taking me in. She's pretty with shoulder-length dark hair and a slim, angular face.

"And I'm Patricia." The other girl runs a finger through her short blonde hair. "We're thrilled to meet you."

"Thanks. I'm happy to meet both of you."

They sip on their drinks, quietly taking me in, before Lilith asks, "So, where do you go to college?"

Great. Here we go. It didn't even take five minutes before the question hit.

"Oh, um…I actually don't go to college." As I play with my straw, my vision bounces between my water and the girl.

Emily tightens a hand around my knee.

"Oh, why?" Patricia's green eyes narrow, and I swear they remind me of Fionn's.

Fionn…

How badly I want to see you again. To tell you about the baby.

If it is his, I don't even know if he'd be happy. Probably not, considering we don't even know each other. But if there's a chance he wants to be a part of his child's life, then I want that too. Bet he'd be a great dad.

I tried looking for him after the money, but neither Emily nor I could locate him. It's like he doesn't want to be found.

I'll have to tell Xander, though. Hopefully he'll agree to a paternity test. There's no way I want him to be a part of my child's life, but I also can't just not tell him. If he is the father, then he deserves to know. I wouldn't do that to my baby.

"I didn't finish high school," I finally answer.

Both of the girls stare at me like I've just told them the world is about to explode.

"Oh…" Lilith attempts to hide her shock. "Do you plan to get your GED?"

"Maybe." I shrug, wanting this line of questioning to stop. "But I do work, and I really need to find a second job, actually."

"Why?" Her thin brows crease.

Emily's gaze fills with sympathy. But screw it. Everyone's going to know sooner or later.

"I found out I'm pregnant a few days ago."

"Oh, shit," Lilith whispers, leaning closer to the table, her eyes about to fall out of their sockets. "I'm so sorry. I can't imagine being pregnant at our age. You're, what, eighteen too?"

"Nineteen," I correct her. "But yeah, it's going to be rough. I haven't decided if I'm going to keep it yet, though. I don't really have parents to help or anything."

"My goodness." Patricia shakes her head, her features twisting with pity. "I can't imagine what you're going through. Is the father gonna help?"

My face turns red. I can feel it.

"Well, I was on a trip with my then-boyfriend, and we broke up while we were still away. But I met this guy there and we kinda slept together?" I slap a hand over my face.

"We're totally not judging!" Patricia says as I look back at them.

"Her boyfriend was a complete douchebag," Emily adds. "So

hopefully he's not the father and it's Fionn."

"Ooh! I love the name!" Lilith's painted-red lips twine up at the corners. "Tell us all about him!"

And I do. I tell them about his kindness and generosity. How I haven't been able to forget him or the magical night we shared weeks ago. But that I knew we were from different sides of the tracks and we'd never work.

"You know, my father owns a hotel not far from here," Lilith says. "And he's looking for help."

"Really?" My heartbeats quickens. "What kind of job?"

Uncertainty washes over her features.

"Just tell me. I'm not picky at this point."

"It's a housekeeper position at Hotel Thalia. The night shift." She grimaces. "I'm sorry. I'm sure you don't want it, but I figured I'd offer."

At this point, I have no choice but to accept. I have the coffee shop during the day, and then I can work nights at the hotel.

"I'd love the job if your father will have me."

She grins. "Of course. Let me call him now."

She gets her phone out, and as soon as he answers, her face lights up.

"Hey, Dad." Her eyes go to mine. "Oh no, I'm fine. I was just calling because I have this friend who's looking for work." She pauses, nodding. "Yep. Can she start next week?" Another pause. "Great! You're the best. Maybe bump up her salary a bit. I won't tell." She laughs, and my heart clenches. I wish I had that. "Love you, Dad. See ya later."

She drops the phone back on the table, and as the conversation about their classes picks up, my eyes wander around the place.

As they do, I stare out the window to my left. A sharp gasp rolls out of me as my eyes catch sight of a man.

No. Not just any man.

A man who looks just like Fionn.

"Fionn?" I call, getting to my feet as he starts to get into a car.

The girls stop talking, staring up at me as I start to dash toward the exit.

"Fionn!" I scream louder.

Emily calls me, but I barely hear her, making it through the maze of tables to head outside so I can see if it's really him. If it's the man I haven't been able to forget.

But as soon as I make it past the door, the black sports car takes off at lightning speed.

"Fionn!" I wave with both hands to no avail.

The car grows more distant. I can't even get the license plate.

He's gone.

"Amara? Oh my God. Was that him?" Emily appears beside me with the other two girls.

"I think so." My pulse continues to spike.

"Oh my God." She cups her mouth.

I sniffle, blinking past the tears. "I was this close to seeing him, and now I don't know if I'll ever get the chance."

"Oh, Amara." Emily tugs me to her chest, while the other two women give me a compassionate look and return inside. "I'm so sorry. We'll find him. And if we don't, I'll always be here for you no matter what."

I grip her tighter. But as much as I love her, I wish I had more.

I wish I had a family to hold on to.

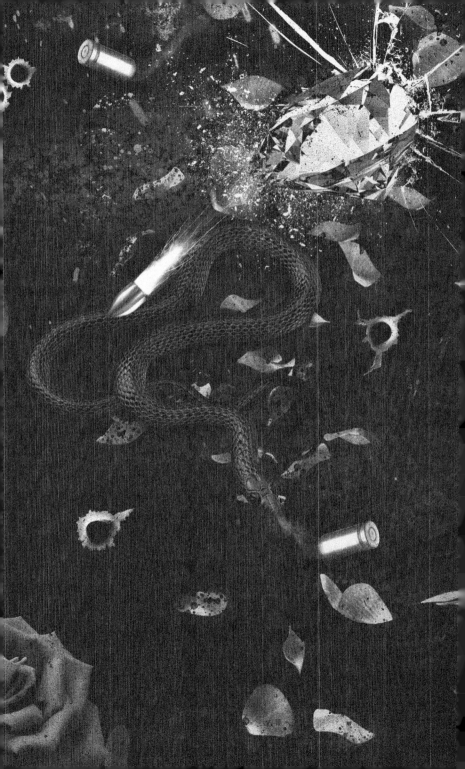

THIRTEEN

FIONN

I swear I thought I heard her calling my name as I drove away from my business deal. That damn sweet voice, as though reaching for me.

But I know it wasn't her. I would've seen her.

I need to get her out of my damn head.

Easing on the brakes of my Rolls-Royce, I stop at the security gate of my family's estate, where I live alongside my brothers.

I head into Caellach Academy, an underground assassin school my father built before we were born.

"Hey, Fionn. How are you doing?" Madison glances up from her computer in the IT department.

But she's not just a computer genius. She's also a skilled killer.

"I'm good. Do you have anything for me?"

Her mouth thins, and I know instantly she's got nothing. I asked her to help me find Emily, hoping she gets something new with facial recognition, but she's clearly got shit.

"I'm sorry. There were no hits." She lowers a palm to my bicep and squeezes, her gaze lingering on mine.

It was one night a year ago, and it seems like she hasn't gotten over it. She's mentioned wanting to date, but I'm not interested. She knew that before we slept together.

I fling her hand off. "Thanks for trying."

Turning away, I head out. Need to get a good workout in and punch something that doesn't bleed. Done enough of that lately.

"Look, Fionn, it may not be my business, but maybe you should forget her."

Grinding my teeth, I turn to her. "You're right. It's not your business. How about we keep it that way?"

"I'm sorry. I just meant—"

"Goodbye, Madison."

Proceeding toward the gym, I find Cillian already there, throwing punches with Tynan.

"Look who's here." Cillian wipes sweat from his brow.

"I'm not looking to brawl. Need some alone time."

Cillian laughs. "What's up with you lately? That girl made you crazy."

"You don't understand," I mutter, marching over to grab some boxing gloves. "I *need* to find her."

"Maybe I don't, but this shit you got going here…" He whirls his index finger in the air. "…is not working either."

"Leave him alone. He's nursing a broken heart," Tynan throws out with a laugh.

"Oh, that's it." A smirk widens as I slip into my gloves. "Now you're both gonna pay for it."

"Bring it, brother." Cillian gets ready to throw some while Tynan stands back. "The loser buys drinks tonight."

"Where are we going?"

"Konstantin's club."

Shit, I haven't been there since before I met her. Had no desire to. Haven't wanted to fuck anyone since I fucked her. Don't see that changing much.

"Come on, don't make me go alone."

Maybe I should go. Maybe I need to get her out of my mind, and this is how I have to do it.

"Fine. But you'll be the one paying for those drinks."

"Yeah, we'll see."

"One bourbon and one whiskey neat," Cillian mutters as music plays low from the speakers.

"You sure you don't need any ice for that bruise on your eye?" I fight a laugh.

"Yeah, fuck off," he mutters.

He hates to lose, but I warned him. I'm in no state to be messed around with.

Once we get our drinks, we survey the crowd. Some of the people are dressed in tuxedos and dresses; the rest are barely clothed. Women in corsets, panties, and high heels. But everyone is given a mask to wear. It's part of the rules.

In Konstantin's club, anything goes. And at one point, I liked it. But now it holds no appeal.

This is the place where I learned that I enjoyed using rope and tested my limits. Now? I want to test them with her. And this is the only place I want to do it. I'd teach and show her how good it can be. I can just picture her eyes taking in everything with shock. That brings a smile to my miserable face.

"Come on." Cillian smacks me on the back. "Let's go walk around."

"Yeah, whatever. I didn't come here to fuck."

"I did." He smirks.

"Right. I'm pretty sure you're looking for *her*."

His face turns tense. "I'm not."

"Come on, man. I know you. I know how much you still want her. What's holding you back?"

"How the hell can you say that?" His glare hits me hard. "Her family killed our mother."

"I know that. But that's not her fault. Sergey was her uncle. She's not the one who did it."

"I'll never marry a fucking Marinov. It'll never happen. The only reason I come to his clubs is because I like it. But to marry one of them? To be connected to them like that? Hell no."

"Fine. What are you gonna do when you lose her for good? Konstantin can arrange a marriage for her whenever he feels like it, and then it's over for you."

"I don't give a shit." But his jaw clenches.

I know him better than he realizes. My brother hates that he still wants Dinara, Konstantin's cousin. They dated for a bit, until he realized who she was and broke it off. Now they both pretend to hate each other.

In that second, we both see her—long black hair reaching the small of her back, her eyes just as deep. As I glance at my brother, his breathing grows harsh.

He's an idiot. I may hate what Sergey did, but my hatred ends with him. Unless the rest of them do some shit, I have no issue with them.

Her eyes scan the room like she's looking for him too, desperate to find him. And as soon as they lock eyes, she freezes like a deer in headlights.

She's in nothing but a white corset around her waist, her tits covered by two jeweled pasties, and I swear my brother's face grows redder by the second.

"Be right back," he mutters, heading straight for her, while I'm left laughing.

He's so fucked.

"Hi there." A blonde woman I didn't see taps my arm.

"Hey." My tone's indifferent, which hopefully means she'll get lost.

She runs a finger up my arm. "Wanna play?"

Her pink-stained lips curl, and beneath her white feathered mask, her dark gaze sways with desire.

"Not interested."

"Well…" She grabs my ass. "Maybe later?"

Tugging her wrist, I gently push her away, my veins filling with disgust. "Definitely not."

You look nothing like the woman I can't stop thinking about.

Turning my back, I order another drink, and seconds later she's walking away.

"Shit," I mutter, running a hand down my face.

I should go home. There's nothing here for me. I'm damn dead inside, and it's all my little rabbit's fault.

I picture her as though she's right here. In a bright red corset and a matching thong.

I'd show her around. Touch her while she watches others fuck. She'd get all shy at first, then once she's turned on, she'd forget where she was, lost to the feelings I bring out in her. I'd have her begging for it before I took her into one of the private rooms, tied her up to one of the horses, and had my fill.

My eyes shut, my cock throbbing. Grabbing it, I stroke through my trousers, the need becoming too much to bear. Gotta get out of here.

"Want me to help you with that?"

Fucking hell.

Looking over, I find another woman, a curvy one with black hair, glancing at the outline of my dick.

And I swear she looks like Emily.

Little rabbit.

My heart beats, the hollowness she left behind filling me up with desperation, even while I know this isn't her. But she's not here, and all I'm left with is a lie.

"What's your name?" I ask.

She runs a finger over a bare nipple, and I imagine it's Emily. Not whoever this woman is.

"Cassandra."

I grab my belt buckle and undo it, glaring hard through my black mask. "Tonight, you're Emily. Understand?"

She laughs. "Anything you want, handsome."

"Drop to your knees."

She instantly does, dragging my zipper down while hungrily staring up at me.

But I have my eyes shut, picturing Emily up against the elevator, her cunt stretching for my fingers the way it did for my cock.

The woman clutches my dick and squeezes, her tongue circling around the crown before she sucks me whole.

Fuck.

"Yeah, that's it, little rabbit. Take it all."

"What?" she asks, stroking me.

I don't even bother peering down at her. Don't want to see her.

"Never mind. Just keep sucking."

She continues on my command, and all the while, I dream of her, wanting her so badly I'd bleed for the devil if he'd send her back to me. Give anything, even my damn soul, if I could just kiss her again.

I've gone crazy, and I know it.

My release fills her mouth, and she takes it all before I'm shoving her off. "You can go now. Thank you."

She snickers. "Asshole."

Frustration returns as I zip up and grip the back of my head.

Wonder what she's doing right now. If she's out there with

someone else.

Shit. I can't think about that.

"Feel better?" Cillian's voice appears behind me, his hair a mess.

"No. I need the real thing. I need her. But it seems like you had a nice time." I smirk, and he groans in response.

"Shut up."

I let out a laugh. "How long are you gonna keep fucking her and pretending you're not into her?"

He runs his fingers through his hair. "I have no idea what you're talking about."

"Right." I shake my head. "I'm going home. I'm not feeling this place anymore."

"Gotta get over her, brother. You're not gonna find her."

"Not happening." I look down at my cell. We haven't even been here for an hour, and I'm done. "I'm leaving. You can do whatever you want."

"Fine. We'll go." He finishes his drink, dropping the crystal cut glass on the bar top just as Konstantin appears.

Tall son of a bitch. A good few inches taller than all of us.

"Gentlemen, how happy I am to see you here. It has been a while, no?"

"Konstantin," I greet him, and Cillian does too.

"Is there anything you need. Anything at all? I can deliver."

"Can you find someone I lost?" A wry chuckle slips out.

"And who might that be?" I can't see his face well through his black mask but I know those cunning eyes are assessing me.

"No one."

The last thing I want is for him to find my girl. He's not coming near her.

"Cillian." He looks to my brother. "I saw you and Dinara a little bit ago. Care to share what that was about? Anything I need to concern myself with?"

"Just saying hello."

"Good. Very good." He slaps me on my shoulder blade. "Let's have a drink, yes?"

"Sure, we'll have a drink." I glance over at my brother to cooperate.

Keeping the peace with the Russians is in everyone's best interest, and Konstantin knows it too.

"Vlad, get me the Imperial Faberge Pearl." He glances at us. "I like to treat my friends to the best."

The bartender brings over an ornate ivory-and-gold egg-style case, pouring us each a shot. Tipping it to my mouth, I toss it back, the liquor scorching its way down.

Damn, that's some good vodka.

"You like?" He lowers his glass.

"Yeah, it's good."

"I'm glad. Have more. Please." He gestures to Vlad to pour us another. "I must go attend to some business, but you enjoy yourselves." As he sets to go, he peers at Cillian over his shoulder. "You know, she's still single." He smirks before walking away.

"What the fuck was that?" Cillian turns to me. "I'll never marry her."

"You could do worse." I let out a laugh. "You know he's been pushing the marriage alliance for a while. Maybe take one for the team."

"*You* take one for the team."

"You're right. Maybe I should. Let me go find her. Maybe after you, she'll want me. Keep it in the family."

As I start, he roughly grabs my shoulder.

"Don't *fucking* touch her."

My body rocks with laughter. "You're an idiot. Did I mention that? Either you marry her or someone else will."

He snaps his fingers around the shot glass, and I know he's thinking about it. But my stubborn brother won't give in until he has to.

I don't want Dinara or anyone else.

I have the one I want.

All I need to do is find her.

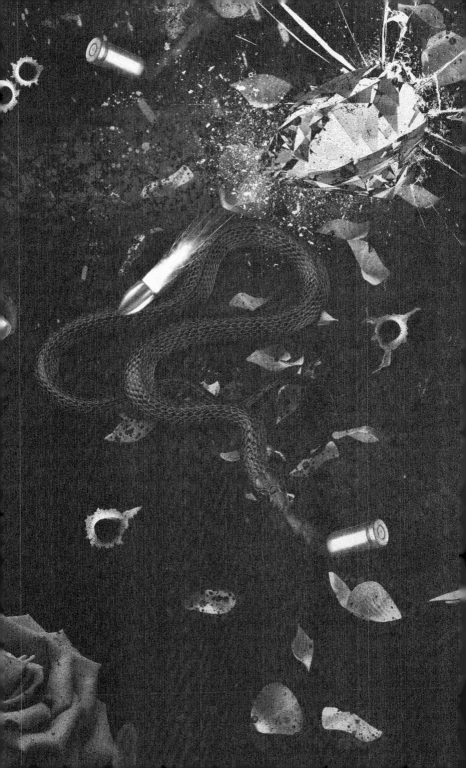

FOURTEEN

AMARA

My stomach is in complete knots as I get off the bus and start the walk toward Xander's house. It took me a few days to gather the courage to see him and tell him about the baby. But I knew I had to.

So many emotions play in my head. Hoping it isn't his. Hoping if it is, that he stays away from us.

On the other hand, I don't want my baby to feel abandoned by her father like I was.

I don't even know if it's a girl, but that's what my heart tells me.

Cupping my belly, I take a deep breath as I continue down his block toward his house on the corner. His parents purchased a five-bedroom home for him, like he really needs something that big. The brown shutters come into view as I approach, and I notice his car isn't in the driveway.

I blow out a rough exhale. Great…

He never got back to me when I texted earlier asking to discuss something important. I figure he's ignoring me. Now I don't even know where he is or when he'll be back.

"Amara?" the older lady next door calls out, waving with a newspaper in hand. "I haven't seen you in ages. How are you, sweetheart?" She approaches and hugs me tight.

"I've been good, Mrs. Windsor." I grin sweetly. "It's just Xander and I aren't together anymore."

"Oh? I'm sorry." She pats my forearm. "Though I will say…" She pulls into me. "I never liked him."

I let out a laugh. "Neither did anyone I knew. Have you seen him, by the way?"

Contemplatively, she scratches the staticky grays at her temple. "Now that you mention it, no, I haven't."

"Oh. Well, that's okay. Maybe I'll just wait around a bit. See if he shows up."

Her thick brows furrow. "You okay, honey?"

"I will be." My lips pinch into a forced smile.

"How about you come inside and I'll get you some lemonade? No point for you to hang here on the street when I'm right next door."

She's got a point. I can't stick around forever waiting for him. If he doesn't show up within the hour, I'm leaving.

"That sounds nice. Thanks."

"Good." Her face brightens. "Come now, honey."

Ushering me up the steps, she opens the door and leads me inside.

"Have a seat on the couch. I'll go fetch you that lemonade."

I settle down on her red velvet sofa while she heads right to the kitchen.

Mrs. Windsor has always been kind to me. We hit it off in the beginning of my relationship with Xander when she knocked over her garbage pail and I helped her clean it up. Since she has no family, I know she's lonely. It was the main reason I agreed to come in.

"So…" She returns with a tall glass of lemonade. "How are you doing? Still at the café?"

I get to my feet and take it from her, returning to my seat as she lowers into one opposite me.

"Yeah." I sip on the sweet goodness. "But I had to get a second job." My fingers slide up the condensation on the glass.

"Oh, why's that? Everything okay?"

I'm trying to get comfortable with the fact that I'm pregnant, even though I don't exactly know if I'm going to go through with it.

"I'm pregnant."

Yep, just spit it out like it's nothing.

"Oh." Her eyes pop. "That's why you're here."

I nod. "Yeah. I'm pretty sure he won't care, but I thought telling him was the right thing to do."

"You're absolutely right."

Just as she's about to say something, a car's engine howls from out the window, and I'm on my feet, staring out. When I find his sedan pulling up next door, my heart grows chaotic, nausea swirling. I'm beyond nervous, but I need to get this over with.

"Good luck," she says as she moves toward me. "If you need anything, I'm here."

"Thank you." I throw my arms around her and hold on tight for a few more seconds before breathing out a sharp exhale and heading out the door.

As soon as I turn left toward his house, he's getting out of the driver's side.

But he's not alone. A blonde with a short skintight pink dress hops out, giggling at something he must've said. Their backs are to me, so they don't see me there yet.

"Come on, babe," he tells her. "Let's get inside so I can fuck you in the new shower."

Maybe I should feel something. Anger. Sadness. But nothing comes. Nothing but disgust. Nothing but shame. What did I ever see

LILIAN HARRIS

in him?

As she dashes around in her five-inch stilettos, she catches me from the corner of her eye. "Um, who are you?"

That's when Xander faces me, mouth jerking as he holds out a hand for her. "What the hell do *you* want?"

They both look at me like I'm gum on their shoe. I hike up my chin, trying to keep my composure.

"Can we talk?" My brow arches as I glance over at the woman for a moment. "Alone?"

He snickers, rounding an arm around her slender hips. "Whatever you need to say, you can say in front of Mindy. She's my fiancée."

Fiancée? Wow. That was fast.

"I think it's best if we speak alone."

"Who is this, baby?" Her voice is mousy and quite irritating.

"It's my ex. No one important."

Screw you.

But I don't say that out loud. Wouldn't want to give the prick the satisfaction. I have more important things to worry about.

My gut churns at the thought of saying the words I need to say, especially in front of this woman.

"Fine." I crush my teeth, pain radiating in my jaw. "I'm pregnant. Thought you should know."

His eyes enlarge before he chuckles and glances at his fiancée, who starts laughing too. "I'm sorry, why are you telling me this exactly? Last time I checked, we weren't even together."

Is he stupid?

Forget I asked that.

"We were together on the island, and it takes a while for tests to pick up on a pregnancy."

"Right." He scoffs. "Like you haven't fucked anyone else since. What about that asshole? Want me to believe you didn't fuck him either?"

My heart drums faster. "Look, I just wanted to tell you so you're aware."

"Great. I'm aware. Now you can get lost."

I curl a fist at my side, my anger simmering. "You're more than welcome to take a paternity test. In fact, I want you to."

"Of course you do." He tightens his arms around her. "Because you're a damn whore."

His chest rises and falls in quick succession, his face twisting with his own rage. I knew he'd react this way. That's fine. I'd rather him stay away from us both.

Reaching into his pocket, he retrieves his wallet. "You need money?" He removes a bunch of twenties. "Here ya go."

He tosses them at me, caught in the wind before settling on the ground.

My eyes burn, but I don't cry. "Fuck you, Xander."

"Please! Don't pretend that's not why you came. You wanted money. Like a damn leech. Well, there ya go. Get on your knees and get it."

The woman's mouth pops a little, shock riddling her features. But she only shows it momentarily.

Good. Glad she sees the real him. Maybe if she's smart, she'll leave him.

Turning around, I leave the money on the ground and walk away with my dignity intact.

I did my part, and now it's over.

For good.

FIFTEEN

AMARA
SIX MONTHS LATER

The last few months have been hard. I'm still working two jobs, though not at the café anymore.

After I was fired for being sick too much, I needed something new.

It so happened I found a stray cat and brought her to the nearby vet. When I did, I noticed that they were looking for a receptionist, and the rest was history.

Working two jobs while pregnant has not been fun, but I've been able to save some money of my own for when the baby comes and I'm out on maternity leave. Both places have agreed to give me two months off after Fia is born.

Fia.

I love her name. It was intentionally close to Fionn's because in my heart, I know she's his.

Maybe one day when he finds us, he'll know I wanted him to be a part of our lives. Or at the very least, her life.

Then this sudden thought hits. Maybe I want something that'll never happen. That not only is she Xander's, but that Fionn wouldn't want us because she isn't his.

"When are you due?" an elderly woman asks as I tour her home, hoping I can rent it. It's in a nicer part of town, and I still have Fionn's money.

"In about three months." Rounding a hand on my small belly, I grin. "It's why I'm looking for a bigger place."

It's been a rough pregnancy, and Mom still thankfully hasn't even noticed. I throw on a baggy sweatshirt and have managed to hide it from her. For all I know, she'll kill me if I tell her—or do something to the baby. I can't risk that.

"What a blessing. And where's the father? Will he not be joining us?"

"Um…"

"He's working. Making all the big bucks," Emily offers, grabbing my hand in reassurance.

I need this place. It's my last hope of getting away from my mother. And this is the best home I can find on a budget I can work with. I'll use Fionn's money to supplement if I need to, but with the new job and nights as a housekeeper at the hotel, I'll come close to being able to afford this place, plus utilities.

I've even gotten a used car recently. Nothing special, but all mine.

"Oh, I understand," the woman says, leading us up the stairs to show us the three bedrooms. "When I had my kids, I wanted the same thing. I raised my three children in this home."

"That's really nice. That's what I'm looking for. Somewhere to plant roots."

Glancing over at me as soon as we make it to the top, she smiles fondly, and I swear, I feel as though she wants me to have this place.

She's retiring and moving down south and wants someone reliable, so if I tell her I'm a single mom, she's not going to rent to me.

"What do you think?" she asks.

I rub my belly some more, hoping that sways her. I'll take anything I can get.

"I want it."

She gives me a thoughtful look. "I have two other applications, but I do really like you." A grin spreads. "Eh, what the heck? I think a young family is just what this house needs."

Phew.

"Great! Thank you so much!" My entire body radiates with pure happiness, and Emily is practically jumping up and down beside me.

"Of course, dear. I'll need the first month's rent and security deposit now, and the rest, you can send via Venmo or mail a check."

"Venmo is fine."

"Let's sign the paperwork and I'll be out of your hair."

I can't stop grinning. I have a home. I have somewhere to raise my daughter.

"This is great. We're gonna live so close!" Emily whispers.

It's going to be tough to be on my own with another life I have to take care of, but it's what I have to do.

My girl and I will be fine on our own. We have to be.

I'm all she has, and I promise to do better by her than my mother ever did by me.

Once the papers are signed, I return home with Emily, needing to pack. I can't wait to be out of here.

As soon as my mother sees Emily bringing boxes out to my car, she grabs my arm. "What the hell is this?"

The bags under her eyes have started to fill up even more. She looks tired. Drugs have done a lot of damage to her. She's always done them for as long as I can remember, though she was a lot more functional back then.

In recent years, it's gotten worse. She's started gravitating toward crack and has stolen money from me to buy it. Sold our TV to get high.

I can't live this way anymore. And I'll die before I let my daughter live the way I did.

"I'm moving out." I straighten my spine, bracing for the fight that's coming.

"Excuse me?" she scoffs. "What the hell you mean, you're movin'? Who told you you're allowed to move?"

"She doesn't need your permission, Desdemona." Emily narrows her glare. "She's been the one supporting you all this time, and it should've been the other way around."

"Who the hell asked you anything, you little rich bitch?"

"Don't you dare talk to my friend like that!" My heart races. "Come on, Emily, we're done here."

I'm leaving my bed and dresser behind. I'll buy another one. Something affordable, but new, because I deserve it.

"You ain't going nowhere." She grabs my arm and yanks me hard, almost causing me to trip.

I clutch my stomach, the instant urge to protect my daughter hitting me like a pile of bricks.

"Don't you fucking touch her!" Emily gets in the middle of us, and as she does, my mother's hazy vision drops to my stomach, now visible from the way I hold it.

"Are you pregnant, you slut?"

The words are like a blow to my heart.

"Don't call me that." My upper lip curls and anger radiates through my limbs.

She laughs. "You think you can raise a child?"

Getting closer, I come face-to-face with her. "I can do much better than you ever have. Then again, that's not saying much." A slow-growing smile captures my lips. "I'll give my daughter everything I can. Do everything for her. I'll be the kind of mother you were never capable of being."

"She's never gonna love you." Her mouth tremors. "Your father never did, either. And no matter how much you've wanted to know who he is, I'll never tell you. He doesn't want you. You know that, right?"

Her words are a sharp bite, but I don't show her how much they affect me.

"He left you while you cried, begging him to stay."

I force away the stinging blinding my vision, but it blinds me anyway. The pain from her words etched in my heart.

"I'm leaving. Goodbye, Mother."

Her face grows ashen. "You can't go. I'll have nowhere to live."

"Get a job. I did. Two, in fact, just so I could pay the rent here and afford to move. I'm done now. Figure it out yourself."

Never in my wildest dreams did I ever think I'd have the courage to face her this way. But having a child, it's given me a reason.

"Come on, Em." I grab her arm and start out.

"You get back here, you ungrateful bitch! You're nothing without me! I made you who you are!"

Opening the door to my blue sedan, I return my attention to her. "You're right. You ruined me and turned me into who I had to become. But that's all thanks to me. You did nothing but hurt me. Now you'll never get to hurt my baby."

Getting into the car, I shut the door on the life that once consumed me.

Now I have hope. A new beginning. And all the possibilities waiting for me on the other side.

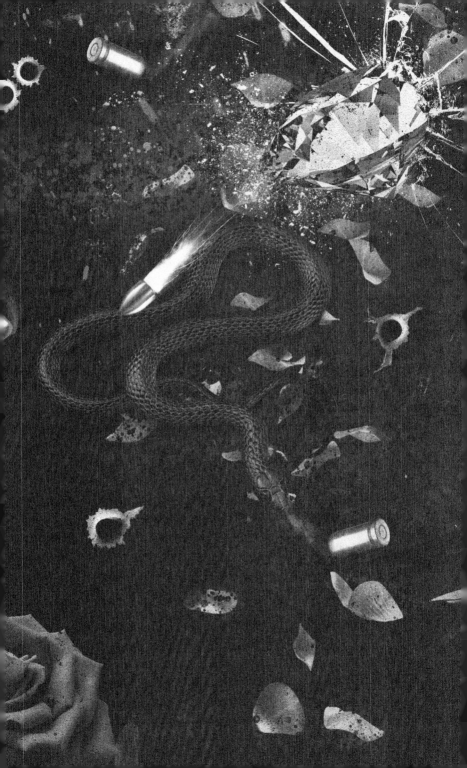

SIXTEEN

AMARA
ALMOST THREE MONTHS LATER

"Push!"

The doctor holds my feet while Emily and Lilith clutch my hands, with Patricia standing off to the side.

I can't believe the last few months have flown by so quickly and I'm about to see my daughter for the first time. My heart aches that she'll have no father, that I'm alone in this. But it's what we have, and there's nothing I can do about it.

"Come on. You've got this, Amara," Emily says. "Fia can't wait to meet her mama."

Tears well in my eyes, and I give one big push until her cry fills the room, and emotions like I've never felt before hit me all at once.

"You have a healthy baby girl." The doctor places her on my chest, and through the blinding vision, I see her face.

Tears fall down my cheeks like rivers. I don't think I've ever known love like this before.

"Hi, baby," I stammer. "I'm your mama."

Emily sniffles, swiping under her eyes.

"She's beautiful!" Patricia gushes, blinking past her own emotions.

"Just the cutest!" Lilith's eyes fill with warmth.

Both of them have become my friends over the past few months. They helped me unpack when I moved, and we all went shopping together for all the things I needed. They all even chipped in to throw me a baby shower at Emily's home. There weren't that many there, but more than I ever expected. Emily's mom even invited some of her friends. I felt so much love.

My mother, of course, wasn't invited.

The shower came as a complete surprise. When Emily told me to register for gifts, I thought that was ridiculous, because who was going to buy me all this stuff? But people have been beyond generous. A new crib, a name-brand stroller, two car seats—one for when she's older—and everything else I could possibly need is already at my home.

All I've been waiting for is her.

My gorgeous daughter.

And now she's here.

I hold her tighter and kiss the top of her head while the nurses wipe her off. For some reason, my mind goes back to the dream of me holding a baby as she slips away, the one I still have from time to time. And I hope it has nothing to do with my own daughter. That I'll never lose her.

"We'll always have each other, my sweet girl. Mommy will always protect you."

And I swear to keep that promise until the day that I die.

Being a mom has been hard. I had a lot of growing up to do in a short time, and I did it. And I'm damn proud of it. Proud of myself for leaving that weaker version of Amara behind. Because in her place I'd like to think I became stronger, for both myself and my daughter. I won't let anyone hurt my girl.

She coos in the stroller, lying in her bassinet as we stroll around the neighborhood.

A whole month has passed since I've had her, and every day I stare at her, I wonder what sort of mother my mom was back when I was this small.

Was she kinder? Did she love me? Did my father? Maybe he was just as awful as her. Who else leaves their child behind?

As soon as we're nearing the house, she starts to cry.

"Oh no. What happened, sweetheart?" I stop immediately and lift her in my arms, placing her against my chest as I bounce her. "Mama's here. Don't you cry. I'll always be here."

"Good morning." A couple passes by, smiling at me.

"Good morning."

My heart fills with joy. This area was everything I needed. No one sells drugs here. I feel safe. My daughter will have a good life. I just know it.

As soon as she calms, I place her back in the stroller and head down the street toward our home.

When I reach the driveway and start for the backyard, a set of tires screeches past me, causing me to stop.

"Is that my granddaughter?"

My pulse slams in my ears.

No. Nonono. She can't be here. She can't ruin this for me.

My eyes squeeze shut, panic sending my entire body drowning in dread.

Footsteps pound closer, and every inch of me wants to run. But I force it all down and turn to face her, standing right in front of the stroller so she doesn't so much as see my daughter.

"What are you doing here?"

My eyes take her in. A pair of jeans and a loose black t-shirt. Her eyes are bloodshot, like she's just taken something.

But she's not alone. I glance at the man beside her, his eyes glassy and dark hair combed back. Probably a new boyfriend.

"Well…I came to see my grandbaby, of course."

"You can't. I want nothing to do with you. Do you understand, Mother?"

She huffs, glancing up at the guy she's with. "Can you imagine ever treating your mom this way?"

He shakes his head, but doesn't say a word.

"Who's he?"

I probably shouldn't have asked. It doesn't matter to me, but he's in my driveway, so I have a right to know.

"Oh, this is Mark. My new boyfriend. He actually lives with me now." She rounds her arm around his tall frame, glancing up at him while he stares at me like I've just killed his beloved cat. "After you abandoned me and left me with no money, I met this beautiful man, who has helped me more than you ever did."

"I'm happy for you." My voice is completely monotone. "You can go now. Hopefully to hell. I think you'd find it cozy." My mouth thins.

"Oh…" She pouts. "Don't be like that." She peers over at my home. "Seems like you're doing well for yourself to be able to afford this place."

My heart races. "I know what you're trying to do. I don't have money to give you, nor would I if I did."

Her laugh is like a cheese grater to my ears. "I wasn't asking for money. Mark is loaded. Right, babe?"

"Mm-hmm."

I bet he is…

"How did you find me?"

We haven't spoken since the day I left. I haven't so much as called her. She probably could've looked me up, though she's not the best with the internet.

"Oh, I followed that rich bitch the other day. Saw her with some toys she was lugging into her car, so I figured she was going to see you, and of course, I was right." She grins, looking proud of herself.

Rage causes my pulse to quicken. "You need to go, and don't ever come back. You understand me?"

"Right. Well, let's go, Mark. Maybe we can catch her in a better mood next time."

"There will be no next time!"

"Whatever you say, darling."

Bitch.

Before I can reiterate that neither Fia nor I will ever have a relationship with her, they're driving away.

And all I can do is watch her go, hoping she never comes back.

"I can't believe she followed me!" Emily shakes her head with disgust. "I'm so sorry. If I knew…"

Placing a hand on her shoulder, I try to quell her guilt. "It's not your fault. That's just who she is. She would've found a way to get to me without you."

She sighs, staring down into her mug of coffee. Fia sleeps in the portable bassinet beside us in the kitchen.

"Are you sure you wanna do this?"

"I have to. She needs to know she can't just show up here again."

"If you think that's best, but please be careful. Especially with that sketchy guy now living there."

I swallow past the lump in my throat. He did look scary. He's probably a drug dealer. She seems to attract them, or maybe use them for drugs. Who really knows with her?

"You sure you'll be okay with Fia? I won't be long. Two hours tops, assuming traffic is okay."

"Of course. I've got her. Don't worry."

"Thank you." Grabbing my handbag and phone, I head for the door, giving my daughter one last look. "I'll let you know how it goes once I'm done."

"Alright. You've got this."

Blowing out a quick breath, I head out toward my car and get on the road.

The whole time, all I do is rehearse what I'm going to say to her. I doubt she'll listen, but I need to try. I'll be honest, with the way she was staring at the house, I'm afraid she'll show up with her boyfriend to rob me.

The cash Fionn left is mostly still here. It's a relief to have it, especially while I'm on maternity leave for another month, not making any money while I'm out.

When I arrive at my mother's, I find her beaten-up Volkswagen in the driveway, but the sedan her boyfriend drove isn't there. Parking a house down so she doesn't see me, I give myself a little pep talk, hoping to remain calm and collected while she hurls insults. Because of course she will. I've lived through it all.

"Okay, it's now or never."

But as soon as I start getting out, I find someone I never expected pulling into her driveway. He doesn't see me as he struts inside, hands in his pockets. But there's no doubt it's Xander.

Confusion mars my features while I try to figure out why in the world my ex is coming to see my mother.

Over ten minutes pass before he returns to his vehicle, and that makes me even more anxious. If he was asking about me, he wouldn't need to be here that long. But what other reason would there be?

When he drives away, I finally step out, grabbing my phone and texting Emily that I got here and who I saw. She's just as suspicious, warning me to be careful.

My heart pumps against my rib cage as I start toward the door, knocking until I hear her muttering that she's coming.

"I thought we were done—" But when she realizes it's me, surprise fills her eyes. "Oh, you," she mutters. "What do you want?"

"Were you expecting someone else?" I cock a brow.

"What? No. I thought you were Mark. What is this, an inquisition?"

"I saw him, Mom. I just saw Xander, so why don't you cut the bullshit?"

"Oh, right." She laughs dryly, scratching her neck. "He was just here for a minute asking where you live and stuff. Of course, I didn't say a word."

She tries to lower her palm to my arm, but I quickly snap my hand away.

"Is that really why he came? Because he was here for a while, so don't lie to me."

"Seriously, what the fuck do you want? He doesn't need your permission to come around."

"You know what? You're right. You can keep him. Better yet, make sure both of you stay the hell away from me and my daughter." I step closer, my breathing shallower, unable to contain this anger she brings out in me. "If I find you anywhere near either one of us, Desdemona, I will ruin your life. So if you like your drugs, I'd leave me alone, or you'll be rotting in prison."

She shakes her head, her glare intensifying. "You'd do that to your own mother?"

A wry laugh escapes me. "Just because I came out of you doesn't mean you're any more my mother than a random woman on the street." Turning away, I stare at her over my shoulder. "Remember what I said. Stay the fuck away from us. Forever."

"Fine! Whatever! Go to hell."

"Been through all that. Don't have any plans to return."

Then I'm back in my car, gripping the wheel tight, my hands trembling as the stress of it all takes over.

But I did it. I told her off. Now it's up to her to call my bluff.

SEVENTEEN

FIONN
EIGHT MONTHS LATER

"I'm sorry, but at this point, we're not gonna find her." In a split second, I have Scotty's throat in my grasp, squeezing the shit out of it. He's the head of IT here at Caellach. He's supposed to be able to find her.

"Back the fuck away." Tynan grabs my arm and forces me back, my anger spiraling. "What the hell are you doing?" he shouts, clutching my shoulders while my breaths howl out of me. "You've gotta stop."

He tries to reason with me, but all I see is her. Those eyes. They fucking haunt me.

"I need to find her. I'm not gonna stop until I do."

"We've tried everything." He sighs. "It's impossible. You need to accept that she's not looking to be found. You need to forget her."

"Never gonna happen," I grit, shoving him off me. "Stay out of my way if you're not gonna help." My attention reverts to Scotty.

"Give me every Emily Daniels you have on file. I'll personally go to every single one since you can't fucking do your job."

The whole IT room stares at me like I've lost my mind. Maybe I have.

"I just emailed it to you," he says.

Turning back, I start to head out, but Tynan's voice stops me.

"You're spiraling, man."

"If this was Elara, you would be too."

Fuck them all.

SIX MONTHS LATER

She's the last Emily Daniels on my list. If it's not her, then it's over. I've followed every single one of them and have been disappointed every time.

Why the hell can't I find her?

She's not a damn ghost.

Gripping the steering wheel, I squeeze until my knuckles go white. "Fuuuck!"

My inhales pound through my chest as I push the door open and get out, heading for the small, quaint coffee shop this Emily works at.

When I walk in, there are a few people behind the counter, all of them around Emily's age. But none of them are her.

She's not here.

She's nowhere!

"God damn it!" I bang a fist on the wall behind me, and every single person here stares at me.

"Uh, may I help you, sir?" one of the girls asks.

"No," I mutter, catching her nametag.

Emily.

She doesn't even look like my little rabbit.

I need to get the hell out of here before I turn this entire place upside down.

When I find my Emily, she's gonna pay for this, and she'll never escape me again.

TWO YEARS LATER

"Where the hell is our money?!" I slam a fist into some asshole's nose, breaking it again.

He spits out blood, holding out his hands as though that'll do anything.

My brothers stand behind me, letting me do all the work. They know I need it. It's the only way I don't think about her. About how I've failed. It fucking haunts me every damn day.

It's been four years, and I've not been able to forget her. It's like a curse, and I can't rid myself of it. When I shut my eyes, it's like she's there, conjured up in my subconscious as though she's actually standing right in front of me with that same baby-blue sundress she wore the day of Tynan's wedding.

Reaching into my pocket, I fist her panties, the only connection I have to her. My heart races, my body buzzing with rage.

Heading toward the wooden table in the storage room on our farm, I pick up a chainsaw. As soon as he sees it, he begs for his life.

"Please, I swear, I don't know! I don't know!"

He chokes on a sob, but it's too late. The vroom of the chain feeds the sickness in me, decaying day by day.

"I don't believe you."

The teeth saw into his thigh as he howls in pain, but I don't stop there. I don't stop until he's nothing but sawed-off pieces of flesh, rotting as much as I am.

EIGHTEEN

FIONN
TEN MONTHS LATER

The Russians called a meeting, and we accepted. It's been a while since we've had a sit-down with them.

Tynan lowers into the swivel chair at his desk, finishing off his bourbon while we're waiting for them to walk into the house.

Settled on the sofa, drink in hand, I wonder why the hell they wanted to see us. I'm not in the mood for them or their shit.

"What do you think they want?" Cillian bounces his foot, anxious as fuck.

Probably because he thinks Konstantin will bring up wanting the marriage alliance between our families he's discussed on more than one occasion. And Cillian knows he's the only one left. They know better than to think I'll touch anyone ever again, let alone marry them.

Konstantin wants this, though, and he's not the kind of man who forgets.

Of course, Cillian wants no part. But he's not stupid. He knows it's coming. Eventually.

There's a knock on the door.

"Come in." Tynan sits up straighter as all four of the Marinov brothers step inside.

"Gentlemen, how good it is to see you on this fine day." Konstantin's mouth tips up before we greet one another.

"Welcome. Please have a seat."

They all sink onto the sofa opposite Cillian and me.

"Drink?" Tynan points to the bar at the corner. "We've got anything you want."

"I'll take whatever you're drinking," Aleksei says to me, his eyes almost as dark as his hair.

"Bourbon." I lift my crystal glass.

"Da, bourbon is good." His mouth jerks, accent as heavy as the rest of them.

"Yes, for me too. Boys?" Konstantin glances at Anton and Kirill.

"Da." Kirill's jaw clenches, the skull and rose tats running up his neck jerking.

"I like vodka." Anton leans back, folding his arms over his chest.

Tynan tips his head, his eyes connected with mine, and I get to my feet, pouring each one their drink and handing it to them.

"So, why'd you come?" Tynan takes the liquor to his mouth, finishing off the drink.

"Well…" Konstantin chuckles humorlessly. "You see, we have a little problem. Call it a family dispute, if you will." His sly grin spreads as he scratches his trimmed goatee.

"And what do you need from us?" Cillian asks, intensity branded on his features.

He outstretches his arms across the top of the sofa. "You see, one of my uncles, my father's brother, he's not a decent man like us."

Pretty sure not one of us here is what the world would call decent.

"In fact," Konstantin goes on, "he wants me and my brothers dead so he can take over the family. You can understand I will never let that happen."

"Sergey's brother?" Cillian balls a fist at his side.

"Yes. His name is Leo. Leonard. You know, Dinara's father." A knowing smile spreads, and no one can miss the way a breath roughs out of Cillian's chest at Dinara's name.

"Don't worry. My cousin is nothing like him. She took our side, and that is why she lives with me now." He takes a long, thoughtful pause. "You should probably know, however, that he wants her dead too. For the betrayal, of course."

"*What*?" Cillian sucks in a breath. "Has he hurt her?"

"You care?" Konstantin smirks right before thunderous darkness washes over his demeanor.

Cillian's nostrils flare.

"Of course you do." He chuckles. "Don't worry. I take care of her, and I always will." His eyes narrow, and his gaze holds Cillian's. "I can promise you that no one will hurt her, and I mean *no one*."

The air is thick with his implication.

"So, what do you need from us?" Tynan asks, breaking the stiff tension brewing between Konstantin and our brother.

"We need assurances, of course." A sly grin emerges on his face. "You know, in case there is a problem and we require more men in the fight with my uncle."

"So you want our help?" Tynan interrupts.

"Nu da." He casually flips his hands in the air. "It's what friends do for one another, no?"

"Sure." Tynan nods, but he definitely wants nothing to do with this family squabble.

"Good. But there is another urgent issue we must discuss."

"And that is?" Tynan pours himself another drink.

"We need to decide how we will unite our two families. It would be good for us. You know, just in case." He huffs a laugh.

What he means is before we find another reason to start a fight between us. A marriage would stop that from happening.

Emily pops into my head. For the fifth time today. The thought of spending the rest of my life with someone who isn't her is like a bullet to my heart. No fucking way.

I'd rather die alone.

Irritation shoots through my bloodstream, mad as hell at her for leaving. Almost five years wasted.

Then it hits. She's around twenty-four now. She could be married already.

My chest rattles with tight breaths. Though there's always a way to take care of that little problem. A robbery gone wrong. Quick and easy. I'd make sure he didn't suffer. Too much. Only as a favor to her, of course.

Why can't I get this fucking woman out of my head? I swear I can still smell her shampoo. Feel her skin on mine when I fucked her. Hear the way she called my name when I made her come.

"I already have someone," I say before I think better of it.

All eyes go to me. My brothers know I mean Emily. They know how consumed I've been with finding her. It's like I see her and hear her everywhere I go. Like she poisoned me and I have no antidote. Not until I find her.

And I *will* find her. I'll get her back, no matter how long it takes. No matter how many men I have to kill to do it. Boyfriend. Husband. The fucking Pope. I don't give a shit. Anyone who gets in my way is already dead.

"Well, then that leaves you, Cillian." Konstantin's voice has me snapping out of my delirium.

"I have someone too." My brother would say anything to get out of this.

A small, dry chuckle escapes from deep in my throat, and that has him glaring at me.

"So you and my cousin…" Konstantin crosses his arms over his chest. "Not interested anymore?" Amusement plays in his tone. "I know you carry a heavy burden with what happened to your mother. But I'm sure with time you can move past it, yes?"

His jaw clenches. "We're just friends. There's nothing between us anymore."

Right. Friends. Pretty sure most people don't fuck their friends. Though I really wouldn't call them that. They both pretty much pretend to hate each other.

Or maybe it's not pretend. I don't even know anymore. All I do know is my brother finds any excuse to go to the club, sometimes dragging me with him and disappearing as soon as he finds her, while I wait until he's done.

He can't help himself. When you want someone that badly, no matter how much you deny it, it's not easy to let them go.

"Okay." Konstantin flips his palms in the air. "Then I will find someone else in your family who will be much better suited for her than you, my friend."

He starts to rise, while Cillian's eyes flash with ire.

"What the fuck do you mean someone else in the family?" His chest rises with a quick inhale. "Like who?"

Someone's mad. I laugh to myself.

Konstantin's mouth quirks up, and Kirill chuckles. "Why do you care? She's not your problem anymore."

"Like hell she isn't," Cillian mutters, expression growing murderous.

Like I said, the fucker can't help himself.

Anton shakes his head with a scoff. "You don't even know what the hell you want, do you?"

"I do know what I want, and it's not this marriage."

"Eh." Konstantin shrugs. "Maybe you'll change your mind, then."

He casually drops his glass onto the bar top, each brother following suit. "It would be such a shame to miss out on this great opportunity for both of our families, all due to past family bickering."

"Bickering?" Cillian slowly rises to his feet, nearing him. "That's what you call what your father did to our mother? Fucking *bickering*?"

Anton and Kirill immediately take a threatening step toward Cillian until Tynan and I are on guard, coming to surround our brother.

"Now, now, we all need to relax." Konstantin adjusts his tie, a sinister expression in his eyes. "We wouldn't want to start something that would end this beautiful relationship we have."

My palm falls on Cillian's shoulder, attempting to calm him the hell down before he starts a fight with the Russians that we absolutely do not need.

"We'll talk about this another day," Tynan says to Konstantin while approaching each Marinov and shaking their hands.

"I look forward to it. Have a wonderful day, gentlemen." He nods a farewell to me and Cillian, and they're all finally out of the room.

Once I shut the door, I face my brother. "Are you out of your fucking mind?"

His fingers flex, anger weaving through his irises as he connects his eyes with mine. "I'm the only sane one around here. After what they did to our mother, I will *never* tie myself to that family."

"You need to understand…" Tynan returns to his seat. "You don't have a choice. We need this to happen. We need an alliance with them so what happened with Mom never happens again."

Cillian snickers. "You're nuts if you think I'll go through with it."

"All you've gotta tell him is you want Dinara, and he'll make it happen." My smirk only infuriates him. "You know you still want her."

"I don't," he snaps. "I don't want any one of them. Understand?"

"So you're okay going to their club, but marriage is off the table?" Tynan shakes his head.

"That's right." He drops two fists across Tynan's desk as he leans in, his rage consuming him. "Marrying into their family means we're connected for life. If we have children, that's even worse. Don't you fucking get it? How the hell do you think Mom would feel knowing her grandchild is someone related to the motherfucker who burned her alive?"

Tynan closes his eyes for a moment before he slants forward, meeting Cillian with an equally deadly stare. "She'd understand. She was resilient. Strong. You need to see the bigger picture."

"Fuck you, man. I told you my decision. Find someone else in the family. A distant cousin. I don't give a fuck who it is. But not me."

He straightens his back and turns toward the door.

As he starts for the exit, Tynan says, "You can't escape this, Cillian. It's gonna happen."

"Yeah, watch me."

Then he's out the door, muttering a curse as he disappears from view.

"Talk to him," Tynan tells me. "Make him understand."

"Come on. You know him. He's stubborn."

Hard laughter slips free. "Aren't we all?"

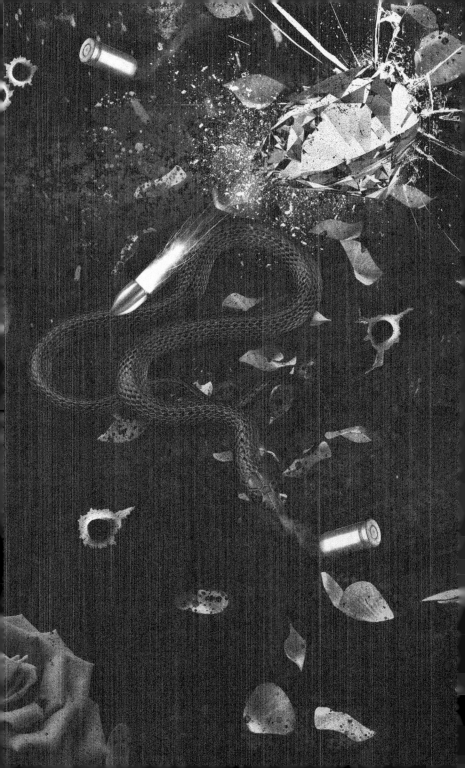

NINETEEN

AMARA

"**M**ommy! Water, please!" Fia calls from her little table, while I rush around the kitchen trying to find my phone.

Where the hell is the sitter?! I'm gonna be late for work.

"Mommy!" she screams.

I huff out a breath, brows furrowing with a smile at my sweet girl, her black strands curling at her ears. She's so beautiful.

"Okay, one second, baby." I grab her water bottle from the fridge, handing it to her.

She sips happily, swinging her little feet.

I wish I could afford preschool, but I can't right now. The sitter I found in the area is a lot cheaper, and Fia loves her.

Finally finding my phone under one of Fia's dishes, I glance at the screen, noticing a missed text from the sitter. When I open it, I clutch my chest. She's in the hospital with a minor leg injury she got from a car accident earlier today.

I shoot back a reply, telling her not to worry and that I hope she's okay, but now I'm out a sitter. Pinching the bridge of my nose, I scramble with what to do. It's the weekend. Maybe Emily can sit for me.

When I call her, she answers immediately.

"Hey, Amara. What's up?"

"Em, I need a favor. Is there any way you can watch Fia today? My sitter had an accident and canceled this morning, and I'm already late for work."

"Oh no! I'm sorry. You know I would, but I'm at a job interview. They're about to call me in."

"I'm so sorry. I forgot! Good luck, okay? Let me know how it goes. And break a leg and all that."

"Thanks! Hey, maybe Lilith or Patricia can help. Did you text them?"

"No, but I will." My pulse races.

I can't lose the job at the vet clinic. It has amazing health benefits. Though I hate leaving Fia with people who've never babysat her. Sure, both Patricia and Lilith have spent a lot of time with her, but they've never actually watched her.

"Let me know what they say! Love you," Emily whispers. "I've gotta go. I'll call you later."

"Love you too. Good luck again."

Dropping the call, I text both of the girls and get replies immediately. Patricia is busy helping her mom at her bakery, but Lilith is available.

LILITH

I can be there in fifteen.

AMARA

You're the best. Thank you!

LILITH

Of course. I love Fia.

AMARA

You don't know how much this means to me.

I text my boss and let her know that I've had an emergency, and she assures me that the other girl can cover until I'm in. Thankfully, she's very understanding, having been a single mom herself. I'm very lucky, but I don't want to push my luck either.

When there's a knock not even fifteen minutes later, relief washes over me. As soon as I open the door, Lilith is grinning, holding a white paper bag.

"I brought my favorite girl some goodies for later."

"Thank you." Giving her a tight hug, I let her in. "Please make yourself at home. Grab whatever you want from the fridge."

"Thanks. I'll be fine."

As soon as Fia sees her, she starts giggling.

"There's my little giggle monster." Lilith rushes for her, tickling her while my daughter laughs.

I'm so thankful Emily introduced me to these girls. It's nice to have a village, and I'm grateful for it every day.

"Okay, Mommy has to go now." I kiss Fia on the forehead and stare at her for a moment, my heart bursting.

I hate to leave her, but one day I hope she realizes how hard her mom had to work to give her the kind of life she has.

"Love you, Mommy."

My heart swells. "Mama loves you too. Be good for Auntie Lilith."

"Okay, Mama." She grins, flashing some of her little teeth.

I turn to Lilith, who waves me off.

"Go! We'll be fine, I promise. I'm used to babysitting. I have a lot of younger cousins."

Blowing a breath, I grab my handbag. "Okay, thanks again. I owe you. I know it's a long day."

She's going to be here until I return from the hotel tonight.

"No, you don't. Have a good day at work."

"Thanks." I give them one last look before I'm in my car and rushing to the clinic, knowing I have to find a new sitter ASAP.

Once I'm done with the clinic, I check in with Lilith before arriving at the hotel, thankful I have this job. The pay isn't all that great, but it's work. I'm able to afford living on my own and supporting my daughter. That's enough.

"Hey, Amara," John, Lilith's father, greets me.

"Hi, sir." I smile timidly.

He's a nice man. Treats everyone well.

He marches past me as I rush to change into my uniform, grabbing a cart filled with towels and supplies before heading for the top floor. I've been instructed to clean all the rooms that have no occupancies. We need them spotless for check-in tomorrow.

Opening the first door, I grab some towels and new sheets, pushing the cart down the hall before scanning the card and walking inside. Keeping the door propped, I make my way past the living area and toward the bedroom. The suites up here are much larger, and there's more to clean. As soon as I rip off the stained sheets, the main door clicks shut.

"Damn it," I mutter.

How the hell did it not stay open? It's fine. Not as though anyone's coming in here anyway.

As I continue, I wonder if this is all my life will be. The dream of one day going to college, working as a paralegal, is still something I envision. Maybe it's ridiculous to think a woman like me could ever attain something like that, but here I am dreaming anyway.

I want not only for Fia to one day be proud of me, but to prove to myself that I can do it. That I can go out there and chase my dreams.

But as nice as that sounds, I need to work. With a deep sigh, I ignore my dreams and focus on the task at hand. A few more hours until I get to go home and cuddle my sweet girl.

As I start for the bathroom to give it a good scrub, I jump back, my heart racing when I hear voices. Men's voices. Coming from the living room.

"Get him inside." A deep tone laces up my skin, the familiar sound causing every cell in my body to awaken.

Because for a moment, it sounded like…like Fionn.

No. Obviously that's not possible. Of course he isn't here. Why would he be?

My mind is playing tricks because I haven't been able to forget him. Not for a moment.

A chill prickles up my back, because it only just hits me. Whoever is out there isn't supposed to be.

Fear clutches around my throat. They could be dangerous. They could hurt me.

Oh my God.

As soon as I tiptoe toward the door to find out who's out there, a man's muffled scream stops me dead in my tracks. My eyes pop wide, body trembling in bathed terror.

"Shut the fuck up," another voice demands, and I swallow past the lump in my throat.

"I told you what would happen if you didn't pay me what's owed, right?" The sinister tone in the first man's voice sends a cold shudder down my spine.

And the more that man speaks, the more it sounds like Fionn. Except he's different. Cold. More sinister. Not like the man I remember.

It's not him. It can't be!

He was sweet and kind. He took care of me. Left me money. He's not this evil guy who's clearly hurting someone else.

I refuse to accept it. I refuse to accept that the possible father of my daughter is a monster.

But the more I listen, the more it sounds like him.

Could it really be him?

My legs refuse to move anymore. I don't want to know. Because once I do, there's no going back. Not ever.

But I have to look. I need to prove to myself that it isn't him.

Sucking in a quiet breath, panic pummeling in my gut, I advance toward the bedroom door, only a crack opened just like I left it. My entire body's riddled with mind-crushing panic, goose bumps spreading across my arms as I pray the floor doesn't make a sound.

Taking slow, easy steps, I make it to the door, finding four men. Yet I only see the faces of three: two with white dress shirts, while another is on a chair, face bloody, eyes swollen.

The one who sounded like Fionn, whose face I can't yet see, grabs the injured guy's t-shirt.

"Where's my money?" he snaps, like he's ready to kill him.

Oh my God. I cup my mouth, afraid they'll hear my exploding exhales.

"I—I don't have it." The man's body shudders.

Please turn around. Let me see you. Prove to me that you're not him. You're not Fionn. You can't be him.

"That's a shame." He straightens to full height, and even the way he walks is just like Fionn.

He turns slowly, almost facing my way.

"This is your final chance," he says, and that's when I see him.

Nonono!

My pulse bangs in my temples, faster now.

There's no denying it.

"Fionn," I whisper, steadying a hand over my erratic heartbeats.

There's no way.

How can this be? How can he be this man? This awful man, hurting another over money.

Did I ever know him? Of course not!

Oh my God. I can't let him or those other men see me. Sweat coats my brow the walls closing in on me until I find it hard to breathe.

He still looks the same. But instead of attraction, I'm catapulted into terror.

There's blood on his knuckles, darkness slicing through his icy gaze. He's ready to kill this man. But there's no way he would. Not here.

Right?

He returns his attention to the man on the chair, and before I can fathom what he's about to do, he lines a blade across his throat.

Oh no! I can't watch him do this!

"Gonna send a message to your family. They pay your debt, or this will happen to them."

With a jerk of his hand, Fionn slices across his throat.

I choke on my inhale as the man gurgles up blood. My feet want to move, to run, but it's like I've been cemented to the floor, unable to do anything except watch the man I once really liked—the man who could be my daughter's father—kill someone.

"Clean this up."

"Yes, sir."

I sniffle, letting out a small cry.

And that's when one of the men zeroes in his glare at the door.

My throat goes dry, my body doused with something hot and cold all at once.

"Sir, I think there's someone there."

Oh no! He saw me.

Go! You have to run! Now!

But I don't. I can't move. Shit, I'm gonna die.

Cunning eyes land on mine, and my gaze expands. My lungs are on fire, heavy like bricks.

That's when I finally snap out of it. Before I know it, I'm racing toward the door separating the room next to this one. It's my only way out.

"Go find out who it is and bring him to me!" Fionn hollers, his tone scarier than even before.

"I think it was a woman."

"I don't give a fuck. She could've seen everything. Get her. Now!" he whisper-shouts.

Shit, shit, shit. I need to get out of here!

Not caring if they'll hear me, I scan my card, running into the adjacent bedroom and placing a chair against the door to help delay their entry.

I register their movements on the other side, and more terror fills my veins. Without wasting any more time, I rush out of the room and into the hallway, praying there's no one there.

I refuse to look back. Refuse to know if they're about to kill me. My footfalls are casual as I step out and dart toward the left, taking the stairs down.

A door opens from above.

"She's running," the same man tells Fionn.

"Oh God!" I whisper-cry, tears filling my eyes.

I can't leave Fia. My baby would be alone.

My heart slices in two.

Mommy's coming. I'm not leaving you.

There's no other choice but to run. From how vicious Fionn sounded, he won't care that it's me. He'd kill me to protect himself. I know that. Whoever he once was is gone, and in his place is a monster.

And that monster wants me dead.

I'll do everything to stop him. Because I have something to live for now.

As soon as I'm on the first level, I scan my card and sneak into a tiny, dark cleaning closet, my heart beating so fast, I grow lightheaded.

The men pass me. I can hear them right outside the door, wondering where I am.

"Find her!" Fionn snaps, and my chin trembles.

Don't hurt me.

"Get the damn security tapes and find out who she is." Icy fury laces through his words, making my tears fall even faster.

Because I still miss the man I remember.

Swiping away at the moisture, I gather some semblance of control. The only thing that matters is getting home to Fia and taking her somewhere safe. If he finds me on the cameras, he'll know who I am and he'll kill me.

Would he kill Fia too?

I choke on a cry, forcing myself to come up with a plan. If I can just get out of the closet and change into my regular clothes, and then get home, maybe I can beat them before they come to the house.

Waiting at least five minutes, I start to open the door, and don't see any of the men. They don't know what I look like. Not until they view the security video.

The hustle and bustle of people checking in makes it easier to split toward the locker room.

"Hey, Amara!" one of the other housekeepers calls from behind me, and my heart stills in my rib cage.

Pivoting, I force a smile. "Hey, Kathy. What's up?"

She turns her gaze into slits. "Oh, nothing. I just saw you coming out of the closet and wondered why."

Her mouth curls. She's never liked me, especially after she found out I get paid more than her. She knows I'd have no good reason to be in there. That's for the janitors.

Think!

"Um, I was looking for some Lysol. Ran out."

"Oh…" Her face twists like I'm an idiot. "But you know we have some here, right?"

A nervous laugh bubbles out of me. "I swear, I can't keep track of where everything is."

"Mm-hmm." She scoffs a laugh. "So, are you on a break?"

Oh God, shut up already.

I swear she keeps tabs on my schedule.

"Yeah, just going to grab some food from my lunch box. I'll see you later, okay?"

"Yeah, sure, no problem."

Waving goodbye, I strut past her toward the door leading to the lockers, my entire body trembling with the need to get the hell out of here.

When I'm inside, I keep eyes on her through the crack of the door, watching her walk away. Rushing toward my locker, I grab my clothes and start changing into them, checking my cell for any alarming texts from Lilith.

If I tell her that I'm coming home, she could call her dad. I can't risk it. I don't want anyone to know anything yet. Once I get home, I can tell her I felt ill or something. Doesn't matter. All that matters is getting home.

Grabbing my handbag, I slip out from the employee exit, the cool air hitting my face as I jog toward the parking lot and get into my car. My fingers jitter as I start the engine. And when I'm finally on the road, I take a breath, emotions plaguing me at the same time.

Memories sweep through my mind like a gust of wind, sending my heart into chaos.

"Why are you being so nice to me?"

"Because someone has to be."

His words echo, the gentleness in them.

Yet there was nothing gentle about the man I just saw. He was someone else.

But he was always that man, wasn't he? He was just hiding it.

The way he grabbed Xander, how angry he looked... I should've seen it. He was dangerous even then. I didn't think he was a murderer, though.

But things are much clearer now. Fionn is not a good man, and I have to do everything I can to keep my daughter away from him.

As soon as I make it back home, I slip the car into the driveway and rush up the cobblestone steps, barely able to get the key in the keyhole.

Lilith jumps up as soon as I step inside, shutting off the TV. "Hey, you're early." But as soon as she takes in my appearance, her face draws with concern. "What's wrong?"

"Oh, nothing. Just felt super ill and they let me go home." Grabbing some cash from my wallet, I hand it to her, my fingers visibly quivering.

"Amara, I don't need money." She grasps my fingers to steady my trembling. "Are you sure you're okay?"

"Mm-hmm. Just need sleep." I push down my emotions and try not to cry.

"Okay... If you're sure."

"I am. Thank you so much."

"Do you need me tomorrow?"

"Uh..." My heart races, needing her to go. "No. I'm gonna take the day off, just in case I'm still sick. I have some days saved."

Her brows draw tighter. "Okay. Well, if you need me any other day, just let me know. I'm always happy to help."

"I know." My arms curl around her. "Thank you."

I barely sound like myself—small and broken.

"Okay...uh, no problem. You're sure you're okay, right?"

"Completely."

"Alright." She starts for the exit, hitting me with speculative glances. "I'll call to check on you tomorrow."

"Sounds good. Thanks again."

"Have a good night."

"You too."

Shutting the door, I lock the double bolt, then hope like hell I can escape before they come for my daughter and me.

TWENTY

FIONN

"**Y**ou give my men access to the security cams or I blow your brains out. You choose."

I cock my nine into the back of the man's head, his body shaking before a set of computers.

"I—I could lose my job. Please—"

The barrel digs in deeper. "You will lose your life, so you decide. You've got five seconds. Because once I kill you, I'll get the footage anyway. May as well save yourself."

His hands quiver, his eyes staring at Pierce, one of my guys.

"Your time is up."

"Okay! Here!"

He jumps off the seat and starts for the door, but before he can get far, Pierce grabs him from behind and puts one into his head, killing him almost instantly. He saw us. There was no other way this could go.

"Hurry up," I tell Pierce. "We need her info ASAP. Then we stuff him into the luggage and get him out of here."

"Yes, sir."

While one of my men keeps eyes outside, Pierce starts clicking keys, eyes concentrating on the footage while I pace back and forth, hating that I have to kill a woman. But she's a witness, and she has to go. I'll make it painless.

"Okay. Got it. Amara Edwards." He shoots off an address. "She lives alone. Young. Want to see her?"

"No." The more I disconnect with this, the better.

"Want me to take care of it, boss?"

It'd be easier if he did.

"No. I've got it. You two take care of this before someone catches wind of what happened to him."

"Don't worry. We've got this."

While they take care of the body and the cameras that could ID us, I head into my car, hating the job I'm about to do.

I arrive at a small one-story home, an older blue sedan in the driveway. The lights in the house are off as I sneak into the back, hoping she isn't looking out the window.

Thought about hiding my face, but it doesn't matter either way. She's gonna be dead.

Removing a small screwdriver from my pocket, I slip it into the lock, thankful I keep this shit on my keychain.

After a few seconds, a click resonates, and when I twist the knob, I know it worked.

My eyes adjust to the surroundings: a small square kitchen, a narrow hallway running perpendicular. The wood floor creaks beneath my feet as I start in that direction, where all the rooms must be.

Fingers curl around the nine at my waist, a syringe in my pocket. I'll drug her, then kill her. Better she doesn't know what's coming.

Don't want that. It's not her fault she was there.

As soon as I step left, a woman's roar causes me to jump back and something hard hits me on the arm. When I look down, I notice the plastic Tupperware bowl.

Was she aiming for my head? That's cute.

I let out a laugh. She was waiting for me.

"I wouldn't do that if I were you, Ms. Edwards. We wouldn't want you hurting yourself."

She gasps with a low cry, but I won't let that affect me.

"P-p-please, leave us alone."

As those words leave her mouth, my heart beats so fucking loud, I almost wonder if I heard right.

It can't be *her*. There's no way in hell.

"Say something else," I demand.

The darkness still clouds her face, but shit, it was her. It had to be.

I should turn on the light and see for myself. But I can't do it. If it is her, it means I came to kill the one woman I've lived and breathed to find these past years.

"I beg you," she whispers.

I close my eyes, that voice feeding this insatiable void I've carried all this time.

"I won't say anything. I promise, Fionn."

Fuck! It's her!

"Emily?"

But that's not her damn name. All this time, I've been looking for someone who didn't exist.

Taking a slow drag of a breath, I attempt to dispel my rage. But it's pointless. Finding the nearest light switch, I turn it on.

It takes me a few seconds to take her in. Those hazel eyes. That dark hair. Curves I've been dreaming about.

It's her. There's no denying it.

The shock of seeing her after all this time sends me back a step.

I'm staring at the woman I've been unable to forget.

And suddenly, the only thing I want to do is take her in my arms and kiss her.

"What the hell?" My tone comes out harsher than I meant it.

She backs away, planting herself against the wall, her body shaking, eyes full of fear.

Of *me*.

Fuck. She saw me kill someone. Of course she's terrified.

Stalking closer, I reach for her face, slowly feathering my fingers over the soft skin of her cheek while she shivers. And that kills me.

"Stay away from me!" She plants a hand between us, but I easily wrench it away.

My pulse pounds, unable to believe she's really here.

"Emily… Fuck!" Anger races through my veins. "That's not your name. I've been fucking thinking about you all this time, and I didn't even know your name."

"Are you serious right now?"

Her head shakes with a scoff, and I finally see it. Disappointment.

"I just watched you kill a man, and you wanna talk about my name?" she whisper-shouts. "You…" She digs a finger into my chest. "…have no right to judge me. Just get the hell out of here!"

A smile winds the corner of my mouth. Because she touched me. She can be as angry as she wants if she keeps touching me like that.

"I thought you were a good guy, but you're a criminal! I can't believe I've spent any time thinking about you at all."

My fingers snap around her wrist, and I pin it against the wall, taking her other one too, both trapped on opposite sides. "You've thought about me, baby?"

Her chest flails, eyes wild with fear, yet I can taste her desire too.

"How many times?"

She visibly shudders. "Not that many." Her cheeks flush.

"Liar." I groan, pushing my body into hers, my mouth slowly

skimming her lips.

She gasps, and that only makes me hungrier for her.

"Amara…" My mouth drops to her ear, teeth clenched. "It's gonna take me a while to get used to calling out your real name while I jerk myself off, thinking of filling your pussy with my cum."

She sucks in a breath. "You're insane to be talking about *that* when you just came to kill me!"

She's just as beautiful as I remember. Maybe her hips are slightly rounder, but I fucking love it.

"You think I could ever harm a hair on your head?" My tone deepens, threaded with my insatiable thirst.

It's been so damn long…

"It doesn't matter. You were gonna kill whoever you thought I was." Her eyes narrow. "I'd never be with you again. I truly hope you understand that, because if not, maybe it's time you got your head examined."

I let out a short breath of laughter, dragging my nose across her throat before pressing a lingering kiss to the spot under her ear.

"I don't remember needing your permission, little rabbit. You're mine now. There's no escaping me anymore."

"Oh yeah?" She pushes at me with her body, forcing me to look at her. "And what are you gonna do? Drag me out of here on your back while I'm kicking and screaming?"

"Sounds perfect." A slow, calculating grin lifts one side of my mouth.

"Stay away from me." Anger stomps through her gaze, like a vicious ocean I'd die to get lost in.

She has no idea how long I've waited for this moment. To find her again. I'll never lose her. I don't give a shit how old she is anymore. Though she's no longer nineteen, so her age is not even a factor now.

She pushes her palms against my chest, groaning when she's not strong enough.

"You fighting me like this only makes me want you more. So please, baby girl, keep going."

My smirk infuriates her, and she lets out a growl before I'm grabbing her wrists and pinning them above her head this time.

"You're a monster."

She's not wrong. I am.

But I'm *her* monster now.

My thumb strolls across her fuckable mouth. "Don't be afraid of me. I'd never hurt you, baby." Clasping a palm across her warm cheek, I stare into her eyes. "My God, I can't believe I'm looking at you. Touching you." I lower my forehead to hers. "I've never been able to get you out of my head."

Pulling back, I feather my knuckles down her throat, and her exhales grow raspier, her body moving into mine like she wants more.

"Please...please just go. I—I won't say anything." But she doesn't sound like she wants me to go, her tone growing huskier.

I tip up her chin with the back of my hand. "Not going anywhere. And I don't think you want me to either."

I can see it in her eyes: that desire to fight me. Fight this connection between us.

But I won't let her forget.

"Please...I—I can't."

With my knuckles, I trace her rounded jaw, my nose sinking into her hair. I can still smell the same shampoo she used last time.

When I look back, her eyes fasten shut, brows knitted.

My mouth lowers, brushing over hers. "Look at me."

When she shakes her head, I say it again.

"Open your eyes, Amara."

She obeys, those long lashes feathering as her sweet, innocent gaze holds mine.

"I can't, Fionn. I can't do this. You're not the man I thought you were. Everything I wanted..." Her voice cracks.

I know she wants this. Needs this.

"Of course I am. You just need me to remind you."

Before she has a chance to resist, I take her mouth in a vicious kiss.

And I know right now, I'm gonna marry her.

Letting out a little moan, she slides her hands into my hair. Mine coast down her back, squeezing her ass and pressing her into my rock-hard erection. It's damn good to feel her hands on me again. She doesn't even attempt to push me away. I knew she'd see reason once she felt how good we are together.

Even if she refuses, it makes no difference. I'm gonna make her my wife.

The way I see it, we both get something out of it. She wants to live, and I get to protect myself and my family if she does something stupid like go to the cops. We've got plenty on our payroll, but not all of them.

Twisting her hair around my wrist, I take her deeper, my tongue invading and taking everything that belongs to me. Her palms push against my chest, and with a groan, I move back a fraction, grinding my jaw as I take in her flushed expression.

"I—I, um…" She traces a single finger over her lips, and a smirk tips up my mouth.

"You felt it too, didn't you? That damn connection we still have." My fingers slide into her hair, fisting all those luscious waves. "I'm never letting you go. You understand that, right?"

"No." Her face turns white. "Please. I promise you that I would never ever say a word. I don't care what you do, okay? Just please walk away. Let that one day we had be how I remember you."

My responding chuckle is low and deep. "It's too late for that. You saw what you saw. My brother's men know who you are. So just because I won't kill you, it doesn't mean one of them won't."

"Oh God!" she pants, terror bathing those beautiful eyes. The ones

I wanna get lost in.

"There is a solution, though."

Of course she won't like it, but she'll come around.

"What's that?" Hope springs in her features, and I'm about to crush it.

"If you want to survive, all you have to do is marry me."

"Um, what?" She coughs a laugh. "You've got to be joking. Please tell me you're joking."

"Not at all." I tug her chin into my palm. "If we're married, you can't testify against me, so my family would have no reason to come after you. That's what we call a win-win." My face curls with a rapacious smirk.

"Are you insane?"

No. Just obsessed with you.

I stroke the outline of her jaw with the back of my hand right before my fingers wrap around her delicate throat. Our eyes lock in a brutal stare.

"Let me explain how things are going to work, little rabbit. You will marry me or you die. It's that simple."

Her ire melts away, and in its place, there's fear. It's almost enough to undo me. To tell her I've changed my mind. Because she has no idea that no one would touch her without my permission. I just needed her to believe she had no choice in the matter. Once she's mine, I'll make her see that I'm still the man she remembers.

"Please, I—"

"Mama!" The sound of a child's cry cuts her words, startling the fuck out of me, like I've gone insane.

Because there's no way she has a kid.

Right?

"Mama!" the little girl calls again.

Amara's face grows ashen, eyes expanding by the second. "Please..."

I don't even know what she's begging for. All I can hear is the child's voice. A child she had with someone else.

My palm squeezes tighter around her throat. "Are you married? Whose child is that?"

Her body trembles, choking on the words that don't come. My nostrils flare while her irises fill with panic. Loosening my grip, I attempt to control this damn jealousy, these murderous intentions.

Because whoever he is, the man's already dead.

"Mama!"

"Please let me go see her. We can talk after, alright? I promise."

"I'm coming with you. Don't fucking try anything, you understand?"

She nods as I tug her hand in mine. Leading us down the corridor, she enters a small room containing a toddler bed with rails on the left side.

And in it is the most beautiful little girl I've ever seen.

She looks just like her mother. Dark curls, and with the nightlight, I can almost tell that her eyes are the same color as Amara's.

Amara. I can't get used to that.

Running a hand through my hair, I stand back as the child curiously glances at me, holding a straw cup.

"I want water, Mama."

"O-o-okay, sweetie. Let me go fill this up for you." She glances back at me, trying to control her fear.

"We'll be okay," I tell her, winking at the little girl. "You can go."

"Who's this, Mama?"

The girl's eyes jump between us, and Amara forces a panicked smile.

"I'm Fionn. Mommy's friend. And what's your name, sweetheart?"

"My name is Fia."

"How old are you, Fia?"

"I'm four." She holds out four fingers in the air and grins, and something hits me hard, something I can't explain.

And I know right now, I'm gonna be her father.

Fia… The similarity between our names doesn't escape me.

A questioning brow arches as I stare at a stricken Amara. "We need to talk after she goes back to bed."

She nods.

The child is four… Could she be mine? The math adds up. But she could also be that bastard's kid.

My fingers curl around my gun, completely hidden from the child's view. If I didn't have a reason to kill that asshole before, I just found another.

It doesn't matter whose blood weaves through this girl's veins, though. She's mine because her mother is.

"Go get her that water, Amara. I'll stay and keep her safe."

My reassurance does nothing but cause her to fear me even more. She grabs the sippy cup, and as she moves toward the door, her shoulder brushes with mine.

"Please don't do anything to hurt her. She's all I have."

Her tears are like daggers to my heart. And when she places a hand on my chest, I slowly unravel.

"I know you've already made up your mind about me, but I'd never hurt either one of you. I swear. Trust me."

She laughs brokenly as she swipes under her eyes. "I'll be right back."

When she rushes out of the room, I'm left alone with the little girl who doesn't even look remotely tired now.

"You have to go back to sleep so you can get big and strong."

"Mama says I'm big and strong already. Look!" She flexes her biceps, snapping her teeth as she giggles.

I can't help but chuckle. "Wow. I think yours are bigger than mine."

Her laughter is innocent and pure, and that voice is so damn cute.

"You're silly."

"There you are, baby!" Amara returns and hands her that cup, smiling at her daughter.

Our daughter.

Let her try to fight me on that. That child is mine, whether she wants her to be or not.

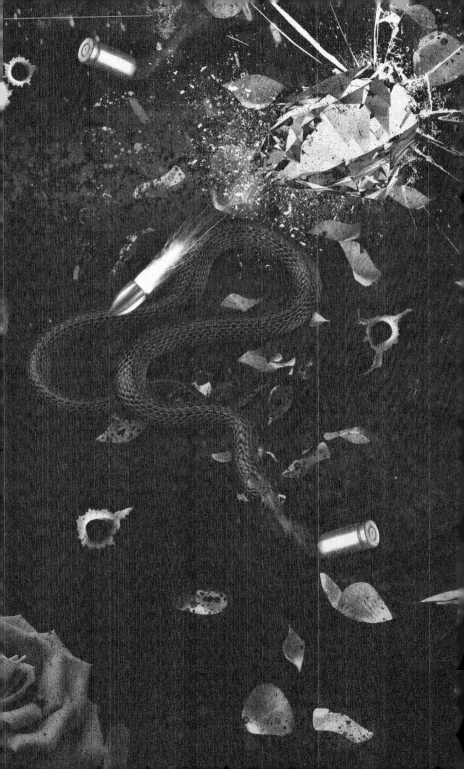

TWENTY-ONE

FIONN

"Be a good girl and go to bed, okay?" Amara tells her.

"Goodnight, Fionn." The child grins, waving goodbye.

"Goodnight, sweetheart. I'll see you tomorrow."

"You will?" Amara's face weaves with shock.

"Sure will, little rabbit." I tug her to my side and she shivers. "You have lots of explaining to do."

She gulps, laughing dryly. "Okay. We'll, uh, see you tomorrow, baby."

"Okay, Mama."

Holding her hand in mine, we exit the room, and Amara gently closes the door. As soon as she does, she turns to me, her anger returning.

"What the hell do you mean, you'll see her tomorrow?" She snaps her fingers out of my grasp. "I told you I need you to go. I will *not*

185

marry you." She blows an exacerbated breath. "This is just nuts!"

A smirk slants over my mouth, my hand cupping her jaw as I near my lips to hers. "Shh. Keep it down, little rabbit. You're gonna wake up our daughter."

"Oh my God, you're insane!" She throws her hands in the air.

"We already established that. And it's all…" I back her up against the wall. "Your fault."

My hands return to her hair, my mouth dropping to her throat.

"This is so not gonna work." She clasps her hands on my shoulders as I kiss and suck the skin above her pounding pulse.

My mouth curls because instead of pushing me off, her head falls backward.

"That's it, baby girl. Show me how much you like it."

"We can't…"

"I think we can."

"You're crazy. And if I allow this, so am I." Her fingernails score my back, her hips gyrating against my dick.

"Sure as hell felt crazy all this time you've been gone." My lips skim down the slope of her throat, tugging the strap of her tank top. "And I promised myself when I found you, I'd take what belongs to me. And I'd never let you run again."

"I'm not yours."

She gasps when my hand slips into the waistband of her leggings, feeling her bare and wet on my fingertips.

"That's not what your pussy says." I back away so I can look into her eyes.

With a finger, I work her swollen clit as she cries, mouth parted, cheeks flushed.

"We're destined, baby. You landed right back in my lap, and now there's no going back."

Before she can protest, I thrust two fingers inside her, playing her clit with my thumb while she tries to keep quiet.

"Fionn!" she cries, and I wrap her mouth with my hand.

"If you don't keep quiet, I'm gonna gag you and make you choke on my tie."

She whimpers as I lower my hand, and when I pinch her clit, she sucks in a breath, eyes lost to her pleasure.

"Please!"

"Please what?" Roughly, I fist her hair, curling my fingers inside her wet cunt. "Please make you gag or make you come?" I swirl my thumb faster over her clit when she doesn't answer. "I can do both. Just ask nicely."

She gasps, begging me not to stop, while images of her with other men fill my mind.

"How many men have you been with after me? Tell me so I can fucking kill every single one."

"Fionn…" Her eyes grasp mine, holding on like a raft.

"Tell me. Just fucking say it and put me out of my misery."

"No one." She shakes her head, her fingers grasping tighter onto my shoulders.

"What?" I still my movements, not believing her.

"Don't stop!"

Her breaths fall faster, and I chuckle as my mouth grows closer to hers, stroking her lips with mine.

"I like how demanding you've gotten."

"Good. Because I need this." Her moans come in gasps.

"I'll give you anything you want. Just don't fuck with me, Amara." Thrusting deeper, I watch her as she writhes in ecstasy. "You haven't been with anyone else?"

She shakes her head, slamming her eyes shut. "Oh my God, that's so good."

"Neither have I."

"What?" Even through the pleasure, her eyes fill with shock.

"I haven't fucked anyone after you."

She's unable to say anything else as I work her faster, knowing she's about to give me what I want. With another touch, she screams for me, and I release a growl, clasping my hand over her mouth.

"Look at how beautiful you are squirting all over my hand."

Her sensual sounds vibrate against my palm, and I bask in the feeling of knowing I did that. I made her come like that.

Me.

When she falls from the high, I slip my fingers out, running them over her lips. "Open up and suck."

She obeys immediately, staring up at me hungrily as she tastes herself.

My teeth grind as I take her in.

Mine. All mine.

I cup her face with my other palm. "Is Fia my daughter?" My pulse beats louder. "Tell me the damn truth, because it's killing me not to know."

Though either way, I'll claim her as mine.

Her eyes go downcast, but I don't allow her to hide, tilting her chin up between two fingers.

"She could be. She's either his or yours, and—"

"She's mine." My breaths rage out of me.

Shock riddles her features, her eyes about to pop. "Don't you wanna know for sure?"

"It doesn't matter to me. You're mine, and so is she. Whose blood runs in her veins makes no difference."

She sniffles.

"What did you think? That I wouldn't want her?"

"I thought it might be a possibility."

"She's your daughter, and because of that, she's mine too. That's all there is to it."

She lets out a small sob.

"Don't cry, baby. You're killing me."

"I—I wanted this for so long." Her glassy vision sucks me in, and all I want is to marry her right now. "I even imagined that you found me and told me this exact thing, but now…"

"Now it's happening." I stroke the outline of her jaw, eyes drowning in her depthless gaze. "Now I've found you and won't let you get away."

"I can't marry you, Fionn. I have to protect Fia. And I don't know who you truly are, but you're clearly dangerous, and I will never allow her to be around that."

As I suck in a rough breath, my chest grows tight. "Oh, baby girl. You're confused." The back of my hand slinks down her pretty cheek. "You *will* be my wife. There's no choice in the matter."

She inhales, air trapped in her lungs as I continue.

"I'm gonna stay the night, and tomorrow after Fia's awake, we'll drive to our new home."

"What?" Panic fills the lines of her face. "No! I will not allow you to just take us! I—I have a job and bills! A life! I—I can't. I won't! Not with you."

Those last words just make me furious, my temples beating. "No wife of mine will work as a housekeeper, and your bills, they'll be paid for. You'll never have to worry about bills again. Not when you have me."

"Fionn, I can't do this. Be reasonable."

"You can and you will."

"I told you I would never get you in trouble," she pleads. "Isn't that enough? My word means nothing to you?"

"I may believe you, but my family won't, and I told you what would happen if you disobeyed me. Now, let's go to bed. We have a wedding tomorrow." I pull her hand in mine, but she yanks it away.

"Wait, whose wedding?"

A wry chuckle slips out of me. "Ours."

She stares open-mouthed, a hand falling to her flailing chest.

I know I'm being selfish. But after what she did, I deserve to be as selfish as I damn well please.

"Don't look so scared." I kiss her jaw. "I promise to be a good husband and father." My lips skim up to the corner of her mouth.

"Are you really going to do this to me? Are you really going to force me to be your wife?"

My wife. That has such a nice ring to it.

I blow out an exacerbated breath. "I'm saving your life. You should thank me."

"Yeah, right." She snorts.

"Try it." A smirk settles on my face. "Come on, baby, try it. Thank you, Fionn, for saving my life." My hips arch into her, still damn throbbing for this woman. "I'm sorry for being such a damn brat and running away from you." I plant my hand around her throat, and she whimpers when I cinch my fingers tighter. "I promise to be a good girl and make it up to you."

"Please, Fionn. I can't…"

"Can't what?" My fingers return between her thighs.

My girl missed me as much as I missed her.

"Can't—oh God!" she moans as I rub her clit.

"Say it or I'll torture you all night, and you know you'll deserve it."

"That's unfair."

"What's unfair is that I had to live all these years without you." Three fingers enter her, stretching her out for what's gonna be one rough fuck.

We both need it.

"Do you know how hard it's been imagining you with other people, forgetting me?"

"I never forgot you," she breathes, shutting her eyes and shaking her head like she can't believe she admitted that.

"Where's your bedroom? And try not to lie this time." My mouth winds, my teeth clenched with frustration and need.

Damn, I want her. It's like no time has passed.

Her vision bounces between me and the ground like she's unsure if we should do this.

"Tell me now, Amara, or I'll fuck you up against this wall." I palm her pussy, kneading into it.

Her lashes flutter, and she lets out a little moan.

"There." She points to the room next to Fia's, and I'm tugging her inside, putting on the light.

She stays frozen by the door while I move toward the bed and settle onto it, taking in her brown furniture and blue comforter. It's simple and very Amara.

My hands run over the fabric of her blanket. "Soft. You play with yourself here thinking about me?"

She visibly shivers. "Never."

That causes my smirk to widen. "Liar, liar."

Uncuffing my shirt, I drag the sleeves up, resting my elbows on top of my stretched-out legs.

I give her body a slow once-over. "Strip."

"What?" she gasps.

"You heard me. I don't like repeating myself." I start removing my shoes, watching that wide-eyed expression as she takes in my movements. "I think I deserve at least that for what you did to me."

"You don't deserve anything." She hikes up her chin. "Plus, I thought you came to kill me."

"I did. But fucking you is a way better use of my time." I wave a finger in the air. "Clothes. Off. Now, Amara. I'm done waiting."

I witness the dread in her eyes before she even says anything.

"Uh…" She grimaces, her chest rising and falling in quick succession.

"What's wrong?"

"Look, I—I can't."

"Why not? You know you want this too."

She curls her arms around herself. "Even if the circumstance of… this wasn't an issue, I just…you know…never loved my body. And, uh, after Fia, it's even less great."

That was hard for her to admit, and it makes me want her even more.

Unbuttoning my shirt, I get to my feet. Stalking closer, I clasp her jaw as I stare down at her.

"You think I'd find your body unattractive after you had my child?"

"Maybe." She grimaces. "My stomach is full of stretch marks. My boobs definitely have seen better days, and you seeing me like that…" Her face burns hot as her voice trails.

"You're perfect. Then and now." As I stare deep into her eyes, my thumb lazily strokes her lips. "Let me show you how beautiful I think you are. You can go on hating me tomorrow."

Her eyes water over, and whatever's left of my fucked-up heart splits right open, letting her all the way in. My mouth lowers, brushing hers softly before I kiss her, taking my time, my tongue parting her lips. I grab her hand and place it against my chest, forcing it lower, running it down my abs until I'm leading it to my cock.

"This is how bad I want you. How damn gorgeous I think you are."

"Fionn, I'm scared," she trembles out, that gaze so damn vulnerable, I'd do anything to keep her safe.

"Don't be. I've got you."

Lifting her into my arms, I carry her to bed and lower her on top of it. Her breathing turns labored as I prop my knee on the edge of the mattress, removing my shirt completely.

With my fingers on my belt, the metal clanks as I pull it out and start on the zipper of my pants, watching her watch me the entire time.

When I'm stepping out of them and pulling down my boxers, her mouth parts as I stroke my erection. Her legs squeeze into one another, and my blood pumps into my hard-on, making it so damn painful.

"Lower your shirt. Show me those tits."

It takes a few seconds of uncertainty before a finger slips into a single strap and she starts pulling it lower, then the other, until her shirt settles on her abdomen.

"Fuck. They're bigger now."

She nods.

"You're so fucking sexy." My voice goes breathless.

"Really?" Her cheeks grow pink.

I let out a chuckle, climbing on the bed and forcing her legs apart as I settle over her body. My thumb feathers over her mouth.

"It's even sexier that you don't know how beautiful you are."

My cock pushes into her pussy, needing to feel it wet and hungry for me again. Lifting off of her a little, I yank her leggings down until they're bunched up against her ankles.

"What are you doing?" she asks as I rise to my knees, forcing her legs over her chest and running a finger through her wet slit.

"I like looking at your pretty pussy."

She tries to shift out of this position, but I don't let her.

"Stop fidgeting, baby, or I'll tie you to the bed so I can do whatever the hell I want to you without disruption."

My fingers sink inside her to the first knuckle, rubbing the wetness over her clit, then I glide another finger into her ass.

"Oh God!" She jolts.

"Does that feel good?" I take her from both ends, watching her drown in bliss.

"Yes…" she groans. "I like that."

"The things I can teach you." I increase my pace. "It's a good thing we've got the rest of our lives for that."

She starts to protest but I don't let her. I fuck her hard, taking what belongs to me. She's so exposed, and I love it.

"Yes, yes, I'm coming!" She fists the sheets, her body undulating in absolute ecstasy.

Needing a taste, I lower my face between her thighs and trace her clit with the tip of my tongue. Her feminine sounds have me groaning against her, sucking her into my mouth until she's screaming my name again.

Her taste on my tongue is like the antidote I've been craving. Ripping the leggings all the way off, I split her thighs open, pushing them down onto the bed. When I stare up at her, I find her flushed, unable to catch her breath.

My palm lands across her cunt, working her clit against it. "It's beautiful to watch you let go."

"That was…"

Grabbing her hips, I flip her on top of me. "It was."

Her pussy rubs against my chest and she looks at me with uncertainty, one arm trying to curl against her stomach while the other makes some attempt to cover her chest.

I chuckle. "Why are you hiding from me? I've seen it all, and I've always liked what I saw."

She lets out a sigh. Pulling her arms away, I let my gaze crawl down her body, arching my hips, needing to fill her.

"You don't hide from me anymore. Understand?" My fingers start at her sternum, tracing down to where we meet. "This is all mine, and I find it beautiful."

I force her higher up.

"What are you doing?" Fear grips her gaze.

"Shut that pretty mouth and come sit on my face."

Her eyes grow larger. "Uh, why? Are you looking for me to kill *you* this time?"

My chuckle fades. "No, I'm hoping to tongue-fuck you until you're squirting on my face. Been dreaming about it."

"Oh God." She squeezes her legs, and my cock throbs for her.

"You want it, don't you, little rabbit? Want to work that sweet cunt all over my mouth until I can't fucking breathe without tasting you. Isn't that right?"

"Yes…"

"Good girl. Now climb up. Then maybe I'll finally get to fuck you."

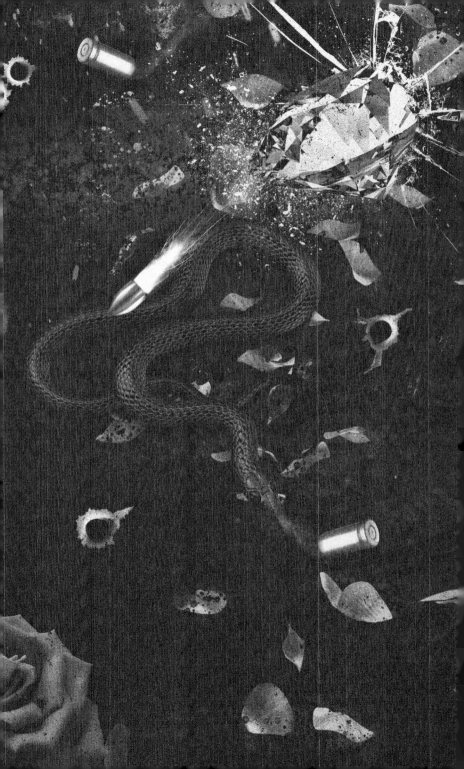

TWENTY-TWO

AMARA

His tongue is like an invasion. An invasion I'd gladly sign up for.

Being with him, it takes me back to the one and only night we spent together.

No matter how hard I tried to forget it—forget him—I never could. And now, I'm lost to the feelings he brought out in me that first time.

One palm clasps the headboard, the other gripping his hair as he takes pieces of me I was afraid to give him. But beneath my fear, there's this dormant desire for the man I've wanted to find.

Now here he is, trying to convince me that he's still the man I remember.

But I know better. Yet I still allow him to do this to me. It feels too good not to. It's been so long since I've felt this. Felt him.

The shame will come. Shame at my weakness and desperation. Right now, though, I'm Emily and he's Fionn, and together we burn like fire.

Though after the flames die out, that's when it'll all come to the surface: who he is and why he truly came.

"Yes," I cry out, my nails digging into his scalp, fingers working through his thick hair as he growls, his tongue sinking inside me.

I concentrate on how amazing this is and not on the fact that he swears we'll be married tomorrow.

He must be joking, right? There's no way.

When he sucks my clit into that warm mouth, a scream dies in my throat, all other noise in my head washing away. With another flick, I fall, eyes rolling back, toes curling in mind-bending pleasure.

Wow. I forgot how good he is. How right this is.

His groaning against my sensitive flesh has me jerking just as he slowly scoots me down to his chest. That smirk and heavy-lidded gaze cause my gut to grow tight.

His tongue slinks out, licking across his lips. "Fucking delicious."

The way his eyes sink into mine, it makes me feel like the most beautiful woman on earth. My fingers reach out, gently feathering over the deep shadow of his jaw. His eyes fasten, body growing languid, and when I stop, he snaps his fist around my wrist, the veins atop his hand jerking as he does.

"Keep touching me."

His stare is deep and intense, and my skin prickles—not from fear, but the demand in his tone, the need within it. I allow myself to touch him more, tracing past his lips, down his thick neck. His abs contract when my fingertips trace each one. He must enjoy the gym to look like this, all built and muscular.

"Fuck." His palm snaps to my ass, and he squeezes it hard as his eyes line with mine. "I need you, Amara."

My heart beats faster, every inch of me wanting this too. "Then have me."

In a flash, he flips me over, fitting his large, towering body over mine. His gaze turns soft, yet there's nothing soft about a man like him.

But when he brushes his rough knuckles down my cheek, I forget. I forget all the reasons this is wrong, and I kiss him. I kiss the man I remember. The man I wanted so badly on that island.

He returns the kiss with equal fervor, fisting locks of my hair, his tongue roughly swirling with mine. When I feel his cock at my entrance, I realize he has no condom.

Pulling back breathlessly, I search his eyes, wanting nothing more than to get lost inside them, the green hue as vivid as I remember. "You need a condom."

He chuckles, mouth locking to my throat as he kisses me there, teeth marking me before his tongue takes the sting away. When he returns his gaze, there's something darker there. Something predatory.

"No, I don't, little rabbit." His thumb rolls across my bottom lip, his eyes following the movement. "Tomorrow, we'll be married, and I plan on filling you up until we have another baby together."

"What?" My eyes widen while he grabs his cock and pushes the tip inside me. The cold metal of his piercings only heightens the sensation. "You wanna get married and have a child together?"

His smug half-smile makes me both turned on and livid.

"That's right."

"You're crazy."

But in the back of my mind, I kinda want it too. Does it make me nuts?

"You keep saying things I already know."

He chuckles all gravelly as he pushes another inch inside me, and I groan, needing this so badly, even as I try not to show just how much.

"You can't get me pregnant when we barely know each other." My voice grows raspier, trying to hide how good he's making me feel, but that only makes him look smugger.

"You know everything there is to know, Amara. There's nothing left."

"Somehow, I find that hard to believe."

"Come on now, baby girl…" He sinks even deeper, his lips latching on to my throat. "You trying to act like your pussy doesn't like this is only turning me on more."

As I shake my head and attempt to roll my eyes, he thrusts himself all the way inside until I'm bucking and cursing out his name.

"Oh God! Yes, please!"

"Now that's more like it." He tugs my head back, my hair still in his grasp, but his movements stop. "Please who?"

"W-w-what?"

"Please, Fionn… Please, sir." His nose rolls up my neck, and goose bumps spread over my arms. "Please, husband. You choose."

"You're not my husband." I gasp as he rolls his hips.

"Not yet."

He slips out and rams back in, causing my eyes to roll back.

"Oh God!"

The need to unravel starts to overtake me. And the more he sees his effect on me, the more he tortures me. Lifting one of my legs, he pushes it to my shoulder while he sinks in slower, deeper, watching me as he does.

His other hand finds my clit, and he rubs it in slow, calculating circles while his cock spreads me wider for him. "Could watch this pussy take my cock all damn day."

"Fionn, please." I grip his bicep, and it ripples under my touch.

"Tell me what you need, little rabbit, and I'll let you have it."

I've never openly talked this way before, but right now, it doesn't seem to make me embarrassed or self-conscious. "Please make me come."

And as though I just opened the dam, he takes my other leg and pummels inside me, like I just unleashed a beast I can never put back. He never takes his eyes off me, and it all becomes overwhelming—both my body and my heart filled with overpowering sensations I

FILTHY SAVAGE

never wanted, not after what I saw him do.

I attempt to close my eyes, needing a reprieve from my overwrought emotions, my release climbing to the cusp until I'm near the fall.

"Open your eyes," his deep gravelly tone calls. "I want you to see what we are together. Don't run from it."

And from that moment on, I look into his eyes and I feel it: that chemistry between us, that pull I'm being sucked into.

His movements grow more urgent while he rubs my clit until there's nowhere to go but down.

"Yes!" With both hands clasped to his back, I fall headfirst into the most intense orgasm, letting go of everything in this very moment.

"Fuuuck," he growls, taking me faster, harder, the sound of skin on skin echoing in the room.

With his next thrust, he releases inside me, pounding deeper while I arch into him, wanting his depravity.

"Yeah, that's it. That's a good girl. Let me fill that cunt."

When I squeeze my breasts together, he mutters a curse, grinding his teeth and slamming harder, hot spurts shooting inside me. His chest rises and falls as his rhythm slows. He lowers his body on top of mine, but makes no attempt to slip out of me.

He remains that way, keeping himself propped on an elbow, eyes on mine as he pushes a strand of hair away from my face.

The possessive look in his eyes as he watches me has me uneasy.

"Are you gonna…"

"Keep my cock buried inside you?" The husky timbre of his tone sends a chill down my body.

I nod.

"There's no way I'm gonna waste a drop. I want you pregnant."

Every hair on my arms prickles. "You really are serious."

His teasing smirk does nothing to alleviate my anxiety. I can't have another child. Not with him. Not now. This is just all too much.

"I never say anything I don't mean, baby girl. Now let's get some sleep." He flips us so we're both on our sides, facing one another.

And his cock, it's still inside me.

He pulls the covers over me, tucking it around me. "Goodnight, baby. Tomorrow is the start of a whole new life. I hope you're ready for it, Mrs. Quinn."

Mrs. Quinn? Oh my God.

Amara Quinn.

Doesn't have a bad ring to it.

The only problem is, I have no idea who exactly I'm about to marry.

TWENTY-THREE

FIONN

I don't know what the hell took over me last night. But all I could think about was getting her pregnant. It consumed me. As soon as I was inside her, that was all I thought about. Maybe it's the fact that I've missed out on the first few years of Fia's life, and I want to make up for it.

Amara tenses beside me while I pick up Fia, holding her tight in my arms while grabbing the spare car seat Amara had in the house.

"Where we going, Mama?" Fia glances between us, grinning all toothy at me, and I can't help but laugh.

Amara clears her throat, probably unsure how to answer our daughter.

"Well…" I tell her. "You and your mommy are gonna have a fun sleepover at my house for a few days. How does that sound?"

"Why?" Her dark pigtails sway as her head slants to the side.

"Because Mommy and I are friends." I glance over at Amara, who's scratching her temple as I go on. "I haven't seen her in a long time and I've missed her, so I wanted us to have a sleepover. I like sleeping with your mother."

When I catch Amara's gaze, her cheeks grow crimson. She catches my smirk, and her face only grows rosier.

Shit, she's so fucking beautiful.

"I like sleeping with Mama too!"

"See, it's fun." I let out a laugh.

"Yeah. Fun." She giggles. "Do you have a poo?"

"Uh, a what?" My brows shoot up while Amara bursts into a laugh.

"A poo!" The kid looks at me like I've offended her.

"Umm…" I grimace.

"You should see your face right now." Amara continues to laugh at my expense.

"Wanna help me out here?"

"Mm, not really." She lets out another laugh before she puts me out of my misery. "She means a pool." Grabbing Fia's hand, she kisses it. "My friend…um, Emily, has one, and she's obsessed."

"Ah, Emily. It's funny, I feel like we already know each other so well."

She rolls her eyes, and as she does, I drop my lips to her ear.

"Only time those eyes should be rolling is when I've got my cock buried in your cunt." When she sucks in a breath, I go on. "Can't get the feeling of your pussy wrapped around my dick while you fell asleep out of my head."

"Can you keep it down?" she whispers, bumping her elbow into my ribs. "She can probably hear you."

"Doubt it." I leave a kiss on the corner of her mouth, and her inhale stills in her throat.

"Come on, kid," I tell Fia. "Let's get you in the car seat. We have a long drive."

"Mommy got all your snacks ready. But hopefully you take a nap." Amara whispers that last part.

"She'll be fine. Right, kid?"

"I like snacks." Fia grabs chunks of my hair while we walk out to my Royce SUV.

I'm grateful it's the one I drove into Boston yesterday.

"Your hair is like a teddy bear." She giggles.

"I'll take that as a compliment." I wink, and she tries to copy me, her high-pitched laugh making me smile.

Glancing over at my pissed-off future wife, I realize I now have a family I didn't know I needed, one already made for me. I'll do everything to protect them. She may not want this—not yet—but I'll do everything in my power to make her happy.

I hand Fia to Amara while I hook the car seat into the back. "Okay, let's get you inside."

Fia's arms reach for me, and I can tell how uncomfortable that makes my little rabbit. That's alright. Eventually she'll realize I'm not the enemy.

I place Fia in the car seat and buckle her in.

Amara hands her a sippy cup. "Be a good girl, okay?" She kisses her on the forehead.

"I'm always a good girl, Mama."

"Yes, you are." She sighs, looking up at me.

"Get in," I tell her, tucking her hand in mine before I bring it to my lips.

She fidgets, darting her eyes to the ground as she whisper-shouts, "This isn't right. You can't just force someone to marry you!"

"I just did." My smirk has her irises burning with a death threat. "I'm protecting you. Don't ever forget that."

"You're really trying to protect yourself," she snickers.

"Well…" My mouth curls. "I never said I wasn't getting anything out of it."

And what I mean by that is you.

"What about my car and my things?" She huffs, her body deflating.

"I'll have everything you and Fia need brought to our home tomorrow."

"Fine. Whatever."

With anger lining her features, she climbs into the passenger side while I get in and start the car. She refuses to pay me any mind while we head toward the highway, staring out the window instead.

My hand clasps her knee, and that finally gets her attention.

"What am I going to tell my friends? They're gonna think I'm nuts."

"Do they know about me?"

"Yeah. But still. They know I met you that one time and—"

"Haven't been able to forget me? I know." I grin. "Me too."

My fingers inch higher, working up her inner thigh while she squirms uncomfortably.

"That's not what I was going to say," she gasps.

"No?" I trace a single finger over her pussy through her pants. "It's a damn shame you're not wearing a skirt."

"Why's that?" Every syllable grows croakier.

"Because I enjoy touching you." Pushing her thighs open while trying to concentrate on the road, I press two fingers over her clit, slowly massaging her there.

Her head falls back, eyes closed, breaths growing needier.

"I love the way you look when you're turned on."

Her eyes snap to mine, our gazes tangled in this unspeakable way. This damn connection I can't explain.

She doesn't even fight it as I slip a hand into her leggings and past her panties, finding her soaked.

"Shit," I whisper, turning up the music so Fia doesn't hear us. "You need this, don't you?"

When her only answer is the tug of her lower lip, I rub her clit, and a cry dies in her throat.

"Answer me when I ask you a question." My jaw clenches, my

cock growing harder the more she tries to fight what I do to her. What I always will.

This woman has been mine from the moment we locked eyes. Denying it will get her nowhere.

Stroking her clit, I slip my fingers inside her. "Tell me you want me to make this pussy squirt. I need to hear it."

She glances to the rearview, eyes tangled with lust.

"She can't hear us," I whisper. "The speakers are right above her."

My fingers dip in and out while she pushes her cunt deeper into me.

I let out a laugh. "So fucking willing to get finger-fucked. My dirty little slut."

Her mouth pops wide even as her walls clench around my fingers.

"You like me calling you that, huh? What else do you like?"

My pace increases, then slows, while I take us on the highway.

My cell rings, and her gaze widens with panic.

"Answer," I tell my car, and when she tries to pry my fingers out of her, I keep them right where they are.

"Fionn! Don't!"

But I ignore her, teasing her clit with my thumb as I answer the phone. "Hey, Tynan. What's up?"

Her core pulses and throbs, her brows knitted tight as she tries not to make a sound.

"I saw you called earlier. Just returning your call."

She holds her breath as I piston deeper, faster, watching her gasp while I let a half-grin take over my mouth.

"I need you to do something for me."

"What's that?"

"That priest you used that night you…you know, with Elara." I glance at Amara—so damn ready to come, I can feel it.

"What about him?"

"I'm in need of his services."

Silence.

"Why?"

"Remember that girl, the one who told me her name was Emily?"

"Of course. You found her?"

"Guess you could say she found me."

My thumb flicks her clit, and she squirts, soaking herself and the seat. Thank fuck it's leather. Her hand clasps around her mouth as she tries not to scream. When she's finally done, I slip out and pop those fingers into my mouth.

"Tasting you is my favorite thing," I whisper.

"What did you say?" Tynan's voice comes through.

Her eyes widen as she shakes her head, like she's warning me not to tell him.

"She's in the car with me. I want the priest at my house in a couple of hours. Want it done today. And I want you and Cillian as my witnesses."

"Alright. We can do that. Need anything else?"

"No. Got everything else arranged."

"See you then." He drops the call while I look at the unwilling bride-to-be.

At least I didn't have to drug her like Tynan did with Elara.

She doesn't say anything for the rest of the way, and when we pull into the gated estate, her eyes widen.

"How much land do you own?"

"This isn't all mine."

I explain how my father set up the houses here for us, and about the farm we run here. She doesn't need to know about our other extracurricular activities. Not yet.

When I pull in beside my other car, I lower the music and glance back at Fia. "We're here, kid."

Amara's awestruck expression as she takes in the towering mansion has me smiling internally. I want to give this woman everything. Nothing has changed.

"Yay! I want to go in the poo!"

"We don't have your swimsuit, baby." Amara gets out, while I follow. "Maybe tomorrow."

"I can get her one. Just give me her size. In fact, I'll make sure to buy her everything she needs."

"She has things at home." Amara starts unbuckling her, me right behind her.

"I'm her father," I whisper into her ear. "I want to get my daughter things. I'm not asking for a lot here."

She laughs under her breath, staring at me angrily over her shoulder. "Yeah, you're right." Her tone is just as low. "Forcing her mother into marriage and moving her and me into your home isn't asking for a lot at all."

Groaning, I grab her hip and kiss the back of her head, knowing nothing I say right now will change her mind.

"Let's go inside. I'll introduce you to my staff."

"You've got a staff?"

I chuckle as she lifts Fia into her arms.

"Right. Of course you do…"

As soon as I shut the door, we're climbing the three stone steps. My guards inside the house open the doors when we approach. Their cells are equipped with cameras, so they know everyone's comings and goings. When her eyes take them in, she shrinks a little.

"Hi! I'm Fia!" My daughter waves, making friends wherever she goes, apparently. Like her father.

Eli and Henry—one of the toughest sons of bitches I've known— smile at her, practically melting.

"Hi," Eli says. "Nice to meet you."

"Where's your hair?" She glances curiously at his bald head, and he starts laughing.

"I shaved it off."

She giggles, reaching for his head to rub it.

"Fia!" Amara scolds. "You can't touch someone without asking."

"It's okay, ma'am." Eli grins when Fia gives it another pat.

"Okay, let's go meet Louise," I say. "She probably baked something for you. I told her you were coming."

"Bye!" She waves to my men, and they return it, while Amara glances at them as we start to walk away, her face filled with fear.

"Who's Louise?" Fia asks, completely ignorant of her mother's anxiety.

"Louise is the nice lady who lives here and takes care of the house. She also likes to cook for me because I can't cook a thing."

Fia laughs as we step into the kitchen, and Louise turns from the stove, shutting it off before coming to greet us.

"Well, who is this adorable little lady?" Her brown eyes brighten.

"I'm Fia."

"Nice to meet you, Fia. I'm Louise." She grins.

"I know. Fionn told me." She slaps on another show-stopping grin.

"She's absolutely adorable." She turns to Amara. "It's a pleasure to meet you."

"Yeah, you too." The women shake hands, but my wife's uneasy expression is obvious to everyone.

Louise has been with me for many years and knows exactly who my family is, but she has no idea about how Amara and I know one another. All I told her was that I'll be getting married today and that I want a nice meal prepared. She knows better than to ask questions.

"Well, I'll let you all get settled. I do have some snacks and lunch prepared just in case anyone is hungry."

"Me!" Fia throws her hand up.

"Well, good." Louise's face lights up, her gaze lingering on her, the pain in her eyes evident.

I know she's going to love having Fia around.

TWENTY-FOUR

AMARA

This is crazy. I can't do this!

I can't marry him and pretend any of this is normal. It's not.

But where do I go? How can I get away from a man like him?

It's simple: I can't.

Yet I can't just go along with this either. Groaning internally, I force myself to calm down. Working myself up will get me nowhere.

Glancing around the house, I find guards at every entry point. Guards with weapons. I saw the guns sticking out from their waistbands.

Is he some sort of crime lord? My God! Just look at the size of this place. What else could he be?

If he sells drugs, that's where I draw the line. I won't let my daughter be exposed to that, not after everything I went through with my mom.

"Would you like me to help you with your gown?" Louise asks.

My brows furrow. "What do you mean?"

"Oh…" She looks at Fionn. "You didn't tell her?"

"Forgot." His mouth quirks while he holds a happy Fia in his arms. "I ordered you a dress."

"What! Why?" I try to keep my tone low, but Fia is too busy munching on a cookie and humming the ABC song to care. "I don't need a dress. This isn't real, Fionn!"

"Either way, I wanted you to have something nice to wear. I got Fia a dress too, just in case you wanted her there with us."

My heart rate picks up. I didn't even think about that. *Do* I want her there? Would this confuse her?

"She's going to ask questions."

"Good. I want her to know what's going on." He drops his mouth to my ear. "I'm her father, Amara. I think it's better she knows that sooner than later."

My pulse slams faster and faster in my ears.

I'm getting married. To Fionn. To the man I wanted for so long.

Though now that I have him, it's all wrong. Like we've been thrown into a blender and the result is messy and inedible.

I don't know how long we'll be here, but I have to tell Fia the truth. She may be young, but she's smart. Once I get the chance to leave him, then I can come up with something else to tell her.

"Fia?"

She looks expectantly at me, crumbs sticking to her chin. My God, I love her. If anything ever happened to her, I'd die.

"So, Mommy and Fionn are going to get married today, and I just—"

"Okay." She continues to bite into her cookie.

Well, that was easier than I thought.

Fionn laughs at my shocked expression.

"See? She's fine." His voice hums across the shell of my ear, and every inch of me grows taut, that husky tone like a switch to my body.

The door opens from beyond, and I register multiple footsteps.

When two men appear with a priest, my eyes almost fall out. This is really happening. His two brothers nod in greeting. I remember them both from when Tynan got married.

"And who is this?" Cillian looks up at Fia.

"I'm Fia." She grins, and he gives Fionn a questioning glance. "What's your name?"

"I'm Cillian." He places a hand on his chest. "And behind me is Tynan and a random priest."

She giggles.

"Damn, this feels like some serious déjà vu." He chuckles, his green eyes filled with mirth as his vision bounces between his brothers.

What the hell is he talking about? Though, if I'm being honest, I don't want to know.

"Runs in the family." Tynan smirks at Fionn, while I grow even more curious.

Nope. The less you know, the better.

"You ready to get that dress on?" Louise takes me out of my thoughts. "I can even do your hair if you'd like."

"Uh, yeah, sure."

My heart picks up speed when Fionn catches my gaze, his tight lips pulling at the corner. I grow warm as his body draws near, his mouth lowering to the shell of my ear.

"I can't wait to make you my wife. Officially."

His hot breath, those words slinking up my body, causes every inch of me to grow tight. My stomach flips as I play his words in my head—so full of meaning, they set my heart ablaze.

It's almost enough to make me forget why this is all happening.

He lowers Fia, and she takes my hand as Louise ushers us upstairs. As I tread farther away, I can sense him watching me. Feel him in every crevice.

If I didn't want him, maybe things would be easier. Maybe I

wouldn't have to reconcile these conflicting feelings. But I can't seem to shut off the part of me that still wants him.

"Right this way." Louise leads me up the spiral staircases and into a wide hallway, white doors on each side and a gray carpet lining the floors. Not a speck of dust anywhere in sight.

She opens the last door on the left, and Fia immediately runs in, squealing when she sees a puffy ivory lace dress on the black tufted bed.

But my eyes are stuck on the wedding gown hanging on the door of what I assume is the closet. It's silk and strapless, tight at the waist, then flaring out in a semi-ballgown style. Simple, yet elegant. Exactly what I'd choose if I were doing this for real.

"It's beautiful, right? It's Vivienne Westwood. The family is good friends, so she flew this in from New York when he texted her last night."

"Last night?"

"That's right." She smiles while I'm shaking from the shock of it all.

He planned this last night. He ordered me a wedding dress and got a priest.

I'm living in some kind of movie. That has to be it. And not the kind with a happily ever after.

"He also got you shoes." She points to the corner. "I'll be right outside if you need help zipping the dress."

"Okay, thanks."

Fia twirls, holding on to her dress, oblivious to my anxious state.

As soon as Louise is out the door, I have a moment to breathe.

It's going to be okay. At least you won't struggle with money. You won't have to work those shitty jobs.

Well, except the vet clinic. I didn't mind that.

I'll have to call both jobs and quit. I feel terrible for not giving them notice, but I have no choice, apparently.

After this wedding, I'll have to call the girls and tell them about this. Emily's going to freak.

"Come on, baby. Let's get your dress on."

"Okay, Mama." She cooperates while I slip it on, keeping her sandals.

When I'm done with her, I grab the white shoebox, Manolo Blahnik written on top of it.

Okay, so I've definitely heard of that brand before.

I find a pair of white slingback sandals inside that match the dress perfectly. Once again, he made sure the heel wasn't big, and that makes me smile. At least he put some effort into this.

Slipping them on, I walk in them a bit and find them comfortable.

Retrieving the dress from the hanger, I run my fingertips over the beautiful soft material, not even wanting to know what a dress like this costs. I've honestly never heard of Vivienne Westwood, but I'm sure this cost a small fortune.

Removing my clothes, I step into the gown.

As I do, Fia's mouth pops open. "Wow! You're pretty, Mama!"

"Aww, thanks, baby. So are you."

She rounds her small arms around my thighs before running toward the full-length mirror, twirling as she watches herself.

"Louise! I'm ready."

As soon as she returns, her hand jumps to her chest. "Oh my goodness, you both look incredible." Her eyes fill with tears, and she quickly swipes a finger under her lashes, clearing her throat. "Sorry, ignore me."

She sniffles, and I wonder what just happened.

"That's okay. No worries." I try to lighten the mood. "This dress definitely isn't as heavy as I thought it would be, and it's shockingly not long on me."

She fingers her chestnut-colored bob. She's probably in her early sixties, a bit older than my mother.

"Oh, yes. Mr. Quinn was very specific about what he wanted for you."

That causes a little twinge in my heart. He didn't have to care about whether I had something to wear, but he did. That means something. He wanted me to feel special. He always has.

No, Amara. Don't do that! Don't act like this is all sweet and normal. He kidnapped you, woman! Stole you from your home and plucked you into a new one. But here's a wedding dress! Such a kind man.

I roll my eyes internally.

"Would you like me to curl your hair?" She puts on a smile, and I can tell she's trying to forget whatever it was that made her break down like that.

"Sure. Thank you."

Heading toward the bathroom, she brings back a hair straightener and a curling iron, plugging both in while I remain seated on the bed.

"Mama…" Fia runs over. "Look at me!" She starts to twirl.

"How pretty!"

Louise glances at her, smiling softly while taking a thick section of my hair and straightening it before curling the end.

"You know…" Louise tells her. "They have ponies on the farm."

"Ponies?" Fia's entire face lights up. "I love ponies!"

Great. So now she's never going to wanna leave.

I swear this child is too mature for her age. She walked by nine months and talked by one. She was always in a hurry to grow up. Though I'm not ready for her to do that quite yet.

I clear my throat. "I think that could be a little dangerous."

"No! Ponies! Please!" She begs with the cutest pout.

How am I supposed to resist that face? It's criminal, really. The way she can make me do just about anything with that pout.

Shaking my head, I succumb to her adorable ways. "We'll see, okay? We'll ask Fionn about it later."

"Yay!"

"I'm sorry," Louise murmurs. "I shouldn't have said anything." She continues working on my hair.

"Don't be. She was bound to discover them anyway." I laugh as Fia entertains herself, making faces in the mirror.

Louise glances at my girl fondly. "I remember my daughter at that age." Her face falls.

"I know. They grow up fast, right?"

She nods. "Too fast."

"How old's your daughter now?"

Her hands still for a moment, her body visibly shaken. And I know right away I should've never asked.

"She would've been twenty-six this year."

The back of my throat stings, and I clasp her forearm. "I'm so sorry, Louise. I really am."

"It's okay. I don't mind talking about it." She sighs deeply before continuing to style my hair. "She was going to prom, and I was doing her hair just like yours."

The pain in her voice tears at my heart. I can't imagine losing my Fia.

"Her boyfriend was driving drunk and killed them both."

Moisture fills my eyes, and I blink past it. "Oh God."

"Geez, I'm sorry for bringing this up right now," she scoffs. "I'm terrible. Today is a happy day." She forces a grin. "I'm really glad for you and Fionn. He's a really special man."

"Right."

Special… I guess it depends how you see him.

She finishes with the last section of my hair and unplugs both tools. "I know what they do, and I'm sure that's scary for you, but behind that, they're a wonderful family who takes care of us."

"What exactly do they do?"

Her brows shoot up. "I should really not be allowed to speak.

Constantly putting my foot in my mouth." She shakes her head.

"No, I—I just wanna know what I've gotten myself into."

She releases a weighty exhale. "Well, I think you should talk to Fionn about that. Because it's not my place. But I will say one thing." She places a palm on my forearm. "I don't know the circumstances of your marriage, and it's none of my business, but I really mean it when I say he's a really good man, and I can already tell how taken he is with you."

I swallow past the thick knot in my throat. "Thank you for the hair."

"Of course." She brings everything back into the bathroom, heading toward the door. "I'm going to go check if Fionn is ready." As she starts to head out, she gives me one last look. "I'm really happy you're here. I know we just met, but I like you already."

Before I can thank her, she's gone.

And I'm left with her words long after.

TWENTY-FIVE

FIONN

Waiting for her in the yard, the priest and my brothers beside me, I keep staring at the double glass doors, needing to see her walk down to me.

It hits me that she's about to be mine for the rest of her life, and with that will come a great responsibility to protect her and Fia from our enemies. There are many of them, and some wouldn't hesitate to hurt our families to get to us. I will do everything in my power to keep them both safe.

Speakers play the traditional wedding march music, and seconds later, I see her. Our daughter is holding her hand, grinning and waving to me.

I give her a wink before my stare returns to the most beautiful woman.

My woman.

My wife.

That dress, the way she looks… It takes my breath away.

Her eyes scan the place, like she's looking for a way out of this. But unfortunately for her, there is none. This is for life.

She will never leave me again. I can promise her that.

When she's in front of me, I grab her hand and tuck her chin in my palm, dropping my mouth to her ear. "You're breathtaking."

"Thanks," she whispers, her hand shivering in mine.

"Don't be scared."

"That's easy for you to say." She hikes up her chin and stares at the priest, ignoring me.

Clenching a fist at my side, I turn toward him.

She will come around. It's just a shock to her right now. I have to believe that.

Fia runs over to me, holding my hand, and Amara tries to hide her shock.

"You look like a princess," I tell her.

"Thank you." Her eyes glimmer.

My damn heart is going to explode. Gathering her in my arms, I nod at the priest to begin while she's nestled against me, her head on my shoulder.

Amara glances over at us, fighting a smile.

Her attention shifts as the priest recites some prayers until it's time for the rings. Tynan hands them to us, and I place one on Amara's finger, then she places one on mine.

"May these rings be a symbol of your faith in each other and a reminder to you of your love. Through Christ our Lord. Amen. You may kiss the bride."

Turning to her, I cup her cheek, capturing her eyes, staring so deep, I know she feels this too—this damn heaviness in my chest that I never even imagined I could ever experience.

"It's like I've been waiting for you all my life," I tell her, meaning every damn word.

Her gaze softens, brows furrowed, and before she has a chance to protest, I take her lips with mine. And just like every other time, she kisses me until we're both lost. My fingers slide into her hair, dragging her deeper, kissing her with all the passion dripping in my veins.

"Geez, get a damn room." Cillian laughs, and that's when she slowly pulls away.

I hit him with a glare, and he only chuckles harder.

The priest finishes his last wish for us, then it's over.

She's mine. For life.

"Fionn." Fia pulls on my suit jacket.

"Yes, love?"

"Do you have ponies?"

Her damn adorable voice… If she asked for the moon, I'd climb up to get it.

"I do. Wanna see them?"

Her mouth pops as big as her eyes.

"Now?" Amara asks.

"Now." I curl an arm around her, brushing my mouth across her ear. "Maybe if you're a good girl, I'll give you a ride on my horse."

"Which horse are you referring to, exactly?"

I jerk back. "Wow, Mrs. Quinn. Did you just make a joke?"

She hikes a brow. "Maybe."

Her pretty pink mouth thins, and my damn chest cinches with emotions I can't name. It feels as though I've known her all my life.

As she starts to walk past me, I snatch her wrist, pulling her flush against my side while staring deeply at her, unable to let go. "You make me feel things I never knew I wanted."

Her eyes flicker with emotion, lips fluttering as though wanting to tell me that this is wrong. That we're wrong.

"Let me love you." My thumb skims across her jaw, pulse quickening.

Her lashes flutter as I bring my mouth closer, stroking her lips until a faint moan slips out, and that's when I kiss her.

And for a moment it feels as though she forgot that she's supposed to hate me and the life we're gonna have.

AMARA

I'm kinda freaking out right now.

I've never been on a horse before, and it's scary up here. Thankfully, I changed out of my dress. Because there was absolutely no way I was going horseback riding like that. He, of course, did too, now in a pair of jeans that hug his round ass as though they were created for him, muscles rippling beneath his white t-shirt.

My arms curl around Fionn's middle, and he tucks my hands in his, keeping me closer. I know I should hate this, but I don't.

Not right now, anyway.

"You okay, little rabbit?" His thumbs draw circles over my knuckles, and tingles spread across my limbs.

"Um, define okay." A nervous, short laugh slips out.

"I promise to take it easy on you." His chuckle makes me pull into him, loving the way it sounds, the way he feels and smells.

My God, I love everything about him. All the good parts I still remember.

Love.

Let me love you.

That's what he said. And I want that. I've always wanted it. Though I can't seem to let go of this fear that his love will never be enough. That Fionn, for all his magic, will be the end of us.

Cillian helps Fia onto the pony that's the perfect size for her. She giggles while he keeps her steady, Tynan riding on his own horse beside her.

"You ready?" Fionn asks.

"Yes."

No.

And I don't mean for the ride.

I mean for us. For this marriage. This life. Can I really be ready when I don't even know who he is?

I know we have to talk. There are too many questions I don't have answers to. But deep down, I already know who he is. I just don't want to say it out loud.

He pulls on the horse's rope, and she starts to walk.

Okay, this is not so bad…

My fingers tighten around him.

"Think if I make her run, you'll hold on tighter, baby?"

My body breaks out in goose bumps from the way he just called me "baby."

"Don't you dare!" I laugh. "I'm already scared as hell."

"Don't be." He brings one of my hands to his mouth. "I'd never let anything happen to you."

My heart skips a beat, and I can't help lowering my cheek between his shoulder blades, needing to be closer.

My stupid, weak heart beats even louder.

I'm hopeless. Utterly hopeless.

I just want to curl up against him and remember how I felt that day we spent together, and how badly I want to return to that.

"Hi, babe," Elara, Tynan's wife, approaches, her blue eyes sparkling with a huge grin, with Brody beside her. I never got to officially meet her at their wedding, but I know who she is.

"Hey, Dad," Brody says, glancing toward Fia and me.

"Hey, bud." He jumps off the horse. "Mo chuisle," he hums, tugging Elara into his arms, kissing her like the world just vanished around them.

When they come back for air, he smirks as he looks at us.

"This is my wife, Elara, and our oldest, Brody. We also have a daughter about Fia's age named Adora."

"It's a pleasure to meet you," she says to me.

"You too."

Fia waves to them. "Hi! I'm Fia."

"Hey, sweetie." Elara walks over to her, giving her a hug.

"Hey." Brody smiles at the both of us before Cillian interrupts with a laugh.

"What's so funny?" Fionn asks.

"Elara, Amara, Adora. I swear you guys planned this."

"Oh my God, he's right!" Elara coughs a stunned laugh. "That's hilarious."

"So can we call you two the 'aras?" Cillian's having too much fun with this.

"Nope." Elara grimaces.

"Absolutely not." Looking at her, I laugh.

"You know…" Fionn grins devilishly. "If you marry Dinara, she'd fit right in."

"Wait, who's Dinara?" Elara looks between them.

"Just someone our boy here can't get out of his system."

"She's out of my system," he mutters with a deathly glare.

"Which system is that?" Tynan scoffs.

"Aww, leave him alone." Elara's mouth pinches before she looks up at me. "You guys should come over tomorrow night. Maybe we'll have a big family dinner and invite everyone."

Fionn groans.

"It'll be fun!" Elara scoffs, throwing a hand in the air. "The girls will have such a great time playing together, too."

"Sure. That sounds nice." I do want to meet everyone.

"Great! Tynan and I will make whatever you want. Any favorites?"

"Um, I'm not picky."

"Only when it comes to husbands," Fionn mutters.

"Shut up," I whisper, smacking his back as he chuckles, all deep-chested and masculine.

"What's that?" Elara pops a brow.

"Oh, nothing. I'm sorry. I was just saying I'd be happy with anything you make."

"What about dessert? Any particular things you like?"

She's being so kind. I can tell how sincere she is just by looking at her.

"I don't want to be a pain in the you-know-what and impose. So whatever you decide on is fine."

Elara rolls her eyes playfully. "We're happy to do it. I swear. So, come on. I love baking."

There's something I did want, but I don't know how hard it is to make.

"I really love baklava. It's this diamond-shaped dessert. I've had it once before when one of my mother's boyfriends brought it over."

"Oh, challenge accepted." Elara's eyes sparkle. "Think we can handle that, babe?" She stares lovingly at her husband.

"Of course." He curls an arm around her and kisses her temple. "Consider it done."

The man doesn't even bother to look at me as he says that, eyes lost on his wife, and I wonder what that feels like. To be that loved.

"Thank you. That's really sweet of you guys."

"We're all very sweet." Fionn tightens his grasp of my hands. "Most of the time." He whispers those words just for me, and I shift uncomfortably at his sultry baritone.

"Well, you guys have fun on your ride." Elara steps back. "Brody and I just came to introduce ourselves."

"Yeah, it's nice to meet you," the boy says as Tynan hops back on the horse.

"You too."

He seems like a nice kid. Maybe around thirteen or so.

"Alright, I promised my wife and daughter a ride." Fionn jerks on the horse's rope.

His wife. My God, why does that sound so good? Though I know I shouldn't like it, I really do.

"Have fun, you guys!" Elara waves as we start down the grass, miles and miles of beautiful green land up ahead.

He gets the horse to go a little faster while Cillian walks Fia's pony, making sure she's sitting upright.

"One of these days…" Fionn tells me. "I'm gonna show you just what she's capable of." He glides a hand down her mane.

As we continue down, I stare out at all the mountains ahead, enjoying myself and realizing I could really get used to living here and finally having a family.

It's what I've always wanted, isn't it?

TWENTY-SIX

AMARA

That night, we tuck Fia into her bed in her new room, one he had apparently set up for her. He even had some clothes picked out. He's managed to get everything she needs just so she's not without anything, even for one day.

"Goodnight, baby." I kiss her forehead before it's Fionn's turn.

"Goodnight, princess." He presses a kiss to her temple. "I'll see you in the morning."

I can't get over how sweet he is with her. How he just fell into this role without missing a beat.

Just as we're about to leave, she asks, "Are you my daddy now?"

The question completely startles me. How do I answer her? The truth is too hard for a child her age to comprehend.

Fionn, though? He's not even fazed.

"I am," he says. "Is that okay?"

My pulse instantly spikes. I can't believe he just said that without talking to me first!

Fia's brows tug before she hits him with a bright grin. "Yes. You're nice."

He smirks. "Your mother thinks so too. Right, little rabbit?"

He wraps his strong arm around my waist, pulling me to his side. Fia's vision darts between us, and for a moment, it feels like we're a family. A *real* family.

I want to be mad at him for not consulting with me before telling her he's her father. But I can't find it in me to be upset. Not anymore. Even if he isn't her bio dad, he wants to be, and that's enough.

My own father abandoned me. My mother treated me like shit. Blood means nothing.

"Okay, kid, you need to go to bed," he says to her.

"Goodnight, Mama. Goodnight, Daddy."

He sucks in a breath and his eyes fill with unspoken emotion, and that only makes it harder not to care for him. His jaw clenches as he tucks her in with the pale pink blanket he bought her.

"Goodnight." He chokes on the word.

"I love you," she whispers.

If he wasn't already melting, I think he just turned to goo.

"I love you too, Fia." The look in his eyes….it does unspeakable things to me.

A big, tough man completely weak for a child? Yeah, I'm screwed.

We shut off the lights and head out, and as we do, he stops, running a hand down his face.

"You okay?" I ask.

The muscle in his jaw pulses, his throat tight on his next swallow before he's staring back at me. "Yeah. I just didn't expect her to say all that."

"Neither did I."

We both stand beside one another, filled with our own emotions.

"I want to adopt her."

Gaping wide, I'm unsure what to say. Everything is going too fast.

Being basically kidnapped. Marriage. And now this?

But it's what I've always wanted. Though that was at a different time, when he wasn't this person. A criminal.

How do I live with him or allow Fia to grow up in such an environment?

"Uh, well, before all that, I think we need to discuss some things."

"Like what?" His face and tone harden.

"Um…" I clear my throat, my pulse kicking up a notch. "You know, like what you really do for a living, for starters. I have no idea who you are." I play with the hem of my shirt, nerves skittering up my back. "And now that we're married, I have a right to know."

Please don't kill me.

His features grow more intense. "You sure you wanna know?"

Our eyes lock, his body moving into mine. The firmness of it pressed up against me brings a rush of yearning unlike anything I've ever experienced.

"Or maybe you're trying to find reasons to hate me when every damn inch of you wants me."

My stomach flip-flops as he pushes my hair away from my face, burying his nose in my neck, inhaling with a slow drag of his breath. Long, thick fingers curl around my waist, pressing his hard erection into me. My breaths grow tight, desire unfurling. His knuckles stroke down my cheek, sending shivers racing up my spine.

"No matter what I tell you, it doesn't change anything. You're my wife, and she's my daughter. You won't be going anywhere." His voice is demanding and all-consuming.

Yet those haunting words somehow make me grow slick between my thighs.

"If you want me to take the paternity test, I will. But if he's her father, he'll sign over his rights to me."

I shudder from the callousness.

"And if he refuses?" I breathe.

His smirk can only be described as deadly. "He won't."

His lips slide down my throat, teeth gnawing before he trails kisses back up, clasping a rough palm around the span of my jaw. He grabs my ass with his free hand, boring his eyes deep with mine while pushing me into the swell of his thick and hard erection.

"I want you, baby," he whispers, his voice thick with lust, my body begging for him.

"Fio—"

He cuts me off with a savage kiss, equal parts longing and passion. A growl crawls out of his chest and a moan slips out of mine, our hands everywhere at once. When he tugs on my bottom lip, I let out a cry, unable to maintain any semblance of sanity.

When he slips his hand into the waistband of my leggings, I know what he'll find.

"Fuck," he rasps, yanking back, his hungered look spreading tingles beneath my skin. "It's like your body's always ready for me."

When his finger sinks inside me, I let out a silent gasp. "Fionn, someone could see us here."

He's got guards everywhere.

His chuckle shoots right into my gut, spreading like wildfire. "Then why did your pussy just clench when you said that?"

He kisses me hard, nipping and tugging, his beastly groans only spurring me on. I want to feel him inside me and get lost in us.

"You wanna get caught, don't you? You want someone to see how hard I can make you come."

"I—I…" I can't seem to speak, drowning in pleasure.

A responding hoarse chuckle rises, and before I can wonder what he's doing, he's lifting me up in his arms, carrying me the rest of the way into the bedroom.

With his eyes on mine, he shuts the door with his foot, lowering me onto the bed. His fingers reach for the hem of his t-shirt, the veins throbbing beneath his large, powerful hands as he drags it up, exposing his toned abs. It does nothing to stop the desire from burning hot and raw inside me.

My thighs squeeze as I watch my husband strip.

It's the very first time since the ceremony that I've said that to myself.

He's my husband. I'm Mrs. Quinn now.

My fingers lower to my core, pressing into my clit through my leggings while he groans, continuing to undress.

"Tell me what you do?" I murmur, hoping he admits the truth while he's all turned on.

His laughter, husky and deep, has me desperate for him. "What do you think I do?"

Another look at his ripped, tanned body has me forgetting what I was talking about.

He removes his shoes, hands on his belt as he slowly drags it out, and I start to wonder how it'd feel if he used that belt on me. Maybe bind my hands behind my back as he took me.

My face heats up instantly. Where did that even come from? Who am I right now?

"I—I think you're, uh…"

"Come on, say it, mo ban dia." His smirk sends hot coals to my gut.

"You're…um…" My voice trembles. "You're in the Mafia." I barely whisper that, like my mind is protecting me from what or who he is.

He laughs until that smile disappears, his face turning dark and haunting, a thick vein in his wide neck jerking.

"And how does that make you feel?" His words creep with an undercurrent of danger, slinking up my skin like a soft caress.

He stalks closer.

And closer.

Like a predator ready to claim his prey.

The belt stretches tight in his large hands as my blood rushes to my head. I drag myself further up the bed, like my body is in fight-or-flight mode, even though I want to know what he's about to do.

"How am I supposed to feel? It scares me," I whisper, swallowing down past the dryness in my throat.

He stops right at the edge of the bed, looming over me with his muscular frame and taunting gaze.

"There's nothing to be afraid of." A single finger drags up the inside of my thigh. "I won't hurt you."

His touch makes me shudder. "What about everyone else? The ones you associate with. Would they hurt me?"

"They'd die before they ever laid a finger on you or our daughter."

A cold shudder drowns me. He would kill them. I've watched him do it.

My stomach churns. My husband is a murderer.

"I can see it in your eyes." His mouth jerks as he winds the belt around the back of my neck, pulling me up to a seated position and towering over me. "You want to run again."

His smirk is a cold, icy chill.

"But there's nowhere to go, baby. Not for you. Not anymore." His hot breath tiptoes across my quivering lips. "You're mine until the day I die. And there's nothing you can do about it." He snakes the belt tight around my neck with one hand, the back of his other stroking across my jaw. "I'll never let you go."

Even through the fear, I grow aroused, enjoying his domineering side.

His hand slips into my leggings, and without warning, he thrusts inside me, stilling a moan in my throat. He keeps me captive, finger-fucking me while he fists the belt even tighter. My breathing is shallower, but it only intensifies every other sensation.

"Oh, yes!" I cry out, needing the release so badly, I'll beg.

Instead, he stops, his gaze menacing.

As he yanks me closer with the belt, his lips skim across mine before he captures them in another earth-shattering kiss. I almost forget how to breathe as he forces me down onto the bed, lowering on top of me, his hips arching between my thighs, his cock nudging into my center.

His fingers tangle with my hair, the kiss turning carnal and forceful, filled with this desperate want. A masculine growl works its way up his throat, my whimpers snaked with the animalistic sounds he makes.

Roughly, he pulls my leggings down, stripping me until his fingers are there, assertive and demanding as they enter me. His thumb strokes my clit until the moans from my lips vibrate over his. He kisses me harder, pistoning deeper like he wants to possess me, take over every inch until I'm his.

The need climbs, filling my veins with burning passion, and when he thrusts into me again, I let go, groaning into his mouth while his own grunts fill with desperation. My toes curl, my nails sinking into his bare back. When my body slows, he pulls away just slightly, eyes crawling with his own desire.

He rises, leaving the belt dangling over my shoulders while he unzips his jeans, pulling the zipper down and sliding out of them. My gaze snaps to his cock peeking through his boxers, which disappear within seconds, leaving him completely naked.

I can't help where my eyes go, especially when he fists his hard-on, stroking it slow.

"If you keep looking at it like that, I'm gonna force it into that sexy mouth."

"Do it," I husk, wanting him to be rough with me.

His hand stills mid stroke. "What was that?"

"Do it." I say it louder. "I want to suck your cock."

Yeah, I definitely don't know what's happening to me, but I don't want it to stop.

"Fuuuck," he growls, squeezing the crown of his erection. Then, suddenly, he grabs both ends of the belt and tugs me. "Stand up."

I quickly follow his instructions and get to my feet, waiting for his next command.

"Take off your shirt."

My body shudders, nerves taking over. But I do it.

When I drop it on the floor, his heated gaze drags down my curves until goose bumps wrap around every inch.

He points to the floor. "On your knees."

My heartbeats quicken, my nipples pebbling.

With bated breath, I lower myself. He snaps the belt tighter in his grasp, popping my chin up with his other hand until I'm forced to stare into his murky eyes. His thumb strokes my lips, jaw clenching.

"Suck me, wife." His tone is soft, yet dangerous, with an edge to it that leaves no room for arguments.

What if I don't know how to do this? I haven't done it that many times. The last time was forever ago. But I want to do this. I want to make him feel good.

With a nervous breath, I gradually lower my lips around the tip, licking around his piercings, cold against my tongue. When he mutters a curse and hisses, I continue, taking more of him into my mouth.

"Oh fuck, that's it." He fists my hair as I take him halfway.

His width and size are more than I've ever had, but I take as much of him as I can, licking and sucking my way down.

"Come on, baby girl, let me hear you gag on it."

My core aches at those dirty words, and I hollow my cheeks, taking him deeper. He snaps the belt tighter, thrusting his hips toward my mouth until I'm swallowing him whole. My eyes water and my throat burns, but I enjoy it.

The sounds he makes, knowing I'm doing that to him... I don't want to stop.

He lets go just enough to allow me some air, working himself in and out of my mouth. "Fuck, baby, you're too good at this."

His fingers tighten in my hair while his words embolden me. I begin moving faster, grabbing his balls to squeeze them.

"Good girl. Just like that." His gravelly tone oozes with erotic intensity, his cock throbbing on my tongue.

I know he's close, and I can't wait to taste him. But before I can do that, he tugs me backward by my hair.

"Get up."

My brows knit in question.

"When I come, it'll be inside that perfect cunt. Not wasting a drop. Not when I want my baby growing inside you."

A chill rolls up my body. I don't even have time to fear the implication of his words. His eyes scorching into mine, he tugs my chin in his palm, feathering my lips with his thumb.

"I'm gonna fuck you and fill you up, and I'm gonna do it over and over and over again. Because I can. Because you're mine. My wife." His features fill with an aura of control. "And I will never let you forget it."

My heart pounds as he pulls me up to a standing position.

"You remember your safe word?"

"Yes." I nod. "Cranberry."

A smirk cracks at the edge of his mouth. "Good girl. Now bend over."

When I just stand there, he chuckles, husky and wicked, before he's flipping me over on the bed, pushing my face down and my knees up.

"Jesus, you're drenched." He strokes me lazily, sinking in and out of my wet center.

I let out a moan, wanting to press my knees into one another, but he keeps my legs wide apart. The belt is in his firm grasp as he winds it around the front of my throat, tugging on it like a leash as he pushes his cock into me, a little at a time.

"I can't be gentle. Do you understand?"

I nod, glancing at him from over my shoulder.

Without warning, he rams inside me until I choke on a cry, clawing the bed, tender and aching. But he doesn't stop. He only goes faster, sliding out and slamming back in with fervor. With need. With possession.

The kind a woman never forgets.

His eyes are demonic. A man who knows nothing else but this.

The feverish way he takes me, sweat beading on his forehead, biceps flexing as he bends my head backward... It's all too much, yet not enough.

He captures my lips once more, taking me in a brutal kiss.

My ass drives into his pelvis, and he spanks it hard while the pain only makes me want him more.

"Oh God."

"Not God. Me. Your husband." With my hair in his fist, he lowers his ear to mine as he takes me deeper. "Say it. Tell me who I am."

The words are like fuel to the fire until I feel it happen, the clawing of an orgasm, needing it badly.

"My husband... Please, please..."

"Tell me what you need."

"Please, please, make me come."

As soon as I say it, he turns even more beastly, grunting as he rams faster. Deeper. I touch myself, needing the orgasm like I need my next breath.

When he pistons inside me this time, I cry out his name, my body soaring so high, I never want to come down.

"Yes, that's it." A husky moan escapes him as his fingers replace mine, rubbing my clit with intensity. "Squirt for me."

With my chest pressed to the mattress, I writhe in a pleasure-filled coma while he continues to possess me, roaring with a growl as his release fills me.

FILTHY SAVAGE

"Don't waste a fucking drop," he demands with ragged breaths before his body stills.

But he doesn't move. He stays that way, while the belt falls from his grasp.

Gently, he takes space behind me, his cock remaining seated inside. He brings his head down, hovering behind my ear.

"Just thinking about my cum inside you, making our baby, makes me wanna fuck you all over again." His words are gruff and tantalizing, causing me to let out a moan.

I'm barely able to catch my breath as he presses a kiss to the back of my head.

My pulse spikes, even as I fight not to be affected by the sweet gesture. "Are you going to stay like this the whole time?"

"Mm-hmm. Until I'm sure your body has taken every damn drop of me."

"You're crazy." I let out an exhaustive sigh.

"You keep saying that like it's a bad thing."

A laugh bubbles out, and I slide in closer. "In some stupid way, I've missed you. Even though we really never knew each other."

The confession shocks me, but it's the truth.

"We knew enough, mo ban dia."

My stomach flips at his endearing tone.

When he gently cups my chin and brings his mouth to mine, I feel it: the reasons why I shouldn't want this slowly coming undone.

FIONN

"What am I supposed to wear to bed?" she asks, nestling against my chest.

I tuck her hair behind her ear. "Nothing. That's the point."

"I'm serious." She shakes her head playfully. "I have nothing here. I swear you planned this."

"Of course I did." I chuckle. "Why do you think Fia was the only one I bought clothes for?"

She gasps, smacking me on the chest.

"Wanted you in my clothes until you get yours tomorrow."

"Is that so?" She pops a brow. "I'm supposed to walk around the house with your clothes on until they get here?"

"Mm-hmm. Pretty sure my shirts would be long enough to cover you." My fingers slink up and down her spine, not wanting to stop touching her for as long as I live.

"You're probably the craziest man—no, not man, person—I've ever known."

"Ah, here we go. The insults that are not really insults." Grabbing a fistful of her ass, I press her closer, kissing her nose. "Promise to have your clothes tomorrow after breakfast."

She sighs. "Fine."

Looking away from me, she runs a circle on my chest. Minutes pass, and she remains silent.

"What is it?" With a finger, I pop her chin.

"I don't know if I can do this. I—" Her brows tug. "I wanted you for so long. Wanted to see you again. Wanted to know if you'd still want me. Want Fia. But now, seeing this, how you live… I—I can't…" She swallows harshly. "My life hasn't been pleasant." Tears form in her eyes, and that makes me want to erase all the hurt she's been carrying. "My father left when I was around two, or so my mother says. And her? Well…" She snickers. "She was no more a mother than a stranger."

Her lashes flutter, her gaze distant like she's thinking about the more painful times.

"I had to raise myself because she was too busy fucking a new guy every month or getting high to care about me."

Another pained laugh escapes while every part of me wants to rip out her parents' goddamn throats. How fucking dare they hurt my wife?

"I wanted so badly for her to be my mother, but she never was."

Moisture builds in her eyes, until it overflows. I'm there to wipe her tears away, thumbs rolling under her lashes as she sighs.

"That day I came back home, after I left you, I found out my dog, Max, was gone."

"What?" My mind starts coming up with ways I can help.

She nods. "You would've loved him." Pain fills her eyes and it completely unravels me. "He was a golden. She said he escaped from the hole in the fence but I never thought that was true." Her voice breaks while anger builds in my chest.

"I think she did something to him." She sniffles, completely broken. "Every day, I keep hoping he's alive and happy somewhere. But I'd do anything…" She pants. "I'd do anything to have him back."

She curls around my chest and cries, shuddering against me.

"Hey, hey, baby. I've got you."

I can just imagine how much this hurts.

Minutes drift until she's pulling back, wiping under her eyes.

"Anyway, I don't know why I just told you all this, except to say my life has been shit and I don't want more of it. And you doing what you do, it scares me." She places a hand over my cheek, and it's like with every touch, she makes me fall even deeper. "I can't go back to that kind of life. I don't want Fia to have that either. It's what I fought like hell to escape from."

Her courage makes me proud. "I'm not your parents. I'd never leave you or hurt you. It won't be that way."

"You can't promise me that."

"I can."

My lips lower to hers, kissing her softly, and I've never been this way—soft and nurturing—except with her. "Let's get some sleep. We can talk more tomorrow if you'd like."

She nods, her exhales warm against my chest.

I turn the bedside lamp off, holding her silky body against mine. Though I can't seem to fall asleep—not for hours—thinking about her dog and what I can do to fix it.

TWENTY-SEVEN

AMARA

The following morning, while Fia happily swings her feet in the chair, I sit across from my husband, eating pancakes while drowning in one of his oversized white t-shirts.

Louise made us breakfast, one fit for royalty. I've never seen such an array before. Pastries, pancakes, an omelet with bacon strips. There's so much to choose from.

Fionn picks up his cup of coffee, already dressed in tight navy dress pants and a pale blue button-down, the sleeves rolled up to expose his muscular arms, thick veins running through them.

I grow warm at the sight of him: that full hair brushed back, eyes as though staring into the depthless sea. The large watch on his right wrist probably costs a fortune. Then again, I'm sure everything he owns is expensive.

I try very hard not to keep staring. Except it's impossible.

His mouth curves as he takes a bite of his bagel. "I'll be gone most of the day, but you're free to do whatever you want."

He motions his head behind me and that has me looking back to find a stern man about Fionn's age coming closer. He's huge and scary. Dark hair and eyes. Who is he?

"This is Roy. He's your bodyguard. Fia will have her own."

My eyes practically fall out. "Oh. Uh, hi."

"Ma'am."

"He's my eyes when I'm not with you." His expression turns tense. "I won't let anything happen to you."

"Where will you be all day?"

"I have some work to do."

"Oh."

Does he mean murder?

When he takes in my face, he chuckles. "Not that kind of work. Actual work. My brothers and I are on the board of our corporation, so I sometimes have to be at the office."

"Okay."

He removes something from his pocket. "I got you a new phone. I've programmed all your numbers in there. Including mine."

When I stare at the latest cell model that I know costs like two grand, I can't wipe the shock from my face. My phone is still upstairs, and definitely nowhere near as fancy.

"Thank you."

When I reach out to grab it, he places his hand over mine.

"You never need to thank me. I'm here to take care of you."

Emotions overtake me and I force myself not to cry, because this is like a dream. And with every moment, I wonder when it'll all blow up in my face.

FIONN

I didn't exactly lie to her. I do usually work. But today, I don't have to.

Today, I have other important things to do.

Arriving at her mother's house, I park across the street, spotting two vehicles in the driveway.

The bitch is home. Which is a good thing. She's gonna tell me exactly what she did to Amara's dog.

Retrieving my gun from the glove compartment, I slip it into the holster at my waist as I climb out. She'll give me answers one way or another…or she'll find herself swimming in the ocean.

Crossing the street, I head for the door, knocking lightly. Shooting my way through didn't feel like a smart plan. Though it was quite tempting.

When she opens the door, she smiles flirtatiously, her teeth as yellow as a lion's ass. "Hi there. What can I do for you, handsome?"

"Who's that?" a man's gruff tone rings behind her until he appears.

Removing my nine, I point it at him. "Get the fuck inside. Both of you."

She gasps, while the man's eyes grow with fear. When he slowly starts to move his hand into his pocket, I fire a shot, the silencer on. The bullet rips through his hand, and when he screams in agony, I shove them inside and lock the door.

"That was just a warning." I lean against the wall, aiming the weapon at him. "Now shut the fuck up before I put a bullet in your throat."

He pants, grinding his teeth and cradling his bleeding hand.

"P-p-please," she begs, "I don't have any money."

"I don't want your fucking money." I trail closer, smelling the stench of something sour coming from the house.

This is how she lived? Fuck. I would've gotten her out of this hell if I knew. If she'd told me.

Damn it, baby. Why didn't you tell me?

"Sit the fuck down, Desdemona."

I don't miss the way her entire face twists with shock at the mention of her name.

"Who…who are you? Wha-wha-what do you want?" she whispers while the prick tries not to make a sound, body shaky with obvious pain.

"You have thirty seconds to tell me what you did to Amara's dog. Or your boyfriend bleeds out."

"Amara?" She snickers. "That's what this is about?"

I push the barrel under her jaw. "You want a bullet that badly?"

Before she lets out her next laugh, I fire one into her foot.

"Ahh! Fuck! You psycho!" Her scream only fills me with irritation.

"Tell me. What the hell did you do to Max?" I dig the barrel into her temple.

"Okay, okay," she cries, wincing as she tries to sit. "I—I sold him."

I'm gonna kill her.

My fist balls at my side. "To who?!"

She shrinks back from my barbaric tone. "Xander, okay? Xander, her ex. Please, please don't kill me!"

That son of a…

"Why him?"

"I—I—I owed him money and hi-hi-his cousin wanted a dog, so he arranged for him to pick up Max while Xander and Amara were g-g-gone."

My fingers curl tight around the grip of my weapon, my pulse pounding in my head. "His address."

The things I'm gonna do to that motherfucker.

She gives it to me without a fight this time.

I start to go, turning to them. "You ever do anything else to harm my wife, I'll kill you both. And that isn't a threat. It's a promise."

"Your…your wife?" she winces.

"That's right." A cold smirk crawls over the corner of my mouth before I'm gone, back in my car and heading to that asshole's place.

I'm gonna have so much fun with him.

He's home alone.

I got lucky. Would've had to kill the witness.

Popping the lock of the back door, I step inside, my footfalls light, the sound of the television coming from somewhere in the house. I follow the noise, stepping past the kitchen. When I make it into the den, I find him on the sofa, his back to me.

He doesn't hear me. Doesn't notice the gun.

Not until it's pressed to the back of his head.

"What the…" He turns, his face growing with panic. "You…"

"So you remember me." My mouth jerks. "Must've left some impression."

"What do you want, man?" He raises both hands in the air. "What's this about?"

The nine remains pressed to his head before I come around. Settling on the ottoman right before him, I let the weapon dangle between my legs, staring hard, letting seconds drift. 'Cause I know with each one, he's even more terrified.

"Look, man, if this is about Amara, she and I are done. I'm with someone else."

I let out a dry laugh. "I know what you did."

"I didn't do shit to her! If she said I did, she's lying."

In a flash, I'm on my feet, towering over him, the barrel digging into his Adam's apple. "You're gonna put on your fucking shoes and we're gonna take a drive to your cousin's house. You know, the one you gave Max to."

His gaze fills with instant terror.

"That's right. Desdemona told me everything."

I can see his eyes working up a plan. Though nothing he says will save him.

"She, uh, owed me money and couldn't pay. You know how it is." He attempts to laugh it off, but when I smash the pistol into his jaw, he's not doing much laughing.

"And you thought taking your girlfriend's dog was the right thing to do?" I snap. "What kind of man are you?"

He cowers, holding his arms up to protect himself.

"Get your ass up!"

I don't wait. I yank him by his shirt, dragging him barefoot out to my car. Opening the passenger side, I throw him inside, then get in.

"Address."

When he doesn't say a word, I remove the gun from my ankle holster and dig it into the center of his chest.

"My temper is running thin. If you don't talk in the next two seconds, I'll kill you."

"Shit," he grits, deciding if he should talk. "My cousin is a good guy, okay?"

"Did he know it was her dog?" I drill him with a sharp look.

Silence.

I scoff. "He's as fucked as you are."

"Please, man!" he begs. "Please don't hurt me. I'm sorry! I'll—I'll apologize to her, okay?"

"You won't get anywhere near my wife again."

He whips his head back. "You...you married her?"

"Yes." A slow, taunting grin climbs up my face. "I'm sorry, your invitation must've gotten lost."

He snickers. "So the kid is yours, then?"

At the mention of my daughter, I dig the gun deeper. "It doesn't matter. She's mine either way."

"Yeah, whatever. Have them both. I don't care."

As soon as he spits out those words, I punch him in the nose.

"Ah! Damn it! I think you broke it!" He clasps it, blood leaking out of both nostrils.

"You talk disrespectfully about them again, and I will break each one of your bones just for fun."

He swallows thickly, chest rising with barraging inhales while blood spills from his face.

"The address. Now."

He shoots it off without a fight this time, and fifteen minutes later, we're there, pulling up next to a small colonial, a black SUV in the driveway.

I hope her dog is there. Because I'm not leaving without him.

"Does he live alone?"

He nods.

Good. Wouldn't wanna break any children's hearts. But that dog is hers, and she deserves to have him back. And I'll be the one to give him to her.

Just thinking about seeing her happy when she sees him again... Fuck, I can't wait.

The gun is aimed at his head as I open my door first, then his, making sure he doesn't run.

"Get out." Grabbing his shirt, I haul him out when he's not fast enough. "Don't try anything stupid."

He flinches at my warning as we make it up the driveway before he's knocking on the door.

"Tee, open up. It's me."

A dog barks in the background.

Fuck. He's in there. Adrenaline pumps through my veins.

"Yo, what's uh..." His words die when his attention bounces between Xander's face and me. "What the hell is going on?" His dark eyes narrow. "What'd you do?"

He's probably not much older than his idiot cousin.

"Open the fucking door before I shoot you."

He trips back a step, and as he does, that's when the dog rushes up beside him.

A beautiful honey-colored golden retriever stares up at me, barking once in warning. But as he creeps closer, he sniffs me, and as soon as he does, he starts barking, tail wagging, excitement building. It's like after all this time, he still recognizes Amara's scent.

"Move." I shove my way in, locking the door behind me.

"What's going on, Xander?" Fear treads through Tee's words.

"This dog doesn't belong to you." I scratch Max behind his ears. "But you already knew that."

"Shit…" he whispers.

"He's Amara's…husband."

Tee's eyes swell when he finally notices the gun. "Yo, just take him, man. I'm cool with it." He raises his palms in the air. "It was wrong, okay? What he did was not cool."

"Yeah, no hard feelings, alright?" Xander chokes on his voice, panic taking over. "Please just let us go."

"Sit, Max."

The dog immediately obeys, settling by my side, staring at the men with their tails between their legs.

I run a hand down Max's head, and he slants closer. "What do you think we should do with them?"

The dog barks.

"I think so too." I nod.

"Wha-what does that mean?" Xander asks right before I put a bullet between his cousin's eyes.

"Oh fuckfuckfuck!" He pulls at his hair. "Please," he cries, staring at his dead cousin on the floor. He raises his palms in the air.

"I've been wanting to kill you from the moment you put your hands on her. I'm only sorry it took me this long."

"Please! I—"

Pop.

He collapses beside his cousin.

At least I won't have to worry about paternity anymore.

"Okay, Max. I think we're done here."

Removing my phone, I call one of my guys.

"Sir?"

"I need the cleaning crew to 555 Main Street in Boston. Two large rooms. Lots of dirt."

"Got it."

The phone goes dead and I'm back in the car, driving home to my wife, unable to wait another moment to see the look on her face once she sees Max.

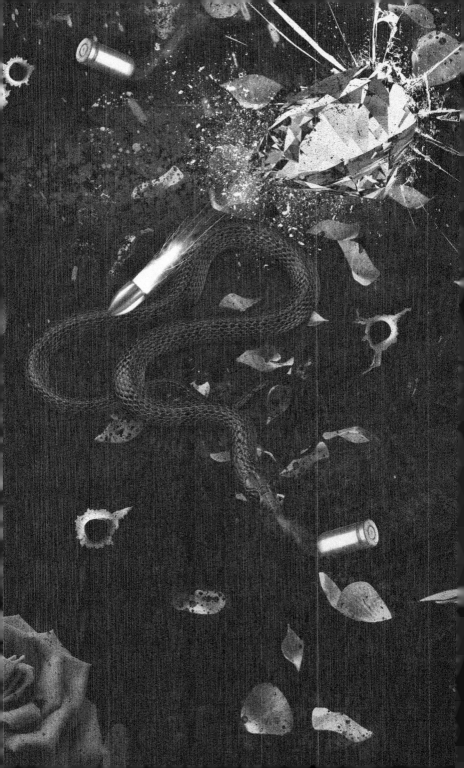

TWENTY-EIGHT

AMARA

"Wait, I don't understand," Emily says through the phone. "You've not only found Fionn, but *married* him? WHAT?!"

Blowing a breath, I hang the last of the clothes Fionn ordered for me, which arrived earlier, including the ones from my house.

"Yeah, basically." I grimace.

Of course she's shocked. I would be too.

"Okay, relax," Lilith throws in. "She's clearly been in love with him since they met, and I for one think this is romantic."

"Aww, I agree," Patricia adds. "I mean, he could be Fia's father. I think it's fantastic, and the fact that he's rich? God, you're never going to have to work shitty jobs again."

So I didn't exactly tell them the truth. Not that I could. What do I say?

Hey, so Fionn is actually in the Mafia and he kidnapped me to prevent me from testifying against him for killing a man. Totally romantic, right?

Yeah. Definitely can't do that. But I *can* pretend we're in love. That we were always meant to be.

Maybe you were.

"He's been great to me so far, and he's so amazing with Fia. He doesn't even care if she's actually his."

"Oh my God, that's so sweet!" Lilith gushes. "I mean, that's a man right there."

"Yeah, he's special."

And I mean that. Because I do like him. That part isn't a lie.

But love? Can I really love someone like that?

"I'm just worried, that's all." Emily sighs. "Maybe we can come over to meet him soon."

"It's sudden, I get it, but I'm okay. I'm happy."

"Well, I can't wait to meet this mystery man!" Lilith says. "Does he have any hot brothers?"

"Uh, yes. Two. Tynan and Cillian, but they're older and one is married."

"How old is the single one?"

There's absolutely no way I can allow my friend to date a Quinn.

"He's forty, so yeah, way too old for you."

"Um, you're younger than Fionn. I mean, there's how many years between you two?"

"Twelve…"

"Ha! Yeah, definitely need to meet this brother."

I roll my eyes. "Sure, yeah, we'll plan something."

"Perfect!" Her voice laces with excitement. "Well, anyway, I think I speak for all of us when I say congratulations. Right, Emily?"

"Of course." Her tone grows soft. "I love you, Amara. You know that. And I kinda hate that you're far away now. I won't be able to see you all the time."

Being over one hundred miles away from one another will be one of the hardest things for me, but there's nothing I can do about it.

"I know. I'll miss that too. I'll miss seeing all of you. But this is good for me and Fia."

Glancing over, I watch her playing with a dollhouse Fionn got her. She's been distracted for hours, jumping from toy to toy. I love seeing her this happy. I definitely couldn't afford all this.

When I register the door opening downstairs and heavy footsteps coming closer, I start for the exit. "Guys, I've gotta go."

"Ooh, hubby's home," Lilith teases. "Bye!"

"Have fun," Patricia says.

"I love you." Emily's voice comes through next. "Call me if anything comes up, okay? Or for literally no reason at all." She laughs, but it's doused in sadness.

"Of course! I'll talk to you guys soon."

When they all get off the phone, I put mine into the pocket of my sweatshirt just as he comes into view, still in the same clothes he left in.

His eyes drink me in, yoga shorts exposing my legs.

"Come here," he calls with a crook of his finger, his gaze seductive and brimming with heat.

My body coils, like it's calling for him. And the closer I get, the hotter I burn. When I'm right in front of him, he clasps his palms over my hips, dragging me close.

"How was your day?" His eyes sear into mine.

"Good," I whisper. "And yours?"

A smirk crawls on his face, his mouth dropping lower.

And lower.

My stomach tightens, body craving his touch.

"Better now," he whispers as that wicked mouth brushes over my lips. He kisses me slow as his fingers ride up my spine, tangled in my hair as the other hand slinks between us, fingers pressing to my core. "I want to be buried balls-deep inside you, little rabbit. You're my undoing."

My hands grip his hard biceps, and the feeling of those muscles, how strong he is, has desire building between my legs. I've never experienced anything like this except with him. Both then and now. Nothing has changed. As though time stood still while we were apart.

Except it hasn't. So much has changed.

"Daddy!" Fia rushes for him. "Look at my toys!"

He growls, nipping my bottom lip.

"Later," he whispers before he separates, kneeling for her to jump into his arms.

As he lifts her, settling her on his arm, my gut flutters with butterflies. It's beautiful to watch the way he's embraced her.

"I know! I heard you got all these cool things."

"*You* got it, Mama said."

He glances at me, hitting me with a half-smile that only makes me want to climb him up like a tree. I never realized how much seeing a man loving on your child can impact your libido, but here we are.

"Maybe we can play together," he suggests.

Is he kidding me? Like, come on. Stop doing that crap! I'm not supposed to fall for you. Hello!

"Yay! I want a tea party."

"A tea party sounds great. I've been thirsty all day." He kisses her forehead as she giggles.

Yeah, I'm done for. I instantly deflate and accept defeat.

"You're funny." Fia gives him a toothy laugh.

He chuckles. "But before we play, I have a surprise for Mommy."

Her little mouth pops. "Did you get her a toy too?"

"Actually, I did." His eyes burn into mine, and I don't miss the meaning of his words, a needy ache hitting my center. "But that's not the surprise."

"Oh?" I stare in confusion.

"Close your eyes."

"Okay?" My brows knit as a tight smile forms.

"Wanna come help me get it?" he asks Fia.

"Yes!"

"Okay, let's go." His eyes align with mine. "And *you* keep those gorgeous eyes closed."

My arms roll with goose bumps from his sweet words. "Got it."

I keep my promise as they walk out, really wanting to know what he got me. I'm not one who needs much. He's already given me everything. I'm mostly curious.

A minute later, I hear them return. The anticipation is killing me, but I don't peek.

"Okay, open your eyes."

Slowly, my lashes flutter open, unable to comprehend what I'm looking at.

My heart races, my vision blurring through the massive river of tears. Because sitting right beside him is…

"Max? Oh my God. Max?" I let out a sob.

He barks, rushing right for me when Fionn drops the leash.

"Max!"

I fall to my knees, crying without shame, hugging him as he excitedly jumps all over me, licking my face. My tears don't stop, my heart unable to contain the love I feel in this moment.

When I look up, he's watching me. My husband. Softness in his gaze.

And right now, a part of me? It instantly becomes his.

"How?" I whisper, holding tightly to him.

"I'll tell you about it later."

"Thank you. Thank you," I whimper. "This means everything to me."

He nods, jaw clenched. "I'd do anything for you."

"Can I pet him?" Fia asks.

"Come on, honey." I hold my hand out for hers while Max starts to settle, his tail still wagging.

"Max," I say. "This is my daughter, Fia."

He turns to her, gently licking her hands.

"He's slobbery." She giggles. "I like him."

When she hugs him tight, it only makes me cry even harder. There's no gift he could ever give me that would be more special than this one.

And no matter what happens, no matter where we end up, I will never forget this. Not for anything in the world.

FIONN

That night, I hold her against my chest, her hands curled under her chin.

Having her here, having Fia…it's all I want now. It's what I never knew I needed until they came back into my life.

But I want more. I want her pregnant. I want to watch our child grow inside her, knowing I did that.

"I can't believe my mother and Xander did this. It makes me sick." She sighs harshly.

My fingers trace up and down her spine. "I'm sorry, baby. It's fucked up. But they'll never hurt you again."

She instantly peers up. "What does that mean? Did…did you do something to them?"

Fuck.

"It depends on your definition of something." I lay a smirk on her, but it doesn't work. Not that I expected it to.

Her eyes narrow. "Fionn. I know you by now."

You're only seeing the tip of the iceberg. There's nothing I wouldn't do for you.

I cup her jaw and stare directly into her eyes so she knows how much I mean what I'm about to say.

"When someone hurts you…" My thumb traces her pouty bottom lip. "They hurt me. So if you want the truth, I'll give it to you."

She visibly shudders, rising up on her elbow. "Is she dead?"

"No. But he is."

She backs out of my grasp, slapping a palm over her mouth as she tries to sit up.

"Don't fucking do that." I have her on her back in a flash, my body pinning hers to the bed. "You asked me for the truth, and now you're gonna live with it." My lips drop to the corner of her trembling mouth, my fingers curling around her pretty little throat. "I am who I am. There's no changing that. And you're my wife now. You need to understand I would never let anyone hurt you and get away with it. Your mother is lucky all I did was leave a bullet in her foot."

"Oh my God!" She cowers, her fear intensifying.

The same fear I saw when I came to kill her.

I squeeze her throat tighter. "I'd do it again." My mouth falls over hers in a soft kiss. One she doesn't return. "No one hurts my girl."

"I don't want you killing anyone for me."

"You don't get a choice. That's not how this works, mo ban dia. Once you became my wife, I made a promise to cherish and protect you." I lay another kiss on her jaw. "This is how I do it."

"That's not normal." She shakes her head, tears filling her eyes. "One day, you'll be the one who dies. What will I say to Fia then?"

The pulse in my temple beats louder at the thought of never seeing them again. "You'll tell her that I loved her from the moment I met her."

Her chin trembles.

"Don't cry, baby." I wipe the tears trapped in her lower lashes. "I never wanna see you cry."

"Then don't kill anyone else for me." She breathes out harshly. "When you're being all sweet…" Her voice drops. "I almost forget who you are for just a moment, and that's when I breathe a little easier."

Releasing a sigh, I flip onto my back, staring up at the ceiling, while she keeps a small distance between us.

"I'm sorry, but this is who I am." My eyes flip to hers. "Your husband. And this is for life, baby, and that's all there is to it."

Even though I know keeping you is the most selfish thing I've ever done. But sometimes a man has to be selfish to get what he wants.

Without waiting for a reply, I turn off the lights and catch her heavy inhales, both of us awake for a while before she falls asleep.

I lie there after, watching her, fingers gently drifting down her hip. Hoping that, with time, she accepts me for who I am.

TWENTY-NINE

FIONN

"More tea, Daddy?" Fia lifts her small pink teakettle in the air, pigtails swinging as she comes over to my side, where I'm seated in a tiny child-sized chair that barely fits my frame.

But there's nowhere else I'd rather be.

"Please, ma'am. This tea is the best I've ever had."

"Really?" she asks, eyes as bright as her mother's, this gorgeous hazel hue.

"Really." With a smile, I glance at Amara, who's fighting her own grin as she observes us from her spot on the sofa, directly in our line of vision, stroking Max's fur.

She hasn't let him out of her sight, constantly touching him like she's afraid he'll disappear.

Fia pours more tea, which is nothing but water, but I still lift up that tiny pink cup and pretend to drink it.

"Mm, so good."

She giggles, returning to her spot across from me in the den and sipping on her own brew.

"Are you looking forward to going to Tynan's for dinner?" I ask Amara.

She's barely said much to me today. I need to fix this, but fuck me, I don't know how. I don't expect her to be okay with me killing that piece of shit. Unlike for me, this is hard for her. I'm willing to give her time to come to terms with her new life, but ending our marriage is non-negotiable.

"I am." She hugs her knees, pressing them to her chest. "It'll be nice for Fia to have someone to play with."

"Yeah." I grab a plastic biscuit and place it on my plate. "Family is important, and my family is now yours."

Her mouth pinches and she stares down at her lap for a moment. "Do the rest of them know?"

"Know what?"

"How I got here and why?"

"No. But you're more than welcome to tell them."

"No." She tucks her knees closer. "I have no plans to say anything."

"Whatever you want, babe. Tea?"

A smirk slips on my face as she shakes her head, while I'm just glad she's talking to me.

"You're good with her."

"Is that a compliment?" A half-grin appears just as Fia grabs a piece of "cake" and pretends to take a big bite.

"It may have been." Her teasing smile makes every cell in my body pulse with awareness.

"I've gotta drop by the office in a bit, but I won't be long."

"Okay." She nods.

I continue playing with Fia until it's time for me to go.

"Daddy will see you later, princess." I lift her in my arms, kissing her temple.

"Love you."

Shit. Hearing her say that is never gonna get old.

"Love you too, sweetheart."

When I place her down, she returns to her tea party while I approach my wife, tugging her chin in a tight grasp.

"I'll see you later, baby." My lips fall to hers, kissing her softly.

And she kisses me back, her fingers dipping into my biceps, like she never wants to let me go. I want to believe that no matter what I do, she'll always kiss me this way, because our connection? It's unbreakable.

"Please be careful," she says softly as I back away.

And I realize right now, in these seconds of her staring at me with concern, that I'm falling for her. Falling hard and fast. And there's nothing I can do about it.

"Are you sure about this?" Tynan asks. "Because you've never made a damn thing in your life."

"Come on, babe." Elara shakes her head. "Give the man a chance."

"Yeah, what she said." I grin.

Brody laughs beside her.

"What's so funny? Think your uncle can't hack it?"

"Not at all."

I scoff. "Wow. I'll prove you fuckers wrong."

"Language." Elara pops a brow.

"Yes, ma'am." I hit her with a salute.

I don't know how she puts up with us, especially a grumpy ass like my brother.

"Baklava is not for beginners. So if you mess it up, it's on you." Tynan grabs some flour, butter, and a bunch of other crap.

But I need to do this. I want to be the one to make it. As soon as I heard her say there was something she wanted, I knew I'd be the one to give it to her, and I want her to love it.

"Yeah, yeah, fine. Stop talking and tell me what to do."

He folds his arms across his chest, and then he's giving me the first steps of the recipe.

Before I know it, I'm making the dough with Brody's help. Or trying to, anyway.

"You have to keep mixing it," he tells me, shaking his head. "It can't be that clumpy."

Yeah, the kid knows more than me.

"Okay, genius." I ruffle his hair as he laughs.

"If you don't do it right, it won't come out good."

"Yeah, listen to my kid." Tynan grabs some eggs and sugar, adding them to another mixing bowl.

"I think it's sweet that you wanted to make her something she asked for," Elara throws in. "That's really thoughtful."

"She's not thrilled with me right now, so I'm trying."

"Well, neither was Elara. At first." Tynan smirks, catching her eye, and her face flushes.

"Yeah, I wanted to kill him. I think I even tried once." She shrugs, a playful look on her face.

"Mom!" Brody's eyes pop.

"I was only playing." She throws her hands in the air.

But as she focuses on me, she shakes her head.

"Definitely wasn't playing," she whispers to me. "Amara will come around. I did. Just give her time."

"Yeah, let's hope this baklava helps." I start on the filling, mixing the ingredients.

"It will. You'll see."

I wish I shared her optimism.

THIRTY

AMARA

B rushing my hair in the bathroom, I continue getting ready for tonight's dinner. Knots form in my gut at the thought of being surrounded by the Quinn family.

A Mafia family.

It's quite terrifying, actually, but I push it to the very back of my mind as I retrieve my knee-length black pencil dress and kitten heels.

The new wardrobe he's purchased for me is beautiful, and I don't know when I'll ever get used to this luxurious life. As hard as my life was, it was mine. I fought for everything I had. This feels like cheating.

"You ready, baby girl?" He peeks into the bedroom, looking as fine as ever in his deep gray suit jacket, two buttons of his white dress shirt popped open.

"Yes." My face flushes when his gaze ravages my body.

Stalking closer, he clasps my hips. "You're so damn beautiful."

I know he means it. I can hear and see it. But most of all, I feel it.

He pushes his hard body into mine and simply stares into my eyes, that sinful mouth feathering over my lips. Yet he doesn't kiss me, though my heart hasn't caught on, beating faster from the proximity alone.

"How did you sleep last night?" His voice is a husky, rhythmic melody, stroking all my intimate places.

Last night, he didn't touch me. He knew I was upset after he told me he killed Xander, and he just held me all night while I tried to figure out how I can accept him and the kind of life he lives.

I never saw myself married to someone who does the kinds of things he does. Yet at the same time, I know he's a good man, a good father, and I can't seem to reconcile those two things.

"You're doing that thing again," he whispers with a gruff timbre.

"Doing what?"

"Thinking about all the reasons you can't fall in love with me."

My stomach flips.

Love.

There's that word again.

His palm cups my cheek, eyes aligned with mine.

I let out a sigh. "Falling in love with you would be the easiest thing in the world. It's all the other things getting in the way."

He drags a shallow breath, thumb stroking my bottom lip. "Well, Mrs. Quinn, we're just gonna have to fix that."

Tynan and Elara's place is only a few minutes' drive from us on the estate. The home is elegant and just as large as Fionn's.

Guards greet us as they let us inside the grand foyer, a housekeeper saying hello as we head for the kitchen, where Elara is placing vegetables on a large platter.

"Oh my gosh! I'm sorry I didn't come greet you guys. I didn't hear you."

She rushes over, giving us both a hug.

"That's okay." I wave off her concern.

"Hi!" Fia grins. "You look pretty."

"Aww." Elara pouts. "Can I keep her?"

"I'd say yes, but I'd miss her too much." I tug Fia to my legs, and she giggles. "Do you need help?"

I glance around at all the dishes on the kitchen counter. Too many to count.

"Absolutely not! You guys go to the dining room. Everyone's already there."

Tynan walks in, nodding in greeting as he picks up two dishes.

"Grab those platters," he tells Fionn, and when I try to help, he shakes his head.

"No, we've got it."

"Okay, if you're sure." But I still feel guilty for not helping out.

"Do they know about Amara?" Fionn asks Tynan, who shakes his head.

"Thought you should be the one to surprise them." He chuckles dryly.

Fionn's eyes go to mine, and my nerves have me jittering.

What do I tell them about us? Do I lie?

"Don't be nervous," he whispers as we stride side by side, stepping into an expansive dining room with over twenty chairs.

All eyes go to us, the sound of conversation turning to a murmur until silence echoes.

"Emily?" Fernanda stares open-mouthed. "I can't believe it!"

"Hi." I shrink back nervously, but his steady palm on the small of my back has me a little less nervous.

"Hi, I'm Fia." She waves.

That has Patrick's thick brows rising in surprise as he glances at Fionn for a moment before he extends his hand to her. "It's nice to meet you, sweetheart."

Everyone greets one another while Fernanda curls her arms around me.

"It's been so long. I never thought we'd see you again. How have you been?" She grabs my shoulders, her gaze searching mine. "*Where* have you been?" She steps in closer, whispering, "Are you okay? I haven't stopped thinking about our talk that day."

"I'm okay. I promise."

"Good." She squeezes my fingers.

"Her name is actually Amara." Fionn smirks, and she gives him a curious glance.

"Seems like there's a story there." Her mouth tightens with a smile. "Either way, it's so good to see you, and to meet this darling little girl. Right, Pat?"

She runs a hand down Fia's head, who smiles brightly at the woman.

"It is." Fionn's dad peeks at my hand, noticing the ring on my finger. "Wait a minute. Did you two get married?"

Fionn slices his fingers through mine, kissing my knuckles. "Yeah, Dad." He glances at his whole family, some I don't yet know. "Amara is my wife as of yesterday, and Fia is my daughter."

Patrick scoffs. "What's with my boys getting married without me there? I'm starting to get offended." He gives Cillian a stern look. "You better not pull some crap like this, son. Ya hear?"

"Mm-hmm."

"You talk funny." Fia giggles at Patrick.

"That's not nice!" I scold, blowing a breath.

"Oh no, she's right. I do." He peers down at her, cocking a thick gray brow. "You know…" His face lights up. "I bet you like ice cream, and they have a lot here."

"I do!" She gapes. "How'd you know? Are you a wizard?"

She plops a hand on her hip, and the room erupts in a laugh.

"Now that I think about it, you've got this whole wizard thing happening." Fernanda's eyes slide up and down his frame.

"Maybe we should get you a wizard hat." Fionn chuckles.

"Ha-ha, you'd all better stop poking fun at a nice old man." Patrick's voice fills with mirth.

"It's okay, Dad." Elara comes out carrying a tray of biscuits. "I'll protect you."

"Aww, see? Now that's love." He saunters up to her, taking the tray and placing it on the table. "Everything looks wonderful, darling."

It's sweet that she calls him "Dad." He must be good to her.

My chest stiffens as I think of my own father and how he could just walk out on me like that. Tears burn my eyes, but I ignore them.

As Fionn and I are about to sit down, a door opens in the distance and multiple footfalls come closer.

When I look to see who it is, I find none other than Iseult and a tall man I assume to be her husband. Her eyes flare as she finds me there, before the corner of her mouth hikes up.

"Well, well…" She struts in, past everyone else, stopping just short of me, black thigh-high boots over skintight jeans. "Look who's returned." A single thick brow arches. "You finally put my brother out of his misery, huh? He was hell-bent on finding you. Did he tell you that?"

Slowly, I turn to Fionn, who smirks wickedly.

I didn't know he tried so hard to find me.

My heart gives a little thump.

"Then again, I'm sure it was his fault you left. So maybe he deserved it." Her amused appearance doesn't make Fionn pleased, a pronounced scowl on his features.

"It's always good to see you, sister. You're such a delight."

But I can't seem to get past what she said.

"You looked for me?"

"For years," she whispers.

He hits her with a glare. "May I talk now?"

She zips up her lips, fighting a grin.

"I looked all over," he explains. "Searching and stalking every Emily Daniels I could find. Even tried with facial recognition. But I came up empty every time."

My heart sinks. "I tried looking for you too. Not as efficiently as you, clearly."

He sucks in a long breath, like he's surprised by the revelation.

"Well, clearly he found you even after all this time."

"Not exactly." He drags in a frustrated breath, staring hard at me with a tilt of his brow.

A questioning expression appears on Iseult's face. "Well, if anyone would like to provide the CliffsNotes version, I would very much love to hear about this reunion."

"Me too." The guy beside her with dark eyes and equally dark hair interrupts. "I'm Gio, by the way. Figured I'd introduce myself since it doesn't seem like my lovely wife will do it for me."

"Didn't think it was important." She fights her smile.

"Yeah, she's really hilarious." He wraps an arm around her, pulling her into his side while she tries to push him off, though it doesn't seem like she's trying very hard. "Welcome to the family. I'd say I'm sorry, but you probably already figured that out."

"Ignore my son." Fernanda rolls her eyes. "The Quinns are wonderful people, and I for one am so happy that you have returned."

As I stand amongst them, I don't feel fear. I feel welcomed and at home. That alone should terrify me, but it doesn't.

A short, slender woman around my age who looks almost exactly like Fionn approaches next, and beside her is a much taller man, his eyes as blue as the sky.

"Hey, I'm Eriu. Fionn's other sister. We've never met, but Iseult told me about you years ago." She reaches a hand for mine. "It's nice to officially meet you, and you!" She kneels to Fia. "I'm Auntie Eriu. It's a pleasure to make your acquaintance."

My daughter shakes her hand with a giggle.

"And I'm Devlin, Eriu's husband." He nods in greeting. His thick Irish accent flanks his tone, just as heavy as Patrick's.

"Hey, you talk funny too! I wanna talk funny!"

"That's called an Irish accent, sweetheart," I tell her.

"Can you buy it for me?"

Patrick laughs, others joining him. "Oh, she's hilarious!"

Brody comes out of an adjoining room, a girl Fia's age with bright green eyes and chestnut curls with him.

"Hey," he says.

"Hi, Brody."

The girl gives us sheepish glances, hiding behind her brother's thigh.

"She gets super timid with new people, but give her some time to warm up," Elara explains.

"This is Adora, Fia." Fionn takes her hand. "She's your cousin. Let's go say hi."

"Okay!"

Fia is a social butterfly. She can talk to anyone, so I'm sure they will be friends in no time.

"Hi. Wanna play?"

Adora glances at her mom, who nods enthusiastically.

Then the girl throws on a smile. "Okay."

She finally steps away from her brother, and Fia doesn't waste a second, taking her hand.

"Where are your toys?"

Adora points left, and they march out of the room.

"Want me to watch them?" Brody asks.

"Please, sweetheart." Elara kisses the top of his head. "But the food is ready, so make sure you're all back in about fifteen."

"Okay, Mom." He follows them to the room next door.

A small black-and-white dog comes running in, growling with a brown loafer in its mouth.

I let out a laugh. "Um, your dog has someone's shoe in its mouth."

Tynan groans. "That's Bubbles. And that's my shoe. We have a love/hate relationship that never quite went away."

"Yeah," Elara laughs. "She's got a knack for destroying his things. But look on the bright side, babe." Her palm lowers to his chest. "At least she sleeps next to you now."

"Lucky me," he mutters.

The dog runs out of view while Tynan shakes his head. "Anyway, let's eat while the food is hot."

He pulls a chair out for Elara, and she gazes at him lovingly, placing a hand on his cheek before she lowers into her seat. Only then does he take his. Fionn clearly was raised the same way, because he pulls my chair out for me too.

"After you, baby." His smirk widens, and those treacherous butterflies roar in my gut.

As I sink into my seat and he does the same, his fingertips roll up the top of my thigh, eyes growing hooded as he drags my chair closer. While everyone starts eating, he places his palm on my knee and leaves it there. My body grows warm and aware, nipples beaded as I force myself to eat, even though it's hard when he has his large hand on me.

"So, how's school been going, darling?" Patrick asks Eriu, while his fingers trace up and down my thigh, making me fidget.

"It's going well. I love my classes."

"Oh, are you in college?" I wonder, trying to ignore the throbbing between my legs.

"Yeah. I'm going for my master's in creative writing."

"Oh, wow! That's awesome."

"Yeah, she's a fancy writer," Patrick offers. "She just published her second book."

"No way. How exciting."

She nods sheepishly, clearly not comfortable with compliments, but her father is obviously proud.

"Yeah, it's been great. How about you? What did you study?"

My heart plummets.

Clearing my throat, I fidget with the fork in my hand, picking on a meatball. "Well, uh, I never went to college. I mean, I wanted to, of course." My pulse quickens. "I wanted to become a paralegal."

Everyone's eyes are on me, and I swear my face is red as a tomato.

"Why didn't you?" Iseult asks. "Go to college."

Releasing a sigh, I go with the truth. "My mother wasn't very supportive. She wanted me to work and be home with her instead. So she had me drop out my senior year and get a job."

"And you still want to be a paralegal?" There's a hard edge to Fionn's tone, which causes me to look at him.

And what I find has my heartbeat thrumming. Every inch of his face is filled with rage.

Is he angry at me or my mother?

"Yeah. I mean, it's what I've always wanted. Stupid, I know."

His jaw tenses. "Why is it stupid?"

"Well, I have Fia now, and she's my priority. She was from the moment I had her."

"Aww," Fernanda gushes, placing a hand on her chest. "You're a good mom, but sometimes we have to also do things for ourselves. I'm sorry your mother was selfish."

"She was a lot of things. Selfish was probably the least of my worries. But she was all I had, and I always hoped she would be a good mom to me." I sag in my seat, embarrassed that I just said all that to a room full of strangers.

"We all want to see the best in our parents." She sighs. "But as we get older, we realize they're just people, and being a parent doesn't make someone a good person."

I know she's right. But it doesn't suck any less.

As the conversation shifts to something else, I still sense Fionn's brooding energy beside me. When I take his hand in mine and squeeze, he returns it, releasing a heavy exhale. As I stare into his eyes, my pulse beats louder with every passing moment, feeling a sense of connection I can't explain.

"I'm sorry your mother was such a damn disappointment." His knuckles cascade down my cheek. "I promise to give you everything you've never had before."

And as my heart skips a beat, he tugs my mouth to his and kisses me.

This kiss…it drifts into my very soul. Like he's asking me to trust him. To trust this.

And right now, it almost feels like I can.

THIRTY-ONE

FIONN

W hile she's in the shower that evening, I play her words over and over, unable to stop this fucking rage from building inside me.

Her mother. That bitch. Should've done more than just put a bullet in her foot.

I grab the video monitor from our nightstand, staring at Fia sleeping in her bed, wondering how anyone can mistreat their own child. I'd do anything for this girl, and I just met her.

Balling a fist at my thigh, I drop the camera back, pulling my shirt off, the pants coming next. I head for the bathroom, needing Amara right now. Needing to tell her that the life she had, it's in the past now.

I may not be able to fix what's been done, but I'll treat her right. I'll give her everything.

The water buzzes behind the glass door as I head in.

She doesn't see me, not at first. But when her eyes fasten to mine, she doesn't hide from me, fingers running through her hair.

"Fionn? What are you doing in here?"

Moving closer, I slide the door open. "I wanted to check on you. We didn't get a chance to talk about what you said at dinner."

Her full lips curve. "And it couldn't wait until I was done?"

"Absolutely not." My gaze rakes every gorgeous inch of skin. "Because then you wouldn't be wet and naked."

Her breathing grows raspier as I step inside, grabbing her hips and roughly pushing her up against the wall, my cock hard and heavy against her stomach.

Popping her chin up with the back of my hand, I lower my mouth and brush my lips with hers. "I'm sorry, baby. Wish I could've helped you back then when you were young."

Her warm exhales scatter across my jaw. "It's okay. I'm okay."

"That's right. You are." My fingers slope down her hip, stroking her clit as she moans. "You have me now, and you'll never have to worry about anything again."

"Fionn…" She gasps, her nails digging into my back as my fingers sink inside her, curling and thrusting as deep as they can go.

My mouth drops to her throat, kissing upward until I capture her lips with mine, working her cunt faster, until her walls clench and pull me in for more.

I wanna get lost in her. Lost in the way she makes me feel. Like I'm the luckiest son of a bitch who ever lived.

I swallow her cries of pleasure. And with another flick of her clit, her hands tighten around me, body quivering.

"Oh God! Yes!" A cry rips out of her, but I only increase my pace.

When her body starts to relax, I decrease my tempo, cupping her cheek with my other hand. "You're so beautiful."

She sighs breathlessly, lowering her head to my shoulder while I stroke my fingers up and down her back.

"Turn around. I'm gonna brush your hair."

"Mmm, okay." I grab her hair comb from the built-in shelf and start to comb her hair from the bottom, working upward, making sure every knot is out.

"You're good at this."

"You sound surprised." I clasp her stomach and push her back into my front.

"Well, you don't have long hair." She glances at me from over her shoulder with a teasing smile.

"It's something I learned from Iseult when we were young. She taught me how to brush Eriu's hair after our mother died when she was five."

"Oh…I'm sorry."

"I know you are." I kiss her shoulder. "But it was a long time ago."

"I'm sure it still hurts."

It does.

I continue to brush her hair, and she shuts off the water when I'm done. Grabbing a towel, I proceed to dry her off, taking my time, looking into her eyes as I take each leg over my propped one, the towel drifting up and between her thighs.

She bites the corner of her lip when I dry her there. Grinding my molars, I force myself to behave, even though it's nearly impossible.

I want her so goddamn bad.

Lifting her into my arms, I carry her out into the bedroom.

"Is that how our showers are going to go from now on?" A smile sneaks over her face. "You carrying me out?"

"You complaining, mo ban dia?"

"Not one bit."

"Good." I throw her on top of the bed, crawling over her.

She welcomes me between her legs, fingertips feathering over my back as I stare into her eyes. My cock grinds against her pussy, her back arching as those eyes grow heavy, laden with desire. Grabbing myself, I work my piercings over her clit, and her eyes roll.

"One of these days, I'm gonna take my time and tie you up, then fuck you."

"Yes, please," she groans, one hand stroking my hair, the other on my shoulder.

"Hearing you beg for it…" My lips skim over her jaw. "…makes me so damn hard."

I take her lips with mine in a hungered, depraved kiss, my cock nudging into her entrance, sinking inch by inch.

With every touch, she sucks me deeper. Until all I know is her. Until all I want and need is to protect her and spend my lifetime loving her.

It's in this moment I know for certain that I do. That I fell in love with her that night almost five years ago.

And now, I finally get to show her just how much that is.

AMARA

I've never slept more peacefully than I did last night. My body was completely satiated in his arms after he made love to me.

And that's exactly what it was. His eyes never left mine. With every touch, he cemented himself into my very core, and now the thought of ever leaving him feels foreign.

My heart lurches at the thought. Like it's revolting at the very idea of never waking up beside him again. Of never hearing him call me little rabbit or his goddess.

With every moment I've spent with him, it's like I belong here. That somehow, this has already become my home.

Rubbing a hand down my face, I groan, stretching my body with a yawn and finding the space beside me warm, yet empty. He must've already gone to work.

Grabbing the video monitor, I check on Fia. As I do, I notice she's missing from her bed.

Panic instantly hits me.

Where is she?

My head spins. My pulse quickens.

What if someone took her? What if it was one of Fionn's enemies? He has to have a ton of them doing what he does.

No, that's crazy. I'm sure she's fine, just wandering like a normal, curious child.

But my mind hasn't gotten the message, my body shuddering from within as I swing my feet out of the bed, quickly grabbing my robe and rushing to her room.

"Fia!"

Where the hell can she be?

"Fia, baby? Where are you?"

There's no one in her room. Nothing but silence.

Once I start for the stairs, voices grow from faint to a little louder.

"Let's let Mommy sleep," Fionn says just as I make it downstairs.

"Okay!" When I register her voice, my anxiety instantly shoots out of me.

Hurrying toward the kitchen, I see them both around the island.

Oh thank God.

"Hey, baby." Fionn peers at me while standing over Fia in the kitchen, cutting into her pancakes.

I place a hand on my chest, trying to control my heartbeat while Max rushes over, licking my hands.

When Fionn takes in my appearance, he lowers the fork. "What's wrong?"

He comes over, clasping my face in his hands, searching my gaze for something amiss.

"When I didn't see her in her bed…"

"Shit," he whispers like he doesn't want her to hear. "I'm sorry." His forehead falls to mine. "Nothing will ever happen to her here. You don't have to worry."

I nod and grab his forearms, not wanting to let go. His strong hands stroke my back, his heart beating next to mine.

"Mama, are you okay?" Fia's sweet tone has me pulling back and smiling at her reassuringly.

"I'm just fine, baby. How are your pancakes?"

"SO yummy!" She tosses another piece into her mouth, foregoing the fork altogether, chocolate stains on her little hands.

"Come on. Let's eat, babe." While holding my hand, he pulls up a chair for me across from Fia's and takes the one beside me.

He fills my plate with pancakes and eggs, then adds to his own. His white t-shirt stretches across his back, every inch of muscle evident. I swear the man doesn't know how to look bad. Even his hair is perfect when he wakes up, brushed back and impeccable.

"I have another surprise for you." There's an obvious glint in his eyes.

"Oh, really?" I cut into my eggs, popping a piece into my mouth. "And what's that?"

"Well, it wouldn't be much of a surprise if I told you." He chuckles. "Now eat so I can show it to you."

What in the world can it be?

I finish the food in minutes, scarfing it down while he sips on his coffee, staring at me with a twitch of his mouth.

"Really wanna know, don't you?"

I nod with excitement. "I love surprises."

"Is that so?" he teases.

"Mm-hmm." I arch a brow. "But I don't want you to think I'm asking for more surprises, by the way." I pop a piece of pancake into my mouth.

He laughs. "Pretty dangerous to tell your wealthy husband you like surprises, Mrs. Quinn, and think he'll just ignore that bit of information."

My belly flips, enjoying the way it sounded when he said husband.

"Come on, let's go outside." Getting to his feet, he reaches for Fia, taking her hand and mine.

I grow eager with anticipation.

"Close your eyes," he tells me as we reach the door.

Once I do, he leads me out, the cool air hitting my face.

"You can look now."

At first, I don't know what I'm supposed to be seeing. A red SUV with tinted windows sits before us.

"Is the surprise in the car?" I glance over at him.

"Kinda both," he laughs. "The car *is* the surprise."

"What!" My widened gaze bounces between the cherry-red vehicle and his adoring eyes.

"It's yours, baby girl. It's armored too, so you and Fia will be safer."

"What does that mean?"

"Means it's bulletproof."

"Oh." My heart gives a little thump.

That's right. Married into the Mob. Got that loud and clear.

"So, do you like it?"

"I love it!" Fia says before I can get a word in, and he curls one arm around her, embracing her tightly.

I huff out an overwhelmed sigh. "It's amazing. I've never had a car remotely this beautiful."

"Wanna test drive it?"

I tug on my bottom lip. "Absolutely."

"Come on, then." He grabs my hand, and we make it down the cobblestone steps together.

"But what about Fia?"

"She's coming with us. I already had a car seat installed inside."

"Yay!" she exclaims while I stare at him with disbelief, unable to stand another second without kissing him.

Throwing my arms around him, I align my gaze with his as I lift up on my feet.

"Thank you," I whisper, my warm breaths mingling with his as I kiss him slowly, enjoying his responding growl.

"You haven't even seen the second surprise."

"There's more?" I say in wonderment.

"Of course there is, baby."

He pushes back, leading me toward the car. The door's already opened, a large yellow envelope lying on the driver's side with keys on top.

"What's that?" My heartbeats echo in my rib cage.

Pushing the keys to the side, he picks up the envelope. "Open it."

Nervous fluttering erupts in my gut, and I start to wonder what it could be. Sucking in a long, deep inhale, I take it from him, pulling open the flap and reaching inside, then dragging a stack of papers out.

When I notice the logo at the top, my mouth pops open. "Fionn? Wha-what's this?"

My eyes scan the letter, a cry catching in my throat.

"You said you wanted to go to college. Now you will."

"Oh my God." My nose stings, eyes blinking past the myriad of tears already filling them.

I read the words over and over.

Congratulations, Mrs. Amara Quinn, on your acceptance to Tomley University.

"I—I don't understand. How?" I choke on my words.

This is one of the best schools in the state, and not too far from here. I can't believe he did this for me.

"The dean is a personal friend of the family. He made an exception because your grades, up until the time you left, were exceptional. And why?" His palm lands across my cheek. "Because I'm your husband and it's my job to make you happy."

Tears leak down my face, and I'm unable to stop them even if I tried. How am I supposed to not fall for him?

"Mommy? Why you crying?"

I grab her hand. "They're happy tears, I promise, baby. Thank you," I tell him, curling my arms around him and pressing my cheek to his chest. "Thank you so much."

"Always, mo ban dia." He drops a kiss to my temple. "Now let's take this Royce on the road and see how fast she can go."

"Uh…" I back away slowly, brows knitted. "I think we're going to stick with the speed limit."

"Probably safer." His smirk widens.

"I think so." I nod, my lips winding. "You're a father now. Safety is important."

"I am." He gazes down at Fia with stars in his eyes. "Best thing you could've ever given me."

The pure sincerity and love within his voice…it sends a pang to my chest. Because this right here feels like the forever I've always been searching for.

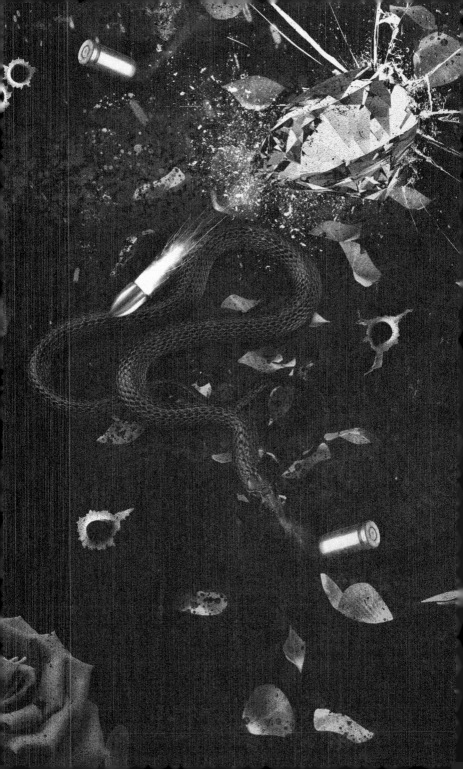

THIRTY-TWO

FIONN

"Xo! Come back!" Her low cries wrestle me out of a deep sleep.

I'm not sure if I dreamed it until she cries out again, begging someone for help. When I flip the bedside lamp on, I find her still asleep. Her face is twisted in pain, her mouth open in horror.

"Baby, wake up." My knuckles stroke her face, but she remains asleep, trembling as I continue to touch her, not wanting to scare her. "Amara, wake up."

"No, stay! Please, stay."

Who the hell is she talking to?

I know it's just a nightmare, but fuck, I wanna help her.

"Amara." I gently shake her, hating to witness her going through any kind of pain. "Am—"

"What?" She instantly pops her eyes open, her labored inhales growing shallower.

When she finally concentrates on me, she whooshes a quick

exhale.

"Did you have a nightmare?" I prop myself on my elbow and look down at her, my fingers grazing her arm, hoping to relax her.

"Yeah." She drops her forearm over her face.

"Want to talk about it?"

"I…um…I've had the same stupid dream since I was younger." She sighs. "It comes and goes, but I don't know what it means."

"Tell me about it."

Lowering back down, I pull her over my chest, my palm clasped to her back.

"I'm in a hospital, around Fia's age, and in my arms, there's a baby. My mother is there, but I can't see her face. It's fuzzy. The baby cries, and I calm her down, but then my mother starts flickering and so does the baby." Her breaths tremble out of her as she goes on. "Then they're gone and I'm alone in a pitch-black room with nothing there. Until I'm swallowed up by the darkness too."

Jesus.

"I kept thinking that maybe it's a sign of some kind that I have to find my father. That I have to know why he left me."

That's right; she told me he left when she was two.

"I wonder if my subconscious is telling me I need to close that chapter of my life," she continues. "That I need some kind of closure from the sense of abandonment, you know?"

"Of course."

"But I don't know his name or anything about him. My mother won't give me my birth certificate or his information."

My fingers feather up and down her spine. "She will to me."

"What?"

"I'll go pay her a nice visit. Maybe bring a plant. Does she like plants?"

"If she can smoke it." She snickers.

"I'm gonna find out everything you need to know, and then you can have your answers."

She bites her bottom lip. "Sometimes I wonder if some things are better left in the past, but I just can't seem to move on from knowing why he left. Every time I look at Fia, I ask myself how he could've just walked out on me like that."

"I don't know either." I cup her jaw and kiss her, my body filling with adrenaline. "But I swear if he tries to hurt you again once we find him, I'm not gonna be able to stop myself from killing him."

Her eyes pop. I drop my lips to her forehead, leaving them there for a few seconds. She can't hide the shock, her face disappearing in my chest.

Once she's asleep, I stay awake, wondering if I should've said any of that.

AMARA

"You okay?" he asks, tightening his grasp on my hand while he shows me around the estate.

But my mind is still on what he said last night. He'll kill my father if he has to. *Kill* him. For merely hurting me.

What does that even mean? What is considered hurt for men like him? Is there a criteria Mafia guys use before they decide to off people? Maybe a checklist?

Ran over wife's beloved flowers. Check.

Said he hated her cooking. Check.

Looked at her the wrong way. Check.

No matter the reasons my father left, I don't want anyone's life on my conscience.

"Yeah, I'm fine," I lie, but from his tight expression, I know he doesn't buy it.

Forcing myself not to think about this, I look out at the mountains up ahead, large and scenic, the smell of freshly cut grass filling my nostrils. I will never get over this view.

When we pass a looming mansion with other smaller ones on each side, I stare at it curiously. "What's that?"

The large construction is bigger than anything I've seen yet, even his home.

"That's Caellach Academy. It's our school."

"Like a real school?" My brows squint in question.

"Not exactly." His mouth twitches. "Want me to show you inside?"

"Okay."

But a wave of apprehension hits me. I don't know if it's because I'm just nervous about what's behind those walls. I guess we'll find out.

Swallowing past the hesitation, I draw in some courage. If Fia and I are going to live here, it's my job to be well-informed about everything that happens here.

He takes me up the steps, pushing a set of brown doors open. The place is mostly quiet, some voices in the distance. Together, we head to the left, down a narrow corridor until we're beside an elevator.

As soon as he presses the button, it arrives, and he takes us inside, holding my hand firmly with his while my heart beats louder.

I didn't have a moment to check anything out. No clue at all what this place even is. Goose bumps thread my skin as the elevator drops, stopping seconds later.

"You ready?" His eyes turn stoic.

"Maybe?"

No. Not at all.

I have no idea what I've just walked into.

He chuckles, and there's a hint of danger within it as he takes me down another long corridor until we appear in front of a solid white door. Nothing to indicate what's beyond it.

Removing his keys, he scans one of them and the door opens.

"Wait, how did you do that?" I stare in wonderment.

It was just a key. A normal-looking key.

He laughs. "The key has a small chip that's scannable."

"Wow. That's crazy."

"We have some of the best minds working here, developing tech for us and our fighters."

"Fighters?" I whisper.

"That's right. You know what we do." He takes me down another narrow path, scanning the same key when we happen in front of another white door. "This is the place we train our next generation."

"As in kids?" I freeze in place.

Are they really making fighters out of children? If that's the case, I can't be here. I can't accept that.

"They're not that young. Sixteen to eighteen, usually."

Okay, not as bad as I imagined, but still. This is madness.

"And what do they do here?"

"I'll show you." He takes my hand, while I do a crap job of hiding my absolute shock.

The further we go, the more voices I start to hear. When we turn left, multiple rooms appear on each side. Within each are different classes. And not the kind that you'd find in a normal school.

To my right, there is a weapons combat class. Two young kids fight one another, guns in their hands, while the instructor criticizes their technique. In the other, a bunch of kids are sitting in front of laptops, typing quickly.

"What are they doing?"

He stands behind me, his hands on my hips, his body so close to mine I shiver. "They're cracking a code, trying to intercept some surveillance."

"Surveillance for what?"

He laughs. "It doesn't matter."

"I can't believe any of this. Is that what Fia will have to do?"

He spins me around, his brows knitted. "Absolutely not. Unless she wants to." His mouth twitches. "Iseult made sure this was a sexist-free environment."

"Well, that's good, I guess, but I still don't want our daughter to be like them." The very thought makes me ill.

"Then she won't." He clasps his palm around my face, his other hand rounding my hip and pulling me flush against him. "I just wanted to be honest with you about all of it. I didn't want you to find out on your own somehow and then hate me for it."

"I appreciate that," I whisper, my pulse speeding as his mouth softly brushes mine.

"Yeah? How much do you appreciate it?" His tone grows husky and deep, making me forget where we are for a moment as he pushes me up against the wall, voices coming from the training room we're beside.

"Stop. We can't do this here." My vision goes hazy, a gasp swimming out of me as his fingers climb up my bare leg, inching up my thigh past my skater dress. "Someone could see us."

He groans, shoving my panties to the side and running a finger through my hot and achy slit. A whispery moan feathers out of me when he strokes my clit, my eyes wide as someone approaches.

"Fionn, someone's coming."

"Good. So will you in about a minute." His smooth, dark chuckle caresses my nape just as a tall man passes, giving us a brief glance before marching away.

My core tightens the more he touches me, and soon I'm lost to the feeling, lost to the anticipation of someone catching us. My body grows taut, craving release like I've gone mad.

"That's it, baby. Come for me." His hushed, gravelly voice makes me dizzy with desire.

"Oh God," I breathe.

"Better keep quiet, little rabbit, or you'll put on a show." He thrusts his fingers inside me with one quick move, a gasp dying off in my throat. "Unless that's what you want."

"I'm so close. Please!" My nails sink into his shoulders, throbbing and needing this so much, I don't care if this whole damn place hears me.

"You wanna be caught, don't you? Look how tight your cunt sucks me in."

"I—"

"Fionn?"

I choke on my reply when I hear a woman's voice. But his towering body covers most of me, so I can't see who she is.

His fingers piston faster, my eyes rolling as the wave hits, pounding through me. A scream dies in my throat as an intense orgasm blasts through my limbs, my teeth sinking into his shoulder to stop myself from crying out.

When my body stills, only then does he lower my dress, kissing the spot below my ear. "I love making you come."

My face heats up, because he definitely said that loud enough for anyone to hear.

When he backs away, both of us come face-to-face with a blonde woman. Her jaw grits when her gaze wanders to me, and I instantly know she wants him. It'd be obvious to anyone.

"Madison." His tone is sharp. "What can I do for you?"

She clears her throat, nervously pushing away a loose strand of hair, the rest in a messy, yet classy bun.

"Well, you asked me for footage of…"

When she glimpses at me, he says, "Whatever you need to say, you can say in front of my wife."

"W-w-wife?" It physically hurt for her to say that.

He runs the fingers that were inside me over his lips, smirking as he sucks them into his mouth. "So fucking delicious."

Her expression turns frostier, and I fight a smile.

"When, uh, did you get married?" Her tone shrinks, like she wants to get swallowed up by a hole.

Fionn is clearly rubbing me in her face, and I don't understand why.

"A few days ago. Remember Emily?" He brings our joined hands to his mouth and kisses the top of mine.

"Her?" Her lips tremble, more with anger than nerves. "But you said…"

"I know what I said, but it wasn't like that with you."

Her heavy panting wrestles out of her, pain evident on her features until it melts away. And in its place is indignation.

She raises up her chin. "Congratulations to you both. I'll leave the surveillance report on your desk."

Without saying goodbye, she hurries off.

"What was *that* about?" I turn to him, hiking a brow. "And don't lie to me."

He palms my hips and tugs me closer, a sly smirk forming. "I have no reason to lie, baby. Madison was someone I had a night with a year before we met. It didn't mean anything to me, but she wanted more, and I told her I wasn't looking for that. When I asked her to help me find you, she told me to stop looking. I never quite forgave her for that."

That brings a pang to my chest. He really did fight like hell to find me.

"Well, it's obvious she never got over you." My stomach turns with intense jealousy.

"Mmm." He pushes me back up against the wall, his mouth grazing my lips. "Must've left a big impact." He arches his hips into mine, and I can hear the smile in his voice.

"Are you trying to make me jealous?"

"Is it working?"

"Yes."

"Good." His eyes turn dark, a muscle in his jaw popping. He cups my jaw, gaze sinking into mine. "I'm yours, Amara. Always. No one will ever come between us."

And when he slams his lips to mine, I believe him. Every word, it's as though he seals it with this kiss. To have and to hold. In sickness and in health.

A vow that only ends…when one of us is dead.

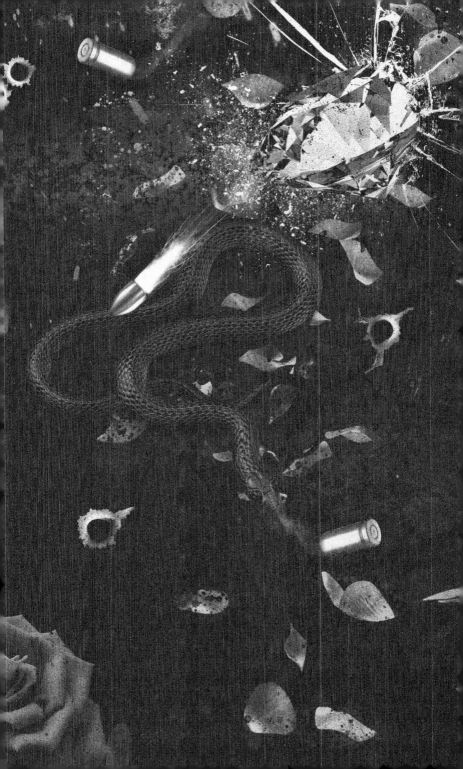

THIRTY-THREE

AMARA

D ays later, my bodyguard, Roy, drops me off at campus. As soon as I step out, a grin spreads. I'm finally here. Finally in college like I've always wanted.

Who would've thought?

The buzzing of students rushing to classes has me giddy with excitement.

When my phone vibrates, I take it out of my backpack and read a text from Em.

EMILY

> Kick ass today!!! I'm so proud of you! Can't wait to see you graduate. With your permission, I would very much like to rub your certificate in Desdemona's face.

AMARA

> I think we can arrange that.

EMILY

It's a date! Now go! Then call me and tell me all about it.

AMARA

I will! Thank you, Em. I love you.

EMILY

Back at you, mama! Talk later! XO

AMARA

XO

Before I can place the phone back in my pocket, another text comes in.

FIONN

I'm proud of you, baby girl. Good luck today.

My body grows warm. It's nice to have someone other than Emily tell me they're proud of me.

AMARA

Thank you for this. I hope you realize how much it means to me.

FIONN

Anything you want, I'll make it happen.

My heart swells. Things have been good between us in these last few days. We've spent time as a family—going horseback riding, playing with Fia, going on walks with Max.

It all feels real.

And though I've tried my hardest to forget what he does and what I saw at Caellach, it's still difficult for me to pretend he isn't two different people: the man he is with us, and the man he is to the rest of the world.

Placing my phone back in my bag, I turn to Roy. "Okay, I'm off. I'll see you when I'm done?"

"I'll be right behind you, ma'am. I'm instructed to go wherever you do."

"Oh." I form a tentative smile as the surprise sinks in. I didn't realize that. "Well, then follow me, I guess."

"I'll do my best not to disturb you."

"Will you be in the classroom too?"

Please say no.

The last thing I want is to draw unnecessary attention to myself.

"I will be right outside."

Phew.

"Alright." I start for the library, a few minutes' walk, and when I arrive, I find Lilith and Patricia both waving at me.

What the...

"What are you guys doing here?"

"Surprise!" Lilith throws her arms around me. "We wanted to be here for your first day and show you around a little. We're very proud of you."

This is the same college all three of them attended. It sucks we couldn't all go together, but that's okay. I'm here now.

Patricia's softened gaze has me giving her a tight hug.

"Thanks, you guys. You're so sweet."

"We know." Lilith gets all sassy. "And look at you with your cute clothes." She gives me a once-over. "Doesn't she look fierce?"

Patricia nods. "So fierce."

She eyes my skintight jeans and black top with three gold-tone buttons on each shoulder. Which, by the way, cost a small fortune. Fionn has spared no expense with my new wardrobe, though it still makes me uncomfortable to wear such expensive things.

"Is that Balmain?" Lilith grins with a curve of her brow. "That man is treating you right, I see."

"No clue." I shrug with a laugh. "I've never been one for brands, so your guess is as good as mine."

She peeks at the tag. "Yep. I was right."

"Good for you." Patricia places a palm on my forearm. "You deserve it after all you've been through."

"She's right. Enjoy every minute of the princess treatment." Lilith curls an arm around my back. "Now the real question is…" She gives me a suggestive glance as we start toward the library. "Does he treat you like a princess in the bedroom too?"

"Stop!" I elbow her with a giggle. "A lady doesn't talk about such things."

"Mm-hmm. He's totally boning the shit out of you, isn't he?"

My mouth pinches, fighting a wide grin. "He totally is."

"Oh shit! I knew it!" She chuckles.

Patricia rolls her eyes at Lilith. She's always been more like me, more timid when it comes to sex. But Lilith and Em, they're open books. I love how different we are and how well we complement one another.

They take me through the campus, showing me the buildings I'll have all my classes in, before we make it back to where my poli-sci class will be.

"Okay, call us if you have any problems." Lilith starts walking backward, grinning with a wave, and almost runs into another student.

"Bye." I shake my head as I get into the auditorium, finding a spot in the middle of the room.

The professor stands before us in front of a large whiteboard—short, trimmed beard, his black-framed glasses sitting across the bridge of his narrow nose. He doesn't look much older than Fionn.

"Alright, everyone, let's begin. My name is Doctor Samuel Wright, and this is Political Science 101."

The lesson picks up, and I take down every bit of information, hungry to learn everything.

FIONN

"What do you wanna see first?" I ask Fia when we arrive at the zoo.

I figured we could have a fun day together while Amara is at school.

"Monkeys!"

"Okay, monkeys it is." Picking her up, I place her over my shoulders as she giggles. "You okay up there?"

"Yes! This is fun, Daddy!" She wraps her arms around my neck, and every inch of me comes alive at hearing her call me that.

"I think they may wanna add you to the zoo. You're like a little monkey too."

"No, I'm not, silly."

Her laughter causes me to grin.

"I love you, princess."

"Love you too, Daddy."

My damn heart right about rips open.

We walk around for twenty minutes, seeing the giraffes and the lions next, her excitement growing.

"I want cotton candy. Please, Daddy?"

I glance to my right at the small stand with someone selling premade ones in all various colors.

"We have to grab lunch first."

You're a dad now. Gotta be responsible and put your foot down.

"Aww, but I really want cotton candy."

Oh fuck. Not that sweet tone of voice.

I'm no match for it.

"What color do you want?"

"Pink!"

We head for the stand, just as a man buys two for his sons.

"Pink, please," I tell the elderly woman.

"Sure. That'll be eight dollars." She glances up at Fia as I hand her the cash. "She's precious."

"She is. Thank you."

I pass the cotton candy to Fia, and as we start toward the next exhibit, she's dripping that sugar all over my head.

But I don't care. Because this is exactly where I want to be. With my daughter. Sugar and all.

As we start toward the next exhibit, my phone rings. When I check who's calling, I find Madison's name on the screen. Hopefully she has the info I asked for.

"Yeah?" I answer.

"I have the intel you wanted."

"You have his name?"

"And the birth certificate."

"I'll be there soon."

Amara will finally have the answers she's been looking for.

AMARA

As soon as I get home, I can tell there's something off with Fionn. He's been tense since the moment I walked through the door twenty minutes ago. Fia told me all about her day at the zoo, while he barely even smiled.

What could be the matter?

"Is something wrong?" I whisper as Fia rushes over to play with her dollhouse in the den.

He drags in a long breath. "I found your father."

My insides tremble with panic, heart beating right out of my chest.

"What?" I whisper, my vision growing hazy as I swallow down the thick ball of dread. "Are you sure?"

He nods. "He had a different name when he lived with your mother. It's why it took me a bit longer to find him because he was careful, but it's him."

Why would he do that? Why would he lie?

I chew on the inside of my mouth. I don't know what any of this means, and I don't even know if I'm ready to face him.

What if he doesn't want to know me? What if he tells me to go?

I bury my hands in my hair, squeezing my head like it's going to help me answer my questions.

"Can you show me? Can I see his face?" I squeeze my temple, a headache forming there.

"Let's leave Fia with Louise and head upstairs."

He disappears into the kitchen for a few moments and returns with Louise.

"Mommy and Daddy will be right back, princess," he says to her, taking my hand in his to help me off the sofa.

Louise looks curiously at me, but doesn't ask any questions.

"Okay, Daddy." Fia continues to play as he leads me toward the stairs, while I'm trying to control my unsteady pulse.

He actually found him. He did what he promised, and now I'll have to face my past. Face that dream of a little girl that has consumed me for far too long.

But I know I need to get this over with. I want to know what he found, then I want to see my so-called father and end this.

With every step, my legs grow heavier, like they're held down by an incredible weight.

"It's gonna be okay," he says, but his words don't bring me comfort.

When we enter the bedroom, there's already a manila folder

waiting for me. My gut twists into knots as I step closer, releasing his hand.

"Is that him in there?" My heartbeats thump louder and louder.

"Yeah. His real name is Lloyd Young. Your mother knew him as Timothy Lee."

With quivering fingers, I lift the folder, settling on the edge of the bed. "Do you know why he had two names?"

He sighs, sinking into the spot beside me. Clasping my cheek with his warm, caring hand, he takes a long pause before he shatters whatever was left of my heart.

"He had two families, baby."

My chin trembles, tears pooling. The betrayal hits me hard.

"He was married and had a son when he met your mom and started up with her. Guess he couldn't do it anymore, so he left."

Sniffling, I pinch my eyes shut. We were his throwaway family. We meant nothing.

"Hey, don't do that, baby. Don't cry, because I can't watch it and not do something to fix it."

Staring back at him, I find his features entranced with equal parts anger and anguish.

"I've thought about killing him for this, but I thought I'd give you the chance to meet him first at least." He cracks a smile, and that has me returning a broken one.

"Right now, you killing him doesn't sound so bad." I bite down on the inside of my cheek, trying to temper my rage and sadness—so deep, I don't know how I will climb out. "I want to see him."

"Now?"

I nod. "I won't be able to sleep unless I look him in the eye and ask him how he could do that to me. How he could've just left his other child."

He nods with understanding. "Alright. We can go. It's only a forty-five-minute flight." He picks up my hand and kisses my knuckles.

"But I swear, baby, if he says one wrong thing to you, he won't survive it."

My heart pumps faster and I nod, accepting his conditions. Maybe a good punch in the face would serve the bastard right.

Even though I know for certain a punch is not at all what Fionn meant.

THIRTY-FOUR

AMARA

We arrive by private jet to an airport on the outskirts of Boston, where my father apparently is. I guess it was easier to jump from one family to another when he lived near each one.

My pulse races, my jaw clenched.

I hate him. Hate what he did. Hate that I wondered why he left, missing him even when I never really knew him at all.

And most of all, I hate that I let him do this to me—make me angry. He shouldn't matter, because no good parent worth a damn would ever purposely leave their child.

If he never loved me, why should I even care?

"You ready?" Fionn asks, clasping my hand in his while I stare at the white colonial home.

Floral design and manicured shrubs line both sides of the front yard, the wooden fence and powder-blue shutters making the home even more inviting. So while we lived in the crappiest part of town, in a home that was falling apart, he was living here, enjoying a nice, cushy life.

The more I think about it, the madder I become.

"Let's go," I tell him, opening the car door before he does.

As soon as I step out, my knees buckle. No matter what I tell myself, I'm nervous beyond belief.

"I've got you, baby." Fionn's a blend of strength and kindness that I fully fall into, holding on to his hand as we walk up the driveway, my heart knocking in my rib cage the closer we get. He glances at me. "I'm right here. Not going anywhere."

I nod and he takes it as permission to ring the bell.

Immediately, we both register a set of hard footsteps drawing nearer. My gut churns, shivers spreading down my arms just as the door opens. I expect to see my father; instead, standing before me is a guy not much older than me with brown eyes and even darker auburn hair.

He smiles tentatively, glancing between us. "Can I help you?"

It's in this moment I realize…

This is my brother. Julius.

He's twenty-six. That's what the file Fionn gave me said. His mother is Soraya, and she's been married to my father for over thirty years.

"We're here to see Lloyd." Fionn's clipped tone has him staring at us curiously now.

"What's this about?"

"It's a private matter. Please get your father."

"Uh, okay. Dad!" he calls over his shoulder. "Someone's at the door to see you."

"Well, who the hell is it?"

His mouth thins. "Who are you, exactly? The old man is a bit cranky with strangers."

"Oh, she's not a stranger." A ruthless smirk tugs at Fionn's mouth.

"She's his daughter."

The color instantly drains from Julius's face. "Umm, Dad, you'd better come and talk to these people. *Now*."

A groan echoes before footfalls pound in the distance, mounting nearer.

"What's the meaning of this?" He practically shoves his son out of the way, giving me and Fionn an irritated look. "Who the hell are you two? And what do you want?"

Nausea swirls, rising up my throat. My mouth refuses to move. I'm unable to do anything but stare at the man with a full head of gray hair, his brows sprinkled with a bit of dark strands.

His eyes are hazel like mine, though his are a bit deeper.

"What do you people want?"

I practically shake, every cell in my body trembling. Fionn holds my hand tighter, as though in tune with me.

"May we come in?" he asks.

"No." He gives him an icy once-over. "Tell me why you're here or get lost."

When I peer over at Fionn, his nostrils flare, and I can tell he's barely holding on to his patience.

"Do you remember Desdemona?" he asks.

In an instant, his face turns ashen, every trace of anger turning into absolute fear.

"Who the hell is Desdemona?" A woman appears behind him, glaring at us and her husband. She plants a hand on her hip, moving toward his right. "Well?"

"Uh…honey, it's nothing." His mouth quivers.

"Didn't sound like nothing to me, Lloyd." She flicks her black strands away from her thin brows.

She seems to be around the same age as Mom, though much prettier. Probably because she doesn't do drugs.

A wrinkle deepens between her brows.

"Julius, why don't you take your mom away so I can talk to these people?"

She scoffs. "I'm staying right here, and so is our son." Her eyes zero in on us. "Maybe you two can tell me what the hell is actually going on."

"My mother…" I clear my throat, needing to be the one to say this, while I use Fionn's hand as my strength. "My mother's name is Desdemona, and your husband is my father."

"WHAT?!" She almost trips, lurching back a step. "Is this true?" She balls her hands. "Tell me you didn't get some woman pregnant!"

Julius stares at me—really stares, like he's trying to find a similarity. But I don't really see much.

"How old are you?" he asks.

"Twenty-four."

"Jesus." He slaps a hand over his forehead.

"You son of a bitch!" she roars, smacking my father on the chest over and over. "I knew you were fucking around back then! I just knew, but you denied it."

She continues to hit him while he covers himself with his arms.

"She's lying! I don't know a Desdemona!"

Fionn laughs, a cold, brutal sound. He takes a step closer to him, right past the threshold, his face nearing my father's.

"Not only are you a deadbeat, but you're a fucking liar too." A vein in his neck bulges out. "You left my wife when she was just two. What kind of man are you?"

Lloyd blinks faster, terror filling his gaze. "I…I made a mistake. I never loved her. I—"

Soraya cries, and her son comforts her, giving his father a dirty look.

"What the hell do you want, huh?" There's a tightness in the lines of his forehead, a flush to his skin. "Did you come here to destroy my family? To get back at me?" His disgust for me is so evident in his features, it hurts. "Are you happy now? You got what you came for."

Tears fill my eyes. "I never destroyed your family, *Dad*. You did that all on your own." I shake my head in disgust. "I don't know what I expected from you. Maybe an 'I'm sorry,' but I can see now you're nothing more than a pathetic old man who never quite knew how to be a father."

He releases a short breath of laughter. "Maybe not to you, but I was a damn good father to my boy. Your mother was nothing but a cheap whore who hung on to me for every dime she could, and when I got sick of her—sick of both of you—I stopped playing pretend."

It takes a few seconds to register what happens next.

Fionn's blow hits him straight in the nose, blood spilling, shrieks and chaos ensuing as he hits him again and again, forcing himself further into the house.

"Stop!" Soraya hollers, while Fionn shoves Julius off of him easily.

"Don't do this!" I call out, grabbing him by the shoulder.

As soon as I do, he stops, fist still clasped around Lloyd's shirt. Tears drip down my cheeks as he gazes at me, brows bending with pain.

"Let's just go," I tell him. "There's nothing for me here. Let's go home to our daughter."

At the mention of her, his grip loosens until my father falls to the ground. Fionn hits them each with a grim stare.

"If you breathe a word of this to anyone, and I mean anyone, I will know about it and I'll come back and kill every one of you."

Soraya nods, eyes popping wide, fingers trembling as they shiver across her mouth.

Without giving them any more attention, he takes my hand and leads me back to the car. Their door shuts, but just as we're about to take off, Julius comes running out.

"What the hell does he want?" Fionn mutters, rolling the window down as he appears before it. "What are you doing here?"

"Look." He shakes his head, exhaling sharply. "What my father said to you isn't right. I'm sorry." His attention bounces to Fionn. "No hard feelings about what you did back there. I would've wanted answers too if I were you. Hell, I want them myself. None of this is right."

"No, it isn't." I muster a reply.

He pauses, staring between us like he wants to say something else. "Uh, maybe this is stupid, but would you be interested in getting lunch sometime? I don't know where you live, but maybe you can take my number and we can, I don't know…" He shrugs. "Get to know each other?"

Hope springs. To have a sibling, to have some family, it means something to me.

I glance at Fionn, and I can tell by his intense expression that he doesn't want me to say yes. But I want this. I want to get to know my brother. Just because my father is an asshole, that doesn't mean he is.

"I'd like that. We're in West Sherwood."

"Great." Julius's lips thin. "Take down my number."

"Sure." I grab my cell from my bag, and he shoots off his number. "Got it. Let me go ahead and give you mine too."

He smiles as he retrieves his phone and saves it. "Well, I'll let you guys get going. It was nice to meet you. Geez, I didn't even get your name."

"Amara." I let out a sigh. "Amara Quinn."

Fionn's palm lands warmly on my thigh, like he enjoyed hearing me say that.

"Well, Amara, I look forward to getting to know you. And I'm sorry again."

"It's not your fault."

He nods, releasing a rough exhale. "Anyway, get home safe."

"It was good to meet you, Julius."

He disappears in the rearview as our car pulls down the road.

When we're a safe distance away, I let out a quick breath, reliving the painful minutes of meeting the man I wanted to meet all these years. Instead, he was just as bad as my mother. Just as cold and cruel. No wonder they got together.

Fury boils inside me. How could he treat me like that?

Curling a fist at my side to steady my emotions, I notice Fionn's bloody knuckles. When I see him this way, it's like a reminder of who he is and how he'd do anything to protect me.

And right now, that doesn't scare me as much as it should.

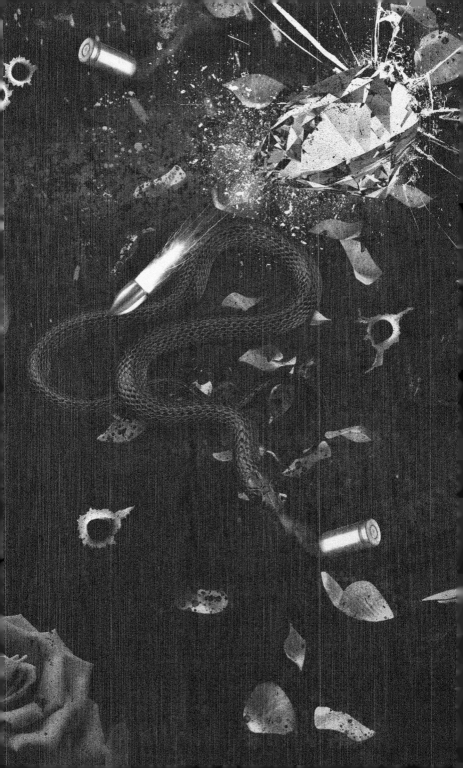

THIRTY-FIVE

FIONN

I've talked myself out of going back to her father's home and ending his life.

The way he spoke to her, the smug look on his face...it was unforgivable. If it wasn't for her, I would've done it.

Though as soon as I heard her voice, it was over. She may think I hold the power, but she's the one who controls me. She can make me do anything.

"I don't think I want you meeting Julius, especially without me." I tell her as she flips the covers on the bed and gets in, my t-shirt climbing up her thighs and exposing a hint of her ass, which I desperately want my hands on.

"I'm not even sure if I will yet. It's all just too much to think about it right now."

"I know." I slip in beside her, rounding an arm beneath her and pulling her face over my chest. Silence greets us as I stare up at the ceiling, my fingers rolling up and down her spine. "I'm gonna take a paternity test."

She jerks back, propping on an elbow, surprise in her gaze.

The realization even surprises me. "It's only because I want to adopt her, and my lawyer said I need to first see if she's my biological daughter."

"Oh. Right." Her brows knit. "I totally didn't think about that. Yeah, that's good." She settles back down.

"I'll have my lawyer come to the house tomorrow and get it done. It's just a cheek swab for her and me."

She nods, and I feel it against me. "No matter what happens between us, she will always be your daughter."

I twist back, fisting her hair, dragging her backward so I can look at her. "What the *fuck* does that mean?" Irritation shoots through my bloodstream. "Nothing will happen between us. Do you need another reminder that you're mine?"

"I didn't mean—"

But I cut her words off in a flash, flipping her beneath me and trapping her as she gives out a little yelp.

"I just meant, you know…" she flusters. "Like in the future, in case things don't work out."

"I swear, little rabbit…" I grasp her jaw, my teeth gnashing. "The more you talk, the more pissed I become, so how about you get those thoughts out of your head?" Grabbing the hem of her shirt, I drag it up, fingertips feathering over her perfect cunt. "Or better yet, how about I help you?"

Her nails sink into my shoulders, a moan escaping as I sink two fingers inside her, slowly dragging them out and repeating it until all that's coming out of her pretty pink lips is my name and those sexy sounds she makes.

"You and I are forever, baby girl." My fingers curl, my movements hard and deep, reminding her that she's mine. "We'll always work out."

Before she can say any more to piss me off, I capture her lips with mine, my other hand wrapping around her throat as I control the pace of this kiss, my tongue slipping into her warmth, her nails scoring my back.

My hips arch between her willing thighs, and it's all I can think about. Need her pleading and begging and tied up.

Would she be willing? Or would she refuse?

There's only one way to find out.

As I drag myself back, she stares at me breathlessly, cheeks flushed, lips pinker and swelled from the brutal kiss.

"Stay right here like a good girl." My knuckles brush over her chin.

"Where are you going?" Her voice is a whispered breath.

"You'll see."

She runs her fingers through my hair, and my eyes instantly close, enjoying the sensation every time she touches me.

Rising to my feet, I head for the closet, reaching up to the top shelf to grab the things I bought the other day. Removing a large black briefcase, I place it on the foot of the bed, watching her watch me as I open it.

She sits up straighter. "What's in there?"

A short laugh escapes as I remove multiple bundles of thick black cotton rope and a bottle of rose oil, and her vision instantly widens.

"What do you do with that?"

Grabbing one bundle, I roll it up her thigh, and a heavy, sensual sigh escapes her.

"Gonna take my time tying you up, then force you to forget everything you just said to me."

Her thighs press into one another, and I know she already likes the idea. She may be nervous, but she's also curious.

"Isn't that dangerous?" Her teeth nip at her bottom lip.

"It can be. If not done right." I remove a pair of shears from my kit, and she sucks in a breath. "These will keep you safe."

"So you're not also planning to use scissors on me?" Relief washes over her face, and I let out a chuckle.

"Shit, babe. You've got a kink I don't know about?"

She titters nervously. "Definitely not that one."

"Not that one? Meaning there are others?"

She shrugs, her cheeks turning crimson.

I definitely plan to have a full discussion about all the things she likes. Just not now.

Removing something else from the briefcase, I place it on the bed, and her lips part.

"What's that thing?"

You'll find out soon enough.

"Don't be scared." Grabbing the scissors, I take her hand. "Stand up."

She doesn't fight it, even while she appears terrified.

With our gazes aligned, I place the shears against the hem of her shirt and start to cut upward. She breathes faster, breasts rising higher, and the more of her body I reveal, the more I want this.

"I won't do anything you don't like."

She nods. "Will it hurt?"

"No. But if something doesn't feel good, all you have to do is use your safe word and it stops."

"Okay." But her features fill with uncertainty.

She shivers as the shirt is split open, her nipples beaded and waiting for my mouth.

Dropping the shears on the bed, I slip off the hair tie she keeps around her wrist. "Turn around for me."

As she does, I wind her hair into a loose bun, my lips dropping to her neck and kissing up to her ear.

My palms glide down her arms before cupping her breasts. "This is about making you feel good."

"Mm-hmm," she groans, head falling backward as I lower my arm to grab the oil, spilling some into my palm. "Shibari isn't just quick and dirty. It's slow and intimate." I work the rose scent over her tits, one hand lowering to her cunt and massaging it as she gasps with low exhales of pleasure. "It involves a lot of touching."

"I can live with that," she breathes while my hands are everywhere, her body glistening before I pick up a bundle of rope.

Spinning her around, I grasp her jaw, kissing her slowly before my eyes slink down her body. "You're beautiful."

She stands there nervously while I untangle the fifteen-foot rope, getting ready to start on my floor work.

"I'm going to tie your arms behind you."

She nods. "I trust you."

"Good girl." The back of my hand feathers down her cheek, and slowly I turn her, placing her arms behind her back.

Winding the rope around her wrists, I form tight knots before bringing the rope back around over her shoulder and twisting it around her body, her breasts on full display. When I turn her fully to me...

"Fuck. You look stunning. How do you feel?"

"A little weird, but good." She laughs nervously, glancing down at herself. "This looks so pretty."

"Let's go to the mirror so you can really see it." Tugging her elbow, I move her toward it, and her gaze flares when she sees herself.

Her tits are pressed between the rope, nipples glistening from the oil. I stand behind her, my thumbs rolling over each tip. When she moans, I pinch one, then the other, until her head falls against my chest. My fingers lower down her hip, slipping between her thighs, where she's already wet.

I enter her slowly as our eyes connect through the mirror, her cheeks flushed as I work her clit until she starts to lose her inhibitions, moaning my name.

Flipping her around, I grab her throat and thrust deeper, fucking her until she's close, her walls clutching me tighter. Right before she's about to come, I throw her onto the bed face-first, ass up in the air. I slap one cheek hard, grabbing the lube from my kit and spilling some into her ass, my fingers working it inside her puckered hole.

"Oh God…"

I stretch her wider with my fingers, enjoying the sensation of her muscles squeezing around me. When I grab the black plug I left on the bed, it vibrates as I turn it on.

Turning her head to the side, she stares at me, tugging on her bottom lip. When it starts to enter her, she gasps.

"You okay?"

She nods, but she doesn't seem sure. Not yet. I push it inside her, seating it all the way deep, rubbing her clit at the same time right before I slip my face under her and lick up her seam.

"Yes!" she cries when I suck her into my mouth, grabbing her hips and forcing her to sit on my face.

My fingers enter her at the same time, my tongue rolling as my mouth sucks her deeper. She cries out with her release, squirting all over my mouth and trying to push off of me, but I only suck her deeper, craving more. Needing her like I need air.

Sliding out from beneath her, I position myself behind her, fisting all that hair. "You don't know how damn sexy you look right now, every inch of you flushed."

"Fionn, that was…" She drags in a shallow breath when I thrust my cock halfway in.

"That was us," I remind her, pounding inside her until all that comes out of her is a silent cry jammed deep in her throat.

With my hand to the back of her neck, I push her into the bed, taking her roughly, unable to hold on to much of my control.

And this time, when her release comes again, it's harder. "Fionn! Yes!"

I ram inside her over and over, like I've lost all sense, until I come too, filling her pussy and marking her as mine. I remain inside her, my cock semi-hard, my palms sliding down to her inner thighs until I grow hard again.

Needing to feel her ass wrapped around me too, I slip out the plug and add more lube, working it around my erection before I go in slow, forcing myself inch by inch.

"Shit," she cries, her muscles shrinking around me.

Fuck she's damn tight.

When she whimpers, I instantly stop.

"You okay?"

"Yes." She nods, brows knitted. "Keep going."

Grabbing her ass cheeks, I spread her wider, pushing deeper, watching myself disappear inside her until she's completely full.

My arm curls around her chest, and I lift her up, my lips dropping to her throat. "You're such a good girl, letting me tie you up and fill your ass like this."

At my words, her muscles clench. She groans when I bite her shoulder, my hips starting to move, slowly at first. My other palm lowers to her pussy, rubbing her with two fingers at the same time. When her body starts to loosen, I work her faster and harder.

"You're mine, Amara. Mine." My teeth sink into her neck, wanting to consume every inch of her. "I won't let you even think about leaving me."

She cries out my name, so close I can feel it.

"Tell me you won't leave me. Need to hear you say it."

My fingers fill her other hole, taking her from both ends as she nods, unable to form words.

"Tell me." My dick throbs.

"I won't leave. I'm yours."

As soon as she says that, I move on autopilot, my desperate savagery winning over as I take her harder with each thrust and release inside her with a deep, possessive growl, needing her to realize that there's no escaping me. No escaping us.

Amara is mine. And there's nothing she can do about it.

THIRTY-SIX

AMARA

When he leaves the house for work, I think about last night.

I've never felt that connected to another person before. The energy between us, like our bodies were feeding off of one another, was something incredible.

Of course, I was nervous at first. Being tied up like that and unable to use my hands was terrifying. But the more he touched me, the more I liked it.

Being in his control was fun.

I lost count after the eighth orgasm, my body incredibly satiated. I fell asleep while he was massaging my body after he took off the ropes. But through the night, I felt his arms around me, keeping me safe even while I dreamed.

"Mommy, look!" Fia rushes over, pulling on my leggings as I finish rinsing the dishes from lunch.

She shows off a new doll Fionn got her. He had it custom made to look just like her, except right now the doll is wearing mismatched pink socks and her hair has seen better days.

"Wow, she's so pretty! But not as pretty as you." I lean in and kiss the top of her head just as Louise enters the kitchen.

"Please don't do that!" She tsks. "It's my job to wash those."

I shake my head with a smile. "I am perfectly fine washing them."

She huffs. "You're not supposed to."

"I won't tell if you don't." My grin stretches.

"Ma'am?" Roy walks in. "The attorney Mr. Quinn sent is here to see you."

"Oh, right." The paternity test. "Come on, Fia. We have to go see someone quick."

"Okay, Mama!" She hops over and takes my hand, and together we make it to the door, following Roy to where a tall man about Tynan's age greets us, holding a briefcase.

As soon as he sees me, his crystal blue eyes glimmer. "I'm Troy Masters." He reaches his hand for mine. "It's a pleasure to meet you, Mrs. Quinn."

"You too."

"Is there somewhere private we can go to?"

"Um…"

Crap, I don't know where to take him. Fionn didn't exactly send instructions.

"Mr. Quinn said his study was fine," Roy volunteers and leads us there, down toward the left-side corridor and the last door on the left.

Fia glances at the man curiously as we enter, and I close the door behind us.

"Hi there." Troy smiles at her. "How old are you?"

"I'm four. How old are you?"

"Definitely not as young as I'd like to be," he laughs. "So, Mr. Quinn told you how this works, right?"

Troy places his briefcase on the cherry oak desk, popping it open and removing a packaged swab.

"Yes, he mentioned it was just a cheek swab."

"That's right. Want to place her on the desk?"

"Of course. Come on, Fia. The nice man is just gonna check your mouth like at the doctor's."

"I'm not sick." She pops a hand on her hip.

"I know, but he's just looking at your throat, to make sure it all looks good just in case."

"Okay. Do I get a lolli?"

"Hmm, let's see." He digs in his briefcase to reveal a chocolate Tootsie Pop.

"Yummy!"

She finally lets me put her on the desk, and not even a minute later, it's over.

Every cell in my body shudders. This is it. This is how I'll finally know who Fia's father truly is.

"I'll inform Mr. Quinn that it was completed."

He starts to walk out as I call out, "When will the results be ready?"

"No more than a few days."

And with that, he disappears out the door and my heart races. Because for a moment, I realize that there's a huge possibility that Fionn isn't her biological father, and I very much want him to be.

JULIUS

Hey, I hope it's okay that I texted. I was just thinking maybe I can buy you lunch one of these days so we can get to know each other. What do you say?

I stare at the text I just got from my half brother, not knowing how to answer him just yet.

I'll definitely need to talk to Fionn about it before I decide if I want to meet with him. He didn't seem all that pleased when Julius gave me his number, and after the way my so-called father acted, I understand why. But at the end of the day, it's going to be my decision.

"Amara? You still there?" Lilith's voice through the cell zaps me back to the conversation.

"Yeah, sorry. Uh, what were you saying?"

"I was just saying that I can't believe your father is such a douche! How could he say all that to you?" she scoffs through the phone.

"I'm sorry, Amara." Emily sighs. "I know how badly you wanted to find him, and to be disappointed like that after all this time…"

"It's fine. I don't care."

But I do care. The hurt, it eats at me.

"Screw him!" Patricia adds. "He doesn't deserve you."

"Whenever Patricia curses, we know she means it." Lilith laughs.

"If he doesn't want to know me, then it's his problem."

"Exactly," Emily adds. "And what about your half brother? Did you get any good vibes off of him?"

"I think so. He actually texted me a bit ago, asking to meet for lunch soon."

"And will you go?"

"I don't know. I haven't talked to Fionn about it yet, but I think I want to." My pulse jumps at the thought. "I've spent so long wondering about my father, and now I have a brother. I kinda want to know more about him and his life."

"Then you should go." Lilith sounds so sure, and it gives me the certainty I was wrestling with.

"So, how's everything else been between you and Fionn?" Emily asks. "Are you happy?"

"What she means to ask is whether he's giving you lots of orgasms, which last time I checked, he was."

My face heats up while Lilith and Emily giggle.

"Trust me, there are no problems there." I bite on my bottom lip, my body warming from thoughts of him and me last night.

"Ooh. Tell us more." Lilith is instantly curious.

"Yes, please let me live vicariously through you." Patricia groans.

She's still yet to find the man of her dreams. There was this one guy, and he broke her heart last year by sleeping with someone from work. She does her best to avoid them, but it's not easy.

"Well, last night…" I whisper as though someone will hear me even though I'm alone, Fia playing with Louise.

"Spill!" Emily utters impatiently.

"He tied me up…with rope."

"Holy…" I don't think I've ever heard Emily sound so shocked in my life.

"Like shibari?" Lilith asks.

I jerk back in confusion. "You've heard of it?"

"Um, of course. Your hubby's a rigger."

"A what?" My brows shoot up.

"Someone who's into using rope like that."

"Oh."

How does she even know this stuff?

"It seems so hot. Was it?" Lilith asks.

"Yes…" My face creeps up with a flush as I recall the way he touched me, taking his time as he tied me up.

"Well, damn! Homeboy is a freak."

"It was scary at first, but I did like it." My body grows hot at the admission.

"Good for you." I can hear a smile in Emily's voice. "After the loser who shall remain nameless, you needed a good bang."

At the mention of Xander, my pulse thunders.

He's dead. He's actually gone, and Fionn is the one who killed him.

My stomach tightens.

"We really all need to plan a day to meet," Emily adds. "I haven't seen you in too long."

"Yeah, we do. Maybe this weekend?"

"Sure!"

"I have nothing to do," Patricia throws in.

"Same," Lilith says.

"Perfect. I'll see if Fionn can arrange for me to go to Boston."

"We don't mind coming to you," Emily volunteers. "I kinda wanna see the house."

"Okay, let's do it!"

At the thought of seeing them, I grow excited. I miss my friends.

THIRTY-SEVEN

FIONN

On the way home from work the following evening, I send Amara a text, almost home for our date. I'm looking forward to having a night out together.

FIONN

Are you ready to go, baby girl?

AMARA

I am. You still won't tell me where we're going?

A smile stretches on my face.

FIONN

You did tell me you love surprises.

She starts to write, but pauses.

AMARA

I do. I can't wait. Are you almost home?

FIONN

Pulling up now.

As soon as I do, I see her in a beautiful cobalt-blue silk gown, her hair and makeup done. Everything was arranged for her before I left this morning. I want her to always feel like a queen.

She stares at me with a glint in her eyes, the same glint I saw a peek of the day we met. But now it seems like her happiness is more prevalent. And I like that—knowing I make her happy.

Roy starts to help her down the stairs, but I cut him with a glare as I get out, and he immediately stops. He knows better than to touch what's mine.

I'm beside her in a flash, taking her hand in mine and kissing the top of it as my ravenous gaze slinks up her beautiful body, unable to fight the urge to feast on it.

I clasp her jaw, my lips dropping to her ear. "You look incredible. Unsure if I can resist fucking you before we get there."

"Get where?" she whispers, her slinky tone making me rock-hard already.

I let out a deep chuckle, eyes flashing with desire. "Trying to get information out of a desperate man?"

"Did it work?"

I shake my head, a smirk tipping up one side. "I've been under much more intense interrogations, mo ban dia."

"Then I guess I'll have to try harder." She wraps an arm around my back, the other sneaking between us and wrapping around my dick.

Hissing, I bite her bottom lip, needing to punish this temptress she's apparently become. "You keep touching me like this, wife, and I'll fuck you bent over the car for all of them to see."

I kiss her slowly, sensually, and she groans under her breath.

"That would be bad."

"It would." I lick across the seam of her mouth. "Especially because then I'd have to kill them for it."

"You have quite the fondness for murder."

"If you think that's bad, you'd be scared of my fondness for you." Sliding my hand to the back of her head, her hair splayed through my fingers, I capture her lips, kissing her with maddening fury.

As I reluctantly pull back, my forehead drops over hers. "We should probably go before we never leave."

"Probably." She kisses me again, and I let out a growl, tugging her head back.

"Behave."

I like this side of her. Want more of it.

"I'll try." Her cheeks are flushed, pink lipstick ruined, but it doesn't look as though she cares.

Taking her hand, I lead her all the way down the rest of the way, helping her into the SUV while saying a silent prayer that I don't get tempted to rip her dress to shreds before we've even had our night out. I mutter a curse as I readjust myself in my slacks before coming around to the driver's side. Getting in, I take us on the road. Her leg bounces, her shy glances making me want to kiss the holy hell out of her. My palm drops to the top of her leg, wanting to touch her any way I can.

She clears her throat. "So, I was thinking of signing Fia up for preschool, maybe three days a week."

Making a right, I look over at her before my eyes return to the road. "That's a good idea. Adora is in one. We can send her there."

"Oh, that would be a lot of fun for her. I think she's already decided Adora is her BFF."

"They're family. No one is closer to us than that."

Her face goes downcast. Fuck. She's probably thinking about that piece-of-shit father of hers, and I use that term loosely.

"Hey, my family is your family now. You know that, right?"

Her tear-filled eyes land on mine as she nods. "I love your family."

Love.

Until this moment, I didn't realize how much I wanted to hear her tell me she loves me too.

"They love you too, babe."

"Speaking of my family…" Her voice lowers, and my pulse kicks up, unsure if I'm gonna like where this is going. She clears her throat. "So, Julius texted me yesterday wanting to grab lunch, and I want to go."

I consider it. I could say no, but that would make me a shit husband, and I really don't wanna be a shit husband. But I don't like that family. I don't care how nice her brother was. Though I know how much she wants to connect to the only family she has. I can't get in her way.

"Okay."

"Really?" Surprise marks her features.

"Yeah. I can fly you there, but I'll be coming with you."

"Of course." She lowers a palm to my bicep. "I want you with me."

When she smiles big and bright, I know I made the right decision.

"Also…" she adds. "I was talking to my friends today, and they want to come over this weekend. Would that be okay?"

"Of course. It's a good idea. I think it's time I met Emily anyway. Don't you?" I let out a laugh.

She grabs my hand and drops her head on my shoulder. "Thank you."

Kissing the top of her head, I squeeze her thigh tighter. "Anything for you, baby."

AMARA

An hour later, we arrive at a trendy steakhouse restaurant, lights dimmed as he takes me up the steps and ushers me inside.

"We're heading to the rooftop," he tells me as a maître d' shows us to an elevator.

As I look around the main floor, I find it empty.

"Where is everyone?" I whisper just as we get in.

"There's no one here but us, little rabbit. I rented it out."

My eyes expand. "Wow. That's sweet."

And expensive.

His fingers squeeze mine as we enter the elevator for a quick ride before we're walking into the upper level of the restaurant. A single round table with a black tablecloth and small votive candles in the center greets us. The overhead canopy is covered in mood lighting, changing between blue, pink, and deep purple.

When a chill crawls up my skin, he shakes off his jacket. "Put this on, baby."

He holds it out as I slip my arms through the sleeves, his expensive woodsy cologne hitting my nostrils. It's like my own canopy of heaven.

He pulls the chair for me, and once I'm seated, he drags his beside me, his leg touching mine. "Did I tell you how beautiful you look already?"

"Maybe." My cheeks hurt from how big I smile, his eyes dancing to my lips with a warm current, making my belly flop.

"I can't seem to stop." The back of his hand strokes my jaw, and my heart lurches, rendering me unable to look away.

A waitress clears her throat, but he doesn't pay her any mind, his attention cemented on me.

"May I get you two something to drink?"

"Bourbon neat for me. And rosé for her. For dinner, we will have all of the chef's specials."

"Coming right up." She places two waters on the table and disappears.

I'm glad for it, wanting us to be alone with his hands on me, those eyes swimming with want and affection.

"The food here is amazing…" His voice grows huskier, his free hand slinking up my thigh, taking the dress with it.

"I don't care what we eat," I whisper, my heart racing uncontrollably as I wonder what he'll do next.

"Neither do I." He drops his lips to my throat, groaning as he kisses me there. "Because nothing tastes better than you."

Before I can reply, he drives two fingers inside me, working me deeper as I fight not to cry out in absolute mind-bending pleasure.

"There you go." The waitress appears, and when I try to move his hand, he doesn't let me, keeping it where it is.

She places our drinks on the table while he thrusts deeper.

"If I can get you guys anything else, please just let me know."

Thrust.

"The food will be here shortly."

Thrust.

"Oh God," I grit, accidently hitting the table with my fist.

"What?" She stares at me, unable to see what my husband is currently doing to me under the table.

"She's just looking forward to eating. Aren't you, baby? Such a hungry little thing."

Thrust.

"Mm-hmm." I nod, my legs quivering.

"Oh, you're going to love everything here."

He chuckles, staring right at me while his thumb works my clit faster. "She's not wrong. So damn delicious."

She smiles politely, strutting away.

That's when I let out a small moan before he assaults me with a faster rhythm, jaw gritted, a muscle in his neck popping as he watches me intently.

"You're so damn wet, you're gonna dirty this dress."

"Oh God!"

I hadn't thought about it, but the fear lasts only a second, because with a flick of his thumb, I'm soaring. As a cry slips out, he seals his mouth with mine and swallows my sounds of pleasure, fingers stretching and pistoning deeper, until another orgasm crests. And once again, he's sending me flying so high, my body fills with euphoria.

When the release ebbs and flows through my veins, he finally slows, sliding his fingers out of me and slipping them into his mouth to suck them dry.

"I was right. Mouthwatering." He fists my hair, eyes tense while I glance down at his erection, wanting to do what he did to me.

I want to make him come. My heart races, but before I lose my patience, I pull the chair back, and he releases his hold on me. His brows draw together, and the shock on his face when I lower to my knees under the table and start undoing his buckle has me smirking.

"Baby, you don't—fuuck." His head falls back when I slide my hand into his pants and grab the crown of his erection, feeling his cold piercings against my skin.

The idea of being caught only excites me. I hide beneath the tablecloth, taking out his cock and stroking it while his palm slips under and pushes my head down.

"Suck me, wife."

At his heated words, I drop my mouth and take the tip, registering his low curses as I suck more of his velvety hard flesh. My fingers curl around the base while I use the other hand to touch his ripped abs through his dress shirt.

"Jesus, Amara. Fuck, I'm gonna fill that dirty mouth of yours and watch you swallow it all."

When I moan around him, he releases a growl, pushing my head down and forcing me to gag.

"Here you are, sir." The waitress returns, and my pulse jumps.

For a moment, I freeze, but he keeps his palm splayed over the back of my head, and I can't help but gag again. When she hears a noise, she clears her throat.

Oh my God, she knows. She has to.

But I continue sucking him deeper, unable to stop. The possibility of her knowing only makes this that much more thrilling.

"Thank you," he mutters, groaning under his breath. "Go. Now."

The next thing I hear is her quick footsteps, growing further away.

"Shit, baby, that's it. Take all of me."

I suck him all the way down. When another animalistic growl edges out of him, it gives me more courage.

"Good girl, sucking me so good."

Twirling my tongue around his crown, I hollow my cheeks, tightening my lips while he winds my hair around his wrist. His movements turn savage, controlling the hurried pace, the sounds coming out of him completely unhinged. And the next thing I know is he's holding me hostage around his cock, shooting down my throat.

"Fuck, that's it. Take every drop."

And I do. I taste him and want more.

My God, I want this man. I've never felt anything like this before. Never will with anyone else.

Because Fionn Quinn is mine, and I am his. And no matter how badly I try to deny it, he's everything I've always wanted.

THIRTY-EIGHT

AMARA

"I can't believe you live here!" Emily gushes as the girls stare around the foyer three days later, after flying here on the private jet Fionn owns.

He insisted on flying them over instead of making them drive.

"Hi!" Fia rushes over with Louise, grinning with chocolate stains on her chin.

"Oh my gosh!" Emily runs over and picks my daughter up, staring at her like she hung the moon. "How did you get so big?"

"I eat lots of chicken! Daddy said it makes me strong!" She flexes a muscle, and Fionn's mouth curls.

Every one of the girls stares at him, and I swear I get a little jealous.

"He's so hot," Lilith whispers in my ear.

That doesn't help the situation, but I know the girls would never do anything like that. I'm just being stupid.

"You really have a beautiful home." Patricia smiles.

"It's our home now." He curls his arm around me and kisses my temple. "Isn't that right, baby?"

The "awws" echo while my face heats up.

"Yes." Warmth cruises down my limbs.

And when I look over at my best friend, emotions riddling her features, I know she's thinking the same thing I am: that after all this time, I've found someone who cares for me like I've always deserved.

"Are you sure you're okay with her by yourself?" I ask Fionn, who places Fia on top of his shoulders.

She giggles from up there, and my heart swells. I love seeing them together.

"I promise we won't feed any gorillas today."

The girls look questioningly between us.

"I wanna feed gorillas again!" she says.

Apparently, the time they went to the zoo, he took her to meet one and she fed him. Gave me quite the heart attack when I found out, but I know he'd never do anything to harm her.

"Not today, princess. We have to be good for Mommy."

I grin. "Well, you guys have fun doing, uh…whatever it is you'll be doing."

He peers up at our girl, giving her a little wink and making her giggle.

"Go. We'll be fine."

He slips his hand in his pocket and opens his wallet, handing me a credit card.

"You forgot this." He smirks, dangling a black card with my name on it, one that's connected to his account.

"Oh, right." My pulse races.

When he handed me the card on the first day of school, I was taken aback. I've never had a credit card before.

"Please treat all your friends. And as I said before, there's no limit."

"Wait. Like, no limit at all?" Lilith whispers behind me.

He chuckles. "That's right."

His eyes burn into mine, and as they do, I'm overwrought with emotions. I'm not used to having all this. Even going to dinner with friends used to be painful, but now I can breathe a little easier, not worrying about how I'll pay the bills. So many people take that for granted—just surviving—but I know I never will.

Throwing my arms over his shoulders, I whisper, "Thank you."

An inhale swells in his chest, and his mouth drops to my forehead. "Never have to thank me for treating you like a queen. Because that's what you are."

His gaze grows heavy-lidded, a thumb tracing my lips before he lowers his mouth to my ear. "Better go before I decide to keep you all to myself." His jaw tightens. "Have fun, ladies. Roy will be with you at all times."

At that, they glance behind them, finding my bodyguard ready to take us to an Italian restaurant in town.

"Bye, Mama!" Fia waves. "I love you."

"Me too." I reach up to kiss her, and he lowers her into his arms.

"Bye, pretty girl!" Emily waves and the other girls follow suit.

"Be good for Daddy, okay?" I tell her.

"Daddy promised me ten s'mores if I eat dinner."

"Did he now?" I quirk a brow, fighting a laugh. "She's all yours if she's too high on sugar tonight."

He grimaces. "Alright, princess. I think we're sticking to five."

"Okay, Daddy."

He gives me a smug look, and my stomach flips.

I instantly wanna kiss him. So I do. I clasp his strong jaw and lean real close, rising on my toes and smashing his lips to mine, forgetting why being the wife of a man who belongs in a world more dangerous than I've ever known is wrong.

And in its place there's hope. Hope for the future. Hope for a family of my own. Hope for something much bigger than I ever dreamed was possible.

Because with him, those dreams seem like a reality.

ONE WEEK LATER

The girls haven't been able to get over how amazing Fionn was that day. They've been gushing about him nonstop. Emily even said how much she adores how well he treats me and fully approves of this marriage now. Not that I needed her approval, but it's still nice to have it.

My stomach turns to knots as we near the restaurant where I'm supposed to be meeting Julius.

After I spoke to Fionn about it, I told Julius I was happy to grab lunch. But with every day, I've gotten more nervous. What if he hates me once he gets to know me? What if his parents find out and stop him from seeing me anymore?

My chest grows tight. I need to stop thinking negatively. It'll be fine.

"You okay?" Fionn squeezes my thigh as he eases the car into the parking lot of the restaurant, and my pulse quickens.

"I don't know. I'm just nervous, I guess. He's the child my father wanted, and I was nothing."

He grabs my jaw and grits his teeth, his irises darkening. "Don't ever call yourself nothing again. Because you're far from nothing, mo ban dia. You're *everything*." His gaze lands on my lips before it crawls back to my eyes. "Your father doesn't matter. What he did or didn't do doesn't define you or your worth. You understand?"

I nod, a knot forming in my throat. He's right. I know he is. It'll just take me some time to get over all of this. But one good thing did come out of it: I haven't had the dream since I came face-to-face with the man who abandoned me.

"Thank you." I grab his wide wrist. "I appreciate that."

"Just telling the truth." He cups both sides of my face and kisses my forehead, and my budding affection for him grows.

"Okay, let's go. I think I'm ready." But the fluttering in the pit of my stomach says otherwise.

He steps out of the car first, coming around to open the door for me before I can do it myself. "I'll be near at all times."

When he helps me up, his gaze drifts down to my tight jeans and simple light pink t-shirt with flats. I don't look like anything special, but from the way he stares at me, it's as though I am.

As I take a deep breath, we start for the entrance and are immediately led toward the back, where Julius is already seated, typing something on his phone. When he looks up, his smile expands.

"Will you also be joining us?" he asks Fionn, getting to his feet and shaking his hand before giving me a hug.

"No. I'll be at the table right there." Fionn points to the one to the left of us.

"You're more than welcome to join us."

Fionn shakes his head and turns to me, grabbing the back of my neck and giving me a quick kiss.

"If you wanna leave at any time…" he whispers across the shell of my ear. "Just scratch your right temple."

I nod, and he lets me go and struts toward his table, his eyes on us as he settles. Clearing my throat, I take my seat from across Julius.

"Thank you for agreeing to speak to me," he says. "I know this must not be easy for you."

"It isn't." I pick up my ice water, taking a few sips. "But I'm sure you feel the same way."

"Yeah." He runs a hand down his face, blowing a breath. "I never believed my mother when she thought he was cheating. I took his side, and I feel guilty about it now." His chest rises and falls with another quick breath. "I'm sorry about how he treated you. I let him have it the next day. It wasn't right."

I can tell from his tight expression that he means it. And why wouldn't he? The man was a complete asshole.

"Thank you. It's all crazy to me. I've spent all this time wondering about him, and he had this whole other family. No offense." I grimace, afraid it came out wrong.

He lets out a short laugh. "None taken. I get it. You were alone while I had him."

"Yeah... Was he a good dad?"

I know I probably shouldn't ask because if he was, that will just sting more. Not that I want Julius to have had a bad childhood or anything.

My God, these thoughts are just so hard to wrestle through.

"He—"

"May I get you two anything to drink?" A waitress interrupts.

"A Coke for me," he says.

"An unsweetened iced tea, please."

"Sure. Coming right up."

Julius glances at me, then down at the table before he speaks again. "To be honest, he was for the most part. I'm sorry if that's hard to hear, but I would hate to lie."

"No, no! Please don't. I want the truth."

He nods with understanding, but there's no way he can ever understand.

"Until the day you walked up to our door, I had never so much as heard him yell. Now, my mother...well, she's a different story." He scoffs. "I've spent my life hearing her tell me I'm not good enough. That I was ungrateful for everything I had."

"Seems like we have that in common."

The waitress places the drinks on our table, and we quickly give our orders before we resume the conversation.

"So your mom was like that too, huh?"

"Yeah. It was just me and her, and she made it her mission to make me feel like dirt every time she could. Didn't help that she had an addiction to cocaine and refused to work, so it was up to me to pay for the bills and keep us alive."

"Shit." His brows shoot up. "I'm sorry."

I twist my mouth. "It is what it is, but I'm free of her now, thankfully."

"Well, now I feel bad complaining about my own mother." He chuckles dryly. "Because at least she paid the bills."

I burst with a laugh, feeling a little lighter. Soon enough, we're discussing his grad school and how I got a B on a paper in poli-sci that I need to discuss with the professor. Julius seems genuinely interested in my life, and I really like him.

"I would love to meet your daughter whenever you feel comfortable with that. She sounds really adorable."

"She's everything to me."

At that, I look over at Fionn, his eyes glued to mine.

You okay? he mouths, and I nod.

"I'm really glad we connected," Julius says.

"Me too. I was so nervous." I scowl. "But I'm glad I didn't chicken out."

"Nervous of me?" He snickers, running a hand through his brown hair. "I'm literally the most unintimidating person you'll ever meet."

He isn't wrong. He has one of those really friendly faces with kind eyes.

As he takes another bite of his veal, his phone rings on the table. When he stares down at it, he grinds his jaw.

"You okay?"

"It's just my mother calling. I'm gonna ignore it." He presses a button. "So, anyway, when are you going to speak to your professor about your B? Even though I think a B is fine. But I get it." He grins. "My sister's ambitious."

Sister.

That sounds so strange.

"I definitely plan to—"

The phone rings again, interrupting us.

He groans. "I'm just gonna answer it, or she'll keep calling."

"Sure, go ahead."

"What's up, Mom?" He pinches the bridge of his nose. He pauses, shaking his head and glancing at me. "Yes, I'm still here."

Another pause, and from the way he's watching me, I would bet anything she's mad that he's here.

"Just stop, okay? Enough. I don't care about all that." He blows a breath, staring at the ceiling. "That's right. That's not my business. I'm doing this for me." He grips the back of his head. "I'm going, Mom. I'll see you later."

He hangs up and places the cell back on the table.

"That seemed intense. Was it about me?"

He stares with uncertainty, but as soon as he lets out a ragged sigh, I know I'm right.

"I don't care what she thinks. Her problem is really with my father, not you. So don't worry about it."

But I can't help but feel bad. "I don't want to cause problems for you. I can sympathize with how she must be feeling, to know her husband not only cheated, but had a child with another woman."

He exhales sharply. "It's a damn mess, but anyway, about your grade. Is your professor an a-hole, or you think he'd be understanding?"

Picking up my iced tea, I take a few big sips. "I think so. I plan to meet with him tomorrow. Hopefully he tells me what I need to do to improve on the next paper."

"Let me know how it goes."

"I will. Thanks."

The rest of the lunch continues uninterrupted, and soon, we're saying our goodbyes.

Julius clasps Fionn's hand before turning to me. "Thanks again for coming. I really enjoyed getting to know you and hope we can do it again."

"Yeah, definitely. Me too." I go to give him a hug, and Fionn practically shakes with intensity, like he hates the idea of even my half brother touching me.

I fight a laugh. It's kinda cute how jealous he is.

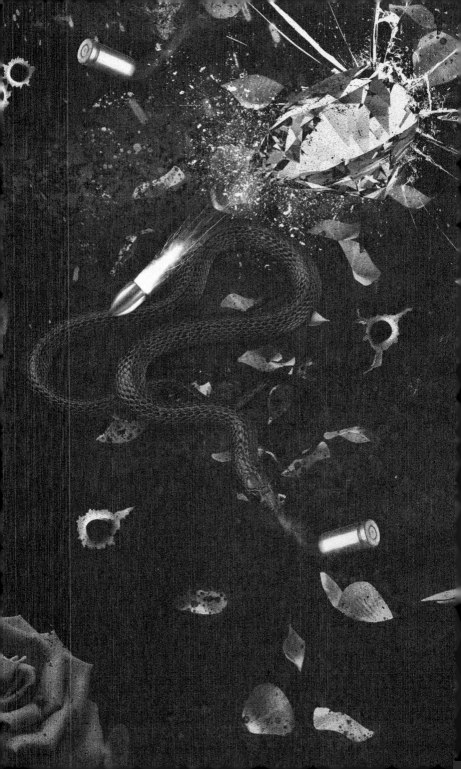

THIRTY-NINE

AMARA

"**C**ome in, Ms. Quinn."

I register the professor's voice before I push the door open. He looks up from his desk as soon as I walk in, jerking his glasses up his nose.

"Thank you for seeing me, Doctor Wright."

He laughs. "You don't have to be so formal here. Mr. Wright or Samuel is fine."

"Oh. Uh, okay." I nervously slip my hair behind my ear, clutching my backpack as I step closer.

"Please have a seat." He extends a hand toward one of the leather chairs before his desk.

His dark eyes narrow as he assesses me, and I grow uncomfortable at the attention, though I know it's innocent.

"Thank you." Clearing my throat, I settle down, swinging my backpack onto my knees before unzipping it and removing my paper.

"So, your grade." He leans back into his chair. "I thought you did well. But not A material. Not yet, anyway." He smirks.

Ouch.

"I'd like to improve, and I'd very much like to know where you felt I needed to do that."

"Well, your arguments about the challenges of balancing individual rights and public safety in policy-making needed to be strengthened with better evidence."

"Oh, I see." I skim the sections he's referencing. "Anything else you felt wasn't done well?"

"I think if you improve your arguments and bolster them up for the next paper, you should be fine. You're a great student. I see a lot of potential in you."

A grin stretches on my face. "Thank you."

"What do you want to do after you graduate?"

"I hope to become a paralegal."

He quirks a brow. "Ah. Really?"

"That's right."

"Well, my wife owns her own law firm. I can put in a good word for you, especially if you continue to do well in my class." The corner of his mouth winds up.

"Thank you. That would be amazing."

It feels like all of my dreams are finally coming true.

"Well, thanks for stopping by, but I do have another student coming in shortly, so unless there's something else…"

"Oh, right. Of course."

I stuff my paper back into a folder and get to my feet, and he follows close behind.

Too close. I can practically feel his body at my back. My stomach gets jittery and a cold rush skitters up my arms, leaving goose bumps behind.

He reaches for the doorknob, and as he does, his other hand brushes over my behind.

My eyes widen. That must've been an accident. It had to be. He's my professor. He's married.

I'm married.

Disgust fills my chest.

When I glance back, there's no indication that he did that on purpose. It was an accident. Of course it was. Obviously, I was overreacting.

"It was great to see you, Ms. Quinn."

"It's Mrs."

"Right. How could I forget?" He laughs. "See you in class."

Rushing out, I stare at the now-closed door, wondering what the hell just happened.

FIONN

"Daddy!" Fia rushes for me when I pick her up from preschool.

Tynan grabs Adora, and we start toward our cars.

"How was your day, princess?"

"Good!" she tells me, excitement rolling in her eyes.

Adora clutches her father's shirt, her face on his shoulder.

"You okay, baby?" he asks her.

When she peers back at him, she pouts. "A boy pushed me."

Tynan instantly freezes, murder in his eyes. "What boy? What's his name?"

His breathing fires out, and I don't blame him because I'd see murder too if someone touched my girl.

"Arthur. He's mean," Fia volunteers.

"Is that so?" he asks.

Adora nods, her bottom lip puckering.

"If he ever touches you again, you push him harder, okay, baby? You don't let anyone do that to you."

"Don't worry, Uncle Tynan. I pushed him back." Fia grins.

"That's my girl," I whisper in her ear, and she curls her arms tightly around my neck.

"I swear, I'm not ready for this." Tynan sighs.

"Tell me about it. I don't know what the hell I'm gonna do when some asshole…" I whisper. "…breaks her heart."

"We'll break his." A short laugh escapes. "Permanently."

"Sounds about right."

"Oh, I forgot to tell you…" He opens the back door of his SUV and places Adora inside, strapping her in while glancing over. "I need you to fly to New York City to meet some new investors for that property we were talking about buying in SoHo."

"When?"

I hate leaving my girls, but work is work.

"Tomorrow. I'll message you the details once I confirm with them."

"Sure."

"So, how's Amara dealing with her new family?" He shuts the door and makes it around to the driver's side.

"As well as she can. But I regret not killing that father of hers after the way he spoke to her. It fucking eats at me."

He clasps a palm on my shoulder, staring straight at me. "If you did, you might have lost her. I think you did the right thing. Though no one says his car can't hit a tree two months from now." His mouth jerks.

"You're right. Those trees, they really come out of nowhere."

He chuckles, getting inside his car. "Now you're thinking, brother."

As soon as Amara got home from school, I knew there was something wrong. She tried to hide it when she greeted me, but her body was tense. I could feel it when I held her.

As Fia eats her pretzels in the kitchen, I walk up to her while she pours our daughter some orange juice.

"Come here," I tell her.

She places the carton down, swallowing nervously while biting the corner of her lower lip.

I tilt up her chin with a finger, searching those beautiful eyes. "Is everything okay?"

"What?" Her gaze bounces to me. "Oh, yeah. Sorry, just thinking about all the work I have to do. I have a test in bio next week, then a quiz in my business class the following day." She smiles uncomfortably.

"You're smart. You'll do great."

"Thanks."

I know she's lying, but I'm not gonna interrogate her. I'll find out what happened on my own.

"How did the meeting with your professor go?"

Did he fucking do something? Just say the word, baby.

"Oh! Yeah, um, it went well." She scratches her temple.

It's him, isn't it?

There's no way she's cheating on me. She's not like that. But I don't know Samuel Wright well enough to know whether he'd cross the line with a student.

I will find out, though. Because unfortunately for him, he now has my undivided attention.

"You know you can tell me anything, right?"

She releases an uneasy laugh, trying to draw my hand away from her chin, but I keep it planted.

"Of course I do. I'm just under a lot of pressure. College is definitely harder than I thought it would be."

I nod slowly, releasing her, inhaling long and deep.

"Mommy," Fia calls.

I've never seen her jump to our daughter that quickly, like she's relieved we're done talking.

"Yes, baby?" Her voice gets all high.

"I want more orange juice, please?"

"Sure, honey."

While she hands Fia the cup she poured, I text Roy.

FIONN

Did anything happen at her school today?

ROY

No, sir.

FIONN

She didn't act strange at any part of the day?

A few seconds pass before he's texting back.

ROY

She had that meeting with the professor, and after that, she was a little quiet. I just thought it was because of the paper. Did I fuck up?

I'm gonna kill that fucking professor.

FIONN

No. Keep your eye on her tomorrow. Let me know if you see him around her.

ROY

Of course, sir.

I slip the phone back into my pocket.

By tomorrow, I'm going to know everything there is to know about her teacher. More than he even knows about himself.

FORTY

FIONN

Slinging a duffle over my shoulder, I head for the door. Amara is holding Fia in her arms.

"Bye, Daddy. I'll miss you."

"I'll miss you more, princess." I clasp the back of her head and kiss her on both cheeks, my damn heart ready to explode.

I'm seriously having second thoughts about leaving for this damn meeting with the investors. I'd rather be here.

I cup Amara's cheek and kiss her, groaning when her tongue twirls with mine. My forehead meets hers, and I inhale her floral scent, needing to get lost in it again like I did earlier this morning.

"I shouldn't be gone more than a day. I'll have the meeting with the investors tonight, then fly back tomorrow."

"Okay." She coughs, clearing her throat.

"Are you sick?" Inspecting her intensely, I start to lower the duffle to the floor. "I can tell Tynan we need to reschedule."

"Fionn." She laughs. "It's just a scratch in my throat. That happens, you know. You don't have to cancel plans for that, especially for work."

"You don't understand, do you?" I clasp her jaw and kiss her hard. "You and Fia are most important to me. Everything else doesn't matter. Not even work."

Her eyes glisten with unshed tears. "I know that."

"Glad we settled that." I smirk.

As soon as I met Amara all those years back, I knew there was never going to be anyone else for me, and nothing has changed since. And with each passing day, I find it harder not to tell her that I may just be falling in love with her all over again.

Once there's a break during the meeting, I call the girls to check on them, but Amara doesn't answer. I try her again, wondering where she is. It's only around dinnertime; they wouldn't be asleep yet.

When she doesn't answer the third time, I call Roy.

"Sir."

"Is everything okay with Amara? She hasn't answered my calls."

"She's been upstairs, sir. Louise is with her. Should I get her on the phone?"

Why would Louise be with her? Something isn't sitting well.

"Get Louise on the phone."

"Of course."

A few seconds later, her voice comes on the line. "Hi, sir."

"What's wrong with her?"

She blows a breath.

I fucking knew it.

"She didn't want me to tell you, but now I'm starting to worry."

My pulse quickens.

"What the hell is going on?" I try to keep my composure, pacing in the hallway like I've gone insane, imagining what could possibly be wrong.

"She's ill. Coughing badly and throwing up."

Fuck. FUCK!

I had a feeling she was getting sick. But this sounds way worse than just a cold.

"I'm on my way home."

"Okay. I'll tell her."

"No, don't." I glance over as Gavin, one of the investors, approaches. "I don't want her upset that she somehow ruined my meeting."

"Okay, sir. We'll see you soon."

"If she spikes a fever, call our doctor. I'll be home in a few hours."

As I slip the phone into my pocket, Gavin grins.

"Leaving already? I hope we weren't boring you."

"No, nothing like that. And please extend my apologies to the others, but I've had an emergency at home that needs my attention. I hope we can reschedule this."

He adjusts his tie, looking smugly at me. "Well, I'm sure we can come up with another date, though it's not a guarantee."

I know what he's trying to say: either stay or we won't see their money. Right now, I don't give a shit.

"I understand. But sometimes family is more important. Good day, Gavin."

I don't give him another look as I hurry out of there, going to where I'm needed most.

AMARA

My lungs ache, and I keep coughing and throwing up. I don't know why.

Louise called the family's doctor, who should be arriving soon.

Hopefully he gives me some strong meds.

"Try to eat a few more spoonfuls of the chicken noodle soup." She's babying me, and I hate being babied, but I'm too weak and too cold to fight it, huddled under a fluffy comforter.

"Okay."

I sit up as she feeds me. As soon as nausea hits, I try to fight it.

"This is terrible. You may have the flu, honey."

"That's what it feels like."

She places a hand on my forehead. "I think you may be starting to get a fever. I'm gonna get you some more meds."

"Where is she?!"

I gasp when his voice booms in the distance, footfalls thundering up the stairs.

"You called him?" I stare at Louise just as he rushes in, his jaw tight, looking crazed.

But as soon as he sees me, his face falls. "Fuck, baby, you look like shit."

A laugh falls out of me, but then a cough catches in my throat.

He gives Louise a tense stare. "You call me next time, no matter what she says."

"Yes, sir." Her shoulders sag.

"And you…" He settles on the bed beside me, the back of his hand stroking my cheek. "If you weren't so damn sick, I'd be angry at you for keeping this from me. I knew as soon as I left the house that I should've stayed."

I grab his wrist. "This was important. I didn't want you to miss it."

"Fuck, Amara. Do you not understand how important *you* are to me?" He clasps my cheek, lowering his forehead to mine.

"Don't do that!" I try to push him back, but he doesn't budge. "You're gonna get sick."

"I don't care. I've missed you."

"I missed you too," I whisper.

He groans, clasping both sides of my face. "I think that's the first time you've ever said you missed me."

Was it?

"Where the hell is the doctor?" He backs away, blowing a heavy breath while retrieving his cell and staring down at it. "He'll be here in five minutes."

"I'm okay," I try to reassure him, placing a hand on his bouncing knee, but it doesn't stop it from shaking.

"You don't look okay, so don't bullshit me."

Just then, someone knocks on the door. Roy walks in with a tall, lanky man who's holding a brown leather briefcase.

"Took you long enough," Fionn clips out.

"I'm sorry, sir. There was some traffic."

"Get to it."

The doctor's thick brows jerk as he clears his throat. "May I ask you to sit, Mrs. Quinn, or do you feel lightheaded?"

"I'm okay to sit up."

Thankfully, the nausea has subsided, so that's promising.

He asks me about my symptoms and how they began, then swabs my nose and throat before handing me a cup for the urine sample. I don't even bother asking why, because all I want is to be back in bed.

Fionn hooks his arm through mine and leads me to the master bath, and as soon as I try to separate so I can go inside, he doesn't let me.

"What are you doing?" My face pales.

There's no way he's going in with me.

"Making sure you don't collapse on the floor."

I would try to look as shocked as I feel, but I don't think I can move much. "Fionn, I can't do that in front of you."

"We're married, little rabbit. There's nothing to be shy about." He leads me inside and shuts the door. "I'll turn around if that helps."

"Got any earplugs?"

He laughs while my face contorts, and my teeth clack when a chill wafts through my limbs.

Screw it. I don't even care right now. Just need to be under my blanket again.

"Okay, fine, turn around."

He does immediately while I quickly use the cup. Once I'm done, I leave it in the bathroom as the doc instructed.

Washing my hands, I dry them before we return to the bed. I breathe a sigh once I'm able to sit down, Louise bundling the comforter around my body.

"Alright, while I wait for the flu and COVID results, I'm going to check the urine sample."

Fabulous. The last time I went to the doctor, I was told I was pregnant. I can't even remember when my last cycle was.

Crap.

"Do you need anything to eat?" Fionn asks.

"She had a little soup," Louise volunteers. "But she was barely able to keep it down."

"Jesus." He runs an anxious hand through his hair, messing it up a bit.

If I was feeling better, I'd appreciate how sexy he looks in his black suit, two buttons of his white dress shirt popped open.

When the doctor returns, Fionn jumps to his feet, approaching him in a hostile manner. "Why the fuck do you look like someone's dead?"

The doctor bounces back a step, holding out a hand. "No, no, it's not bad."

"Tell me!" he spits out.

His eyes loop between us. "Your wife is pregnant, sir."

"What?" I whisper just as Louise gasps, a smile stretching.

"She…she's pregnant?" Fionn almost falls backward, his voice raw and deep, eyes filled with emotion—so much of it, I feel it pouring out of him as he gazes down at me. "Are you sure?"

"Yes, absolutely." The doctor finally relaxes his stance. "She probably got a bug and this illness has nothing to do with the pregnancy, except maybe the nausea. I always check these things before deciding on medication."

He moves to inspect the other tests he took. "She's negative for everything, but there are many viruses out there, and when a woman is pregnant, her immune system is lowered, so it's easier to pick things up and also feel much sicker."

"Is there anything she can take?"

"Some Tylenol for the fever, aches, and pains, as well as Zofran for the nausea. If it gets worse…"

But I stop listening, my mind still coming to terms with the fact that I'm having another baby.

The last time I was told I was pregnant was different. I was scared. Alone.

Now, things are better. I have Fionn, and he's already an amazing dad. We're a family.

"Feel better, honey," Louise says, rubbing my back. "I'm thrilled for you both. Congratulations."

"Thank you." Tears cloud my vision.

Fia is going to have a brother or sister. This family of ours is growing, and after hearing it out loud, I realize how badly I want this.

Fionn sits beside me, wrapping his arms around me. "I'm so damn happy right now. I just wish you weren't sick."

"Me too. About both," I whisper.

His mouth falls to my forehead, lips remaining there for several seconds before he pulls back, an affectionate look in his eyes. "Lie down, baby. You need some sleep."

"Will you stay with me?"

"Of course. I won't be going anywhere."

I lower my head onto the pillow, and he climbs in beside me, strong arms surrounding me and holding me tight.

Slowly, I drift off to sleep, knowing he'll be right here when I wake up.

FORTY-ONE

FIONN

It's been five days since the doctor told us the pregnancy news, and it has finally hit me.

This is really happening. We're gonna have a baby.

I glance down at Amara's stomach, wanting to see it grow with our child. I missed out on so much with Fia. I won't ever let that happen again. I'll be here for every single moment.

"I can't believe I'm going to have another grandbaby. Lucky man, I am," Dad says, with Fernanda beside him.

I wasn't going to have the family over with Amara just starting to feel better, but she insisted.

"Congrats." Tynan smirks. "Poor kid."

"Yeah, yeah. Shut up." I chuckle. "If you can do it, so can I."

I won't admit it to him, but I'm nervous I'll screw up this kid. I've wanted her knocked up from the moment she came back into my life, and now that she is, I'm fucking terrified.

What do I know about being a dad? I like kids, and I know I'm good with them, but it's different when it's yours.

What if he hates me? What if I'm not good with newborns? I've never even changed a diaper before.

Fuck me. I don't know shit, do I?

"I think he'll be great. He's been amazing with Fia." Amara gazes up with those adoring eyes, a hand on my chest, and everything snaps into place.

Every insecurity about fatherhood washes away in an instant. Because if she believes in me, then maybe I should too.

"Aww, that's so sweet," Elara gushes, looking over at Amara. "How are you feeling, by the way? Any morning sickness?"

"I feel okay." She shrugs. "Nauseous some mornings, but nothing too terrible."

"Well, you know if you ever need anything at all, you just call me."

"I'm always available too," Fernanda adds. "We're all here for you."

Amara practically radiates with happiness. With the shit of a mother she's had, I can see why. We may have our flaws, but we'd do anything for family.

"Do you think it's a boy, Uncle Fionn?" Brody asks, sitting across me beside his mother while the girls play.

"I don't know, kid. We'll find out soon."

"I think it's a boy."

"I think so too." I wink, and he hits me with a grin.

Sometimes I look at him and remember the boy he once was when Tynan first adopted him. He didn't talk for a while after his parents' death. But when Elara appeared in his life, he got better. It's damn good to see him doing so well.

"Lunch is ready," Louise announces.

"Alright, how about we eat?" I tell them. "Thankfully, I didn't cook."

Tynan scoffs. "Yeah, you'd burn the house down."

"Whatever, man." I shove at his chest.

"Well, I, for one, thought the baklava you made was very good." Amara winds her arm around me.

"Thank you, my beautiful wife." I kiss the top of her head, glaring at my brother. "At least someone in this family appreciates my culinary skills."

Tynan bursts with a dry laugh. "Have you actually looked up skills in the dictionary?"

Elara sighs. "Aren't they awesome?"

AMARA

Staring at my poli-sci paper the next day, I'm filled with dread.

He gave me a C.

There are barely any marks on the paper. I don't understand why I can't seem to do well in this class. Every time I think I'm heading in the right direction, I just do worse. I did everything he said. My arguments were rock solid.

As he dismisses the class, I descend down the stairs toward him, while the voices of my classmates dwindle down until they disappear.

"Professor?" I call.

He peers up, pushing at his glasses. "Ms. Quinn. How can I help you?"

I don't miss the fact that he called me *Ms.* again, but I don't correct him.

"It's just, I don't understand this grade. I did everything you told me to do, and I did worse."

He sighs. "Okay, how about you come to my office and we can see what we can do? I don't want you to stress about this."

My body deflates with a heavy exhale. "Of course I'm stressed.

This is the only subject I'm doing terribly in."

He flings the strap of his brown satchel over his shoulder as he starts up the steps, me following beside him.

"There's still a chance for you to save your grade, so don't worry too much." He gently pats my forearm.

I grow uncomfortable, but manage to push those thoughts back. He's just being nice. That's all.

Was he nice *when he touched your ass?*

That was clearly an accident.

When we exit the room, Roy is there, following us as we make it to the professor's office. Roy stands offside as we enter, the professor shutting the door before dropping his satchel onto his desk and taking a seat.

"You can sit down, Ms. Quinn."

"Mrs. Quinn."

I don't know why he keeps doing that. Is he just not used to calling his students Mrs.? But this strange part of me thinks he's doing it on purpose.

A smile spreads before his expression turns stoic, almost angry.

I recoil.

"Your paper lacked depth, *Mrs.* Quinn. There was nothing in there that gave me an idea of how you truly felt about the polarizing views. Instead, you gave me both sides without choosing one. I wanted you to choose."

"I thought I did."

"No." His eyes turn to slits. "You did not."

His gaze slinks down to my chest before returning to my face. Suddenly, I feel naked, stripped bare. I need to get out of here.

"If you want to redo the paper, I'll see if I can bump up your grade."

"Really?" My eyes widen with hope. "Thank you so much. I won't disappoint you."

"I hope not."

I start to get up, and he follows after me…standing too close.

Goose bumps spread across my nape, a sense of fear taking hold. He presses his body into me as he grabs the doorknob—so close, I can feel him hard against my behind.

My heart races, nausea crawling up my throat.

This can't be an accident. How can I even consider that it is?

Just open the door and go!

But it's like I'm frozen, unable to move or do anything, my heartbeats pummeling faster and faster.

His hand slithers out, fingers feathering over my hip.

"You have three days to get that paper to me," he husks into my ear, and my body shivers from absolute dread.

Go! Just leave! What's wrong with you?!

His fingers roll down my leg before they disappear completely, opening the door.

Panic. Pure panic rolls through me.

When Roy catches my eye, he moves at lightning speed, glaring in front of the professor's face. I reach out a hand for his chest and quickly shake my head, my gaze widening for him to stop. The last thing I want is for him to start a fight at school and get me kicked out.

The corner of the professor's mouth lifts at Roy before he snaps his attention to me. "I'll speak to you next week, Mrs. Quinn. Keep up the good work."

I don't say a word, rushing away, needing to get as far as possible, while Roy follows me.

"Mrs. Quinn? What happened in there?"

"Nothing, okay? Nothing at all. And don't say a word about this to Fionn. I don't want him to overreact."

My heart flutters so fast. If Fionn finds out, he's gonna kill him. I just know it.

Sure, the man's a creep. That's obvious. But I don't think I want him dead for it. Maybe I should just accept the C and ignore him for the rest of the semester.

Then a thought hits.

How many other girls have there been? And what has he done to them?

FIONN

"Daddy, can I have chocolate milk?" Fia gazes up at me, while I'm unable to stop thinking about the text Roy sent a bit ago.

That fucking professor.

He did something to her. He did something to *my wife*. And he's gonna fucking pay for it.

But first, I'm gonna get the truth out of her before I decide what sort of punishment Mr. Wright deserves.

I did my digging on him. Married with no kids. Nothing to indicate he's been inappropriate with his students. But that doesn't mean shit. He could easily hide all that.

"Daddy?"

"Oh. Sorry, princess." I glide a hand down her hair. "I'll get you some milk."

My chest tightens with this immense sense of devotion I have for her and her mother. No one will survive if they ever do anything to harm them.

I pour some into a paper cup and place it before her on the kitchen counter. She sips on it, watching a show on her tablet.

Staring at her, I wonder if I'm her father. Her biological father. Because shit, I wanna be. I deserve to be. She's mine.

This strange feeling gnaws at me, though. Like it's telling me the paternity results won't be good. It's why when Troy called today telling me he has them, I told him I don't wanna know yet. I'm not ready.

When I register the front door opening, I know it's Amara.

"Can you keep an eye on Fia?" I ask Louise, who's cutting up some zucchini for dinner later.

"Of course." She waves me off. "Take your time."

"I'll be right back, baby." My mouth falls to the top of Fia's head before I'm marching to the foyer, just as Amara removes her backpack and shoes.

"Hey, little rabbit. Did you have a good day?"

Her lips tremble. She can't even fake a damn smile.

That son of a bitch. If he touched my wife, I'm gonna string him up and cut off every single one of his limbs before I kill him.

"Yeah," she says rather enthusiastically. "Absolutely great."

My jaw clenches. "Don't lie to me."

"What?" Her eyes round, gaze bouncing between Roy and me.

"Yes, he told me." I stalk closer, tugging her chin in between my fingers. "Roy doesn't keep anything from me." My thumb rolls over her mouth. "We're gonna go upstairs and have a talk."

Her bottom lip quivers. "Okay."

That voice comes out so small, I can't help but hold her to me, breathing in heavily.

"I'm not mad at you, baby. I just wanna know what's been going on."

"Okay." Her small fists clutch the back of my shirt.

Pitching back, I stare into her eyes, palms cupping her face. "I want you to know you can tell me anything. You're safe with me, baby girl. I'll always protect you."

Tears fill her gaze. Taking her hand in mine, I bring her fingertips to my lips, kissing each one before we climb the stairs and enter our bedroom. When I shut the door, she wipes tears from under her lashes.

When I lead her to the chaise, she sinks into it, running a hand down her face, while I stand there waiting for her to start talking before I lose my fucking mind, imagining the worst.

"I shouldn't have gone into his office that second time. I didn't know if what happened the first time was even on purpose." She shakes her head, blinded by her tears. "I wanted to think it was a mistake and—"

"Amara…" A pulse pounds in my head, a fist curling at my side. "I need to know what the hell he did, because I swear, baby, the shit that's going through my head right now isn't healthy."

"He touched me…"

The rest flashes like a blur, every detail just making me grow infuriated.

"I'm so sorry!" She grabs my wrist, her face ashen, body visibly shaking.

"What are you sorry about? You didn't do anything wrong. You know that, right?"

He's the only one who's going to be sorry.

"I just feel like it's my fault. I must've given him some kind of wrong impression, but I swear I told him I was married more than once!"

"Hey." I clasp a palm over the side of her nape. "He won't get away with this."

She sucks in a breath. "What are you gonna do?"

"You don't have to worry about that. Just know he'll never hurt you again."

"Please, Fionn. Don't do anything crazy."

Has she met me?

"I'm your husband, mo ban dia, and it's my job to protect you. What he did to you, he'll never be able to do again."

"Just promise you won't hurt him. I don't want that on my conscience."

"I won't hurt him."

I'm gonna kill him instead.

FORTY-TWO

FIONN

I wanted to make sure his wife wasn't home. It'd be much harder to kill him with a witness.

It took me two days to learn of his daily patterns. Like how he gets his coffee every evening on the way back home. The way he likes to sit in his driveway to scroll on his cellphone, looking at college coeds before heading inside.

When he gets out of his car, he doesn't notice me approaching from behind, silently trailing his smaller frame. He's too busy with his cell to notice a damn thing as he heads up the driveway.

He doesn't realize I've punctured his throat with a needle until it's too late.

As he clutches his neck, the coffee collapses at his feet, black loafers covered in brown liquid.

"Good evening, Professor." I hit him with a tight, crooked smirk.

He stares at me through my opaque sunglasses right before he passes out.

Holding on to him, I adjust my hoodie with one hand, looking in every direction for potential witnesses, then throw him in the back seat of my car. The camera by his front door was already disabled, and so were all the ones in a mile radius from here. No one will suspect me.

No one will even know what happened to him. I'll make sure of it.

Slipping into the driver's seat, I get us on the road and to the farm, dragging him out and tossing him into one of the stables.

"Wake up, asshole." I slap him hard on the face a few times before he's finally groaning.

The dose I used was only enough to keep him quiet until we arrived. Now he's more than welcome to scream as loud as he'd like.

"Who...who are you?" His words are hoarse and his eyes glassy as he blinks up at me.

"My wife told me all about you." I start undoing my cuffs, dragging each sleeve up to my elbows.

"Who? Who's your wife?" he stammers. "Please, just let me go."

He's visibly shuddering, and it's a pathetic sight.

"Amara Quinn." I kneel before him, grabbing a fistful of his shirt. "Your student. That's who."

His eyes expand. "I didn't do anything to your wife. I—I—I was helping her. She's the one who came to my office, wanting extra attention."

My blood swirls in my veins, burning hot through my marrow. "Are you trying to insinuate that this was my wife's fault?"

"No, I just—"

Before he can say another word, my fist lands square on his nose.

"Fuck!" he hollers, holding it as blood shoots out.

My fist tightens. "You touched what's mine, and for that, I'm gonna have to kill you."

"What! No, no, please. I swear. I—I'm sorry. I didn't mean to do that. I'm weak. I'm—"

I punch him again and again and again. So many times, I lose count after twenty.

When I stare down at him, I can barely make out his face. "Say something now, you son of a bitch."

But he doesn't.

Placing two fingers on his throat, I don't register a pulse.

Well, that was easier than I thought.

Washing my hands at a nearby sink, I dry them before grabbing my cell from my pocket and calling one of our men.

"How can I help you, sir?"

"There's something I need you and the boys to get rid of. Need it done so no one finds it. It's at the barn."

"We're on our way."

Staring down at my shirt, I find blood everywhere. Slipping it off, I leave it here to have my men destroy it. I don't want Amara to see me like this. Things have been going well between us, especially with the baby now, and I don't want to jeopardize it.

Heading home, I find Amara putting on Fia's shoes.

"Hi, Daddy!" Fia rushes over, wrapping her arms around my thighs, and I use one hand to hold her to me.

Amara inspects me suspiciously. "What happened to your shirt?"

"Just tore it riding."

"Oh…" Her brows snap. "I didn't realize that's where you were."

"Where are you two going?" I quickly change the subject.

"I'm just gonna take her out to the swings and let her run around before dinner."

"That's a good idea." I clasp the back of her neck and kiss her softly. When I gaze back at her, my damn heart beats even louder. "I love you, Amara."

Maybe it's wrong to say it now, to tell her the truth after I just murdered someone. But I want her to know. I want my wife to know that I love her.

She gasps, unable to contain the emotions coasting through her wide gaze.

Seconds pass while I wait for her to say it back.

Instead, she continues to stare, unable to. Or maybe not wanting to.

And I wonder if she ever will.

AMARA

On the way to school the next day, I keep replaying his words in my head.

He loves me. He actually loves me.

I wanted to tell him I loved him too, but I got scared.

What if I don't know what love is? What if it's just attraction?

But it feels like more. This has to be love. What else can it be?

Roy trails close behind as I enter the Humanities Building, heading for my poli-sci class.

When I walk in, I'm greeted with the heavy murmur of students as a woman rummages through papers in the front of the room. Her hair is pulled back in a tight bun, and she's dressed in white suit pants and a blue blouse.

"Who's that?" I ask the student beside me.

"I don't know," she whispers, eyes filled with the same confusion I'm feeling.

"Settle down, please," the woman calls, and the murmurs drown into silence. "I'm Professor Cortez. I'll be filling in for Doctor Wright for the rest of the semester."

Hushed voices echo, and my heart skips a beat, thoughts racing in my head.

Did something happen to the professor? Is he hurt? Is he…

No. Fionn wouldn't do that. Not after he promised that he wouldn't hurt him.

"What happened to Doctor Wright?" someone from the front row asks.

"The school will be sending an email about that, but for now, let's open our books to chapter seventeen."

The lesson flies by in a blur while my cellphone burns in my bag. I need to text Fionn and find out if he's involved, though I'd rather ask him in person.

The hours pass slowly, but I'm finally heading home, nerves skittering in my stomach.

What if he was involved? What if he hurt the professor…or worse?

No. I can't think like that. I'd rather know for sure instead of speculating.

As soon as Roy parks, I'm hopping out and rushing inside, heading toward his deep husky baritone drifting from the kitchen.

"Mommy!" Fia runs up to me as soon as I step inside, her arms snapping around my thigh.

I hold her close while my gaze fastens to Fionn's, wondering if he's capable of lying to me so easily.

"Hey, baby girl. How was your day?" He comes over, leaning in to kiss me.

His mouth on my skin feels so good, I almost stop myself from talking to him about this. My mouth thins as he pulls back, his eyes narrowing when he examines me again.

His jaw clenches, a muscle in his chin popping. "Louise, would you excuse us?"

"Of course."

"Come on, Fia," she says. "Let's let Mommy and Daddy talk."

"Okay." She takes the woman's hand, exiting toward the den with her.

"What's wrong?" Fionn cups my cheek.

But all I feel is anger and sadness. Anger about the possibility that he lied, and sadness that I may have caused someone's death.

Gathering the courage, I just blurt it out. "My professor, Dr. Wright, never showed up for class today. The sub wouldn't tell us why. Do you know something about it?"

As soon as his nostrils flare, I just know. He did something.

"Oh my God." The edges of my vision blur, angrily stepping backward. "You told me you wouldn't hurt him! You promised."

My body grows shaky as I back away even more, needing to get as far as I can from him.

Instead, he cuts the distance, sharply inhaling as he backs me up against the wall, his features twisted in fury. He doesn't say a word, two palms caging me, his gaze dark and dangerous.

Fear crawls up my arms.

"I told you I wouldn't hurt him," he says. "I never said I wouldn't kill him."

My heart sinks, the words like hot burning flames. I slap a palm around my mouth.

"Please tell me you're lying," I whisper. "That this is some kind of sick joke!"

I'm blinded by my own tears.

"Amara…" He places a hand over my forearm, the touch so soft and warm, I almost forget it belongs to a murderer.

How many people does he have to kill for you to see him for who he is?

"Don't touch me!" I fire out. "I can't even look at you right now. You lied to me!"

With the tips of my fingers, I swipe under my eyes.

"I did this for you! He fucking *touched* you. Did you want me to wait until he raped you to do something? Is that it?"

An ache weaves its way through my chest. "I can't be here right now. I can't look at you." I fight the tears that come. "I'm gonna go for a walk. Don't follow me."

As I march past, he grabs my wrist and tugs me flush against him. "You may hate me right now, but that's okay, mo ban dia. I'll never stop loving you."

Pushing off of me, he stalks away, while I'm left collecting the broken pieces of the progress we've made.

I don't know how long I've walked, not wanting to come home and face what he did. Max sniffs the grass, pulling me while my mind plays Fionn's words over and over, like a broken record.

He killed my professor.

He *killed* him.

How did he do it? Did he send someone? Did he do it with his bare hands?

I don't even want to know.

Is this going to be our lives? Where he just kills people at the drop of a hat?

"Amara?"

I register Elara's voice behind me and pivot to find her strolling with Bubbles. Our two dogs sniff one another, Max wagging his tail. He clearly likes her already.

"How are you?" she asks.

"Eh, you know."

But she doesn't know.

Then again, maybe she does. She's married to Tynan. She has to know what they do.

I need someone to talk to, and maybe she can be that person. I'll tread lightly and feel things out before I tell her more.

Letting out a sigh, I tug on Max's leash as we continue down the acres of open green grass. "I'm having a hard time with this life, you know?"

Glancing at her from my periphery, I find her nodding.

"Oh, yeah. Believe me, I get it. We've been married for so long that sometimes I forget, or maybe make myself forget, but I understand the fear you're experiencing. It's perfectly normal."

"Yeah, exactly. And I just don't know how to deal with the stuff he does. Especially when he says he's doing it for me. But when it comes to hurting others, I don't want him to do that to protect me. It's not right."

She pauses, narrowing a curious gaze, and my pulse flutters.

Did I just put a foot in my mouth? Crap. Crap!

"Are you talking about something specific?"

Oh, Amara, you're an idiot. Tynan is gonna kill you for talking to his wife.

"Never mind." I clear my throat. "I was just being stupid. I'm okay."

I start to stride past her, but she rushes after me, grabbing my wrist.

"Amara, hey!" She pivots to stand in front of me. "You can talk to me. I know everything, okay? Everything they do. So you wouldn't be telling me anything new."

Running a hand over my face, I breathe a sigh of relief. "He killed my professor."

"Oh." Her brows shoot up. "I think this conversation at least deserves some margaritas."

I let out a laugh before a groan comes through. "I'm pregnant, remember?"

"Oh, for me, girlfriend. Not for you."

Once we make it back to her place, we settle in the den, her with a margarita, me with a virgin daiquiri, and I tell her everything. All about my past, my fears for the future, what he did and why.

"I get it." She takes a sip of her drink. "It's not easy being a Mob wife." As soon as she says that, she grimaces. "When I say it out loud, I still can't believe it's my life. But I love him like I've never loved anyone, and that's enough for me."

My heart tugs, afraid that I may be in love with Fionn too. That it's either accept my place beside him as the man he is or tell him to let me go.

Yet the thought of never being with him again, imagining him with someone else, looking at her the way he looks at me... It's like a knife to my chest.

"I think you have to decide what you can live with," she tells me. "This life of theirs, or a life without him." Her eyes brim with compassion. "And it doesn't have to be today or tomorrow, but you will have to choose." She leans back into the sofa. "Though if you choose to walk away, you need to know one thing."

"What's that?"

She angles in closer. "These Quinn men, they don't just let things go without a fight."

A shiver runs down my spine. "Is that how Tynan was?"

She laughs. "Oh, yeah. My husband has a knack for getting what he wants. Especially when it was in the middle of the night while I had my suitcase packed to run from him."

"Oh, wow." I stare at her with shock. "So, what happened?"

"Well..." She folds her arms over her chest. "I'm here, aren't I?"

Then she's telling their whole story, not holding back, and even through it all, I can tell just how much she loves him.

And I'm left wondering whether we'll somehow get there too.

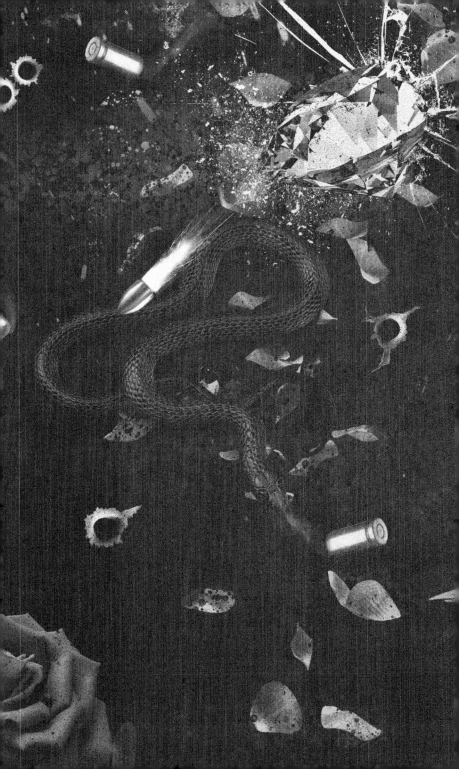

FORTY-THREE

FIONN

"I don't want you picking up anything heavy," I tell Amara, grabbing the grocery bags from her.

Tynan told me that Elara talked to her yesterday, running into her by chance, and I hoped that it would've made a difference. But she's still pissed at me, barely saying a word after she came back from her walk.

Not much has changed today, either.

"I'm fine. The doctor said I'm perfectly okay carrying things." Her lips grow with a faint smile, jump-starting my heart.

Glancing down at her stomach, I can't wait to watch it grow with our baby. We've just returned from her latest doctor's appointment and everything's going well, though it's still too soon to find out if it's a boy or girl. It doesn't matter to me either way, but I'm not a patient man, and unlike my wife, I hate surprises.

"We should talk names." I drop the bags on the floor, tugging her body to mine.

Fuck this wedge between us. I won't let it get in my way from touching her.

"We probably should." Her voice is small, and I fucking hate it.

I let out a harsh sigh. "Please, baby, tell me how to fix this."

She shrugs. "Just give me time, okay? That's all I'm asking."

Clasping the back of her head, I bring her to my chest, inhaling the faint scent of her floral shampoo. "You can have anything you want, but just so you know, this changes nothing. You are mine, Amara Quinn. And there's no escaping it."

Her breath hitches, like the thought scares her.

I tug her tighter. If she wants to divorce me, she'll have to kill me first.

Hours later, my brothers and I are in Tynan's study entertaining the Marinovs, who've come for a meeting to discuss the situation with their uncle. He has apparently begun to advance his plans to get rid of Konstantin.

"In exchange for your thoughtful decision to support us, I want to gift you all a little something." A smirk cracks at the edge of his mouth before he turns to Aleksei.

The younger brother gets up, exiting the room momentarily before he and another man bring in three large duffels. They throw them on the floor, and he unzips them.

Weapons and ammunition.

"That's very generous." Tynan gets to his feet.

"Consider it a thank-you. I'm always most generous when people extend a helping hand."

"Hopefully your uncle has a change of heart once he realizes we're backing you."

"Oh, not likely, my friend. My uncle is motivated and stubborn. Those are not the best qualities to have together."

"His loss, then." Tynan rubs at his chin.

"It very much will be," he taunts with a grin, snaking his attention to Cillian.

Talk about stubborn…

"By the way, I did want to tell you something, Cillian."

That has him looking up sharply.

"I have found Dinara a husband."

"*What?*" he growls thickly, dropping both elbows on his knees, face turning tight and enraged.

"I know. It's wonderful news, isn't it?" Konstantin's mouth curls. "I did tell you I would move on from you, yes? Of course, I had to mourn the idea of joining both our wonderful families together." He sighs dramatically. "But I didn't want to push you anymore. You know? Call me a softie." He chuckles. "But yes, she will be married, and I do think she'll be much happier too."

Cillian's nostrils flare.

"He's the son of one of my other associates. The marriage will, of course, benefit me." He laughs humorlessly. "But he will be a very good husband to our girl, I assure you."

His features turn dark, but Cillian's turn even darker. He hates this. He's fucking crazy about her.

"Now, if you'll excuse me, I need to use the little boys' room." His cold sneer grows. "I do hope to see you at the wedding."

Getting up, he heads out the door, while all three Marinovs stare hard at Cillian like they're ready to kill him. He glares back with equal disdain.

Probably not a good idea to have them all pissed at each other with these weapons lying around.

AMARA

"Come here, Max!" I whisper as he chases a ball down the long corridor. "Max, come!"

But he completely ignores me, continuing to sprint toward the ball while I grow nervous following him.

Fionn's study is the last door on the right, and I know he's having a meeting, which I don't want to disturb.

"Max!"

Just as I rush after him around the corner, I bump into an incredibly tall man, his body hard as stone.

"I'm so sorry!" I have to force my head back just to look at him.

"That's okay, daragaya." The man with a thick Russian accent hits me with a half-grin, but it's the dangerous and wicked kind.

One that turns my veins to stone.

Is he who Fionn is having the meeting with?

Max sits beside him, wagging his tail while peering up at him, as though waiting for his command or maybe an ear rub.

"What a good dog. Beautiful, too." He scratches the top of his head. "It's very important to surround yourself with loyal people *and* animals." His mouth tips higher. "And I can see this dog is very loyal, aren't you…" He looks to me for a name.

"Max. His name is Max."

"Ah, Max. I have a cousin named Maxim. Very loyal too." His grin spreads. "Tell me, who are you? We have never had the pleasure of meeting."

Without an invitation, he picks up my hand and kisses it.

"I—I'm Amara, Fionn's…wife." I don't know why that was hard to say.

"Ah…so, you're the one he was looking for?"

"You know about that?" Shock tramples through my words.

"Oh, maya milaya, I know everything about everyone. It's part of my charm." His grin widens while an icy chill remains on my skin, like my head knows he's one to fear. "That man was scouring the entire state of Massachusetts looking for you, so I heard…"

His intense stare causes me to shiver.

"Are you not thrilled about your marriage? Is he not up to your standards?" He continues to stroke Max, and for a second, I wonder if this man is some kind of witch, controlling my dog the way he is.

His eyes hold mine, and my gut rolls with absolute terror. He's dangerous. I can feel it.

"No, he's great." For a moment, I shift my stare to the floor, needing to avoid his intensity.

"Oh…" He shakes his head disapprovingly. "Lying is not one of your strong suits, I'm afraid. So I ask again, why do you not want to be married to him? He's not a bad man, and believe me, I know bad men."

"He does bad things, though…" I suck in a breath immediately.

How could I have said that out loud? And to him!

"Ah, I see. You're not from our world." He takes a step closer, and Max follows him. "You must understand men like us, Mrs. Quinn. We do what we must for those we love. For those who matter to us most. And you, I'm sure, matter a great deal to him." His eyes turn deeper, even though they're already dark. "He will do everything in his power to make sure you are safe. It's how it's done in our world. And who can fault us for that? Can you?"

He pauses for a moment, as though waiting for me to reply. Instead, he continues.

"If you had the power, wouldn't you protect the people you love at all costs? Would you kill for those you love or would you let them be killed because of your own morality?"

I consider what he says, and part of me can see his point. People like Fionn don't see things like the rest of us do, where if someone does something bad, they get arrested.

In his world, they die.

And maybe Fionn was right. Maybe the professor would've done something worse to me if I had said nothing. What if he already did that to some other girl? What if Fionn stopped him?

"I'm sure you are scared," he goes on. "And you don't yet understand how people like us do what we do, but I promise you, maya daragaya, the rest of the world is just as bad. While we may kill with our bare hands, they kill in other ways. It's just much easier to stomach that for people like you."

The corner of his mouth twists, and even though he's frightening, I find some comfort in his words because he's not wrong. Us humans, we hurt each other in many different ways.

"I'm certain he loves you very much, and love is a powerful emotion." He scoffs. "One that corrupts while it empowers. It's why I don't want it." He quirks a brow. "But he does, and you're lucky for that." His dark gaze bores deeper. "Because with him, you'll always have someone who will make sure you're protected at all costs. Not many people have that."

Before I can reply, he gets set to go.

"I hope you have a wonderful day, Mrs. Quinn." He glances back. "I do hope to get to know you better."

He starts down the corridor, and I find myself staring after him, wondering if I just had a conversation with the devil.

FIONN

As we get ready for bed, I watch her in front of the vanity, putting her hair up in a messy bun, my white t-shirt rising up to her upper thighs.

She catches my gaze in the mirror, my cock practically jutting out from my boxers. It's been over a day since I've fucked her.

Over twenty-four hours of her being mad.

I could've just taken her, but I wouldn't do that. I want her to want it. To want me.

She lowers her arms and flips around to face me, her nipples beaded beneath the thin fabric. Grinding my jaw, I force myself to look at her instead of that sinful body I constantly crave.

Every time I think back on those years we were apart, how riddled with obsession and anger I was, I'm grateful to have her. Even while she's pissed.

"Can we talk?" she asks, tugging on the hem of the shirt, her glance bouncing between me and the floor.

Relief hits me. Talking is good. I can do that.

"Sure." Stepping close, I curl my palms around her hips. "What do you wanna talk about, little rabbit?"

Her eyes fall to a close before she's gazing up at me, and what I find within them gives me some damn hope that she can forgive me.

"I had some time to think…"

"Hopefully good things." I smirk, but she doesn't return it. "This is killing me, Amara." I grab her jaw. "I love you, baby. I love you so fucking much." I lower my hand to her growing belly. "I love our baby too. I love our family. I don't like feeling like we're breaking."

Her brows bow, emotions treading in her features. She places a palm across my cheek, staring deeply into my eyes, and I feel it everywhere.

"I love you too, Fionn Quinn."

I suck in a breath, the weight of her words strong enough to crush me.

"I never thought I'd hear you say that." My mouth strokes hers while my fingers sink into her hair, tugging gently.

"I'm sorry," she breathes, and that has me pulling back.

"Sorry for what? You have nothing to be sorry about."

Her face falls. "I just wanna explain, okay?"

"Of course, baby." I clasp a palm across her nape and search her gaze, needing her to keep talking.

"You have to understand that this has been hard for me. It may always be hard. But..." She trails, and my pulse spikes. "But I've come to realize that I know you're just trying to protect me in your very unorthodox ways." She finally smiles, but it's barely there. "I also know that no matter what, you're never gonna let me go."

That's a fact.

"But today I realized something else."

"And what's that, mo ban dia?"

She brings her lips to mine and kisses me. "That I want to stay. That I want to try to understand you and the way you live." She throws her arms over my shoulders, and I finally feel at ease. "Because I don't see a life without you."

Tears fill her eyes, and I feel them heavy in my soul.

"Thank fucking God." My forehead falls over hers. "There's never been a life for me without you either, not from the moment we met."

She lets out a small cry just as my mouth crashes over hers. My unrelenting desire for this woman, the longing...it all comes to the precipice. Lifting her into my arms, I lower her onto the bed, ripping off her shirt before my clothes are gone too.

Every inch of her is mine for the taking.

Every hole mine to fill.

And I do. I take her hard and fast, flipping her onto her stomach after making her come with her knees up over my shoulders. Her hair tangles with my fingers, her moans of pleasure filling the space around us.

And I'm finally at peace. Finally knowing she loves me just as much as I love her.

All those years I waited for her have been worth it.

FORTY-FOUR

AMARA

"Where are we going?"

Fionn fixes my blindfold while I squeeze my thighs together when his large hand rests on my leg.

"It's a surprise." His gravelly tone tiptoes up my body, making me weak with desire.

His fingers slide up my leg through the long slit of my black silk gown. All he told me was that we'd be heading somewhere fun for our date this evening. I'm definitely excited, but nervous beyond belief.

It's been three days since I told him I loved him, and things between us have been stronger than ever. I realized that even with all his flaws, he's an amazing man. An amazing father. There's absolutely no one who can love me and our daughter the way he does.

I want to be with him, and nothing will change that anymore. Whatever comes, I'll deal with it the best way I can.

Because I want to be Amara Quinn. I want to be his wife.

He rests his hand over my stomach, rubbing a thumb over it.

"How's our boy doing?" That huskiness sends tingles down my body.

"We don't know if it's a boy yet." My smile widens.

I know he says it doesn't matter, but he wants a boy after Fia, and I want to give him that.

"You're right, we don't. According to the stuff I read, he or she is the size of a blueberry this week."

I let out a laugh.

Yes, my Mafia husband has been reading all about pregnancy since we found out. I think it's adorable, which is not at all how everyone else would describe him, but it can be our little secret.

"The doc said we can find out soon with that blood test he mentioned," he adds.

"Do you wanna find out? Because I kinda want it to be a surprise."

He laughs. "You and your surprises." His thick fingers feel so good on my skin. "Whatever you want, baby girl."

"Really?"

"Mm-hmm." Not being able to see him makes his raspy voice sound so much sexier than it already is.

My core throbs, and it's like he knows it too, his fingers lowering to my thighs again. My sex drive has been at an all-time high lately, and he definitely read that too and has been taking full advantage.

Grabbing his wrist, I lead him just where I want him.

"Mm. Already wet for me." His gravelly groan as he rubs my clit has a cry escaping from my lips.

He eases two fingers inside me, curling them while his thumb works me slow, then fast, until I'm ready to explode.

"Not yet, baby. I want you to save that for later."

I have no idea what he means, but I don't think I can last in this state through dinner.

"Please," I beg, needing it so badly.

Instead, he removes his hand while I gasp in protest. And then I notice that the car has stopped.

"Where are we?" I ask as he pulls my blindfold down.

As my vision adjusts to the surroundings, I notice we're at an industrial brick building, people all around, dressed up in gowns and suits. But that's not all...

They're all wearing masks, like those masquerade types. Super fancy.

"What is this place?"

His smirk grows. "It's a private club. Owned by Konstantin. I heard you ran into him in the hall the other day."

My eyes expand. "Oh. Him. I probably should've mentioned that."

Nerves pummel in my gut.

"Don't worry, he did." He laughs.

"Who is he, exactly? And please don't lie to me."

"I have no intention of lying, baby." Picking up my hand, he holds it in his lap. "He's the head of the Russian Mob. The Pakhan, as they call it."

My heart races at the revelation.

I was talking to the head of the Russian Mob... Holy shit.

I swear, this all sounds like a movie.

"And what kind of club is this?"

He chuckles just under his breath. "A sex club."

"What?" I laugh, because of course this is a joke.

Right?

When he stares at me with a serious expression, my pulse hikes up.

"Oh my God, you're serious."

"Don't be nervous." He strokes my jaw with his hard knuckles, his gaze narrowing and turning heavy-lidded. "We don't have to do anything. We can just watch. Or I can take you to a private corner and fuck you while everyone walks by, knowing exactly what I'm doing to you."

My pussy clenches. "What else?"

A salacious grin grows on his perfectly sculpted face. "Or…I can take you into a room and have my way with you."

"How?" My voice drops, my body tight from the orgasm he denied me.

"I'd use my rope, lift you up in the air and eat your pussy while they watch, then fuck you. We'd draw a nice crowd too, with the way you'd be screaming for me."

"Oh God." I shift in the seat, completely turned on.

Could I actually do all that?

"You'd be in a mask. So would I," he assures me. "It's required."

"So no one would actually know it's me?"

His fingers lace up and down my knee while my breaths come in heavy pulls. I want to try everything he just described, but I've never been naked in front of people before.

"No one except Konstantin."

My gaze expands. "And that doesn't bother you?"

His mouth picks up on one side. "That he gets to see how beautiful you are, but can't do a thing about it?" The pads of his fingers slide between my thighs, tracing over my core. "It actually turns me on, little rabbit." He flicks my clit and my eyes roll back. "Knowing he can't touch you. That you're mine. Like I'm dangling you in front of them all. But no one gets to enjoy this beautiful body but me."

He thrusts inside me, fingering me so deep that my nails sink into the leather, needing to be taken out of my misery.

But just as before, he slides out of me, torturing me again.

He pops open the glove compartment and removes two masks, handing me a black one with gold crystal-encrusted loopy designs that end with a feather above one eye. "Put that on."

I slip the elastic around my face while he gets his on, a simple black half-mask.

Adjusting it on my nose, I open the mirror above and stare at myself. I don't even recognize the woman staring back at me. No one else will either. But Konstantin seeing me without my clothes on still makes me uneasy.

His devilish smirk slowly spreads, making my nerves swell. "You ready to go, mo ban dia?"

"No." I grimace. "I don't think it's something anyone is ready for, but I'm willing to try."

"If at any point you want to leave, just tell me and we will."

That puts me at ease.

Getting out of the car first, he comes around to open my door, taking my hand in his as I step out onto the street. Cars are all around us—so many, I wouldn't even be able to count.

Together, we make it toward a security guard with a red devil's mask, waving a device in front of a couple before us.

"What is he doing?"

"Scanning masks. Each one has a chip, which is connected by a number to our membership information."

"Membership?"

This is insane.

"Yeah, it's invite-only."

Geez!

"And you've been a member for how long?"

If he's been here, then he must've participated. I know it was before me, but my stomach goes all twisted at the thought of my husband touching other women and doing God knows what to them.

"A while." His arm wraps around my hips, lips lowering to my ear. "But I've wanted you here with me from the time we met."

I want to ask more, but it's our turn now. As the man silently scans us, I think it's better not to know anyway. Anything that happened before me doesn't matter.

"Phone," the guard says, holding out a clear plastic bag.

"Oh, uh…" I glance at Fionn, who's already throwing his phone in it.

"It's for everyone's protection," he explains. "That way no one takes photos or videos."

That makes sense. Reaching into my handbag, I grab mine and put it in with Fionn's. Once we're done, a woman in a red strapless gown ushers us inside toward the elevator, which arrives in seconds.

My heart echoes in my ribs as we enter. She follows us silently, pressing a button. Her black hair is up in a tight bun; a black mask and bright red lips make her appear like she's attending a fancy party. There's nothing about her or the building that indicates we're about to step into anything remotely like what Fionn described.

"You okay?" he whispers across the shell of my ear.

"Ask me later."

He chuckles just as the elevator brings us to the top floor. As soon as we step out, we face heavy-looking red doors, two men with tuxes and black masks like Fionn's standing on each side.

They let us in immediately, and we're instantly assaulted by dimmed colorful lights, low sultry music, and fully clothed people dancing everywhere.

Fionn holds my hand tight as I stare around. Nothing about this smells like sex.

"He likes to change locations of the club every time," Fionn tells me.

"How does that work?"

"They're called pop-up clubs. The members get a text with the address and time, then it disappears."

"Wow. That's crazy."

By the look of how packed this room is, I gather people really like his club.

"Do you have to pay to become a member?"

"Yeah, ten grand."

"What?" I flip my face to his. "Oh my God."

He chuckles.

"I guess to people like you, it's not much."

He grabs my hips, turning me toward him, forcing my body flush against his. "To people like *us*, little rabbit. You're my wife. And what's mine…" He traces my bottom lip with a thumb. "…is yours."

His voice dips with a husky timbre, his mouth lowering to mine and brushing lightly, setting me ablaze.

He starts to dance, flipping my back to his front, and I can feel how hard he is. The music and my body take over as I move along to the erotic rhythm. His palms stroke up and down my hips, lower, to my thighs and back up. We dance for several minutes, one song leading to another, and my greedy body aches for more.

"Come…" His tone takes a darker turn, making my unsatiated desire grow, and when he grabs my hand, I follow him like a moth to a flame.

We descend down a narrow space, doors open on both sides, sounds of pleasure coming in waves.

In one, a woman is hung from the ceiling being whipped, her legs spread and cuffed, her wrists bound above her. The man is naked and hard, wearing a demon mask, while hers is angelic.

My heart races. This is crazy.

In another, two men are with a woman. She's on her knees, over something that looks like an elevated straddling contraption. One man takes her from behind, while the other is forcing his penis into her mouth. I find myself pausing to watch, and he lets me, palms running up and down my shoulders from behind.

"Do you like that, baby girl? Like watching her get fucked by two men?"

"Yes…" My breathing turns heavy, my core aching.

"You can watch all you want…" His knuckles trace down my hip, forcing his palm between my thighs through the dress. "But that'll never happen." The friction of the dress causes me to moan. "My cock is all you're ever gonna get."

Roughly, he slides his hand through the slit of the dress and drives two fingers inside me, stroking my clit at the same time while the woman cries out in pleasure, and I join her, so close I can feel my release taking over.

"You're not gonna come yet, little rabbit." He bites my earlobe. "Not until I have you so damn desperate, you'd let me fuck you anywhere."

"Please, Fionn." I clutch his thighs, barely able to get a grip through the rippled muscles.

He takes my hand, pulling it behind me, and places it against his massive rock-hard erection. "I wanna have your glistening cunt on display while I fuck it over and over."

I stroke him, and he hisses a curse.

I'd agree to anything right now.

"Let's keep walking," he says across my ear, dragging me down the rest of the hallway until we make it past a large open space with a stage and seating that's currently empty.

"What happens here?"

"Auctions."

The little hairs on my arms stand up. "What kind?"

"Marriage, virginity. All kinds."

"As in women being auctioned off for *that*?"

He glances back with a smirk. "Mm-hmm."

My God. I never even imagined a world like this existed. I've been so naïve.

When we pass one room, I find a woman hanging from some metal bar attached from the ceiling, which she's tied to. Her legs are up to her chest, rope around her thighs and ankles, more around her stomach, hips, and chest. She looks amazing, while the man uses a toy on her, driving it deeper while she cries out shamelessly.

It must be so freeing to do this here and not even care. I want that kind of freedom.

"You like that?"

"Yes…"

He pushes his palm into my core, massaging my clit with it. "I reserved the room next door for us."

My heart skips a beat. This is really happening. I push down my fear as he leads me to the room, the same metal bar hanging from the ceiling, and my body suddenly feels cold, apprehension taking over.

"It's okay, baby. You're safe with me." His hands glide up and down my arms, cupping my breasts and pulling on my nipples through the dress.

Before I know it, my body is aflame, needing this man inside me. I barely notice when he slips off the straps of my dress, sliding them down my body until I'm bare, facing away from the door.

My head falls over his chest as the music hums low through the speakers above. My small heels clack as he takes us toward a black leather chaise.

"Sit." Lowering me down, he walks away momentarily, opening a closet and returning with a black briefcase. "I had this brought here before we came."

I nod as he opens it, removing two bundles of red rope. He places the briefcase beside me before heading toward the far right and pulling on a lever on the wall. It automatically brings the circular metal bar down.

He begins wrapping one of the bundles around it, creating intricate loops, then picks up the second bundle and ties it to the other rope.

Tension settles in my body, my stomach heavy and filled with dread—yet excitement too.

When he stalks toward me, I notice people have gathered to watch us, and that causes panic to settle in my gut. My arms come to cover myself, and when he notices that, he tilts my chin up with the back of a finger, forcing me to look at him and only him.

"Drop your arms. Show them how beautiful you are."

My inhales grow more rapid, but I obey, gradually lowering them to my side even while I grow nervous with heady anticipation.

Is this really happening? Am I actually doing this?

"Good girl." His mouth drops to my breast and he sucks a nipple, eyes connected with mine as he does the same to the other.

He grabs the briefcase and takes my jaw, kissing me roughly before I'm being pulled toward the bar.

Holy crap, this feels so good.

Opening the briefcase, he grabs another bundle of rope. "Wrists together."

The command in his voice has me obeying instantly, pushing down the anxiety as I grow incredibly turned on.

"If at any point you want to stop, use your safe word, and I will cut the ropes off."

I nod as he continues to tie my wrists, forcing my hands behind my head and using more rope around my arms and chest.

My heart races uncontrollably as I try to forget that I'm naked right now.

He comes around to admire his work so far, twisting my achy nipples between two fingers, his mouth dropping to my throat to kiss down my nape. His hot breath on my chilled skin has me even more aroused. His fingers drag up and down the insides of my thighs, up my stomach and breasts, until every single cell in my body wants this.

He continues to coil more rope around the rest of me—my thighs, my hips, except my stomach—until it's time to attach me to the ceiling.

Oh my God. I never even imagined I'd let a man do this to me. This is both insane and exhilarating.

Before I know it, I'm fastened by my chest and each of my legs, being lifted up until I'm suspended in the air.

Crap. This is kinda high.

Don't think about it. You're fine. Everything's fine.

People are watching you hanging naked from the ceiling. Pretty sure you don't understand how fine *works.*

"Are you okay?" he asks.

"Mm-hmm."

"Any discomfort?"

I shake my head, unable to get the word out.

"Good." His smirk curls. "You look so damn good."

I'll take his word for it.

He shakes off his jacket, placing it on the chaise, while I try not to look at the people staring at us, waiting for him to begin. His eyes never leave mine as he takes his time, undoing his cuffs one at a time. His shoes come off next, then he starts on the buckle of his pants, the sound reverberating through the large space before he's sliding off his trousers and boxers to reveal his massive thighs.

I shut my eyes, forgetting anyone else exists besides the both of us.

His rough fingertips roll up my thighs, gliding over my clit before they climb down my other leg.

"You're beautiful." He grabs the insides of my legs and forces himself between them. Pushing my body higher, he throws my legs over his shoulders, his mouth descending to my needy flesh. The tip of his tongue circles around my clit, and it's over from there as he sucks and thrusts at the same time.

My release comes crashing down in an instant. But he doesn't stop there, forcing another one out of me, his fingers taking me roughly while I cry out shamelessly.

"Yes!" My hands ball tight, my body falling hard and fast as they all watch me fall apart.

Though I no longer feel shame. I feel strong. Somehow being suspended in the air, knowing we're being watched, is something I enjoy.

He strokes himself, working his cold piercings against my clit, and with one thrust he's inside me, pounding into me with hard strokes.

The sound of my skin slapping against his, his croaky growls as he takes me faster…it causes every inch of me to burn with need.

He pounds even deeper, circling his hips as he does. I whimper out his name, and when he slams harder, a strangled moan gets lost in my throat, and stars erupt before my eyes.

"Yes, that's it. Squirt on my cock." His beastly growling rips through his chest until his warm release fills me.

I don't know how long he takes me, using my body in whatever way he pleases, until he cuts the rope and secures a robe over me, holding me tight as he kisses my forehead.

"How are you feeling?"

A smile stretches. "Tired."

That was incredible.

He rubs his palms across my back, the silk of the black robe warming my skin. "Let's go home and get you in bed."

"Mmm, that sounds nice."

He shuts the door, hiding us from the crowd. Bringing me back to the chaise, he lays me down, staring down at me with a clenched jaw.

I really let him do this to me. And the crazy thing is, I'd let him do it again.

His large hands massage every inch of me, making me feel so good after being bound like that. Like he's worshiping me.

He kneels on the floor and kisses my stomach. "I love you, Amara."

Tears spring into my eyes. Because for once, I'm safe and happy.

"I love you too."

FORTY-FIVE

AMARA

"Wait, he took you to an actual sex club?" Lilith stares, open-mouthed.

Emily and Patricia both appear as though their eyes are about to pop out.

"Yep…"

"And you liked it?" Emily can't believe it.

"I did." My lips purse. "It was scary at first, but fun after I stopped caring."

Picking up my soda, I drink a few sips at the restaurant we all decided to meet at. It was pretty last-minute, but after a series of texts, Fionn arranged for me to come meet them for brunch since I had no classes today.

"You know that feeling right before you go up on the roller coaster and you're terrified, but after it's over, you can't wait to go again?"

They nod.

"Well, that's exactly how it felt for me. I'm actually excited to try it again."

"And it's okay while pregnant?" Patricia whispers, a flush creeping on her face.

"Yeah. Apparently he asked my OB about it before he took me. She said as long as I don't put pressure around my stomach and don't lie flat as I progress, then I'm fine."

"Wow, who knew you'd be the freak amongst us girls?" Lilith laughs. "But now I wanna try it."

My other two friends grimace.

"Meh, I'll pass." Emily pops a tortilla chip into her mouth. "I don't think screwing around in public is my thing. The rope sounds cool, but I'm too chicken to try it."

"Yeah." Patricia scratches her temple. "I'm with Emily on this one."

"Never actually thought I'd see the day you two agreed on something regarding sex." Lilith stares between them with a laugh, her attention bouncing back to me. "So, think you can ask Fionn how I can get into this club?"

"Uh, well, you need ten grand and you need to be approved."

"Whoa!" She jerks back with shock. "Now that's crazy."

"I know, right?"

Glancing at my cell, I check the time, knowing I need to get Fia from preschool soon. Luckily, the flight is only forty-five minutes. Fionn would've done it, but he had to attend a meeting with his brothers at the last minute, and that's a few hours from home.

"I'm gonna run to the ladies' room," I tell the girls. "If the waiter comes back, can you guys get me another Coke?"

"Sure," Lilith says.

"I'll come with you." Emily rises, heading down to the restroom with me. She throws an arm around my shoulders. "I'm really happy for you. Fionn has really proven to be good for you."

"I know." My body grows taut at the mere mention of him. "I can't wait to see Fionn love on this baby." I cup my small belly, loving this child already.

"I can't wait to be an auntie again!"

Just as we head inside, I accidentally slam into a woman. "I'm so sorry!"

She smiles, heading out while Emily walks into an empty stall.

As I'm about to head into another, I notice that the woman dropped something.

An envelope.

"Excuse me!" I call for her, picking it up, but when I rush out onto the restaurant floor, I don't see her anymore.

Crap. I'll have to pass it to the manager.

Intending to go there after I'm done, I start for the stall, and as I do, something slips out.

"What the…" I look down at a photo printed on plain paper, and it takes a few long seconds for my brain to catch up to my eyes.

My heart gallops up to my throat, my skin turning ice-cold.

Because in the photo is my daughter sitting on a chair, holding a teddy bear, fear in her eyes.

"Oh my God," I pant.

Someone has her. Someone took our baby!

When I turn the photo around, I read the words, unable to make sense of any of it.

We have her. Come alone. If you tell anyone, she's dead. 746 Tavern Lane. Boston.

"Oh my God!" I stumble, bracing myself on the wall so I don't collapse.

Panic grips me, and I'm unable to breathe, my hands shaking as I get my phone and call her preschool.

The phone rings and rings just as Emily comes out.

"Amara? What's wrong?" Concern hits her features instantly, while I lift a finger in the air, indicating for her to hold on.

"Hi, may I help you?" the secretary asks.

"Hi, this is…uh, Amara Quinn." My voice shakes, the phone almost dropping from my jittery clasp.

"Oh, yes. Hi there, Mrs. Quinn. Is there a problem?"

"My daughter, Fia. Is she there?"

Silence.

Nonono!

"Uh, she's not… She was picked up about an hour ago."

"What! Oh my God." I collapse onto the ground, the phone falling out of my grasp while flickers of light erupt before my eyes like stars.

"Amara! What's wrong?" Emily helps me up, getting the phone for me, while the photo of Fia is tight in my palm.

I can't let her see it. I just can't. Whoever they are, they told me no one can know. I can't let anything happen to my daughter.

Oh my God, my baby!

I start to cry.

"What do you mean, she was picked up?! By who?" I holler through the tears, swiping at them.

"Uh, let me check that for you." She pauses. "Is everything okay?"

"No! It's not okay. I don't know who picked up my child."

I dig a fist into my chest, unable to pull in air, my left side heavy like I'm having a heart attack, but it's panic. I felt this before growing up, panicking every time my mother was high.

"So, the ID of the person who got her is Desdemona Edwards."

I choke on a gasp.

"Should we call the authorities?" she asks.

"No!" Terror grips me.

No cops. My mother is unstable, especially when she's high. She could be with someone who wants to get money from me for Fia.

"I'll take care of it. Thanks."

Hanging up, I try to slip the phone into my bag, but it jitters and crashes on the ground again.

Emily picks it up, alarm in her gaze. "What's going on? Does someone have Fia?"

Someone walks into the bathroom, and that has me keeping my tone low as I pull Emily out. "I need you to do something for me."

"Of course! Anything."

"Stay here for five minutes so I can sneak out from the back without Roy finding out. Can you do that?"

"Amara, you're really scaring me. If Fia's in danger, you should call Fionn."

"NO!" I grab her wrist, showing her the photo and the words on the back so she understands that she can't say a damn word.

She gasps, cupping her mouth.

"My mother has her."

"I swear…" Her voice breaks. "If she hurts that girl, I'm gonna kill her."

"Me too." My heart feels like someone's carving it out.

And it's right at this moment that I realize maybe I'm not so different from Fionn. Maybe Konstantin was right about it all.

When those you love are hurt, there's nothing you wouldn't do to stop it.

I pick up my cell from the cup holder for the third time, wanting to call Fionn, wanting to tell him. But I chicken out at the last minute. Countless thoughts go through my head.

What if I call him and she ends up dead? What if not calling him will do the same?

I don't know what to do!

"Ahhh!" I let out a wild scream, gripping the steering wheel tight in my hands.

A woman in the car beside mine glances at me like I've lost my mind as we both wait for the red light to turn green. As soon as it does, I accelerate, gunning down the road, hoping the cops don't stop me. But I can't waste time.

All I have is this address. Some house on a residential block. Not a bad area, either. Why would my mother be there? Maybe her boyfriend lives there?

My pulse beats through my temples, my heart ready to give out. This woman has taken so much from me. She won't take my daughter too.

The phone rings, and I find Fionn's name staring back at me.

My body breaks with hives, my heartbeats shuddering in my chest. I click ignore, but he calls again. And again.

By the time he finds me, I'll have Fia back. He can be mad then. At least that's what I hope happens. In the back of my head, though, I fear we may both end up dead.

Twenty minutes later, and I'm in front of a red brick two-story home, the white picket fence open, obviously waiting for my arrival. With my body trembling, I step out, holding my phone in my hand, my legs weighing a million pounds as I rush up the steps, trying the door.

It opens instantly.

Silence greets me at first—so thick, I suffocate on it.

"Fia? Where are you?"

Silence. Until…

"Mama! Mama!"

"Fia, I'm coming!"

Running toward her voice at full speed, I make it only a short distance before I register pain in the back of my head and collapse on the ground, the world around me spinning.

I don't know what happens next, because everything goes black.

FORTY-SIX

FIONN

The buzzing in my head grows.

Something's fucking wrong. I called Amara to find out when she's getting Fia, but she never answered, even after my texts.

Roy hasn't, either.

"Did you call Roy again?" I ask one of our guys.

My brothers are at my house with me after we left our meeting early.

"He's still not answering."

FUCK!

I try her again, but the phone keeps going to voicemail.

"We're tracking her, sir," he tells me.

She has no idea that her wedding band has an embedded device that gives me her location.

"Hurry the hell up!" I pound a fist on the wall in the foyer.

If Roy is somehow involved, he's dead.

"I just got the security cams from the restaurant." Cillian marches up, holding his cell.

The video plays, and she's there, rushing out into her car from the back.

Ice fills my veins.

She drove off. Is she running from me?

No. She wouldn't do that. Things between us have been good, and she'd never go without Fia.

"The preschool just said she called to ask about Fia," Tynan adds. "They told her Fia was picked up an hour ago by a Desdemona."

"That bitch! I should've killed her when I had the chance."

"We're gonna find them both." Tynan clasps a palm on my shoulder, and I nod, my entire body tight with rage.

"Sir, we know where she is."

He shoots off the address. Some house in Boston.

"Call the pilot," I tell him. "We're going now."

I start for the door, my brothers behind me. Adrenaline rushes into my veins. If something happens to my girls, the entire world will pay.

As soon as we're each in our cars, driving to the air strip at one hundred miles an hour, I call Emily.

She answers immediately. "Uh, Fionn, is…is everything okay? Is Amara with you?"

The nervous tempo of her tone, the way she asks about my wife, I know instantly she knows something.

"Where the hell is she, and don't you dare lie to me!"

Swerving past a vehicle on my left, I register her low cries.

"Emily, she could be dying! Fia's missing too. What happened?!" I try to control my rage, but it's impossible.

She should've come to me.

"Oh God," she sobs. "She was so scared. She told me not to say anything."

Fisting the wheel tighter, I grow damn impatient. "Tell me."

"We went into the bathroom," she sniffles. "And some woman—she wasn't paying attention to who—dropped an envelope. Inside was a photo of Fia holding a teddy on a chair. They gave her an address."

She tells it to me.

God damn it!

That's where the tracker said Amara was.

Blood pumps louder in my head. "Anything else?"

"No," she whimpers. "I'm so sorry."

"I've gotta go." I hang up the phone, racing faster.

Her mother and anyone else involved are going to pay.

Please, baby. I can't lose you. Can't lose either one of you.

AMARA

There's a buzzing in my head, a pummeling heaviness I can't shake.

I don't know where I am.

My lashes flutter open, but only darkness surrounds me.

Panic hits all at once, and when I try to move, I realize I can't. My hands, they're…they're tied behind my back.

"Mm!" I try to yell for help, but all that comes out is a groan.

My mind starts replaying whatever I can remember before now.

The house. I went into the house.

Why? Why did I…

Fia! Oh my God, my baby!

I shake my body, fighting the binds, my feet bound too. There's something over my eyes, something that makes everything seem dark.

It reminds me of that dream. The one of me as a child.

Is this a dream?

No. It can't be. I can sense the pain at my wrists, my lungs aching as I try to scream, but it's just unintelligible mumbling.

"Let's get this shit over with!" a man says, but my mind's too loopy to make out his voice.

But in the back of my head, I think I've heard it before.

A woman snickers. "I've waited years for this moment. And you think I'm gonna blow it away because you're impatient?"

Oh my God.

My breathing turns labored.

It can't be. No. It…it can't be.

Tears fill my eyes as I recognize both of them, hoping I'm wrong. That my head is making me imagine it all.

"Not happening, buddy." She laughs. "If you don't like it, just leave. I can do this on my own."

"I don't fucking trust you," he spits out, and I choke on a cry.

Why are they doing this to me?

My body quivers, fear like I've never experienced taking hold. I don't understand what's happening.

"We're both working for the same thing, aren't we?" she continues. "I just want my time with her before we kill her. Okay?"

Kill? NO!

"Yeah, whatever. Make it fast."

"Ah, I think she's awake already." Footsteps draw closer.

In seconds, she's ripping off the blindfold, and my eyes blink against the bright lights, unable to see anything clearly at first.

"Shh, don't cry," Lilith says. "It's gonna be okay."

"Mm," I shake my head, shuddering as I come face-to-face with both of them.

Julius glares, his face tight.

The dual betrayal hits me so hard; I snivel, unable to catch my breath.

He never wanted to know me, did he? It was a ploy. It had to be.

But for what? To hurt me? I don't understand what's going on.

Lilith drops her head to the side, a sympathetic look on her face as her mouth forms a thin line. But her eyes are bleak and cold, something I've never seen in my friend before.

"Now, if you promise to be a good little girl, I'll remove your gag, okay?" She makes herself sound syrupy sweet, but in a deranged kind of way. Like one of those serial killers in movies that act all nice before they slice your throat.

My gut heaves.

Oh my God, Fia.

What have they done to her?

I start to fight my binds again, but she gives me a disapproving look.

"What did I say?" she scolds me like a parent would scold a child.

All I do is cry, panic pounding in my chest. Why is she doing this? Why is he? How do they know each other?

I'm gonna throw up.

"I'm going to give you one chance. If you fuck this up and decide to scream, I can't promise he won't kill you." She kneels, a grin stretching as she whispers, "He has a gun."

Her grimace makes every hair on the back of my neck stand up. How have I never realized she's insane? Though there was never any indication.

I want to ask her why. What have I ever done to deserve this? What has Fia done?

She slowly rips the tape off, and I groan from the pain.

"Where is my daughter?" I whimper, emotions clogging my throat.

"She's safe," Julius grumbles. "My girlfriend has her. Once we're done here, she'll be returned."

"Done here?" I look from him to her. "What does that mean? Do you really plan to kill me? Why?! What have I done to either one of you?"

He hits me with another glare, refusing to answer.

"Please, Lilith, why are you doing this to me? To Fia!" My sobbing grows. "She loves you. *I* love you. Why?"

Something dark passes in her features. "Oh, Amara, I really did like you. I just couldn't handle them anymore, always going on and on about you." She rolls her eyes. "I wanted to punish them, you know. I wanted to hurt them the way they've been hurting me."

"Who?" My pulse skips every second beat, the pressure on my chest intensifying.

"Enough of this already!" Julius shouts, and in a split second, everything changes.

One moment, he's holding a gun out to my head. The next, she whips out hers, shooting him right in the chest.

"Oh God!" I gasp as he falls to the ground, blood pooling around him while his chest rises and falls.

She marches up to him, a wide grin on her face. "I told you to be patient, didn't I?" She shakes her head. "Silly boy. If you'd behaved long enough, I would've told you she wasn't even your sister."

"Wh-what?" I choke out, just barely. "What is happening?"

"Oh." She grins, pivoting toward me. "Don't worry about him. He wanted you dead. I helped you."

She's insane. I need to get to my daughter!

"Please, you have to get Fia! That's all I care about."

"Of course we will." Her brows furrow, and she comes over to me, placing a hand on my forearm. "But now that he's gone, we can finally have the chat I've been dying to have since the moment we met. Because, you see, I've waited so long for this."

I blink past my tears, every inch of me buzzing with confusion and terror. "For what? Please tell me what's going on."

She plops down in front of me, crossing her legs. "I couldn't believe it when I found you. All those years of hearing how special you were. How I was overshadowed by your disappearance, but there you were. I knew I had to know you. I had to hurt them for everything they had done."

"Who, Lilith?" My question sticks in my throat, croaky and heavy. "Who hurt you?"

"Our parents, silly."

All the blood drains from my veins, as though she's sucked it out with three little words.

Our. Parents?

"N-n-n-no. I—I—I don't understand. You're my—" I choke on the rest of the sentence, my head spinning.

"Yes, I'm your sister. And I'm sorry to tell you this won't be the reunion you've been waiting for."

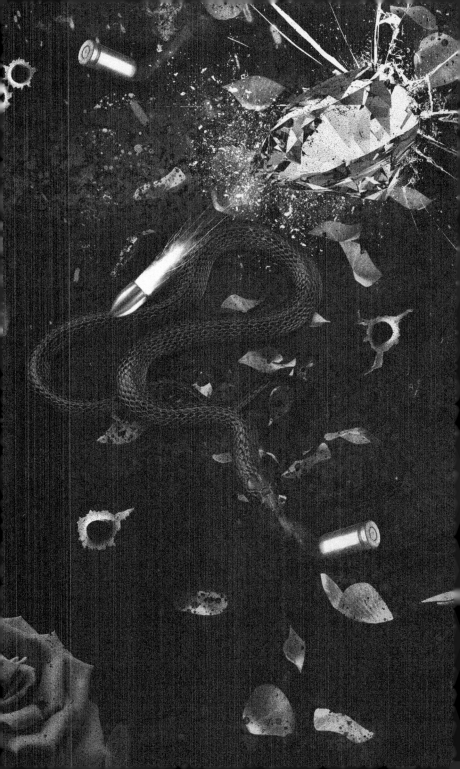

FORTY-SEVEN

LILITH
HOURS EARLIER

"Now, now. Don't get your panties in a twist, Mom." I laugh.

My father's nostrils twitch—so much anger for one tiny man.

But I get it. They're pissed. I've had their precious daughter for the past several years while they cried themselves to sleep every night, thinking about what happened to her when she was two.

She was taken from the hospital the day I came into their life.

ME! The daughter who's always been here. Always begging for an ounce of love.

But they saved it all for her. The favorite daughter. Even her nursery still looks the same as it did the day she vanished.

"How could you not tell us you found her?!" my father shouts. "That she worked for our hotel? We would've done anything to be reunited with her!"

"Yikes, Dad. Don't give yourself a heart attack."

My mother slaps me hard across my face, shaking her head at me in disgust as tears continue to fall. "What is wrong with you?! She's your sister! Our daughter! Don't you care? Don't you love her?"

"Love?" I grit. "You wanna talk about LOVE?!" I get into her face. "Where was your love for ME?! The daughter who was alive and well? The daughter who was by your side all these years, begging for a tiny piece of this so-called love you like to throw around! Where was that, huh, Mom?" I grind my teeth, unable to hold back at the hypocrisy. "I'll tell you where: it was with her! Instead of focusing on the daughter you have, you saved all your love for the daughter who was dead. I should've been enough! Me! But I never was."

"She's not dead." My father's icy glare hits me and I barely feel it.

I return with a thunderous look. "That's what you have to say after I just spilled my heart out to you? Figures." My upper lip curls. "You don't deserve her. And after today, you won't have her at all."

"What the hell does that mean?" Mom's eyes flare.

Before she can wonder, I remove the taser Julius got me and zap my father first before I zap her too, striking both of them hard on the head until they groan. Removing a pair of zip ties, I tie my father's hands behind his back, tazing him again before I bind my mother's arms too.

I wait for them to both come to, standing above them and staring with a smug look.

It's finally happening. I'll finally take her away from them for good.

"Now you both stay here and think about what you've done, and once your angel daughter is gone, we can all finally be happy."

"Wait!" Mom calls. "Please, sweetheart, whatever you're planning, don't do it! We can all be happy together. I promise!"

I let out a snort. "Oh, Mother, you had your chance with me, and you blew it. But don't you worry. I'll make sure she dies quickly."

"Stop!" Dad hollers. "We love you, baby, please!"

"Hush. I have places to be."

And a brat to pick up from preschool.

I drag the fake ID out of my wallet. It pays to have friends who know how to hack a school's computer system and add Grandma to the pick-up list.

Now let's hope the school doesn't make me take my sunglasses off.

"Please, Lilith!" Amara begs, and I almost feel something.

Almost. But it's not enough.

"I'll do whatever you want," she cries. "Don't kill me and my babies."

Oh, right. She's pregnant. I almost forgot. That's too bad.

"You can save your tears, dear sister. They're a damn waste."

"I love you, Lilith. Please! If you tell me how to fix this, I will! We can be a family! I wanted one for so long! You know I did."

I blow out an exhausted sigh. "That'll never happen. You ruined my life!"

She jerks back from my shouting. "How?"

"Every single day you've been alive, every day they looked for you and swore they'd find you, was a day that I lived in the shadows." I get to my feet. "And when you're gone, we'll all finally be happy. I'll give them the closure they've always needed." My mouth curls. "I'll give them your death."

She sobs, unable to control her pathetic emotions. "When did you know? When did you find out we're sisters?"

"Oh, I knew before I inserted myself into Emily's life. Became her instant BFF just so I could get to you."

My grin is smug, and why wouldn't it be? None of them knew

shit! I deserve an Oscar.

"I took an ancestry test online, and surprise, we matched."

"Oh my God. You're…you're GS!"

"Ding, ding."

"I—I messaged you! I thought maybe you were my dad's child or something, but you never wrote back."

I snicker. "Of course not. I couldn't tell you I discovered who you were. And when I followed you to Julius's house, I put it all together. Because our parents always suspected someone who worked in the hospital took you. Then I discovered Julius's dad worked as security there when I was born, and voila! I had the story."

"But my mother never wanted me," she whispers. "I don't understand."

I shrug. "Don't know what to tell you, sis, but that's what happened. He took you."

She starts to cry again. My God, she's pitiful. What did my parents ever see in her?

"Why Julius? Why did he want me dead?" She pants. "What did I do to him?"

"Oh, that. Well, his father had a change of heart or something. Wanted to add you to the will. And Julius being Julius, he wanted to prevent that from happening."

"Oh my God," she whispers as I continue.

"He told me his father wouldn't hear it, and after he failed to convince him not to give you any money, Julius decided you had to die. Isn't he a peach?"

She studies my face through her grief, like she's seeing me for the first time, and I hope she likes what she sees, because I'm damn amazing.

"If you ask me, I think his dad just wanted to play nice with you so you wouldn't go digging."

She cries.

Aww, she actually looks sad. How cute.

Flipping my hair back, I continue with the story. "After I followed you to the restaurant where you met him, we struck up a conversation. He didn't exactly know I was your sister." My grin grows. "I told him you were my crazy friend, trying to come between my family and me, and he bought it. I don't think he cared what the reason was. He just wanted a partner."

"How could I have been so blind?" she whispers.

"There, there. We played you well. Don't fret too much, sis. No one can blame you."

"Please, I need to see Fia. She's probably so scared." Big tears drip down her cheeks.

"Don't worry. Fia will be home soon. I already texted Lena to leave her at the local hospital. I would never hurt our girl."

She shudders, eyes puffy from all that crying. "You don't have to do this. Please just let me go."

"No can do. I'm afraid this is where your story ends and mine begins." I lift my gun in the air.

Pop.

Amara's eyes widen.

Blood leaks down into my eyes, and when I touch my forehead...

Is that my blood?

Well, this didn't go as planned. Of course, she always ruins everything.

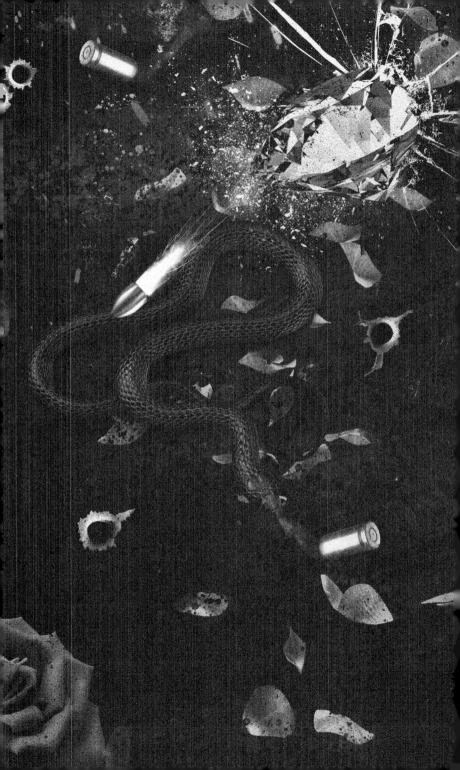

FORTY-EIGHT

FIONN

Sisters.

Fuck!

I can't believe I didn't see this! I had her at my damn house. Who knows what information she was collecting? I should've caught this! It's on me.

I continue listening as we finish surrounding the place, taking our positions quietly, needing the perfect time to infiltrate. My teeth rattle as I steady my breathing, trying like hell not to rush in there and save Amara before it's too late.

"You don't have to do this. Please just let me go."

Fuck, hearing my baby's voice all broken like that… I just wanna get in there and fucking get her out, but I know I have to be smart.

I can see everything from one of the side windows, and even though she's got her back to me, I spot Lilith's gun at her side.

One wrong move, and she could fire at Amara. I won't risk that.

I peer back at my brothers, all of us knowing it's gonna be go time at any second. As soon as we're out of here, we're going for Fia. My men already have the perimeter around Lena's house locked.

She doesn't know who she fucked with. But she will soon.

"No can do," Lilith says. "I'm afraid this is where your story ends and mine begins."

As soon as she lifts the gun, I put a bullet in her head, glass shattering as I do.

Within seconds, she falls to the ground, and I'm running through the door.

"Amara! Sweetheart, are you okay?"

Her body shakes with heavy breathing, eyes locked on her dead sister.

"Amara! Talk to me." I kneel before her, cutting her zip ties with a flip knife and giving her a quick once-over for any damage.

She seems okay. Physically, anyway.

She looks right past me, as though not seeing me at all. Like she's in damn shock, though who can blame her?

"We've gotta get moving," Tynan says. "We need to get Fia before anyone else they may have working for them tips off that other bitch."

I nod, kissing Amara on the forehead as I gather her in my arms, keeping her tight against my chest as I carry her out. "We're gonna go home soon, I promise. We just have to get our baby back first."

She doesn't say a word even at that, staring aimlessly, and that fucking terrifies me.

Because what if, after everything, she's not okay? What if I've really lost her?

I see her before she sees me, sitting in front of the TV, eating a bag of pretzels while the woman who took her paces with a phone to her ear.

If I were to guess, she's calling her now-dead boyfriend. It's a shame he'll never witness what I do to her. And it's an even bigger shame I didn't get to kill him myself. The amount of rage I have inside me right now for what these assholes did to my family would scare even the craziest motherfucker.

As though sensing me, Fia looks to her right, her eyes expanding as she catches me from the edge of the small rectangular window.

I place a finger over my mouth so she knows to stay quiet.

She nods, while Lena continues to pace.

"Hey, kid, stay here, okay? I need to get some water."

"Okay," Fia says, glancing toward me.

I motion for her to stay quiet once again, and she does.

"On my count," I whisper to my brothers and our men. "Then you storm in through the back while I go through the front. You get her, and I'll grab Fia."

They nod.

I raise a finger. Then two. Once I hit three, chaos erupts.

Within seconds, Lena's scream for help dies out as I rush for my baby girl. Before I can pick the lock, she's there, opening the front door.

"Daddy!" Fia runs into my arms as I drop to my knees, her small body crushing into mine.

"Are you okay?"

"Yeah." She backs off, her chin trembling. "That lady said she was Mommy's friend and that Mommy had to go to the doctor. I didn't wanna go, Daddy, but she made me." Tears fill her eyes.

My veins turn ice-cold. She made my daughter cry.

"It's okay, baby." I cup the back of her head, and even through my fury, heavy relief hits me.

Both of my girls are okay. They're alive. I don't know what I would've done if…

I don't even want to think about that.

"You ready?" Cillian's voice rings behind Fia, and she turns toward it.

"Hi, Uncle Cillian."

"Hey, love. Are you okay?"

"I'm okay." She pouts. "I wanna go home. I want Mommy."

My eyes lock with my brother's before I'm cupping her face. "Mommy's in the car. Go with your uncle to see her. Daddy just has to talk with the lady before we go home, okay?"

"Okay, Daddy." Her eyes light up at hearing that Amara—who didn't say a word on the way here—is waiting for her.

It'll break Fia's little heart if she doesn't talk to her either.

She gives me one last look as Cillian grabs her hand.

Getting to my feet, I drop a kiss on the top of her head. "I promise I'll be quick, okay, baby?"

"Okay, Daddy." She heads out the door, while I prepare to end this.

As soon as I make it to the kitchen, I find Lena on a chair with tape around her mouth, eyes stricken with fear as she takes in the six men here, including Tynan.

Her gaze widens even more when I step inside, towering over her. My mouth curls as I rip the tape from her face.

"Please! I—I didn't do anything. I was just supposed to hang out with the kid. I didn't—"

"Shut your fucking mouth. You won't speak unless I tell you to speak."

She nods, tears filling her eyes.

"You took my daughter. Mine!" I smack a palm to my chest.

"No! It was all him! He helped that girl fake an ID. He hacked the school to get her on the list. I was just making sure she was safe!"

My temples fucking throb. That school is gonna pay for this. But right now I'm gonna start with her.

"You're gonna die today, and I wanna tell you how before it happens."

"P-p-p-please, I beg you!"

Removing a nine from my waistband, I fire one into her thigh, the silencer keeping the sound at a minimum. Her scream just makes me want to kill her faster.

"That's what you get for not listening to instructions. Now…" I lower the gun. "As I was saying, I'm gonna put a bullet in your head. Then, my guys are gonna chop you up into tiny pieces, just because, before we burn you and toss your ashes."

She sobs, bottom lip quivering.

I have no sympathy. None. She brought this on herself.

"But don't worry. Because I'm a nice guy, I'll make sure you and your boyfriend burn together."

As she continues to cry, I raise my gun to her head.

"Please!"

Pop.

It's over.

Now I can finally take Amara to the doctor, and I hope like hell that he says she'll come out of this.

I hold Amara in my arms as she shakes and cries, unable to come to terms with the utter betrayal.

Neither can I.

She still hasn't spoken since we got her to the underground hospital run by Gio Marino and his family, but at least she's feeling it all. That's progress.

We did end up finding Roy in the parking lot of the restaurant the girls ate in, stabbed in the throat. There were no cameras to catch her, but I think it was Lilith who killed him.

"She's just in shock right now," the doctor explains. "She and the baby are fine physically. But she needs to be home and taken care of right now."

"Are you sure that's it? That she'll be okay?"

I'm damn worried about her mental state, but maybe he's right. She needs to be home with family.

"I've seen cases like this. It's not uncommon. Just give her time and space to heal."

I blow out a breath. He'd better be right.

"Mommy?" Fia cries. "Mommy, say something."

I hate hearing my daughter so sad and scared. But she's one tough kid.

"Let's take Mommy home. She just needs rest."

Fia wipes under her eyes. "Okay, Daddy. Let's go home."

FORTY-NINE

AMARA
ONE WEEK LATER

I t hasn't hit me yet. I don't know if it ever will.

She was my sister. Lilith was my sister, and she tried to kill me. She would've done it if Fionn hadn't come at just the right time.

Reliving her death every day makes me ill inside. She was broken. Hurting. But what she did wasn't right.

And Julius… I don't even know what to think about that. About what his father did to me.

When I told Emily and Patricia about it yesterday, they cried, unable to believe it too. How could our friend have been such a psychopath? I don't know what other way there is to describe her.

"Are you ready to go inside?" Fionn asks as my leg bounces, parked in front of their house.

Roxanne and John. My parents. My real parents.

I want to meet them. They definitely want to meet me.

Fionn spoke to them when I couldn't. And after he rescued me, he sent his men to check on them, knowing what Lilith was capable of, only to discover them tied up in her bedroom. He told them who he was. Told them their daughter was dead. One, anyway.

The other? She was a little dead inside too.

I didn't speak to anyone for two days. Everything was locked up tight. But slowly, things unraveled, and I let myself feel it. Feel this immense agony in the center of my chest.

My life was stolen from me. So many other lives destroyed. I could've had a sister. A real family. But that was taken away. And for what?

It didn't take me long to realize that the dream I've had of myself as a little girl wasn't about being abandoned by a father who was never mine, but about what he did to me.

What *they* did.

Lloyd and Desdemona were arrested a few days ago. Fionn made sure of it. They're waiting for trial, and I cannot wait to testify against them.

"I'm ready as I'll ever be," I tell him.

My heart races, but I have to do this. I have to meet them. It's what I've been waiting for without even knowing they existed.

When I step out of the car as soon as he opens my door, he clasps his hand in mine, kissing my knuckles.

"It's over, baby. It's gonna be okay from now on."

I nod, a knot in my throat.

But nothing is okay. None of this is right.

Dragging in a shallow breath, I get ready to meet my parents. The two people who never forgot me.

He leads me up the three steps before we're in front of a plain white door. Nervously, I knock on it, my stomach gnawing.

Footsteps rush over before the door is quickly pulled open.

And then I see them. Mom with her hazel eyes just like mine. Dad with brown ones, both of their hair a similar brown shade.

"Thalia?" Mom cries.

I almost forgot that's the name they gave me. The name of the hotel I worked for, not knowing it was named after me.

I rush into their arms, all of us sobbing. And being held by the people who gave me life, it completely shatters me. I felt so alone in this world, abandoned and unloved, but none of that was true.

They really loved me.

"Oh, baby, I'm so sorry," Dad cries. "I should've been watching you. I should've been there."

"It's okay, Dad. It's okay." I wrap my arm around him tighter. "I'm home now."

We stay together, desperate for every moment, feeling the weight of our reunion and separation all at once.

And though this story has a bitter end, there's still some love left to go around.

Days later, and we've returned to my parents, Fia playing with their Cavalier King Charles named Rami.

When my parents invited us over for lunch, we immediately agreed. I wanted them to meet their granddaughter. I want her to meet them too.

Fionn clutches the results of Fia's paternity test in his hand, finally wanting to find out. I think he was just afraid to know the truth because the reality that she isn't his would crush him. I figured we can do this with my parents to give them something after all they have missed.

"May I have another cookie?" Fia asks, and her toothy grin has Mom in a pile of goo.

"Oh, honey, you can have ten. Cute little thing like yourself." Her eyes glisten with unshed tears. "You remind me of your mother. Same smile and all. Right, John?"

He nods, choking on his own emotions. "Right, sweetheart."

It's been hard on my parents, reliving what happened to me when I was two. Apparently Lloyd was hooking up with Desdemona, who wanted to have a kid with him, probably to trap him. But he didn't want that. When she wouldn't stop pestering him about it, he decided to take matters into his own hands.

The day Lilith was born, he found me lost in the hospital, so he took me, ruining my entire life in the process. He told Fionn from jail that he regrets what he did because he never loved my mother; he just liked sleeping with her. He stayed with her for another six months after he took me, and then he left, growing sick of bouncing between two homes.

The very idea makes my stomach turn. I'll never forgive either one of them.

"I can't believe she's gone," Mom whispers, swiping under her lower lashes. "No matter what she thought, we loved her with all our hearts. We told her time and time again, but she wouldn't see past her own jealousy for still keeping your memory alive."

I lean over and clasp her hand from across the sofas. "I believe you, Mom. She was just sick. None of us saw it. I was her friend for years, and I never saw it either."

She sighs, glancing at Fia, her mouth thinning as she tries not to cry.

"So…" She clears her throat and looks over at Fionn. "Are you gonna tell us the results, honey, or are you gonna keep us in suspense the whole day?"

He laughs. "Alright. Fine. Fine."

His fingers clench and unclench before he's ripping the flap open and staring at the paper inside. Seconds drift, and my heart turns into a mess of erratic beats.

"What does it say, babe?"

He gazes up at me, his face unreadable at first.

"She's mine." His eyes glisten. "Fia's mine."

"Oh my God!" I jump out of my seat and into his arms, my face buried in his chest as he holds me.

"I knew it," I cry. "I knew she was yours from the moment I had her."

"She's always been mine, mo ban dia." He cups my face between his loving hands, his gaze shining with so much love, I drown in it. "No test would ever change that."

When Fia runs over, he brings her onto his knee, his other arm coming around her.

And I remain there, in the arms of my family—my *entire* family— knowing how lucky I am to have them.

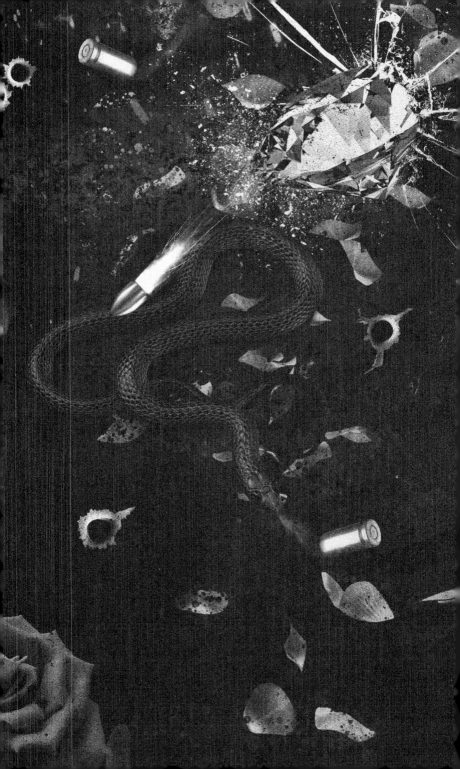

FIFTY

FIONN
TWO MONTHS LATER

W hen the Russians invite you to a party, you don't say no.

While Amara gets ready in the bathroom, I check my phone for the text I've been waiting for from one of my men.

CAHAL

> It's done, sir. Both are busy indefinitely.

That brings a smile to my face. Amara never has to know I was involved. That I ordered the hit on Lloyd and Desdemona while they were in prison. A lot of bad things happen in those places.

Tynan was right, after all. But sometimes it's not a tree.

As soon as the door opens, she struts out, taking my breath away in a knee-length pink-floral-and-white dress that hugs her growing belly.

"My God, I'm a lucky son of a bitch."

She holds out her hand for mine, and I grab it, lowering my palm over her stomach.

"I can't wait to meet our baby," I tell her, my mouth dropping to kiss her there.

"Me either." She sighs. "Though I'm not all that excited about this weight gain."

"I don't know what you're talking about, because I love this ass." I grab her backside and push her into my stiff dick.

She shakes her head. "Come on, let's go before we're late."

Letting out a laugh, I follow my beautiful wife, my fingers slicing through hers as we climb down the stairs, our daughter waiting for us.

Tonight should be fun. Konstantin's throwing Dinara's brother a tenth birthday party.

I'm sure it's going to get crazy, especially with Cillian and Dinara being in the same room together.

AMARA

This isn't just a party; it's an affair. Balloon twisters, fire blowers, a magic show. Women in old-fashioned gowns and wigs walk around with trays filled with pastries wrapped around their midsections like walking dessert tables. There's even a popular singer they hired who is performing on a stage while hundreds dance.

"This is crazy," I whisper as we head to find Konstantin to say hello.

"This is how they party."

When we lock eyes with Konstantin, he approaches.

"Ahh, there you two are. And, Mrs. Quinn, may I just say how ravishing you look tonight?"

"Hey," Fionn snaps. "Keep those eyes to yourself."

"Oh, my friend, love looks good on you." He clasps him on the shoulder.

"And what about you, Konstantin?" I ask. "No special lady in your life?"

"You amuse me, daragaya." He chuckles dryly. "No, I prefer my life to be a little less complicated, at least in that aspect." He smirks.

"It isn't that bad," Fionn throws in. "I'm sure even a man like you could get used to someone actually tolerating him."

"Ha! You're a comedian, I see." He slaps a hand across his back. "Why don't you go get something to eat? Your family has already arrived."

He points to a table at the left corner of the outdoor area he had transformed with tents, a dance floor, and more tables than I can count. We head over there, the whole gang greeting us.

"Some party, huh?" Elara says, glancing at Adora and Brody, who are watching a man swallowing fire.

"Wanna go with them, baby?" I ask Fia, who nods.

When Brody sees her, he waves, and she goes running.

"Where's Cillian?" Fionn asks, pulling out a chair for me.

"He was here a few minutes ago." Patrick looks around. "Not sure where he went."

As my eyes scan the area, I catch sight of Cillian with a beautiful woman with long black hair.

"Isn't that your brother?" I whisper to Fionn, and he follows my line of vision.

"It is. And it seems like he hasn't wasted any time arguing with Dinara." He chuckles. "The woman he won't admit he's obsessed with."

I continue to watch them as she digs her finger into his chest, and when he grabs her wrist and smirks, she slaps him.

"Wow!" I say. "What do you think he did?"

"Knowing him, a lot of things," he scoffs.

"Well, she doesn't look happy to see him. That's for sure."

"She never is. It's a game they both play. Except they don't know they're playing it."

Someone clinks their glass and the voices dim, the music instantly stopping when Konstantin stands in the center of the dance floor.

"My dear friends and family. It is a pleasure to welcome you all into my home. To share my food and my hospitality with each one of you for our dear Gregory's birthday is a gift to me." His eyes go to the boy, who stands across from him, dark hair and eyes like his sister's. "Come, come."

Konstantin waves him over, and he walks over to stand beside him.

"Gregory and his two sisters, Tatiana and Dinara, mean a lot to me. I'm sure they know how much I love them. And it's why today is a special day. Not only because our dear Gregory is practically a man, but because today, I announce something else special to me. Something that I have planned for a very long time."

"Shit," Fionn mutters, glancing at Cillian and Dinara, both of whom stare in horror at Konstantin, and I don't know why.

"What's going on?" I ask, but Konstantin starts again.

"Tatiana, may I please ask you to come here with me?"

A gorgeous, tall young woman who looks like a spitting image of Dinara comes strutting down in her short black minidress.

"My Tatiana turned eighteen not too long ago, and I wanted to find her a suitable match who would provide her with the same care I have provided her for these past years. And who better than you, Cillian Quinn, wouldn't you say?"

"Oh shit," Fionn mutters, looking over at Tynan, who doesn't look thrilled.

"What the hell is he doing?" Patrick whispers. "Is he trying to start a war?"

Cillian curls a fist, while Dinara stomps forward toward her cousin.

"Are you crazy?! What are you doing?" she shouts at Konstantin.

"Is this a problem?"

Her face flushes from pure anger. "Of course it's a problem! You know how I feel about him! How much I despise the man!"

Every one of the guests stares with shock, like they're watching a bomb go off.

"Of course I know that, but Tatiana doesn't have to hate him. Right, my darling?" He glances at the sister, who nods sheepishly.

This is even worse than my own complicated family history.

"So, what do you say, Cillian? Will you accept this marriage arrangement so we can finally unite our two families?"

"Over my fucking dead body," he growls. "I'll never marry her. Or *her*."

His glare lands on Dinara.

"Ha!" She marches to him. "You think I'd ever want you? Maybe you think you're some prize every woman wants to be with."

"You once thought so." A cocky half-smile momentarily appears on his face.

"I'm not that girl anymore. You're nothing to me, Cillian Quinn. Nothing!"

He snaps his teeth while her chest flies up and down.

"Nothing, huh?" He takes a step forward while she hikes up her chin.

"That's right."

"Say it again." He takes another step, while I wait to see what happens next.

"You're. Nothing."

As she flips around to march away, he grabs her around the back of her head and kisses her.

People gasp as she fights him, but that only lasts seconds, because no matter what she just said, she's crazy about him too. It's obvious from the way she melts into him. The way her tense hands start to release the lapel of his jacket, holding it gently now.

"Let's raise a toast to the new happy couple. Dinara and Cillian!" Konstantin takes a shot one of his men hands him, then everyone is clinking glasses and cheering.

What the hell just happened?

Dinara and Cillian pull away, both horrified at what they just did, staring at Konstantin with shock and rage.

"So, this is normal?" I ask Fionn.

He laughs.

"Never mind."

"My brother has been denying that this is gonna happen for a long time, but he can't run from it now. If he tries, I don't know if any of us will be ready for the war he'll throw us into."

"A war?" My pulse hammers.

"We have a long, complicated history with the Russians, and it's in both our interests that we maintain our truce."

"Oh…"

I will never understand any of this, but I've accepted it because the alternative means I lose him, and I can't live in a world where he isn't mine.

The music starts, and everyone returns to whatever they were doing, dancing and eating.

"Cillian may pop a vein," Tynan says. "I think I'm gonna go talk to him."

"Alright." Fionn takes my hand. "I'm gonna go dance with my wife. What do you say, Mrs. Quinn?"

"I think I'd like that."

He helps me up and takes me to the dance floor, his arms clasped around the small of my back, mine looping around his neck as we sway to a slow song while Fia spins around in circles, her pink tulle dress twirling with her.

And for a moment, I remember. I remember the pain of growing up. The fear of the future with a mother who never quite wanted me.

And I let it all go.

Because the woman I've become, she's everything I always wanted to be. I'm finally happy. Finally home.

And there's nowhere else I'd rather be than right here, with the people who matter most.

THE END

THANKS FOR READING!

Want more Fionn & Amara? Scan the code below for a bonus scene!

I hope you're ready for *Wicked Savage*, the final book in the *Savage Kings* series. This enemies to lovers age gap story is going to bring all the fire.

Wondering if Iseult & Gio have a story? They do in *Twisted Promises*!

And everyone's favorite, **Konstantin**, is getting a book! You can pre-order that now!

BONUS SCENE

PLAYLIST

- "I'm the Sinner" by Jared Benjamin
- "Call My Name" by GRAHAM feat. Henrik
- "Moon" by Austin Giorgio
- "Dusk Till Dawn" by Camylio
- "Flames" by Donzell Taggart
- "Baby You're Worth It" by Kina
- "Do It for Me" by Rosenfeld
- "Dusk Till Dawn" by ZAYN feat. Sia
- "Littlest Things" by Camylio
- "Parachute" by Camylio
- "Faith" by Camylio
- "Higher" by Croixx
- "Are You With Me" by Nilu
- "Temporary Love" by Ben Platt
- "Beautiful Crime" by Tamer
- "Chokehold" by Austin Giorgio
- "Never Alone" by Garrett Kato feat. Elina
- "Talking to the Moon" by Sam Tompkins
- "Rest" by Dean Lewis feat. Sasha Alex Sloan
- "Darkerside" by David Kushner
- "Overgrown" by James Blake
- "Paper Cup" by Thomas Day
- "Found a Home" by AG feat. Nilu
- "Breathe" by Kansh
- "Over Me" by Camylio
- "Toxic" by Sayge

- "You Put a Spell on Me" by Austin Giorgio
- "Smoke" by BOBI ANDONOV
- "Apartment" by BOBI ANDONOV
- "Close to You" by Gracie Abrams
- "Maybe Next Time" by Jamie Miller

LISTEN ON SPOTIFY!

ALSO BY LILIAN HARRIS

2. *Brutal Savage* (Tynan & Elara)
3. *Wicked Savage* (Fionn & Amara)
4. *Filthy Savage* (Cillian & Dinara - May 5th, 2025)

Marinov Bratva Series

1. *Konstantin* (September 8th, 2025)
2. *Aleksei* (Winter 2025)
3. *Kirill* (Spring 2026)
4. *Anton* (Winter 2026)

Standalone

1. *Shattered Secrets* (Husdon & Hadleigh)

WITHIN EVERY HEARTBEAT,
THERE'S A STORY.

For Lilian, a love of writing began with a love of books. From Goosebumps to romance novels with sexy men on the cover, she loved them all. It's no surprise that at the age of eight she started writing poetry and lyrics and hasn't stopped writing since.

She was born in Azerbaijan, and currently resides on Long Island, N.Y. with her husband, three kids, and lots of animals. Even though she has a law degree, she isn't currently practicing. When she isn't writing or reading, Lilian is baking or cooking up a storm. And once the kids are in bed, there's usually a glass of red in her hand. Can't just survive on coffee alone!

FIND LILIAN ONLINE!

Printed in Great Britain
by Amazon

55371564R00245